There is a place we go
when we sleep,
a world that exists
between life and death.

VRIN: ten mortal gods

Contents

To my precious wife Joan
for the many grueling hours spent
editing and refining my vision.
You are a gift from the Creator
and I am diminished without you.

To Nate Dudley-
You were inspiration
when it was needed most.

Chapter One

A GOD AWAKENS

1 0 1 0 1 1 0

So there I sat, wondering how long I had been staring at the same page of my book. My head was fuzzy, and my thoughts were scattered. I could remember starting the book, and I knew it was important that I finish it, but not much more would come to me-- including my name.

Somewhere a log popped.

I pulled my eyes from the page and tried to focus on the lavishly decorated room around me. Light from a fireplace scattered dancing trails of orange on bookshelves lining the walls and in the corner a spiral staircase wound its way up to a balcony where statues of mythical figures sat balanced on delicate podiums.

I shook my head; something was wrong with my vision. The effect was subtle, yet distinct. Every color in the room shimmered with a life of its own and my eyes tingled from the influx of shades and tints. I closed them and gave a squeeze, but the problem persisted. I looked down. Even the hands gripping the strange leather book had a color fluctuation, as if they could not decide on a proper shade of tan.

How long had I been sitting? I reached up and rubbed the back of my neck. The stiffness there indicated it had been awhile-- but I was unable to draw upon any workable memory to confirm that conclusion. Scenes passed before me, but their meanings ran like frightened shadows. Face after familiar face pushed forward from the murky pool of my consciousness, but who these phantoms were and how I knew them was a mystery. *Am I dreaming?*

I shook the jumbled images from my head, pulled forward in the chair, and put weight on my feet. They tingled but had not yet fallen asleep. Placing the heavy volume aside, I stood and shuffled over to the fireplace where a variety of framed pictures sat lining the mantelpiece. The colors continued to dance, but I managed to bring things into focus. There were several portraits: a family gathering, children in color, a couple in black and white-- and a panting dog next to a smiling man holding a trout. I sensed these images held a secret to my past, but whatever that secret was, it eluded me.

Something caught my eye, a trophy tucked behind one of the larger portraits. I moved the picture to get a better look. The inscription read, "1976 Bar Harbor Golf Tournament, Second Place, Jason Tardin." *Jason Tardin?* Was that my name? There was a faint recollection. But nothing more.

Again I surveyed the room. There was such familiarity in this place. No. More than familiarity-- a sense of security-- like a childhood hiding place. I felt safe here, but safe from what, or whom?

My eyes came to rest on the book I had placed on the end table. I could remember nothing of its contents and yet-- there was *something* in it I needed to know. I walked over and looked down at the volume. On the cover emblazoned in gold were the words, *Davata Notrals,* and a line of letters I assumed was the author's name. I started to reach for it, but froze. Why could I remember nothing *before* holding this book? Could it have been tainted with a poison or some kind of drug? Crouching down I examined the worn out pages from the side. They appeared to be stained from age but-- could the stains have been caused by something else?

7

Using a nearby pencil I turned to the first page--then stared in confusion. It was written in a foreign language! I flipped to the next page, and the next... They were all the same. I stared long and hard at the stylized calligraphy, hoping my mind would string the characters together in some meaningful way, but it was no use. I let the pencil fall from my loosened grip. It didn't make sense. I could *remember* reading this book. But *how?*

The door to the study creaked open and a finely dressed man stepped in. "Master Tardin, a gentleman is here to see you, sir. Shall I show him in?" His voice was deep and his manner showed the distinct signs of cultured refinement.

The astonishment on my face must have painted a pretty picture. "Uh, I'm sorry. *What?"*

"You have a visitor, sir."

"--Who?" I asked, trying to appear calm.

"A Mr. Sajin Barrows, sir."

Sajin Barrows? The name held no familiarity. I straightened. "Uh, yes. Show him in."

"As you wish." He bowed, and without so much as a raised eyebrow, turned and exited.

Show him *in?* What was I thinking? I didn't know who this man was-- I didn't know who *I* was! I felt my head. There was no damage, nothing to indicate an injury. What then? Was this a mental institution? Was I a part of some psychological experiment? Had I been started on some new drug that was messing with my mind? *Is that the answer?* They've drugged me because I'm crazy?! No. Crazy people don't *wonder* if their crazy. They're just crazy. That's all.

Footsteps approached in the hallway. Frantically I looked about. The colors continued to shimmer; the room shifted at odd slants. It *had* to be drugs! I needed to get ahold of myself! Just let things play out. Go with the flow. *Don't give anyone a reason to believe you're crazy!*

Regardless of what had caused this problem, the best course of action would be to pretend there *was* no problem. Until an appropriate opportunity presented itself-- if I could just play along-- maybe the answers would come. The doorknob clicked.

I gathered my wits for the performance of my life.

A man entered the room, a distinguished looking gentleman in an elegant gray suit. The material was flawless, almost too perfect, and at his side he wore-- a sword? My memory was messed up, but I was pretty sure I'd never seen anyone wearing a sword before, not in real life anyway. I fought to keep my expression from revealing my confusion.

The man had a strong physique and his short black hair shadowed the determination on his face. Keeping his eyes lowered, he cautiously strode forward and reached out his hand. "Greetings, Lord Tardin. I have been sent by Vrin's ruling house to welcome you to our world."

Our *world?* I shook his hand and kept my expression neutral.

"I am Sajin Barrows." He looked up and offered a smile. "But of course you already know this."

I returned his smile.

"The Prime Median, Daru, apologizes for his absence, but his reason for not being here is my reason for coming. I have come to implore you to consider a matter of grave importance to my people. I have no knowledge of how your kind communicates so if I cover anything with which you are already familiar, please forgive me."

I nodded stiffly, wondering what he meant by my "kind".

"Since the awakening we have no doubt witnessed indescribable wonders, things we never would have experienced on our own in a thousand years, and most of my people are thankful for the intervention of the gods. We

9

believe the ancient prophecies and we believe you will one day deliver us to Ethral..."

Gods? I was immediately thankful for the quasi euphoric state I was in.

"Nevertheless, there are some who are profoundly affected by the seemingly incidental acts of the gods, and it has caused in my people a troubled heart. We want to believe, we want to trust, but it is difficult to reconcile the contradictions. We need *you* to lead us to reason." He paused.

This guy was *good!* If he was acting, he was totally believable. *Fine. If this is the game, I'll play along.*

"Too which 'incidental' acts are you referring?" I said, trying to sound broody as I imagined a god would sound.

"My apologies, lord. I meant no disrespect."

"None taken. Please continue."

"It is the war which weighs most heavily on my people." He looked at me, as if I knew to which war he was referring.

"I'm sorry. You will have to give me more than that. There are many wars."

He lifted his brows. "The battle between-- Armadon and Rath?"

"Oh. That war."

His brows then furrowed. "We know of no other war in which the gods fight."

"Of course. You wouldn't," I said, hoping to cover myself.

"Why do they fight amongst themselves? Does the ancient text of the Marathil not describe the gods as joining together to destroy the evil of chaos? Even as we speak my people are dying by the hundreds, yet the others look on with indifference. Why?" He stared at me expectantly.

His acting was *impeccable.* His expressions and tone of voice completely believable. There was no hint of pretending as the fairy-tale words fell from his lips.

It wasn't hard for me to stay in character.

"I am very sorry for the hardships your people have faced."

He straightened himself with resolve. "Then you will help us? The others are unwilling to help. You may be our last hope." Again he stared at me expectantly.

"And-- what makes you believe I am any different from the others?"

"But why would you refuse us?" His voice held a hint of desperation.

What was I supposed to say to that? How long was this little experiment going to last? "--Ah, things are a little *confusing* for me at the moment."

"We are desperate people. Surely you can see that."

"You don't understand..."

"Then *help* me to understand!"

I wanted to scream at him. *I* don't understand! All I had were questions-- questions I didn't dare share with *him*-- for fear of who might be studying me, *if* there even *was* anyone studying me! The asylum concept was growing sketchier with each passing sentence. None of this made *any* sense. Crazy people don't have *meetings* in large expensive studies with butlers and strange men with swords!

"Will you help us, lord?"

Was this guy for real? "I..."

The sound of breaking glass startled us and I twisted around to see a man dressed entirely in black crouching before a shattered window. In his grip, was a crossbow, and upon his features, a look of vengeance. Slowly the man rose from the debris, carefully aimed the weapon at my head, and began a slow advance.

11

"Put that down, Dirm! You cannot harm him, he is one of the Ten!" came Sajin's voice from behind me.

"They die!" His voice dripped with hatred. "And I will prove it!"

Was this for real!

I had to think fast. Think! These men *actually* believe I'm a god! Okay. *But am I indestructible?* The man with the crossbow apparently had his doubts. If I gave him any reason to trust those doubts he *would* kill me! "Do you love your family?" I found myself saying, with a tone of warning that shocked even me.

I must have struck a chord, for my would-be assassin paused his advance. "What do you mean by *that? Demon!"*

With all my strength I suppressed my fear, put on my best poker face, and looked the man dead in the eyes. In a cold calculating tone, I asked, "What kind of terror would a demon unleash on your family, should your assassination attempt fail?"

Sajin's voice was near panic. "Listen to him, Dirm! You have seen what they can do!"

I kept my countenance solid and my eyes locked on those of my adversary. I sensed this was not the first time I had stared down an opponent, and something told me I was good at bluffing. Very good.

His hand remained steady on his weapon as he searched my face for a hint of fear. But he found none. Slowly the tension in his stance visibly melted away. His body went limp with despair. With a muffled curse he lowered the crossbow and held it loosely in his grip.

Sajin stepped forward and relieved the man of his weapon. "We told you to stay out of this," he said in a low voice. "It was agreed we would seek aid, not incite war. I know your son is dead, but this will not bring him back. Nothing can bring him back."

"Nothing?" The man's eyes lifted, he glared at me with contempt. "Can *they* not bring him back?" His inflection was filled with bitter distrust.

Sajin turned to me. "My humble apologies, lord. We had no way of knowing he would act in this manner."

"No harm done," I said, trying desperately to keep my voice from shaking.

"You can be assured he will be severely punished for his actions," he said, gripping the man by the arm.

"Please, don't," I said.

Both men looked up, surprised.

Sajin bowed, "You are very merciful."

"It is not mercy. His anger is justified and not deserving of punishment. However, I'd like to assure you, I had no part in the events which claimed his son's life."

"Our understanding is limited. We do not know the workings of the gods, we can only judge by what we've seen-- and there has been much pain. Pain which has blossomed into this violence. Thankfully it has ended here. If he had succeeded your death would have no doubt caused a revolution.

A revolution? Against gods?

Sajin sighed. "My people are painfully divided. I wish it were not so."

"Have we caused only hardship?" I said, surprised to note it was a genuine question.

"It is mixed, lord. Some have been generous, picking up the pieces where the two have done battle, but others protect their own interests, or stay out of the affairs of man altogether-- unless they are directly affected."

"I see."

"If only we could speak with Gaza," he said, almost to himself.

I paused a moment, contemplating his statement. "You think Gaza can change this?"

13

"He is the Maker, the god of birth. The great book reveals that none among the gods are more powerful than he, with all due respect, lord."

"You speak highly of my brother Gaza," I said, now irrevocably submerged in my role.

"As your leader, does he not decree the conduct of the gods?"

I dodged the question. "He does as he pleases."

"Would you consider waking him to ask if he will give our Prime Median an audience in his court?"

"This is all you ask, a meeting with Gaza?"

"Yes, lord." He bowed.

"I will think on it," I stated curtly. "You may go." With a wave of my hand, I ended my performance and turned toward the fireplace.

As the door closed behind me, my body loosened, and I was left to sift through the preposterous mystery I'd found myself entangled in. If this was a trick it was an elaborate one-- but if it was not-- I was in *way* over my head.

For a long moment I stood motionless, then slowly sank back down into my comfortable chair, feeling considerably *less* than comfortable.

λ

After some time I sat forward; I had come to a conclusion. Although the events occurring were preposterous, it was apparent that I was in fact a part of them. And unless by some stroke of fortune I should wake to find this all a dream, I was going to have to dig to find some answers. Looking about, I took note that my vision had stabilized. *That* at least was a good sign. I stood, hoping the landscape beyond the wind-tossed curtains might jog my memory-- but I didn't make it to the window. Instead a full length mirror caught my eye and I was irresistibly drawn to it. Would I recognize the face staring back at me?

I stepped in front of the glass and could not believe what I saw. My *eyes!* They were *glowing!* Even with my memory loss, I was sure my eyes had never looked like *this* before. I moved in closer to examine them. They were cold and hard like steel, a deep blue color, strangely absent of irises or pupils. I experienced an involuntary shudder. *Is it true?* Cautiously I raised my hand to touch one, then the other. I poked at them until tears soaked my cheeks. I didn't know how, but they were real. I let out a cynical laugh; some god I was, confused and paranoid.

For several moments I stood quietly observing the curious stranger looking back at me. Aside from the eyes, I appeared to be a fairly ordinary twenty-something, with black hair, dark eyebrows, and slightly darkened skin. I was

15

of Italian descent but there was something else thrown in there as well. My clothes were basic: hard cotton shirt, blue jeans, a pair of brown climbing sneakers. Coiled around my left pinkie was a gold ring, curious, but quite unremarkable. There was nothing impressive about my visage. I looked like an ordinary guy-- with glowing blue ball bearings for eyes.

I pulled my gaze away and proceeded toward the window. Careful to avoid the shards of broken glass I stepped over the sill and out onto the balcony. The wind tugged lightly at my clothing.

Below, a beautiful lawn with large flower beds encircled by rock spread out before me. In the distance, three moons hovered above the horizon, shedding an eerie blue blanket on the dark silhouettes of the night. In the center of the yard a statue of a woman stood opening her arms to the heavens. The workmanship was breathtaking, every detail captured precisely. Whatever this place was, it was beautiful.

At the edge of lawn a line of trees danced in the wind. As I stood staring at them a strange feeling washed over me. As if *I* were a part of the dance. I began swaying back and forth to their slow rhythm. And the wind grew stronger. Nature itself was moving to the beat of my heart and the world was alive around me. I could feel its power soaking into my skin and permeating my senses.

I longed to be walking along the path which twisted away just beyond the flower beds when suddenly a burst of energy coursed through me and I found myself surrounded by thin blue strands. They traveled away from me in every direction. Oddly enough, however, I was not shocked by their presence. Somehow I knew it was my will that had brought them to life, and instinctively I knew their purpose.

Caught up in the chain of events, my body responded to the force of my will, my essence melted into the strand that would bring me to the path, and with a crackle of energy, I found myself standing on the spot I had wanted to be. The wind brushed harder against my face. The sweet smell of flowers filled my nostrils.

I turned and looked back up at the balcony. The strand I had used was still floating in the air. The others had vanished, but this one still had a glow to it.

It seemed Mr. Barrows had been correct, I did possess some sort of power. I wanted to be on the path and the threads had reacted to my will. I looked around. Could I *consciously* control the threads? I spotted a small rock. *Be an egg,* I thought. There was no response. I increased my concentration and felt another energy burst. It started from behind my eyes and worked its way down to my hands. I waved my arms back and forth. Although I couldn't see the threads, I knew they were there; my arms tingled as they passed through them. Then all at once the web was alight once again.

I looked down at the rock. Like everything else it got its shape from the blue threads, which acted like an internal skeleton or a wire cage. The colors and textures of the rock were wrapped around this framework. Using the energy emanating from my hands I tried to bend the wire structure. I touched a nearby thread, closed my eyes, and pictured a sphere. Energy left my hands and when I looked down, the rock was completely round.

The web faded away-- and there I stood, smiling at my creation.

"Deep in thought?"

I looked up to see a beautiful young Asian woman, perhaps in her late teens or early twenties. Immediately I found myself drawn into her eyes. They were exquisite, like two blue embers casting a soft film of sapphire across her lovely features. They were similar to my own, only much brighter. My gaze drifted downward. Her tiny form was distinct under the thin colorful fabric of the dress

17

which fluttered slightly in the wind. She was absolutely *breathtaking.*

"Who..." was all I managed to utter, followed by open mouthed speechlessness.

A chuckle escaped her lips. "Who am *I?*"

"Yes, ah... That was what I was hoping to say."

"Well. Who are *you?*" she asked playfully.

"N- no one of consequence."

She straightened and gave a smirk. "Humble-- for a god."

"A *god. Yeah...*"

She began to back away.

"About that..."

"You should not be in such a rush to find answers. You may miss the moment. And *this* moment is going to be like nothing you have *ever* experienced." Her eyes sparkled. "Want to have some fun?"

She did not wait for an answer, but turned and bolted down the path. "Follow me!"

There seemed to be no other option. I looked back at the mansion. No one else was around. She was my best chance to find answers. I burst into a run.

Her braided ponytail swung gracefully behind her and her soft black shoes made padded thumps on the stone pathway. Each side of the path was adorned with manicured shrubs which acted as walls. In some spots they formed archways crossing overhead. I was surprised to find myself enjoying the exercise; her playfulness set me at ease.

When we emerged from the path we found ourselves on the edge of a steep cliff overlooking a large expanse of blue ocean. Far below, a village sparkled on the water's edge. Millions of tiny reflections danced on the distant waves, like fireflies playing in the moonlight.

"That's Trinador!" The wind blew at her words. *"It is my village! I built it from the power of the web! Would you like to see it?"* She looked *absolutely* magnificent

silhouetted against the night sky, her delicate oriental curves were highlighted in the soft moonlight which played upon her garments as they rippled in the wind.

I couldn't imagine wanting to be anywhere else but with her.

"Sure! Why not?" I hollered back. *"How do we get down there?"*

Her eyes twinkled. *"Fly, silly!"*

And with that she fell backwards over the edge.

In reflex I grabbed for her, then scrambled to see her plummeting to her death toward the jagged rocks below. I didn't want to watch but was frozen in *horror.*

With violence her arms snapped wide and caught the vibrating wind in the fabric of her dress. With a graceful sweep she rose up in an arc-- and hovered before me.

I stared in open-mouthed amazement.

"Come on!" She laughed. *"Don't just stand there gawking!"*

I marveled at the scene before me: the young woman soaring through the air with graceful movements, her form melting into the peaceful backdrop of the twinkling village. She was completely at ease floating in the currents of the wind and there was an expression of total freedom on her face.

Suddenly I felt invincible. I looked down at the rocky coast far below-- but it didn't frighten me. I could sense its curves in the power of the web. With a thought I could easily turn the rocks into sponges. I could change the direction or the strength of the wind. I could do whatever I wanted. In this world, *I* was in control. Somehow I was now sure of this. And whatever doubts I may have had, evaporated.

I stepped to the edge and jumped into the void.

The wind smacked hard against my body. My heart pounded. My eyes overflowed with tears. *Exhilarating!* I willed the web to appear once again and saw that the strands were guiding the wind in upward and downward currents. I needed to be lighter for the currents to hold my weight. I focused on the structure of my body and decreased my density. With this my frame became lighter and the effect of the wind increased. Now all I needed were a set of wings. I transformed the shape of my shirt and spread my arms and instantly I began gliding upon the wind with ease!

The young woman was quite a distance below me now so I put my hands to my sides and dropped like a bullet.

With a twist she turned and rode a current on her back. *"I told you this was going to be fun!"* she called. She caught an updraft and screamed with elation.

We glided back and forth a number of times, exchanging glances and smiles. I didn't know this young woman-- but somehow I felt a kinship with her. *"I don't believe I've ever had this much fun!"* I yelled above the wind. As I spoke the words a feeling passed over me. I was certain I had never allowed myself to be wild or impulsive. But with this young lady it was easy to let go. I felt the urge to laugh at the top of my lungs. So I did! The laughter was contagious and soon we were both twisting and laughing, gliding effortlessly through the night. I wanted this moment to go on forever. But all too soon I began to feel the misty salt air on my face. The lights below grew larger and brighter. As the ground drew nearer, the girl turned and headed toward a strip of beach near the village. I followed.

It wasn't the smoothest of landings. I hit the ground in a run which quickly transitioned into a series of sand flicking tumbles, ending up with me on my back, laughing.

The girl swooped in, rose up for a moment, then landed gently on both feet. Her smiling face appeared above me. "Are you hurt?"

"Just my pride." I laughed. "That was *amazing!"*

She giggled. "You will be long discovering the wonders of this place."

"Of that I have no doubt." I rolled over with a grunt and got to my feet, brushing sand as I went. I brought the web to life once again and molded my shirt to its original shape.

"You are making great progress," she said, smiling. "Come. I would like to show you my palace." Gently she took my hand into hers. We headed up the beach to a path leading to a brown needle road. Thousands of sparkling lights lined its edges.

Trinador was like nothing I had ever dreamed or imagined. Enormous trees had been painstakingly carved out into separate living units all the way up the majestic tree trunks to the delicate canopy of leaves overhead. Slanted wooden walkways provided easy access all the way up to the lofty penthouses. And rope bridges criss-crossed over the brown needle road. Glittering lamps hung everywhere, filling the village with a soft glow.

The workmanship surrounding us was extremely advanced. It would have taken hundreds of sculptors hundreds of years to create these wonderful works of art, yet the villagers appeared completely at ease moving among the fantastic architecture. I was awestruck.

"You *made* this?" I said, craning my neck."

Thunder rumbled in the distance, and the briefest look of concern crossed the girl's features. Lightly she tugged on my arm. "Come. This way."

I gazed in wonder as she drew me along. There were no cars here, only sturdy horses and an occasional cart. As the villagers scurried about tending to their nightly routines, I noticed that the colors of their clothing matched the green and brown hues of their surroundings. Their expressions reflected a general look of contentment. They stopped and bowed slightly as we passed. I wondered if this was a standard greeting, or an acknowledgment of station.

21

Either way, I decided to bow back. I did take note, however, that my companion did not.

An old man looked down at us from his second story stoop. He rocked back and forth and smiling a toothless grin. An unsettling feeling washed over me. He was out of place in this fantasy setting. The scenery around us was without blemish, oddly unaffected by age or weather, but this man had a measure of decay. I looked about. Where were the rotting logs and dead branches? Aside from this one old man the village was perfect-- too perfect to be real. We continued on.

We rounded a bend. Towering before us with majestic grace stood the palace in all its splendor. Carved out of a tree much larger than the rest, thick branches traveled off in all directions. Ornamental carvings wrapped around the trunk in fantastic designs. A set of polished stairs traveled deep into its heart.

The young lady dropped my hand and flashed a brilliant smile. "So, what do you think?" she said with her arms spread wide.

"It's *magnificent*. You *made* all this?"

"Yes." She giggled.

"It must have taken forever!"

Her lovely eyes lit up. "It did take awhile, and I must admit my first few attempts were rather poor. But the villagers were very supportive."

"The villagers were here before you?"

She nodded. "I stumbled upon their village quite by accident one night. They were familiar with who I was, so I was treated like a queen. That is why I decided to stay. That, and the fact that they needed my protection from *Rath, the...*" Her jaw tightened and she leaned in close, "*the nastiest,* most *vile,* spoiled rotten little..."

There came another rumble from the sky and the villagers quickly retreated into every nook and knothole.

"Oh, now that hurts my feelings, young blood." A deep voice resonated across the open area. *"How many times do I have to tell you, Kitaya, if you blaspheme my name, I will make things most difficult for you."*

The voice unnerved me to my very core.

"Rath!" Kitaya clenched her delicate fingers into fists of rage. *"Where are you?* If you hurt my people, I will make you pay! I swear!"

"Easy, young one," the voice boomed out. *"You might burst a vessel in your head. Then where would you be?"* I looked up to see a giant disembodied head filling the sky. It was aglow, and there was a twisted smile upon it. *"Who's your friend, strumpet?"* The voice dripped with arrogance. *"He doesn't look like much from up here."*

I felt a presence breeze by my shoulder, and turned to see a man whose face matched the image in the sky. Instinctively I looked back up. And immediately regretted it. A hand grabbed my throat and my back slammed hard against the matted ground. Rath hovered above me, his hand still on my throat.

"Leave him alone!" Kitaya screamed.

"If you do not interfere, little one, I'll stop the games for a bit," he stated smoothly, never taking his eyes off mine. I reached up to pry his hand free from my neck-- but his strength was enormous. "You're not going to give me any trouble, are you, newbie?" He smirked, re-emphasizing his hold on my neck. *"I* am the ultimate ruler of this world. If you resist me, you will *die. That* is rule number one." He released his grip and moved away.

I caught my breath and arose cautiously, eying him in case of further attack. I tried to take a non-threatening stance, so as not to invoke any further hostility to my neck. Or any other part of my body for that matter.

He paced back and forth with hands on his hips, an ominous figure of a man, yet unnaturally charismatic. He wore a strange suit of black and red rubber armor. His curly blond hair rested against his padded shoulders. And a scar ran diagonally across his right cheek. His eyes, like mine, were blue metal spheres. Cold and lifeless.

"Conspiracy!" he said, glaring at me and pushing his finger toward the sky. *"You,* with us no more than an hour and you're *already* conspiring against me!

"Y- You must be mistaken."

"Silence!" He drew up his shoulders. "I will not be made a fool! I know conspiracy when I see it!"

"You see conspiracy in *everything,* Rath!" Kitaya yelled. "All we want is to be left alone!"

He snapped around to face the girl. "Then why is it your troops stand on my border this very minute prepared for invasion?"

She stared at him in disbelief. "They are not there to *invade!* It is a defensive line. And it would *not* be there if you would stop your silly games!" Her lovely almond shaped eyes glared at him.

"Oh," he said unexpectedly, his expression taking on an air of sudden understanding. "My apologies young lady, my mistake," he said insincerely.

A horse materialized beside him and in one motion he spun and lifted himself onto its back. His cold eyes met mine as he leaned forward in the saddle. "I'll be watching *this* one," he stated with finality. The horse bolted off leaving a flurry of needles in its wake.

We watched until he was out of sight. "Wow," I said, beating at my clothing to get the needles off. "That's the second time I've been accosted since I arrived."

Kitaya shook her head. "It is always something new with him."

"So what do I do now?" I asked, feeling a renewed concern for my safety.

Kitaya looked up at me with a sullenness unbecoming of her beautiful face, and said, "Practice."

Chapter Three

THE CHILD KING

$$\alpha$$

Since I wasn't quite ready to be on my own I decided to take Kitaya up on her offer to stay the night in her palace. She informed me that we didn't require sleep, so I figured this would be a good time to push for answers. I gathered she knew the condition of my memory and I hoped we'd be able to spend several hours discussing the questions plaguing me, questions like: who am I, who are you, and *why don't we need sleep?*

She left me in what she called her "living chambers" while she attended to her nightly routine, so I looked about and took in my surroundings. In the center of the large room was a huge stone fireplace, magnificent, though apparently unused. I circled the enormous structure. All four sides opened like insidious mouths complete with teeth running across the tops and bottoms. An immense chimney reached to the ceiling high above.

The rest of the room reflected the artistry and earthy motif of the village. The walls were alive with vines and vibrant flowers. A small stream gurgled along the base of one wall, emptying into a fountain in the corner. At the far end of the room thick glass doors stood slightly opened, revealing a balcony. The doors merged perfectly with the surrounding walls as though finished glass were a natural part of an outdoor scene. It was nature with structure, a work of art, and I wished to compliment the artist.

A servant brought a platter of delicacies for me to sample. I thanked him, he departed, and once again I stood waiting. I was anxious to find out what Kitaya knew about this world. I thought back to what Sajin had asked of me. He wanted to meet with Gaza because he thought Gaza could stop the war between Rath and Armadon. I wondered if Kitaya would agree. I also wanted to find out more about Rath. He was obviously unstable and apparently had a particular interest in me. This did not settle well in my stomach.

Kitaya entered and my thoughts evaporated. Again I tried desperately not to stare. She had changed into a thin silk evening gown with iridescent fabric clinging gently to her small curves. She gestured and I turned to see two comfortable chairs next to a crackling fire.

Impressive.

We settled in and I gazed at her radiance, desperately trying to bring my mind back to the questions at hand. She raised her arm slightly and began making a circular motion with her finger. Presently a cup and saucer materialized in her gentle grasp. The smell of sweet tea reached my nostrils, so I decided to make a cup of my own. First I visualized a cup and saucer, the threads formed the frames. I then added material, black porcelain with gold trimming. And finally the tea, Earl Grey, hot.

Kitaya spoke. "Are you feeling any more relaxed?"

"As relaxed as possible under the circumstances." I took a deep breath. "I've been tense since I awoke-- but somehow in your company..." I gave a warm smile. " I feel much more at ease."

"That is good to hear." Her eyes lit up. "You must have questions."

"Indeed. Unfortunately they all fall into the same category of urgency, I hardly know where to begin. I guess, first and foremost, I'd like to know who I *am.*"

She frowned slightly. "I am afraid I cannot help you there but I do know what the people of this world call you."

"And that is?"

"Sam' Dejal, the god of reason."

That's odd, I thought, *the butler at the mansion called me Tardin.*

"What's your title?" I asked.

"I am Ki' Janu, the goddess of the wood, or more accurately, the goddess of nature."

"That is fitting. You do seem to love trees."

"You mean because of the village? I created this village more for the people's sake than for my own. Trees are wonderful and I like nature and all, but I would not consider myself connected to it in any way." She shrugged and took a sip of her tea.

I studied her a moment. Then spoke again. "Do you remember anything from before this place?"

She shook her head. "I do not."

"Then you must have been as confused as I was when you first awakened."

"Hmm. Probably not. I did not have time to be. Rath was on me from the beginning." She tilted her head. "But that is a long story, you probably would not want to hear it."

"On the contrary, if you wouldn't mind telling it."

"Very well..." She sat up straighter and furrowed her brow. "Well, when I first became aware, I was in a large, lavishly furnished tree house." She paused and her eyes took on a distant look. "I was reaching into a kitchen cabinet to get something but I could not remember *what.* I felt strange and everything looked so *funny."* She paused a moment, then gave her head a little shake. "Anyway I heard someone knocking so I found my way to the front door and looked out. Just outside standing on a large branch was this *magnificent* looking man in dark glasses. When I opened the door he greeted me with a bow. I was instantly taken in

27

by him, he seemed harmless enough, so I invited him in." She looked at me and smiled. "After all I had a lot of questions.

"But listen to this. He convinced me he was a *genie* and that I had called to him in my dreams. At first I thought he was nuts, but then he took off his glasses, and, well I think you can understand why I believed him. He wove this elaborate tale about how he was genie to the throne and how his search for a bride had led him to me. He said he did not want to be too forward but he wished to court me. It would be a long courtship and in the end, if I was not completely taken with him, he would return me to my planet with whatever riches I desired." She raised her eyebrows. "That sounded like a good deal to me."

"So," I interjected, "you didn't doubt him at all?"

"No." She shook her head. "I did not. He was very convincing and *very* handsome." Her gaze drifted away again. "--No, I did not doubt him. So we traveled to the castle to meet the 'royal family' to whom, he *said* he owed his service and loyalty. And of course our means of transportation was a flying carpet. This made me believe him even more. He brought me into a room full of lavish gowns and expensive jewelry so I would be 'presentable' when he announced my arrival. I put together the most exquisite outfit: an elegant silk dress, white gloves, diamonds... When I was ready he escorted me to two enormous doors but before they were opened he gave me a blindfold. He *said* it was customary for the royal family to look upon the bride-to-be before she was allowed to look upon them.

"Finally when he opened the doors I could hear the voices of what I *thought* was the assembled nobility. He led me forward several paces into the room but then stepped away. As I turned to reach for him someone shoved me hard and I landed on my chest with my face pushing deep into something foul! I slid downward until finally I stopped and tore the blindfold from my head. *Thousands* of eyes were looking down at me from row upon row of a *huge* amphitheater. I was *mortified!*

"What did you *do?*" I said, feeling shocked and somewhat thankful for my own experience.

"I did not know *what* to do! Then this man who I thought was my *friend* announced, 'BEHOLD, THE GODDESS KI' JANU!' I swear the whole arena shook from the laughter. I struggled to my feet in the slippery mess, wiping the crud from my arms, and looked behind me. I had slid down a slide covered with what I think was grease and human waste! Into a pool of manure!"

"You must have been livid!"

"Oh I *was!* And my anger must have ignited something because all of a sudden the room went dark and all of the voices fell silent-- except *Rath's*, he laughed louder! But then I noticed that my hands were *glowing* orange! Now *I* had to laugh because I thought, *I* am a genie! But I was so humiliated and hurt and *angry!* I opened my arms and currents of electricity shot out toward him."

"Did you get him?"

"Yes. But he fell to the floor and just kept laughing, saying, 'Is *that* the best you can do?'" She gave me an exasperated look. "But then the room filled with the blue strings and somehow I knew they were reacting to my thoughts. I thought about the flying carpet and there it was. So I jumped onto it and took off like a flash." She raised her chin in defiance. "I never looked back."

"Wow!" I said, shaking my head. "Did you ever manage to get him back for that?"

"I have tried a few times." She shrugged. "But he is extremely smart. He usually finds some way to twist things around to his advantage."

"Why do you think he's he so cruel?"

29

"I do not... I honestly do not think he understands he is being cruel. He is like a spoiled child."

"Do you know what happened when he first arrived?"

"No, I have never thought to find out."

"--Maybe he had a really bad experience."

"Maybe-- Hmm. How could we find..." She put her hand to her chin and looked thoughtful. "Oh!" She looked back at me. *Moota!*"

I gave her a sideways glance. *"Moota?* What's a *Moota?"*

"He is a sky searcher." She smiled.

"--Oh, o-*kay."* I returned her smile. "That helps."

She shook her head. "Let me explain. A *sky searcher,"* she annunciated the words, "searches the sky for fragments of the past, which were put there by what is called... Hold on. I will let *him* explain. Her eyes dimmed and her head tilted slightly to the side. After a short moment she looked up. "I called him. He is on his way."

I squinted at her. "What did you just do?"

"I have a strand attached to those I keep in contact with the most. It allows me to speak to them."

"Oh. --You'll have to teach me that trick."

She smiled. "It is easy. Just bring up the web and break a strand with your fingers." I did as she said. "Good. Now touch one end to my neck just below my ear." I reached out and placed my finger under her ear. Her skin was soft, I could feel her warmth. "Now attach the other end to yourself and close your eyes. There. Now to establish a link all you need to do is picture me in your mind. *Good. Now no matter where we go we can always communicate with one another. And if for any reason you do not wish to talk with me all you need to do is detach the strand from yourself."*

"This is fantastic!" As I pictured her my thought turned to vibration and traveled to her through the strand.

My thoughts were energy now, as were hers. *"I can think of no one else I'd rather be attached to."*

I heard a giggle inside.

"Really." I opened my eyes. "I want to thank you for helping me. I've been feeling pretty lost," I said aloud.

She opened her eyes and gave a tender smile. "We are both lost, but perhaps we can find the way together."

"I'd like that," I said, reaching out to put my hand on hers.

"And in so doing..." She stood and turned toward the door, "may we fix the damage caused by our own. --He approaches."

The doors opened and a tiny man entered. I stood and suppressed a smile. He looked more like a gnome than a man; stout and sturdy, with a green shirt, tan vest, soft pointy shoes. And upon his face (which showed the wrinkles of many years) a pair of shiny glasses straddled his fat little nose. Yet despite his appearance he had a look of intelligence about him, like a scientist-- granted, a very *short* scientist.

Kitaya giggled.

"Um," I whispered out of the corner of my mouth. "how do I drop our connection?" "Blank out your mind," she whispered back in like fashion. I did as she suggested and felt her presence push from my mind.

"You called for me, precious one?" The little man swept low in a courtly bow.

"Yes, we have need of your talents. But first allow me to introduce you. Moota, this is Sam' Dejal. Sam, this is Moota."

"It is a great pleasure to meet you, lord." He bowed again.

"Likewise," I mused.

"Did you bring your event cells?" Kitaya asked.

"Right here in my bag, great lady."

"What is an event cell?" I asked.

31

The little man looked at me with aged and somewhat bloodshot eyes. "It is a device which allows a person to relive the past. You see around our world we have a layer of gas called the cognosphere." He gazed up as if through the ceiling. "The cognosphere acts as a mirror to what was. In it is the imprint of our entire history. Unfortunately, however, the information is scattered and the only way to access it is with an event cell." He paused. "Shall I continue, lord?"

"Please. How does it work?"

He examined me briefly, then continued. "When placed at an event, the cell sends out a pulse which marks the cognosphere. Then later, that same device, tuned to its own harmonic, can search the cognosphere for the same pulse. The cell finds all the pieces of the original pulse and combines them into one. When a mind enters the cell it encounters the reflection of the event and is able to interact with it.

"Interesting," I said, intrigued. "What if I were to enter an event cell which had never been used?"

"Oh, very bad, very bad," he said shaking his head.

"Why?"

"Imagine this planet's entire history fed into your mind without any cohesion, it would be like... like drinking water from the base of a waterfall. What it would do to a god we do not know, but to a mortal man..." He shuddered at the thought. "With all due respect, lord, I do not care to speak of such horrors in the presence of a lady." He turned back to Kitaya. "What do you wish of me Ki' Janu?"

She smiled and nodded. "Thank you, Moota. We would like to hear of Rath's arrival and witness the event you recently acquired."

"You heard about that," he said, sounding like a mouse caught in a trap.

"I have never forbidden any of you from pursuing that which pleases you. You are an inquisitive old sot. I like that about you."

"Thank you, your holiness." He bowed so low I thought his nose would scrape the ground.

Kitaya sat, brought her knees to her chest, and wrapped her arms around them. She gestured for me to sit then turned back to the little man. "Alright, Moota, teach us."

He thought for a moment, then spoke. "When at first he arrived, Rath, known as the god of fire was seen only occasionally, always in the same manner, walking aimlessly through a town late at night, apparently drunk out of his mind." As the old man talked he used elaborate hand movements and animated facial gestures. "And he was always babbling to himself. At first we thought he was talking to the other gods, but soon it became clear that he was delusional; the conversations were erratic and broken. As you can imagine the spectacle was quite unnerving for the local residents. Sometimes people would muster up the courage to come out of their homes and greet him, but he would usually look right through them and keep on his way, *if* they were lucky. Sometimes he would fly into a rage. So most people avoided him completely.

"Strangely however, the children loved him. Anytime there were children around he would become coherent and quite amiable. He seemed to truly enjoy their company; his eyes would light up as he handed out treats and gifts he'd created. In fact his affinity toward children was so great that he decided to visit hundreds of orphanages around the world. Some children were scared of him, but most were captivated by his kindness and interest in them. He promised to care for them and allow them to do whatever they wished if they joined him. For most it was an offer they could not refuse. Countless children responded. But after awhile he became restless.

33

That's when he seized control of the country of Pagnia. He walked straight into the royal castle, declared himself ruler, and stated that all who challenged him would be extinguished. Those brave enough to stand forth were silenced in horrible ways."

Moota looked about then came in close. "Of course-- he told the people of Pagnia-- that the royal family had been relocated-- to another kingdom on the other side of the world. But we know that was not the case. Our informants tell us he had his child army go in and remove all the residents of the castle by force, save for members of the royal family, who were locked in the dungeon to perish along with their home. I recently acquired the event cell placed at Mount Dastra. It shows what was to be the pinnacle of the incursion." He reached for his pouch and pulled out a dark glass square with smoothly sanded edges. "This is the event cell." He tapped the cell with a hairy finger. "It will allow you to interact with the reflection that was marked. Which one of you would like to go first?"

Kitaya looked at me. "Would you?"

"Ah, okay. How does it work?" I stood and reached out my hand.

"Notice the top." He handed me the device and pointed. "It is malleable, slightly firmer than a sponge. Press that edge to your forehead and the moment will be sent to you. You will not actually be present at the event but you will perceive a physical body.

"What if I want to stop it?"

"Close your eyes and blank out your mind, this will terminate the link, and your consciousness will return to your actual body."

"Sounds simple enough," I said, not feeling the confidence I portrayed. I placed the soft black cushion on my forehead and instantly found myself standing in a field of knee-high grass. Hundreds of people were traveling up a dirt trail. I looked around. A short distance up the path something big was going on. I made my way to the road and followed the stream of refugees. No one paid any attention to me.

Moving up a steady incline, I looked behind and saw the origin of their trek, a large village surrounding a huge stone castle. Apparently these were the residents of Pagnia, and judging by the multitude, it looked like Rath was planning on destroying more than just the royal castle. I spotted a young child walking along the edge of the crowd, digging a stick into the dirt as he walked. He was wearing the same kind of red rubber armor I'd seen on Rath. *He must be one of Rath's children,* I thought. Slowly I turned and scanned the outskirts of the crowd. Sure enough, there were others dressed in the same peculiar apparel.

Topping a slight incline I encountered several small gatherings of women and children sitting about with their belongings piled around them. In the midst of the smaller groups, talking furiously amongst themselves, was a large group of men. I headed in their direction. As I weaved my way through the various groups, I couldn't help but look down on the faces of these poor displaced families. I felt for them; there was great sadness in their eyes. What right did anyone have to push these people from their homes? It was outrageous!

"This is an outrage!" came a voice from inside the circle. I saw an opening and stepped inside. Three men stood talking in the center. Their clothing stood out from the rest in both quality and design. *They must be from the ruling party,* I thought. The same man continued. "Will we not *stand* and protect our property? He is but one man!"

"We are not fighters, Fyousa and even if we were, he is too powerful."

The man grimaced. "We are not *fighters* because we choose it not, not because it cannot be! We *cannot* stand still in the face of this *aggression* and do *nothing!* He has snatched our homes, taken the land we have worked *so hard* to nurture and protect! Our people have worked for centuries to build that kingdom! We *cannot* let Rath take what is not his to take!"

The third man spoke. "Be calm my friend." He placed his hand on the man's shoulder. "Does it not state in the great text that the brothers and sisters of light would one day join us? Is it not so they created this planet and our people from the dust of the cosmos? Then is it not fair for them to reclaim the land which is rightfully theirs?" The crowd watched intently as he turned and addressed them. "Tul' Naydor is no saint but he has demonstrated the power of the gods. He is one of the Ten. He has every right to place his claim on our land! Now disperse! Go back to your families and tell them not to despair, for although things look dark, we must trust that the gods have shined on us this day!"

Reluctantly the crowd began to disperse, and the old man looked back at Fyousa. "Let us not hear any more talk of revolution, my friend," he stated smoothly. "Is it not better for us to live in the dark, than to die in the light as if we never were?"

The two of them stood in silence watching as the others moved away.

Then-- through the sea of moving bodies-- I saw him. The god of fire, sitting with his legs crossed, staring out at the village. I made my way over and crouched before him. If he saw me he made no indication. His eyes were scanning the sky intently as he rocked back and forth; he was exerting some kind of force on the clouds. I looked up. Slowly, almost imperceptibly, pure white melted into a massive pool of brown undulating liquid. Deep dark colors swirled about in pockets of chaos, blocking out the sun, hovering like a blanket of death. Everything in the valley took on a dim brown hue. I looked back at Rath. His eyes were blank. In eerie oblivion his children played behind him.

36

With a wicked smile he stood and faced the crowd. Without warning the brown liquid fell to the earth, it burned and smote everything it touched, filling the entire valley, dissolving everything in its path. Leaving nothing but a smoking hole and a memory of better times.

The people watched in horror, clinging to each other with tears in their eyes as everything they had ever known dissolved before them. Their past was erased, and their future looked as dark as the charred ground below.

Rath looked pleased with his handiwork. He paced back and forth in front of the multitude of grief stricken faces. Finally he stopped. His hands moved rapidly in the air in a series of gestures which ended at his mouth and when he began to speak his voice was amplified. "The life you once knew is now gone!" he announced. "*I* am now your ruler. For those of you who do not know me, I am Tul' Naydor, the god of fire. But you may call me Rath. You do not realize this yet, but this is a glorious occasion. From this day forth *I* will provide you with comforts no mortal ruler could. You will never again go without food and you will never again be forced to walk about in tattered rags while the kingdom sucks taxes out of your empty pockets. Under *my* rule there will be no taxes! These things and many more are the benefits you are now entitled to as residents of *my* kingdom. No more will disease claim the lives of your family and friends, and no more will you struggle to provide the necessities of life. From this day forth you may pursue whatever endeavors please you, so long as they do not conflict with my own."

The people hung on his every word; every statement offered a glimmer of hope. Their faces reflected a great yearning as he played upon their desperation like a master musician.

"What I ask for in return is your infinite loyalty and worship. If you treat me well I will return your goodwill tenfold, but if you defy me," he leveled his eyes at them, "I will make things most unpleasant. Now! *Behold,* as I create our new home and the core of my empire to come!"

With that he turned toward the scorched pit and began creating his new kingdom. He had already designed the buildings and other items he wished to put down. I could see their wire frames floating in the sky. Now it was simply a matter of stamping the objects where he wanted them. In the valley building after building appeared out of thin air. The last of which was his castle, rising from the center of the city like a tall white skyscraper. It shone like a beacon of light, radiant in its beauty. But I knew its insides were dark-- because I knew its creator.

By the end of the day Rath had turned the ugly blackened valley into a paradise of beauty. Those used to living in overcrowded, broken down, hovels were now faced with the proposition of living in brand new homes, with a patch of land to boot.

I followed Rath through the streets as he created large stores of food, necessities, and other assorted treasures. The peasants took what they wanted. It was clear by their excitement they had all but forgotten the injustice and were willing to accept Rath as their new ruler.

My stomach felt uneasy. They were pleased with his gifts and promises, but what would be the cost? I felt sure after the initial excitement died down, they would remember the life they had left behind, and regret their loss.

I had seen enough.

I closed my eyes and blanked out the scene. When I opened them I found myself looking at my companions in the exact same positions I had left them in. "How long was I gone?" I asked.

"Not long," said Kitaya, "fifteen seconds maybe. How long did it seem?"

"I'd say five, six hours."

"That is a long time." She frowned.

"It went by fast."

"Alright, let me do this before I change my mind." She stood up and took the box. Gently she placed it against her forehead. Her body tightened and for a few brief moments she was completely occupied. I could only assume she was witnessing the same events I had witnessed, except perhaps from a different perspective.

Her hands dropped and she looked at me in astonishment. "Thank you, Moota. That was extremely enlightening." Her expression became cold as she turned from us and slowly walked toward the balcony.

"Do you require anything else Ki' Janu?" he called after her.

"No, that will be all thank you. You may go." She seemed disoriented.

"Are you okay, Kitaya?" I trailed after her.

"Gaza has not been sleeping," she said softly, staring through the balcony doors.

"What does that mean?"

When she looked up her face was wet. "A long time ago during the foundation of the world, it is said that Gaza went mad. Creating Vrin was too much for him. The ancient book says he became apathetic and fell into a deep sleep, a pool of forgetfulness. It is that sleep which has protected Vrin from his madness these many centuries."

"I don't understand. Why did Sajin wish to speak with him?" I said, half to myself.

"Sajin is a purist," she said with disdain. "He believes the gods are incapable of fault. He does not believe Gaza is mad. I wish I shared his naivety." She turned back toward the balcony.

"Kitaya-- what did you see in there?"

She gazed blankly at the glass doors. "I followed a group of Rath's children into his new castle." She looked back at me. "I climbed a staircase to a balcony overlooking an enormous library. Down below I could see Rath and another god I did not recognize at first. But when he spoke

I realized it was Gaza. They were in a heated conversation. I'd missed the first part but it was clear he was very upset. He said something was wrong with the people of Vrin and something about searching for a perfect match..." She stopped and a look of panic flashed in her eyes.

"Kitaya?"

"He said, 'Fear me for I am the maker. This world will pass away if I do not get what I want!'"

"He-- threatened to *destroy* Vrin?"

"Yes." Her face hardened. "And he said he would return us to the void."

"The void?"

She nodded slowly. "I have flashbacks from before this place. The emptiness. The loneliness. Floating through boundless space with nothing but the web to keep me company." She looked up at me in desperation. "I for one, do *not* want to go back."

Her description sparked a memory. Nothing but the web. No body. No environment. It made me shudder. "Yes, I remember," I whispered.

"Then remember the misery and hold it close-- for we are about to do battle over the abyss." Her eyes turned to the ground and her voice lowered. "And I will probably be the first to go."

"Why would you say that?"

Her chin trembled. "--Because he saw me."

Chapter Four

THE FACE OF THE ENEMY
1 0 0 1 1 1 0

ζ

The morning sun heated the curtains as fingers of
light pierced through the gaps between. The dust particles.
They did not swirl about as expected, but merely hovered
there, motionless, as if their presence was only for the
visual effect. Even when I blew at them, they didn't move.
What IS this place?

I stared. And the questions filtered through my mind
for the hundredth time. If Gaza was all-powerful, then why
did he need Rath's help? And why would Gaza destroy his
own creation? Did I need to contact Sajin? Would it help or
hurt for him to know that Gaza's solution to the problem
was not a viable option? Although dissolving the planet
would invariably stop the conflict between Rath and
Armadon, there would be no one left to appreciate it...
Kitaya's words echoed in my mind. *"He is looking for a
perfect match."* What did this mean?

Though the long night had brought me no closer to
a solution, my path at least seemed clearer. I needed to find
out what Gaza was looking for, and why. If I could find the
solution to this mystery, perhaps it would bring me one step
closer to solving my own.

It became obvious that I could no longer deny the
pain in my back. I had been crouching in the corner far too
long. I stood, stretched, and shuffled across to the full-
length mirror. A bath would have been pleasurable but was
unnecessary. I could alter my appearance in any way I

chose. I brought up the web and molded clothing similar to those of the townsmen, simple and comfortable. Pleased with the result I headed down to bid good morning to my lovely hostess.

She was on the terrace overlooking the ocean. A warm breeze pushed in as I opened the glass doors. She looked up at me with a lovely smile, her face so young and perfect. Her spirits had apparently lifted a bit since the evening before. "Good morning, Sam." Her smile brightened. "Do you mind if I call you Sam?"

"You know." I furrowed my brow. "I thought about it last night and I think I'd like to be called Jason, Jason Tardin. Back at the mansion I was addressed as Lord Tardin and I saw the name engraved on a trophy in the study."

"Hmm, Jason," she said, trying it out. "Yes, that is nice. It does seem to fit."

"Good. Then it's settled. Jason it is." I sat down and lifted my face to the morning sunshine. "Beautiful day."

She nodded her agreement. "Did you come up with any solutions?"

"Nothing earth shattering."

She looked thoughtful. "What *I* cannot figure is, if the event we witnessed last night took place some time ago, then-- why are we still here?"

"I don't know. Maybe he's still looking."

"It is possible, but he sounded like he was at the end of his rope."

"I guess he found more rope. What do you think we should do?"

"I do not know. I have kept pretty much to myself here. I am not familiar with what is going on in the rest of the world. I would not know where to start looking for answers."

"Is there someone close to Gaza, someone who knows him better than anyone?"

"Well-- there is Humphrey. He was the second. Gaza was still active when Humphrey came to Vrin."

"Where can we find this Humphrey?"

"Good question. He has chosen to live as a hermit. All I know is that he lives in the woods somewhere outside of Ristol, and that he refuses to use the power. I saw him in an event cell once. What was it he said to Gaza? Oh yes." She made a stout grumpy face. "I have no interest in playing *God,"* she said in a deep gruff voice.

I found her impersonation amusing. "So he chooses to live like a regular person?"

"Yes, he lives off the land as much as possible."

"Independent, I like that."

The door opened and a woman stepped out onto the terrace. Kitaya looked up, her eyes brightened. "Corel!" she squealed. The woman smiled back with brilliant enthusiasm as Kitaya jumped up and gripped her friend in a warm embrace.

Corel looked to be middle aged but she wore her years well. Her wavy brown hair was swept back in a long ponytail. She was wearing an outfit much like that of a climber, very sleek, and very feminine. Her muscular arms gripped Kitaya around her tiny waist as she lifted her off the floor.

"I have missed you! Where did you go off to?" probed Kitaya.

Corel drew away. "I've been exploring again. This time in the Adilian Mountains. The people there have a *fascinating* culture, and you know me. Besides, I needed a little break from all the crap Tiko was shoveling. Come see what I brought you." Kitaya shot me a smile as she followed her friend back into the palace.

I sat there, unsure of what to do. I didn't want to be left out, but I didn't want to tag along uninvited and appear overly eager. So I decided to create another cup of tea. If they wanted to talk with me, they would call.

Corel had the blue fire in her eyes. It was obvious she was one of us. Was Tiko as well? Apparently there was some friction between them. I hoped it wasn't as bad as the blood between Rath and Armadon. With this thought I was brought me back to the problems at hand. From what I could piece together, Gaza was very powerful and extremely resourceful. After all, he created this entire world. I doubted I could do the same. If we were going to confront him we would need to enlist the help of the others.

First we needed to know what he was looking for and why. If we knew that we would have a better chance of finding a peaceful solution, if there was one. We also needed to know why he hadn't let anyone besides Rath know about the search. And why *Rath?*

I gazed out over the ocean and considered going to find out what Kitaya and her friend were up to, but decided against it. It frustrated me that under more casual circumstances I would have been thoroughly enjoying this place. I wanted to spend more time experimenting with my new powers. I couldn't *wait* to fly again, but I couldn't afford to let my guard down. There was no telling what might happen next or what danger lurked around the next corner. I imagined the worst, me, strapped helplessly to a rock in the desert, birds pecking at my face. I shuddered at the thought.

A small movement on my left pinkie made me look down. My ring-- was *moving!* I let out an involuntary yelp and almost fell over backwards in my chair. I jumped up flailing, desperately trying to shake the ring from my hand. After several seconds of this ridiculous behavior I stopped and held my arm out straight. Reluctantly I moved my hand in to get a closer look. It was still moving. I stared wide-eyed as the little ring unwound itself from my finger and began rubbing its tiny head against my knuckle. I reached out with my other hand to touch it. It was a cute little thing. It wiggled around. I let it into my palm.

"Well, hello," I said softly.

It responded by lifting its head in acknowledgment.

"Do you understand what I'm saying?" I asked, incredulous.

It nodded in the affirmative.

I couldn't help smiling. "Do you have a name?"

It paused for a moment then twisted its tiny body into a shape and held the position.

"I don't understand."

It repositioned slightly.

"N? Are you making the letter N?"

It looked up and nodded, then outlined another letter.

"O?"

It nodded again.

Next was a T and then what looked like an L. "L?"

It shook its head no.

Then it hit me. "Ohh! One?"

It nodded feverishly.

"N, O, T, One, Not One? *That's* your name?"

It shook no.

I was puzzled. "Are you trying to tell me-- it's not just one name?"

It nodded happily.

"Then what should I call you?"

It appeared to go into deep thought then rubbed its head hard against my palm.

"You want to be called palm?" I smiled.

It shook no madly.

"I don't know, poke, itch, rub, scratch?"

The last one got a response. It began to wiggle around happily.

"You want to be called *Scratch?*"

The little creature nodded.

"O-*kay*. Scratch it is."

45

My tiny new friend seemed satisfied but the exertion must have tuckered him out, because he began to slow down.

"You okay?"

He nodded once, then slowly wiggled over to my pinkie and wrapped himself around it. His skin became hard and it was once again, a tiny gold ring.

I pulled the ring off my pinkie and examined it. I never would have known there was anything special about it; it looked just like a regular old ring. As I replaced it on my finger the two women strolled back out onto the balcony.

I stood politely and Kitaya addressed me first. "I am sorry, Sam, I mean, Jason. I should have introduced you. This is my friend Corel. She has been away for awhile. She likes to travel."

"Good to meet you." I offered my hand. "I'm the new guy on the block." I took note that Corel wore a similar ring, and that Kitaya, did not.

"Good to meet you as well." Corel shook my hand firmly. "Kit has informed me of Gaza's plan. I find it to be very disturbing."

"I would have to agree with you."

"She says you want to try to find Humphrey. I doubt he'll be very helpful. If you do manage to find him, there's a good chance he won't even talk to you. He is *very* stubborn."

"In light of the alternative, don't you think he would at least give us some information?"

"I doubt it." She looked thoughtful. "I think we need to speak with Armadon. No one knows Rath's movements better than he."

"But isn't he as dangerous as Rath?" I asked.

"He can be but he is a strategist at heart. I'm sure he will at least listen to what we have to say. He understands that information is the strongest weapon."

46

"Then let us waste no time," I asserted.

Corel looked at Kitaya then to me. "We'll have to join hands."

As she grasped my hand I felt her power bleed into my body and mingle with my own. With a burst of blue energy we rose in a flash, high above our surroundings, until the world was nothing more than a wire globe far beneath us. The sphere turned until our destination was visible, then, as quickly as we had departed we were once again standing firm footed.

Before us stood a magnificent castle, the architecture unique in its design. The outside was encased not in stone, but in a smooth flawless metal which shone in the mid-day sun. It hurt my eyes to look directly at it. Corel stepped up. "Shall we knock and see if he's home?" she said smartly.

A deep wide chasm filled with thick mist surrounded the castle. I stared down into the darkness but could not see the bottom. Corel touched something near the edge of the pit and the ground shook as a bridge of land pushed its way across. In no time the way was passable.

We continued on toward the towering entrance and as we approached, there came a voice from the battlement. "Open the gate!" The massive barrier made a tremendous noise as its iron structure slowly lifted to allow us passage. A man scurried out to greet us. I guessed he was from the royal court as he was wearing an outfit of ruby red with bands of gold metal. His head was cocked to the side and he appeared to be talking into his wrist. "Corel, Kitaya, and an unknown sir."

Corel spoke with authority. "We wish a meeting with your lord."

The man bowed slightly. "It is my esteemed honor to welcome you, Lady Corel. The Holy One awaits you in his throne room."

"Thank you. Lead the way please."

He turned and we followed him through the massive gates. Several soldiers moved about performing various tasks, but I saw no civilians. We traveled up an immense set of black slate stairs and through an enormous set of doors. Cracks between the large stone floor tiles let off a yellow glow, filling the room with a mystical ambiance. To the rear was a magnificent throne like nothing I'd ever seen or imagined. Exotic jewels embedded in its design glimmered brightly in the soft lighting. --*I* was impressed.

The figure upon the throne was no less impressive, an intimidating hulk of a man, at least nine feet of solid iron muscle. His face was like chiseled stone. Deep dark sockets encased burning blue eyes. Now *this* guy looked like a god!

As our party approached, Armadon's voice boomed out. "WHY do you disturb me?"

Displaying cool confidence, Corel explained. "There is a matter of great importance developing. We wish to trade information."

"Are you in league with children?" he asked deeply.

"We are not."

"Then continue."

"We have news of a great darkness which is about to befall Vrin. Gaza is not the angel of peace described in the Marathil. He plans to destroy Vrin."

"WHAT!" bellowed Armadon, his voice filling the room.

"He is looking for something and has chosen Rath to help him. He told Rath he would send us back to the void if he does not find what he seeks. We have come to you because you know Rath better than any."

"Yes. I do. And your words explain much." Armadon brooded. "I thought Rath was a fool for dividing his resources, but it seems he had no choice. My informants tell me he is looking for a woman and a girl child."

"An exact match?" I blurted.

48

Corel shot me a warning glance as if to say I should not speak out of turn.

"Yes," said Armadon.

"Can you guess why he would go to Rath only, excluding the rest of us from the search?" Corel asked.

Armadon shifted in his throne. "He might not want us to know, should we decide to resist his efforts-- but that would mean his efforts are worthy of resistance." He brought his massive hand to his chin. "I do not see what harm a woman or girl child could do."

"Will you join with us against him," Corel asked boldly, "should we be forced to act?"

"Yes. But first we must find out what he is planning. It isn't wise to go against an opponent unprepared. We need to be careful and move without his knowing."

"He already knows." Kitaya stepped forward.

Armadon leveled his gaze at her. "And *how* do you know this?"

"I witnessed his conversation with Rath in an event cell-- and he saw me."

"What?" Armadon stood up. "That's not possible!"

"He saw me. I am sure of it. The question is, did he see me six months ago when the event took place, or twelve hours ago when I was in the event cell?"

Before anyone could comment, a loud siren filled the air. Armadon's head cocked to the side. He jumped up and he bolted past us. "We are under attack!"

"May we join you?" Corel called after him.

Armadon was almost to the door. "If you wish!"

We had to race to keep up with him, through broad corridors, across enormous chambers, up immense stone stairways. Eventually we emerged onto the battlement overlooking the castle grounds. We joined Armadon at the edge of the wall. Far below several ghost-like beings were ramming one by one into the massive gate of the castle. Their actions were systematic, void of thought or reason.

49

"What are those?" I found myself saying.

Looking down on the eerie scene Armadon seemed genuinely puzzled. "I've never seen anything like them. I doubt they are agents of Rath. He has never come against me with anything but mundane troops."

The dark figures tore at the metal gate with phantom teeth. Sparks ignited around them at each impact. In the flurry, I tried to make a count. It looked like six, maybe seven. With a hideous scraping noise one of the creatures broke through.

I bolted to the other side of the battlement and peered down into the courtyard. Like a snake the ghastly specter weaved in and out of men and architecture. Its eyes glaring back and forth. Seeking its prey. Its tail trailing behind like a gossamer cloth.

It chewed into its first victim and my stomach wretched as the man let out an awful scream. I brought up the web and attempted to pull at the demon's threads. --But they wouldn't move! In desperation I created a hole beneath the man. He fell and I sealed the hole with a flat piece of metal. The creature bit wildly at the barrier. I had prevailed for the moment but this was a small victory. More demons had broken through.

Kitaya reinforced the front gate while Armadon, Corel, and I fought hard to isolate the specters from the soldiers. After much effort they were finally contained. Three were trapped in the center of the courtyard, four outside the gate. They wailed and bit but the barriers stood.

"Why don't they just fly over?" I wondered aloud.

Armadon answered. "They seem to be hovering by air propulsion. See the sand below them pushing away? It must not be strong enough to lift them any higher."

Troops moved into position above the courtyard with crossbows at the ready. The tips were set on fire and they waited. I looked at Armadon.

His face tightened. "Fire!"

50

A volley of burning wood descended into the trap. The demons' wailing pierced my eardrums and increased in pitch until I found myself covering my ears-- yet the others seemed unaffected. Then it dawned on me, earplugs! I made some and quickly and stuffed them in. Unfortunately the humans did not have the same luxury. Screaming in pain, delirious from the excruciating noise, two soldiers fell to the ground from the battlements.

The wailing ceased and I looked down into the courtyard trap. Nothing remained of the creatures; the fire had consumed them utterly.

Corel made her way back over to the group. "Could these be Gaza's?"

Armadon nodded. "That would be my guess."

Kitaya cried out, "They are gone! I only turned away for a second!" Her voice was shrill and panicked.

We gathered on the outside edge of the battlement and looked down. The trap outside the gate was empty.

Kitaya looked nervous.

Corel looked concerned. "Before this gets any better," she said in a low voice, "it will probably get a lot worse."

"Much worse," said Armadon. "We need to formulate a plan."

α

After much deliberation it was decided that *I* should be the one to go and look for Humphrey. I knew little about Rath or Tiko and I felt confident that I could get Humphrey to talk. No one else, however, shared my optimism.

Corel and Armadon made preparations to infiltrate Rath's camp to find out more about the woman and child. According to Armadon's sources this information could be found inside a small black box. If they found the box, they were to contact us through the web.

Kitaya and I shared a private moment on the battlement of Armadon's castle. I wanted her to come with me to find Humphrey but everyone else thought it would be better if she went to find Tiko. He was known to be a womanizer, and Kitaya would undoubtedly have the best chance of persuading him to join us. Not only was she beautiful but Tiko had never seen her before-- and he was always looking for a new plaything.

The thought of Kitaya using her beauty to entice Tiko into cooperating with us bothered me to no end. Though we'd met only yesterday, somehow I felt I'd known her forever. And secretly I hoped that one day our relationship would grow into something more. Perhaps when this whole thing was over I would tell her this. But not now. So we parted ways. And my heart felt heavy.

Armadon advised me to seek the aid of Sajin Barrows. As it turned out he was the second most prominent figure on the planet.

The architecture of the capital city of Oonaj, like forms in a distant dream, towered in magnificent splendor. Their phantom shapes were familiar but their origins could not be attained. I knew them from another time and yet somehow the structures did not seem to go together; pyramids and battlements, marble temples and stone monoliths? In the midst of these a mighty skyscraper reached up into the clouds. It was breathtaking to behold, yet it left me with a sense of foreboding.

In the center of the city, rising up with majestic grace, stood the royal castle. Inside this massive stone structure stood a smaller building. I studied the capital building from a distance. I didn't want to just walk in through the front gate. *That* would catch Gaza's attention. After all, it wasn't every day that Sam' Dejal, the god of reason, popped in for a visit.

I circled the building and decided to go in through a barred window of what looked like a large empty storage room. I melted the bars quickly, climbed in, and silently moved across the room to the door. The door gave a faint creak as I carefully opened it and peeked out. A man passed by and I made a quick mental note of what he was wearing. Energy leaked from my hands as the threads twisted and bent to form the image of the man's clothing. Piece by piece the shapes formed in wire frames and then material was added. When I was finished I ran my fingers across the odd fabrics. Each item had its own distinctly different texture, weight, and smell. They couldn't have been any more real.

I was still a little slow at making things from the blue threads, but given time I was sure I could make anything no matter how complex. All I needed was a vague idea of shape and material and the web did the rest. I closely examined the cotton shirt. I had simply thought: *cotton* and it had appeared out of nothing. Every pore was present, every stitch in place. *Fascinating.*

Now all I needed was a way to hide my eyes. It took a moment but then an idea came to me. I created a handkerchief and a white cane. I would be a blind man. Using a trick I'd learned from Kitaya I made the cloth visible from only one side. To everyone else it was a thick covering, but to me it was as transparent as plastic wrap.

I stepped through the door and started walking down the hall casually tapping the cane for effect. A woman passed by giving plenty of room, but she took little notice of me. It was the same with the two soldiers standing guard at the next intersection. I continued following the hallway around in a large arc and passed by several more intersections. Each had two men standing guard, but no one paid any attention to me.

For several minutes I searched up and down the long corridors. I couldn't put my finger on it-- but something was wrong. Like the architecture of the city the objects and people here didn't seem to fit together. Paintings of all sizes littered the walls, some ornately framed in precious metals, others surrounded by brightly painted wood. In some areas images were carved directly into the finely sanded surfaces and in other spots crude cave drawings could be seen. Soldiers, statesmen, and an assortment of employees rushed about their daily tasks wearing suits and swords. Some carried briefcases, others held rolled up scrolls.

After awhile the corridors began to blend into one another, but then I saw a man who looked like he might be able to help me. He wore a security badge. I waited until he finished speaking with two guards then followed him down to the next corridor. I checked in front and behind. All was clear.

"You, sir, could you help me please?" I stated loudly.

He stopped and coolly replied, "What do you need? I am very busy."

I moved closer and revealed my face.

His eyes widened. "I am sorry, your holiness. I- I did not recognize..."

"I do not wish to be recognized. Will you help me?" I asked gruffly.

"Y- Yes. Yes of course."

"I am looking for Sajin Barrows."

"H- he is in the council chambers. I am not authorized to go in-- b- but I know someone who is."

"Can we trust this person?"

"Yes."

"I will emphasize I do *not* want it known I am here. I am trusting you will keep this in confidence."

"You can count on me, lord."

"Go then. I will wait." I tapped him on the shoulder, attaching a thread. He quickly departed and I brought up the web to keep an ear on him. He did what he said he would and soon returned with another man.

"This is Randal. He can help you."

The man wore a fine blue suit. White curly hair covered most of his burly face. He reminded me of Santa Claus. I uncovered my eyes.

"Follow me please," he said gruffly.

I followed him down an endless string of hallways until the man slowed to a stop. As he opened the heavy door to the council chamber I quickly scanned the interior. Around a large granite table in the center of the room were twelve men in business suits. The table formed a symmetrical dodecagon. A man sat before each flat edge. Papers littered the table.

Randal spoke in a lowered voice. "One moment, I will get him for you."

55

Sajin was on the far side of the table apparently in a heated debate with the man next to him. As Randal spoke in his ear he looked up quickly, then excused himself. I couldn't help noticing how tired he looked. This was no great surprise, he was a man with a lot on his mind.

"Greetings, Lord Tardin." He spoke quietly. "What an unexpected surprise. Why do you come in such secrecy?"

I looked at Randal. "Thank you. You may go." I reached out and shook his hand and deposited two rather large diamonds. His eyes widened. "I trust you will keep our meeting *secret,*" I said, looking him in the eye. "And make sure the other man receives his share."

"Yes, sir. Thank you, sir." He bowed and left.

I turned back to Sajin. "Is there a place we can talk privately?"

"Yes, this way."

He led me to a chamber and as he opened the door the scent of strawberries wafted out. Inside many candles were burning. A fire crackled in the fireplace. In the center of the room, a cloaked figure sat poring over a thick brown book.

I looked at Sajin, slightly annoyed. "I said I want to go somewhere *private.*"

He gave me a puzzled look. "This is private, lord."

I squinted at him. "Then who is *that?*" I pointed to the slumped figure.

"Again, I find I must apologize. I did not wish to state what I thought you already knew. His name is Charm. He is our sky searcher. Last night he was found here, frozen in that position." He looked toward the figure. "I do not believe he can hear us. We may speak freely."

I did not respond to Sajin but moved toward the silent shadowy form. Completely motionless. Frozen above a thick leather book. The man's dark features appeared distorted in the flickering firelight. His expression was one of total astonishment, as though he had uncovered something of great importance. My heart skipped a beat as a haunting realization took hold of me. "What book is this?" I asked, fighting to keep my voice even.

"That is the sacred tome, lord."

I looked up. "What is it *called?*" I asked shortly.

Sajin looked at me questioningly, then stated slowly, "Davata Notrals?"

The room began to swim. I reached for a table.

"Are you all right, lord?"

"I'm fine," I replied through clenched teeth. "I am-- merely experiencing-- entrance fluctuations." *Entrance fluctuations? That was a pitiful excuse.* Gradually my head cleared and I took a long hard look at the figure in the chair. Who *was* this man? Why had he frozen in place the night I arrived? And *more* importantly, what did that *book* have to do with it? I needed to know more but didn't want to let my guard down in front of Sajin. "Sajin, what is your understanding of Davata Notrals?"

He furrowed his brows. "It is a gift."

"Is that all you have to say about it?"

He thought a moment. "I understand it is alien to our world and that its text is ever changing." His eyes took on a distant look. "It speaks of lands which do not exist and of great men who have no history in Vrin. It has puzzled our scholars for centuries. They have sought after an answer to the singular God depicted within it. This God is referred to as the God of All, perhaps inaccurately, by our sky searchers." He gave a slight pause, perhaps hoping I would step in with some universal truth. He appeared disappointed and continued. "We have used it as a guide to living a pure life and have utilized its principles in the development of our world's government. Although we have seen the stories of the people in it change, the message of the law does not. It is this law which has kept Vrin at peace

57

for centuries, that is, until the gods returned." He stopped abruptly. "I beg your pardon for my frankness."

"You speak the truth. I will not hold that against you." I looked him in the eye. "You're right. War has returned to Vrin and for that I am sorry. But you have to understand, not all the gods wish it. I can't change what Rath has done, it is tragic and criminal. But a new threat has surfaced which is far more menacing..." Again I wondered how much I should disclose.

"Lord?"

I threw caution to the wind. "Gaza is on the verge of destroying Vrin. We are gathering forces against him."

He stood dumfounded. "I- I do not understand. He created this world. Why would he want to..."

"We do not know much at this point. We're not sure what his intentions are, but we can't allow him to follow through with the threat. We need your help."

"My help?" He looked surprised. "What could I possibly do to help the gods?"

"I'm looking for Humphrey. Do you know where he is?"

"I don't. But I know someone who does."

"Can you bring him to me?"

Sajin looked doubtful. "I can bring *her* to you, but I cannot guarantee she will cooperate; she is a refugee of the war. Before the war, she stayed with Lord Humphrey for a time because her father died in his service."

"I thought Humphrey was a hermit?"

"He is. That is why her father's services appealed to him."

I waited for him to continue. Then asked, "What do you know about Humphrey?"

"Sir?"

"Tell me everything you know about him."

Sajin again appeared puzzled by my lack of knowledge. He furrowed his brow and began. "Humphrey was always too stubborn to use his power for even the smallest pleasure or necessity. So every time he went into town the people gave him a hard time because he wouldn't bless their community with treasures. Humphrey swore he would not use the power and was not willing to make any exceptions. He had decided to move on but that's when he met Janod, Thana's father." Sajin hesitated. "Is this what you wanted to hear?"

"Yes. Go on," I said, eager to learn as much as I could.

"Janod was a local businessman and fairly well to do. He approached Humphrey with a proposition. His only request was that the old god bless his daughters with a touch. In return he would bring supplies directly to Humphrey's cabin. Humphrey informed the man that his touch would not do the children any good, but that did not matter to Janod; he believed in his heart that it would protect them.

"And so it was. For four years Janod brought fresh supplies, and often Humphrey invited him to sit and talk. The children would come out and play near the river and over time a bond developed between Humphrey and Janod's family.

"But then one day Thana came in the place of her father. She told Humphrey her father was ill. Humphrey went with her to see him. He was indeed very ill and the local healer said there was a good chance he would not survive. Humphrey sat with him for several days providing what comfort he could but it was not enough, and on the sixth day, Janod died. Janod's wife knew Humphrey's convictions yet she could not bring herself to forgive him. So she packed up her belongings, and her children, and moved away. After a time Thana returned to let Humphrey know that she was not angry with him. Like her father she believed Humphrey was a good man and she understood his convictions. He invited her to stay as long as she wished; he missed the company of her family very much. She stayed for a short time but soon left to go back to her mother and sister."

Sajin stopped and furrowed his brow. "But when she reached home, she found both of them dead."

"Dead?"

"Yes. Because of the war between Rath and Armadon." Sajin shook his head. "And now she is the leader of the resistance group called SCAR. I believe you remember Dirm. He is one of them."

I let out a small laugh. "It's hard to forget a guy who points a crossbow at your head."

Sajin gave an apologetic smile. "So I realize Thana is unstable, but I know of no one else who could lead you there. Given the circumstances she would be foolish not to help."

"Do you think she will refuse?"

"We won't know until we ask."

"That is acceptable. Where do we find her?" I was anxious to get on with my mission.

"I will have to bring her to you. She will most likely want to meet in a public place, perhaps in the square."

"That will be fine. Lead the way."

The town square was bustling with merchants and peasants. Anything and everything was for sale and barter was alive and well. Sajin was unsure how long he would be but I told him not to worry, I would amuse myself.

The alleyway in which I found myself was filthy, but I paid no attention; I was engrossed in my conjuring. The fragile blue threads glowed around me, filling the air with a web of blue. I waved my hands through them and the strands became brighter. The power created by my thoughts spoke to the threads in a language which communicated need and imagery. From thought came energy, and from energy, substance.

I pictured a balloon in my mind and with a subtle shifting of perception the web responded to the thought. The threads filled the air with their ghost-like essence and at once began to bend and form to the shape of my desire. A solid frame appeared before me, balloon-like, but empty inside. I knew as soon as I added texture to the glowing frame the balloon would become real. I willed the balloon shape toward me. It responded.

My intention was to test the theory behind the threads. First was a test for substance. I made the balloon solid rock and it fell hard into my hands. It had the look of a bright red balloon but was heavy and solid with a rough stone surface. I studied it for a moment before stripping the texture, returning it to a hollow wire frame.

Next I turned it into an actual balloon. It was much lighter and the surface appeared smooth and shiny. I let it go and tried to keep it afloat with my mind. It did not respond. Apparently once the texture was applied it reacted to the laws of physics governing this world. I thought back to the magic carpet. How did it work? Perhaps in order for an object to have magical qualities it needed to be created with special material which would react to thought energy.

I started from scratch and applied a new texture to the balloon frame, a material that was an approximation of what I thought flying carpet threads would look like. It was ugly but would it function? When I let the balloon go it floated awkwardly. When I willed it to move, it did. Quite pleased with myself I moved on to the next test.

I wanted to know about an object's inner space, whether it was solid or hollow, after the outer material was added. I stripped away the magical texture of the balloon and brought the wire frame back to my hands. *How about a balloon apple?* I mused. The texture became red and glossy and its weight seemed correct for an apple of its size. I lifted it to my mouth and took a bite. It was sweet and juicy.

I examined the reaction of the threads to my physical influence. New threads formed to make up the shape of the bite mark and a new texture appeared, simulating the apple's interior. Carefully I turned the apple around and stripped away the skin opposite the bite mark. I peeked inside. Nothing but darkness. The apple was hollow. Without the threads glowing on the surface the large balloon apple *looked* real but I now knew, that it was not. It seemed this entire world was made up of material being simulated by an unknown source. It gave me chills to think about it. *Hollow apples.*

I continued fiddling with the threads and time went by. Then something very odd happened. A thread passed by very close to my face and suddenly I was aware of something. Something was *inside* the thread! I pulled it closer and examined it. *Amazing!* Inside its dark center, so tiny and easily missed, something was moving. I squeezed the thread between my fingers and it flattened. I looked closer but still could not make out what it was. I needed to stretch it to increase its surface area. But *how?* I visualized the thread becoming flatter and thicker and with much reluctance it reacted to my desire. I pulled at its sides until it was finally wide enough for me to make out the object of my interest. My jaw dropped. It wasn't possible! It *just wasn't possible!*

A hand touched my shoulder. Quickly I willed the threads to vanish and blinked up at the two figures standing above me. Slowly I got to my feet, gathering myself on the way up. "That was fast," I said, brushing the dirt from my pants.

"I did not mean to startle you." Sajin looked at my hands and down to where I had been crouching. "What were you looking at?"

"Nothing." I offered no further explanation. Apparently he could not see the web. "You must be Thana,"

I said, offering my hand to the young woman at Sajin's side.

It was refused.

She was obviously not interested in sharing pleasantries. "Right then! Where do we start?"

"Thana has agreed to be your guide as long as you agree not to use your powers." Sajin's expression was one of apology.

"If that's what it takes then I agree." I smiled at Thana.

The smile was not returned.

"You will be traveling on horseback. Humphrey's is about a day's journey from here."

An entire day on horseback did not sound like my idea of a good time. I would have to tell the others my mission was going to take longer than expected. "Would you excuse me for a moment? I must use my power one last time before we begin our trip."

It was impossible to miss the annoyance on Thana's face as Sajin turned her toward the street.

I brought Kitaya's image into my mind.

"Hello, Jason." Her thoughts where warm.

"How are you faring?" I asked.

"Tiko does not stay in one place for long. That makes it difficult."

"I'm experiencing some complications as well. I don't have time to explain but it looks like I'll have to finish my journey without using my powers, so it's going to take awhile."

"Oh that does not sound good."

"I know. If things get too hairy, I'll use them but only as a last resort. --Well, I guess I have to go. --I look forward to seeing you again. I... It's nicer when you're around."

I felt her giggle. *"I miss you too."* Her words were so light and innocent. *"Take care."*

"Thanks. I'll do my best. You take it easy on Tiko. Okay?"

"Alright."

As much as I hated to, I pushed her from my mind. I stood for a moment, letting her words wash over me. She missed me. I felt like a little kid.

Now to check on Corel. *"Corel?"*

"Yes, Jason?"

"This is going to take more than a day to finish up. How are you and Armadon faring?"

"Not sure. Armadon is very meticulous. Could take hours before we depart from here. Do the best you can, Jason. I will try to inform you if things change."

"Good luck then." I broke the link.

While Thana was out of sight, I took the opportunity to consider my situation. It was difficult enough trying to combat Gaza's minions using the power of the web. Without it, it would be much more difficult-- if not impossible.

I needed a weapon.

I remembered my discussion with Armadon. I had asked him why his troops used primitive weapons such as bows and arrows and swords. He had replied that he didn't know how to make a firing mechanism. He knew what a gun looked like and how to use one, but he didn't know how they functioned.

Fortunately for me, I did. It was odd how my memory was fragmented. I could remember intimate details of pistol firing mechanisms, but I had no idea who had taught me, or where I was when I'd learned it. I brought up the web and created the items I would need for my trip including a pistol and a holster, which I neatly hid under my shirt. Last of all I made a backpack in which to carry everything.

"Well, I guess I'm as ready as I'll ever be," I said, emerging from the alleyway. "Thank you for your help, Sajin."

"My pleasure, sir. Good luck." He backed away as we moved past him and mounted the horses waiting patiently nearby.

I looked at my quiet partner. "Lead the way," I said, trying to sound cheerful.

Silence.

Oh yeah, *this* was going to be fun.

Chapter Six

EXPELLING A DISTORTED MASK

Traveling by horseback would probably be on the bottom of my list of preferred transportation, if I had such a list. Horses simply lacked the speed and comfort of an automobile. By now I would have had the air conditioner on and the radio blaring. But instead, the sun was burning a hole through the back of my neck, and my inner thighs were becoming sufficiently tenderized.

Thana was doing an excellent job of ignoring me. I made several attempts to pull up beside her but each time she spurred her horse ahead. It was clear she wanted nothing to do with me, so I rode quietly behind her for several hours.

Finally I could stand it no longer and with difficulty managed to pull my horse up next to hers and keep pace. "Where's the fire?" I joked.

Silence.

Somehow I had to get through to her. I wasn't such a bad guy. If she could just take two seconds away from her grumpy schedule, she would see that. "Listen, what do you have against me anyway? You know, if we're going to work together we are going to have to communicate. Our lives may depend on it."

I felt the chill from her shoulder.

"Look, Thana, I feel greatly for your loss but *I've* done nothing to you."

66

I must have touched a nerve because without warning the floodgates crashed open. *"What!* You think you've done *nothing? All* you people *do* is meddle! You have *no* respect for what we've worked for. You come here sticking your noses into everything without asking us what *we* think. We've been here for *centuries.* This planet is our *home!* We've put our sweat, tears, and memories into its construction, but that doesn't seem to matter to your kind! You snap your fingers and a mountain is a valley. You wiggle your fanny and a lake is a dessert. Well it's *wrong!* And thousands of my people have died senselessly in the faithful service of the *gods.* But their deaths have no meaning because the cause is *worthless.* Peace? Hope? You don't seem to understand the meanings of the words that come from the very book that spoke of your intervention. You don't *know* us! This isn't your planet and..."

"Now wait a minute! You don't know *me!"*

She glared at me. "I know your *kind,* gods indeed!" Her voice dripped with sarcasm. "It's amazing that the fabric of the universe should choose *you* as its supreme beings. You can scarcely see beyond your own noses. Life is not something you bend to suit your fancy. It's hard and it's rewarding, and it's the journey that makes us who we are! But to the so-called *gods* nothing is sacred. There's a quick fix for everything!"

"That's *enough!"* I clenched my hand into a fist. "You have no right to judge me!"

"What are you going to do, destroy me? Silence me for the things I've said? That *is* how your kind deals with their problems isn't it? If you don't like it, change it. Well, go ahead! Snap your fingers and make me disappear. I don't want to live if I have to live under the whim of *juveniles!"*

I stopped my horse and enunciated through clenched teeth. "Listen closely, *Thana* for I swear to you on all that is precious if it were in my heart to do so I would destroy you where you sit for your ignorance. But I am not the monster you think I am. If anyone is short sighted it is *you*. *I* am working toward peace yet you don't see that. *You* superimpose on me the sins of others. *I* am not *them*, and if you took a moment to get to know me, you would see that. I will be the first to admit, I'm not perfect, but I'm doing the best I can! So save your little *attitude* for someone who deserves it!" I pulled on the reins and turned away from her. She wasn't worth the aggravation. There had to be another way to find Humphrey!

I was about to spur my horse when her voice interrupted me. "I'm sorry," was all she said, and it sounded like the words tasted bad in her mouth. I still had my back turned when I heard her horse start back up along the path. I sat grumbling to myself for a few moments, then grudgingly followed.

She was so stubborn and *angry.* --But I guess I couldn't blame her; she'd lost her entire family. That was a lot of pain for a young woman to carry. But she didn't have to take it out on me! I had my own problems. At least she still *had* a home. The home I remembered was nothing more than a fragmented collection of jumbled images without a single personal memory to build from. I was lost in a strange world. Everyone I had ever known was gone. At least she had the memories to hold on to. But-- then again, maybe that wasn't such a good thing.

We traveled on in silence. The river we were following was beautiful, but I could barely appreciate it with everything filtering through my mind. The shadows were growing longer. I pulled up next to Thana. "Would you mind if we stop in that clearing up ahead? We don't have much daylight left and I'd like to stretch my legs, if you don't mind."

She gave me an examining look.

She probably thought my suggestion was made out of selfishness so I added with annoyance, "I don't require rest or sustenance but you've gone quite awhile without eating or drinking. Stopping will do us both some good. Then maybe we can start fresh, okay?"

She slowed her horse, and gave me a nod.

The clearing was surrounded by large maples and evergreens. Leaves rustled in the breeze and the sweet smell of pine filled my nostrils. I climbed down and looked about. The road behind us trailed off into the hills and the road ahead disappeared into a stand of pines. This was definitely a good place to stop. It was open and grassy and the river looked inviting.

I led my horse down to the water's edge. She took a long drink then started grazing. I looked over my shoulder to see Thana rummaging through her pack, searching for something to eat no doubt. We had traveled a long way and she was probably famished. I still found it strange that I did not experience hunger. --Apparently I drew *my* energy from something other than hollow apples.

I pushed my face down into the crystal clear water. It was cool and refreshing after the long hot day. I removed my pack, sat back against one of the trees, and looked out over the water. There was a relaxing quality to this area, and for a moment I almost felt like I could put this nightmare out of my mind. But as I closed my eyes the eerie specters from the morning came back to haunt me. Scenes from the sinister ordeal paraded through my mind like a spooky picture show. I let out an involuntary shudder.

Thana's voice interrupted my dark thoughts. "What is *that?*"

I looked around. Up the river, silently drifting toward us, a ship of some kind penetrated the dim evening air; an ominous haunting figure, its shape dark against the setting sky. This did *not* look good.

I climbed back up the bank to where Thana was quickly putting her things into her pack. "Here, let me help you," I said, kneeling down.

"No thanks."

"Okay then I'll keep an eye on the ship," I said shortly. My patience with her was growing thin.

I got up and moved back to the edge of the bank where I could keep tabs on our dark guest. It wasn't a large ship, but was heavily armored and rigged for combat. I was not looking forward to tangling with it. As I quietly watched its unearthly form creep toward us, fear welled up inside my chest. I hoped it would just pass by. But as my luck would have it, it stopped directly across from us. And just sat there. Defying nature. The current and the wind continued to apply their forces to the vessel, but it had ceased to pay any attention to their influence. They must have dropped anchor, but why here? Why now?

With a thunderous clank five large plates opened on the side of the ship. Startled, I jumped back. "Are they going to fire on us?" I asked with sudden urgency.

Thana had packed and untied her horse and was preparing to mount. I followed suit. As I lifted my leg over the horse's back a shrieking noise cut through the air. My head snapped around to see balls of fire emerging from the side of the ship.

"Ride!" I yelled, spurring my horse. Thana's feet snapped back and her steed bolted. Both horses dug in and we took off down the road. Nearing the turn that would bring us away from the river I looked back. The fireballs were following us. They swirled and weaved around each other in pursuit. *"Stay toward the water!"* I yelled.

Thana looked back, my terror reflecting in her eyes.

"If we're going to survive without my power we'll need the protection of the water!"

Her horse pulled to the right and followed the river's edge. I checked behind. The fireballs were gaining ground. "We'll have to jump in the water!" I yelled. But as soon as the words left my lips iron bars began shooting up

70

out of the ground near the water's edge, blocking us from its protection.

Gaza's work, no doubt.

I spurred my horse faster, but the bars kept ahead of us. "Now what?" I looked behind again. The fireballs were getting dangerously near. "Can I use my power *now?*" I pleaded.

"No!" she screamed insistently, urging her horse even harder.

I would have to wait until the last second. If I acted sooner I would jeopardize my mission.

"There!" She pointed.

There was an opening in the rock wall to our left. We made a sharp turn and entered the rocky mouth. Behind us explosions could be heard. I turned hoping to see our pursuers burning at the entrance, but they had only scraped the edge coming in. We had made some headway but wouldn't keep the distance for long. I could hear the crackling of fire echoing off the crevice walls behind us as we weaved in and out. Then without warning, our horses nearly sat down as they skidded to a halt. The crevice had ended, and so had our escape.

I leaped off the horse and faced the advancing demon fire. "Can I use the power *now?*" I called behind me.

"No! I am ready to *die,* if that is my destiny!" she screamed back.

Oh brother. Well *I* wasn't ready to die. I raised my arms with the intent of applying the web, but the fireballs came to a sudden stop just before me. They were so close, I could feel the heat from their baleful flames. They hovered silently-- as if in contemplation of their next move. What were they *doing?* Why didn't they just finish us? Abruptly, they began to change. Flames fell apart and sprinkled down toward the ground. In the spray, humanoid fire creatures began to take form. I looked on, more with curiosity than fear, and soon five fully formed lava creatures stood before us.

I stood my ground. "What are your intentions?" I stated with confidence. I had already devised a plan of attack in case they made any hostile moves. It involved lots of water, and I was feeling more sure of myself by the second.

One of the creatures spoke. "Do not continue." Its voice crackled and fizzed.

"Why? What are you afraid of?"

"If you continue, you will die." Its smoldering eyes bore into mine.

"Are you *threatening* me?"

"If you continue, you will die," it repeated.

"Yes, I caught that. Who sent you? Gaza?"

"You have been warned," it finished. In a blinding flash, the creatures dissolved before us.

"What was *that* all about?" I fumed. "Is Gaza trying to scare us? Well I'm not giving up!" I looked up at the sky. "You hear that, Gaza! I'm *not* giving up! You'll have to kill me first!" As I fumed I felt a squeeze on my pinky. It was Scratch. I'd forgotten all about the little guy. It squeezed again. What was he trying to tell me? I looked around and saw a shadowy figure standing in the dusty haze. Was Scratch trying to warn me? I started moving forward.

The figure turned and began walking away. "Hey!" I called. It was hard to see through the dust. I broke into a jog. "Hey!" I called again moving faster. The figure disappeared behind a rocky corner. As I came around I braced myself for an attack. But there was none. I jogged farther until the dust was much thinner. He was gone. Whoever it was.

I rubbed the little gold ring. "Keep me posted, little fella," I said quietly.

Back at the horses, Thana didn't look happy. But then again she never did, so I paid no attention to her.

72

We traveled farther up the road to a clearing deep in the pine forest. I gathered wood, she made the fire, and we settled in for the night.

The three moons hung in the night sky, one white, the others slightly different shades of blue. They filled the air with a misty aura. Spaced in perfect harmony they made a remarkable sight. I looked over at Thana on the other side of the fire. "You know, I think it was darker at dusk," I said thoughtfully. "How are you holding up?"

"Fine I guess," she replied softly.

"How far would you say now?"

"We'll reach the village tomorrow late afternoon. From there it's not too far into the woods. But we'll have to go on foot, the terrain is too hostile for horses."

"Very well then, get some sleep. We'll leave first thing in the morning."

"Mr. Tardin?" she said through the fire.

"Jason, please call me Jason."

"I want to thank you, Jason, for respecting my wishes earlier, even though it put you in great personal danger."

"I'm doing my best to make you feel comfortable with me."

"I may have misjudged you. I know this now. I regret that I was harsh but you have to understand, my people have made *so many* sacrifices. We prayed for centuries to the gods, always expecting that when they came they would answer our prayers. Can you imagine our disappointment when we came to realize the gods didn't know our hearts and that they'd never even heard our prayers? I am as much a mystery to you as you are to me. We wanted the answers to the universe. Who are we? Why are we here? Where do we go when we die?" Her eyes watered slightly. "Instead, you play games with us and use us as pawns in your wars, showering us with gifts and then

73

pain, taking away our strength and replacing it with dependence."

I felt for her but what could I say? "--I wish I had answers, Thana but I am as confused as you are. I've been lost since I arrived. For all I know I could be dead and this is my afterlife. I don't believe I possessed these powers in my last life. And I can assure you I am no god. I am just a man caught in some very unusual circumstances."

Thana studied me for a moment. "Humphrey said the same thing. He doesn't believe he is a god either. He says he's an impostor and that the real God would punish the Ten for their arrogance. He didn't want any part of it. Gaza went to visit many times in the days of the awakening but Humphrey didn't want anything to do with his schemes. He used to say, 'We have no right to influence these people's lives on any level.' Gaza would argue that he created Vrin and that it was *not* God's work. He claimed God was deaf and that he did not hear the prayers of man. They spent many nights in philosophical debate, which usually ended with Gaza leaving in anger.

"I believed in Humphrey. Even when my father died, I believed there was a higher purpose, a purpose even the Ten didn't understand. But then when my mother and sister died in the war my faith was shaken. I began to wonder if the God of the gods had his own god. I wondered if it went on forever in a chain, like some sick joke. I wondered if there was *anyone,* God or man who knew the answers to the universe. These past few years the only thing that's kept me sane is my devotion to Vrin's purity. I thought if I could stop the Ten perhaps I could break the chain and restore understanding." She put her head in her hands. "But I guess I won't get that chance if Gaza's going to destroy us. We'll be returned to the cosmos and the chain will continue."

"Not if I can help it."

74

She looked up. "I don't think you can stop him. From the stories Humphrey told me as a child Gaza is *extremely* powerful. Humphrey called him the blind genius." She offered me a lackluster smile. "He could build a human but lacked the ability to understand his own creation. Old Humphrey said that he himself was no intellectual slouch but he couldn't even begin to understand the mechanics of the human brain. He could create the shell of life from the web but there would be no substance."

Like the handgun, I thought. Any one of us could have created the shell of a handgun but without the knowledge of its inner workings, it would be useless.

"Humphrey said the body was almost as complex as the spirit. Humphrey is a master of the spirit. Gaza could never best him in that. But I'm afraid to say Gaza is the master of creation and who better to destroy this world than the one who created it?"

All this talk of Gaza made me anxious to continue my research with the web. "Yes, who better. --Well, it's getting late. Why don't you get some sleep. We have a long ride tomorrow."

"But I want to talk some more."

"I'm enjoying our conversation as well but you need to be rested. There's no telling when Gaza will strike. We should have plenty of time to continue our conversation on the way to Humphrey's."

She gave in grudgingly and crawled into her sleeping bag.

Silently the three moons floated in the sky. Their soft blue light permeated the landscape. They were truly breathtaking to behold-- and yet, I felt a certain sadness.

Their light removed the stars.

I missed the stars.

α

As soon as I was sure Thana was asleep I brought up the web. Slowly and quietly I walked around the outskirts of our encampment, setting a trip wire a few inches off the ground; in case there was trouble while I was gone. The other end I attached to my wrist. I didn't go far, just far enough to be out of sight in case she awoke. It wouldn't look good if she caught me waving my hands around and mumbling to myself.

I settled in and crossed my legs. The web glowed lightly against the night as I reached out and plucked a strand. With my mind I stretched the thread until the moving area was once again visible. Black translucent letters flowed by like blood in a vein. I studied the odd script. It was indeed what I had thought, modified machine code. Innately I understood it. mmc was an advanced computer language specifically designed for scientific research. But why would such a code be present in these threads? It didn't make sense. If this was a computer generated environment, it was like nothing I had ever seen. It was far too real.

I examined the code for several hours trying to figure out the purpose of the programming. If I focused I could make the text move by faster. Each time I reached the end, there was a space, then the code started over from the beginning. I could string the pieces together easily but it was an enormous program and each time I read it, it grew. It was continually growing and adapting, as if it were alive.

Then suddenly, I realized something. It was acting like the cognosphere! It was storing data, keeping track of variables, watching, and learning. This program controlled the flow of information about this world. Every detail was on record. Every action was being observed and reactions were being applied.

If I were to throw a ball the program would figure out how far the ball would fly, its speed and velocity, and what laws of nature would have to be applied to it. The program would regulate the ball's response to my application and the cognosphere would store the results so the next person going by would find the ball lying on the ground. Every person on this planet, the Ten included, were continually writing the program. And it was Gaza who had designed the program. I looked up.

Gaza isn't a god! He's a programmer!

I stood. My legs were cramping from sitting too long. My mind was on fire weeding through the possibilities of this new information. How much did Gaza know? Was he responsible for bringing me here? Were the people of this world computer simulations, or were they real? Where did the woman and child fit into it? What type of environment was this that the computer could keep track of it? It wasn't virtual reality, at least not like any I was aware of. It was *far* beyond any technology I'd ever seen. Somehow I felt sure of this.

I sat back down and quickly started a search for my own essence. If I could find myself in the program, then perhaps Gaza could find me too. This made me uneasy. As I searched, a character on the page caught my attention. It represented a sub-directory and was classified as 'created items'. Perhaps I could find the cup of tea I had created at Kitaya's.

I opened the directory into a thread of its own and the contents scrolled before me. It contained everything that had ever been created from the beginning of Vrin to the present time. *Unbelievable!* Laid out before me was creation itself!

Each item had a sub-directory, containing every detail, right down to its smell. I could change anything in Vrin without even being present with it. I shuddered. With a thought I could erase any of the items that lay before me. It was too much to comprehend.

I continued looking for my essence in the program but after an exhaustive search I gave up; the program was immense, with far too many sub-directories. It would take a lifetime to follow all the paths. This realization brought me comfort for it would be a monumental task, even for its creator, to track anything in a program this vast.

My mind was filled to capacity and I was about to quit for the night-- when something caught my eye. A peculiar entry moved up the thread. A new line. Someone must have just added it. I examined it closely. It was nothing like the other entries-- It was complete gibberish. I studied it for a moment then suddenly realized, it wasn't gibberish! It was backwards! I reversed the line and decoded the statement. Much to my astonishment, it wasn't a program line at all but a message. It read, "Test 4:12 pm: Robert, can you see this?"

I stared at it. *Should I try to answer?* Maybe the sender would be able to shed some light on things. The message included the time. I recognized the format, from the world just on the other side of my memory. Perhaps if I could make contact I could find some answers.

I focused my concentration on the strand. Just as I could apply textures to threaded structures I was sure I could apply text to the program. Sure enough it responded. On the thread before me lay my words in: "Yes. I see it."

I sat, staring at my words, wondering if the sender would see the reply, and wondering if I even wanted the answers to my questions. The text continued to scroll by for what seemed an eternity and I continued to watch. Every time it started a new loop I found the original message and decoded it. Each time I was disappointed. Until...

A buzz began emanating from one of the threads. I watched with curiosity as it twitched and hummed. Periodically the noise would fade and I could hear a faint voice mixed in with the chaotic signal. Someone was trying to communicate but the thread wasn't amplifying the sound properly. I wasn't sure if this would help but I clamped the thread on either end and pulled it taut. As I suspected the act of tightening caused the buzzing to fade and the voice became clearer. It was a masculine voice. "Marker test twenty-eight. Can you hear this?" Pause. "Marker test twenty-nine. Can you hear this?" Another pause.

I smiled. The owner of the voice didn't realize he had gotten through.

"Marker test thirty. Can you hear this?"

"Yes," I responded. This was no time to play games.

"Oh my God! Robert! You did it! Hold on! Dr. Solomon is on his way."

"Who am I, and what is this place?"

"I'm sorry. I'm not authorized to give you any information. Dr. Solomon will be here any second." He sounded nervous.

"Well can you at least tell me who *you* are?"

"Although I don't see how it can hurt I have to follow protocol. I'm very sorry."

I was getting annoyed.

He'll be here in a minute. Are you in any pain or discomfort?"

"No."

"Are you in any danger?"

"Not at the moment."

79

"Then we are doing just fine."

"*Right--* I guess that depends on your interpretation of *just fine.*"

"Here he is!"

There was a short silence, then another man began to speak. "Hello, Robert. Remember me?" His voice sounded familiar.

"My memory is a little scattered but I think I recognize your voice, although I don't remember from where."

"That's okay. That's a response we expected."

"Where am I?"

"Let's take this one step at a time, Robert. Where do you think you are?"

Great. I wanted answers not more questions! But I bit my tongue. If I was going to get anywhere I would need to cooperate. I took a breath. "Well, I'm on the planet *Vrin.* From what I can tell it is the twenty-first century but these people never moved beyond the middle ages."

"Is the experience believable?"

"Yes for the most part, but I've noticed discrepancies."

"Can you describe them?"

"Well, everything, *almost* everything, is far too perfect but there is a lack of detail in some of the natural effects."

"A lack of detail? Such as?"

"Such as particles in a sun beam that don't move, and the total lack of insects. And when I first got here there was a weird color problem but it has either corrected itself or I've gotten use to it."

"That is a very interesting analysis."

"Now let *me* ask a question. *Where am I?*"

There was an awkward pause. Then, "--I'm not sure you want to know that yet."

"Try me."

"This is a very delicate matter. We should approach it with caution."

"Well we need to do it quickly because I don't know how long this world is going to *be* here."

"What?"

A tinge of fear and adrenaline shot through me. *Should I have said that?* What if this was Gaza? --No, it couldn't be, these men were definitely surprised I had gotten through. Still...

"Robert?"

I threw caution to the wind. "There is a madman here and he says he's going to destroy Vrin."

"My God! Why?" The man sounded genuinely alarmed.

"I'm not certain but from what I know of him, he can do it."

"Are you doing anything to stop him?"

"I'm afraid I can't share that information with you." If there was any chance this *was* Gaza I didn't want to put my friends in danger.

"I understand." He paused.

The pause lasted too long for my comfort. "Hello?"

"I'm sorry, Robert. My assistant was asking a question. We were discussing who that person could be."

"So you are aware of the others?"

"Yes. There are ten of you."

"Who are we and why are we here?"

Again there was a long pause.

I began to lose my patience. "If you don't tell me who I am and why I'm here right now I'm going to cancel this communication!"

It was a bluff and he called it. "You don't want to do that, Robert. You need answers as much as we do and you know deep in your heart that I am your friend. I know you are confused and believe me I am sensitive to that. But there is too much at stake to go blindly ahead. I'll tell you what. I'll give you half of what you've asked for. Perhaps it will help you to remember. Your name is Dr. Robert Helm. You are a scientist and a programmer. Unfortunately, I can't tell you where you are or why you're there just yet. We don't know what that information would do to your psyche. We have a psychiatrist here and we are consulting..."

"Jason?" That was Thana's voice.

"Gotta go."

"Robert, we need... "

The web vanished and I stepped out of the bushes. Thana was standing in the campsite with her back to me.

"Over here!" I called.

"Where did you go?" She sounded concerned.

"I just stepped into the bushes to... well, you know." I gave a crooked smile.

"Next time could you let me know?"

"You looked so peaceful. I didn't want to wake you." I feigned a stretch. "Well, it looks like the sun is coming up. Think we should get started right away?"

"Yes. I think we'd better."

It was nice we were actually talking now but as we chatted my mind kept wandering back to the conversation in the web. Who could I trust? Everywhere I turned, there seemed to be a conspiracy.

I was beginning to feel like Rath.

Chapter Eight

THE BRAVE KIND SNEAK
1 0 0 1 1 0 1

Ɛ

We continued our journey to Humphrey's, this time side by side. My rapport with the young lady had completely changed. We shared some pleasant conversation and even a joke or two.

"I don't know," I said. "I give up. What *is* a dyslexic agnostic insomniac?"

Her eyes twinkled. "Someone who stays awake all night wondering if there really is a dog."

It took me a second but when I got it we both broke into a roar of laughter. "Did Humphrey tell you that one?"

"Yup. He had to explain dyslexic to me though. He was always teaching me lots of new terms. When he told me what that one meant I thought I would never stop laughing."

"Humphrey sounds like a good man."

"Oh, he is. The two things he loves most in the world are making people laugh and arguing. What's really fun is when he's arguing with one person and making another person laugh at the same time. He used to have fun twisting my father's words around. Then he would smile at us when Daddy became flustered. Humphrey's quite the character."

"Is that the village up ahead?" I pointed.

"Yes, that's Ristol. We should stop there and replenish our supplies. We'll need them for the second half of our journey."

"Good idea. Lead the way."

Ristol had definitely seen its share of hard times. The buildings, most of which were made of barn board, were worn and lacked maintenance. And the people didn't look much better. They appeared tired, weathered, and very poor. But their eyes reflected strength and determination. Life was tough on them no doubt but I sensed that they stood strong and faced life's challenges together.

I should have put my blindfold back on, but it was too late. The news of my arrival spread like wildfire. People came out and stared as we passed through town.

A woman came running out of a building. "Lord, wait! I beg of you! Wait!"

I slowed my horse and looked down at her filthiness. Her appearance was haphazard, as if she had lacked the proper time to get ready for the day. She was aged beyond her years. Desperation marred her otherwise pretty eyes.

"Lord, my son is very ill. I have given everything I own that he may be cared for but he is slipping away and I can't afford to pay for an expensive doctor to come in from the city. Please help me. You've got to help me!" Tears ran down her dusty face.

My heart hurt to see her pain. I looked at Thana. Her expression was one of sadness. "Can I help her?" I asked softly, not wanting to put Thana on the spot.

"If there is a physical way I will help too." She dismounted and approached the woman. "Shesu, where is he?"

"He is inside." She looked up at me, her eyes silently pleading for help. I sensed she did not welcome Thana's presence but she did not voice her thoughts. I gave her a shrug.

We entered the hovel where the woman's son lay on a cot. The room looked like a medical combat zone. Jars, pillows, dishes, ointments, and other various articles littered the floor and counters. She had indeed been very busy. I stepped over to the cot and looked down at the ashen face of her son. He was visibly sweating. His pillow was damp. "Do you know what caused his illness, ma'am?"

She moved to my side. "He was running in the field behind our house when he stepped on a metal spike. Soon after he began to get sick."

I went to the base of the cot and lifted the blanket and was shocked to see the piece of metal still protruding from the boy's foot. I looked at Shesu, my mouth gaping. "Why has this not been removed?"

"The healer said removing something from a wound that deep might release his soul from his body. I didn't want to take that chance."

I looked at Thana, then back to Shesu. "What foolishness! The boy could have *died* from infection! Bring me some hot water, several clean rags, and some pure alcohol if you can get it. Thana, put something in the boy's mouth so he doesn't bite his tongue."

Shesu quickly put a pot of water on the fire then ran out the door. Thana rolled up a cloth, put it in the boy's mouth, then gently took his hand. He watched as I firmly took hold of the spike. He turned to Thana with pleading eyes.

"Sorry, son," I said. "But this is going to hurt. Brace yourself." I pulled gently, then harder. There was some resistance. So I gave a firm tug then stumbled backwards as the spike came free.

The boy twitched in agony, then passed out.

Shesu returned with the cloths and a large flask. I took one of the cloths and applied pressure to the wound to stop the bleeding. Once the bleeding slowed I dipped another cloth into the hot water and carefully cleaned the infected area. After removing as much of the oozing puss as I could I poured a liberal amount of whiskey over the wound. It was fortunate for the boy, and us, that he was unconscious.

The young man began to move his head, mumbling something unintelligible. His mother moved quickly to his side.

"This should stop the bleeding," I said as I finished wrapping the area. "And hopefully any further infection. You will need to change the cloth three or four times a day and keep the area around the wound as clean as possible. As for your son's fever, it should go down if you tend to his foot properly."

"How can I ever thank you?" she asked, kneeling before me.

"You can thank me by taking care of your son. It is my hope that his condition will improve. Use this if it does not." I handed the woman a coin. "Rub it softly in your hands and pray to me if your son's condition worsens. And do not go to that healer again. Do you understand?"

She nodded.

"Have faith, and he will be okay."

A crowd had gathered in front of the woman's house. We mounted our horses and began to move but it was difficult to get through. "Make way!" yelled Thana. The people began to move aside but it was still slow going. Pleading eyes looked up at me. I could have easily delivered these poor folks from their poverty but Thana would not have approved. Was there anything wrong with offering a little comfort to these unfortunate souls?

I thought back to what Thana had said earlier. *"You take away our strength, and replace it with dependence."* Perhaps she was right. Pain makes a person stronger. Without sorrow growth is hindered. Who was it that said through pain comes change? I couldn't remember but it made sense. If I were to take away the challenges of these people's existence what service would I be doing them? It would take away their sense of accomplishment, maybe their sense of purpose.

Humphrey may have been right to a certain extent but I felt his convictions were a bit extreme. I didn't think offering a little help could hurt-- but then again where would I draw the line? If there *was* a divine plan I was given my power for a reason. To use it irresponsibly would be wrong. I knew this. But to not use it at all would be just as bad.

Eventually we reached the other side of the bewildered crowd. Thana turned to me and spoke. "I think we shouldn't stop for supplies. We should have enough for now and Humphrey will take care of us when we get to his cottage."

"Whatever you think is best."

"Again I feel I need to thank you for respecting my wishes-- and also for helping Shesu and her son."

"You don't need to thank me, I enjoyed helping them." I smiled to myself. If the woman ever did rub that coin she was in for a surprise. When their backs were turned I had used the web to create a solid gold coin covered in brown chalk. It was worth enough to pay for a certified doctor and then some-- just in case. Again I thought, *a little help can't hurt.*

The mighty Dessa Forest appeared on the horizon. It was extremely dense and as Thana had said the horses would not be able to get through. We found the hiding place her father had cleared out long ago. It was a small pocket just inside the wood, partially overgrown from years of disuse, and cut out at the site of a natural spring. The horses would have grass to eat as well as plenty of fresh water.

Thana located a crude gate made of twisted sticks and brush, disentangled it from the overgrowth, and pulled it across the opening. The gate had a dual purpose. Not only did it camouflage the hiding place but it would also keep the horses from wandering off.

The path through the gnarled wood was still partially formed so we didn't have to hack much. An occasional tree branch needed to be cut but for the most part, it was passable.

My mind drifted. So many bizarre things had happened in this strange world, it was hard to sort through it all. The thing troubling me most was the fact that I was apparently playing a part in some kind of experiment and the guys running it were unwilling to tell me where I was, how I got here, or the purpose behind it all. If I could only unravel that mystery then maybe I'd be able to figure out the dynamics of this place-- which might help us to combat Gaza.

Before my contact with the outside world this place had been mystical, almost awe-inspiring. But now that I knew others like myself were in control somehow it wasn't the same. The magic was watered down; it saddened me.

As I had thought all along, I was no god. I merely possessed the power to effect this place. The others were no different. --But what I couldn't figure out was how the *people* of this world fit into the mixture. They must have been created for the experiment, synthetic simulations perhaps, but they were *so real*. When I helped the woman and her son not once did it occur to me that they might only be computer simulations. I was completely immersed in the event. Even if I'd felt sure they *were* simulations I still would have felt compelled to help them. After all, who was I to judge?

I looked at Thana walking in front of me. Every detail about her seemed real. She approached a branch, reached out, snapped it, then continued on. Her shoes crunched upon the leaves on the ground and her hand absently brushed a strand of hair off her face. I could faintly smell her musk oil perfume. If she was a simulation she was the most complicated simulation I'd ever seen or heard about.

It ate at me. This place was too real to be virtual, yet too different to be real.

A person under hypnosis could enter a dream-like state in which everything would *seem* completely real. But hypnosis was a suggestive state, and here, in this world, I was in complete control of my actions, or at least I thought I was. And if it *was* hypnosis then I should have been able to bring myself out at any time because hypnosis is a state of consciousness which has to be accepted by the subject. The hypnotist cannot control a person under hypnosis unless that person is willing. I couldn't remember where I'd learned all this but somehow I knew it to be true.

I could have been asleep and dreaming but this experience was far more real than any dream I'd ever had. From what I could remember my dreams usually consisted of brief imagery with an emotional base. If I were to dream about a beautiful girl she might be an amalgamation of many women, perhaps changing identities as the dream progressed. For a time she might be an old girlfriend or a girl I met at the grocery store then later turn into a baby-sitter I'd had as a child.

Somewhere in the depths of my broken memory, words from an old textbook echoed. *As the characters and events of a dream shift, the dreamer continues to feel comfortable because although the dream does not make sense to the conscious mind, it makes perfect sense to the subconscious mind. If a man were to dream of swimming down a river, it might flow through a house he once lived in. He could swim to the edge, get out, and the river would be gone behind him. Regardless of the inconsistencies he would continue to feel right at home in the outlandish twists and turns of his mind.*

That's how dreams tended to work. So, although this place had its twists and turns, there was far too much solidity for this all to be a dream.

I let out an involuntary sigh.

Thana looked back at me. "You okay?"

"Just thinking."

"Anything you want to share?"

"Not especially. Maybe another time."

She shrugged her shoulders and turned back to the path.

Even that brief exchange bothered me. Her response was *so* real. *What IS this place?*

We walked for well over an hour before the path opened up a bit. Thick tree trunks rose up like pillars, supporting the leafy roof. The uneven ground crunched as we walked. And I could hear the sound of rushing water coming from up ahead. The waning light of the sun flickered through the trees' gnarled wooden fingers. Soon it would be night again.

A feeling of uneasiness crept over me. I peered into the darkening woods. At first I didn't see anything. But then the shadows began to move. The movements were subtle at first but soon there was no question. Someone, or some*thing*, was there.

"How much farther?" I asked in a low voice.

"Not far."

"Then we should pick up the pace a bit."

"Why? What's wrong?" She looked around.

"I'm not sure, perhaps nothing."

A snarl filtered through the trees.

"Perhaps something." I nudged her to speed up.

Out of the corner of my eye I saw a quick movement low to the ground. The snarling increased, as did our speed. We were now at a slow jog, ducking and dodging branches. I looked over my shoulder to see three enormous gray wolves emerging from the brush. Their graceful forms began weaving in and out through the branches with deadly skill. I was unsure if they were following us or just going about their normal business. Desperately, I hoped the latter.

Thana let out a scream. I snapped back around. Two more of the giant beasts were sitting on the path before us.

"Are these friendly or unfriendly wolves?" I asked in a low voice.

"I've never seen wolves in this forest," she said, her voice quivering.

The wolves stood baring their teeth and growling a deep guttural warning. "I'm going to go with unfriendly."

I needed to do something fast, or we were going to be dog food. I pulled my pistol from its holster and checked the clip. It was fully loaded. "What I'm about to do is *not* magic," I said defensively as I quickly stepped in front of Thana. I aimed the weapon into the air and let off three quick bursts. The wolves jumped back.

I turned to see the shots had startled the wolves behind us, as well as Thana. Her eyes were so wide each iris looked like a tiny island in a sea of white.

"Sorry. I should have told you it was loud.

The enormous animals paced back and forth. For the moment we were at a stalemate, but I was sure it wouldn't last. I wanted to use the web but didn't want to lose Thana's trust. I looked around for alternatives. I could attempt to shoot the wolves, but there were five of them, and only one of me. Most likely they would overtake me before I could deal a lethal shot to each.

The beasts began to advance again. I *needed* to use the power but I didn't want to jeopardize my mission! Then it came to me. It was a simple plan but I thought it just might work. With Thana to my back I brought up the web. Threads appeared all around us but she was oblivious. I examined the network of crossing lines, chose the few that would do the trick, and turned them into metal twine. They

91

formed a fence between the wolves and us, and from where we stood they were not visible.

"Get down!" I screamed behind me. Thana dropped to the ground. Two rounds roared from the pistol. The first one missed. But the second found its target and the wolf let out a yelp. After a startled moment the wolves in front began to charge but rammed headfirst into the wires and fell back dazed. I fired two more rounds. "Keep your head down!" I yelled at Thana. She dug her face deeper into the dirt. The wolves clawed at the metal lines, but I took them out one at a time, all the while circling Thana, yelling, and kicking up dirt. When I was done I quickly removed the substance from the threads and the fence vanished.

"Stay here," I said.

All the wolves were still except one. It lay on the cold ground beneath me, panting in the clutches of death. Its coat was sticky where blood had seeped out; its breath was shallow. I pointed the gun at his head and quickly put the animal out of its misery.

I shuddered to think what would have happened if this monstrous beast had gotten hold of us. All of the thoughts about the reality of this place were moot in the face of such destructive power. As I stood staring down at the dead animal a disturbing question crept into my mind. Could I *die* in this place?

Thana approached. "What is that thing?" She pointed at the handgun.

I looked at her blankly, then realized what she'd said. "It's a pistol," I said defensively, lifting it up to show her the barrel.

She squinted at me.

"Look. A piece of lead is pushed through this metal tube." I pointed at the gun barrel. "It's similar to a blowgun, only instead of using air, the driving force is a chemical reaction. When charcoal, sulfur, and potassium nitrate are mixed and ignited, they create an explosion which in turn creates pressure and pushes the lead down and out the end of the barrel."

Her expression sat fixed as if to say, "*What?*"

I sighed. "Trust me, it's not magic."

She grudgingly accepted my explanation, though it was clear she didn't have a clue what I was talking about. I could have cracked open a bullet and given her a chemistry lesson, but I don't think it would have helped. Besides, we were budgeted for time.

It was clear we were being watched, and most likely by Gaza. But I had a feeling these creatures were not meant to stop us. Like the fire creatures they were probably sent as a warning or as a scare tactic. I continued to find myself fighting with the notion that I was nothing more than a puppet in an elaborately constructed game. Anger welled up in my chest. Why didn't Gaza just face me and get it over with? Why was he *toying* with me? I did *not* like being toyed with, not one bit!

I felt a squeeze on my pinkie. This time instead of looking down at the ring I crouched and peered back into the woods.

Thana turned. "What is it?"

"I don't know," I whispered. My eyes scanned back and forth through the murky wood. The sun's light was dim making it difficult to see but I knew he was there, somewhere.

There! I burst into a run and the crisp ground snapped under my quick footfalls. In the distance I could just make out a dark figure walking through the shadow of the trees. A branch snapped me in the face making my eye water but I didn't slow. As I neared the spot the man became clearer. He was watching my approach. I veered left desperately trying to keep him in view. Crap! He passed behind a thick tree. I reached my destination and came to a skidding halt, my chest heaving from the exertion.

He was gone.

"No!" I kicked at some leaves. "Crap!" I swung at a branch with my hand and snapped it off. "Crap! Crap! *Crap!*"

Thana caught up with me. "What was that all about?" She breathed heavily.

I scowled at her. "I took care of the puppets. But what I really want is the puppet master. Gaza was here pulling the strings all along." If Thana hadn't been with me, I could have used the web to instantly transport myself to him. I looked at her and let out one last, *"CRAP!"*

"What?" She backed up defensively.

I brushed by her. "Never mind. I'll get him next time. Let's go."

Again we followed the winding path, this time, a little more watchful-- and a lot more jumpy. Every little noise startled us. "How much farther is it?" I asked. "Maybe we should stop and make camp."

Thana halted suddenly and I almost ran into her. She was looking down over a steep ledge overlooking a deep leafy crevasse. "It's just a little farther," she said.

To our left, a magnificent waterfall spilled its crystal clear water over the edge. Directly before us stood a faded sign:

BEWARE THE WRATH OF GODS. DO NOT ENTER.

The crevasse seemed unnatural somehow, as though the ground had been pushed down in an even line. The trees below matched the trees on the upper level, like they had once stood side by side. I looked down over the edge. "What *is* this place?"

"This is the only thing Humphrey ever used the power for. He could not live among us because his eyes gave him away, and since my people wouldn't leave him

alone, he created this place. The only way to get down there is to use this pulley system."

Just off the edge of the cliff a metal weight with a red cushion upon it hung in mid air. A rope ran from the center of the weight to a pulley hanging from a tree above, across to a second pulley, then down into a hole in the ground.

Thana explained. "This is a balance system. Inside the walls of this cliff are pipes that funnel water from the river. The water is used to fill the counterbalance. See this hole?" She pointed to where the rope entered the ground. "This tunnel reaches down to the bottom of the cliff. At the end of this rope is the counterbalance to that seat." She pointed at the red cushion.

I looked at the tiny cushion floating in stark contrast to the large expanse of the crater, and it dawned on me, that she had used the word "seat." My jaw dropped. "I have to sit on *that?*"

"Yes, and see that lever down there?" She pointed to a rusty iron bar protruding from the cliff face. "You'll need to pull that up to empty the water from the counterbalance below. When you start to drop, push the level back down." She chuckled. "Otherwise it will be a very fast ride. Oh! And when you get to the bottom you'll find another lever. This is very important. You must pull that lever *down* for ten seconds before getting off the seat."

Again I peered downward. It was quite a drop, a couple hundred feet anyway. I looked up and opened my mouth to refuse, but then remembered my experience with Kitaya. If I were to fall, I could always fly. "--So, when I get to the bottom-- I need to pull the lever, down?"

"Yes down, for ten seconds."

"And what does that do?"

"When the counterbalance gets to the top it will be filled with water. When you get off you will be taking your hundred and eighty-some-odd pounds with you. The lever will empty the water from the counterbalance to even out the weights."

"So the seat doesn't come shooting back up. Right. I understand."

"Good. Are you ready?"

I looked up at the pulley in the tree. "Are you sure it still works?"

"No."

I shot her a look.

She laughed. "It's fine. Humphrey always keeps his things in good working order."

I looked again at the little red seat. "Alright. Here goes nothing." I reached out and grabbed the rope. It was rough in my hand and burned slightly as I drew the seat toward me. Carefully I placed a leg over, and soon was swinging out over the gulf below. Fear took me immediately. The height was dizzying. Whether this world was a figment of my imagination or not made no difference, vertigo was still a very real phenomenon.

"Now pull the lever."

"I don't want to," I said, clinging to the rope.

"Some god you are." She laughed, reached down, and pulled up on the lever. Within seconds I was plummeting to my death. I could only hope she would remember to push the lever back down.

I seemed to fall for an awfully long time. It was much farther than I'd expected. But eventually the ground became visible, then more defined, then branches rushed by me until I touched down with a thud.

I sat for moment. "Someone has to talk to Humphrey about this death trap!" I muttered to myself. "I don't care what anybody says I will *not* be returning this way."

In front of me on the face of the rock was the lever. Clearly marked above and below were the words, FULL and EMPTY. I pulled it down and counted to ten. Carefully

I dismounted the contraption and stepped back. It rose up slowly and disappeared into the branches overhead. I scanned my surroundings and found nothing out of the ordinary. Many varieties of brilliant flowers blanketed the landscape. Their aroma was sweet. Humphrey's hand no doubt. The river flowed by not far from the site of the pulley system so I perched on a rock and stared off into the falling water. Such power and beauty. The waterfall's song was medicine to my tired soul. Its thunderous sound echoed off the cliff walls as it weaved its way down into the deeper forest to my right. I sat taking in the sights and listening to the playful chatter of the birds. I took a deep breath and let it out slowly. For a brief moment I felt at ease, and the sensation was foreign to me. I'd had so few opportunities to relax in this strange world.

It wasn't long before Thana touched down with a thump. She held tight to the rope as she dismounted, then scooped up a metal hook that was buried under some leaves and secured the weight so it would not rise back up. "I hope you enjoyed your ride." She smiled.

"More than words can say." I smirked.

She chuckled and headed down the path, I hopped off the rock and followed. We passed over a wooden bridge and into a clearing. To our right the river poured into a lake, and on the lake's edge was a log home. As we approached I could see a man out front chopping wood. He was an old fellow in a red flannel shirt and green work pants. A long white beard dangled before him. Each swing of the ax was powerful and accurate; he was definitely not a frail man. Suddenly, seemingly unprovoked, he began jumping about and flailing his arms in the air with quick jarring motions, back and forth, like a madman. "Go away!" he yelled. "*GO away!*" Soon his wild motions brought him to the ground with a crash, then all we could see were the old man's arms and legs stabbing up into the air from the thick grass. "Leave me in *peace!*" he yelled out. *"Go AWAY!"*

For a moment I thought he was hallucinating, but then I spotted the object of his misery. It was a tiny bird, a humming bird. It hovered over his flailing body for a moment then turned and shot off across the lake. I guess the old man was too much of a challenge for the little creature.

"Humphrey?" I asked.

"Humphrey," she stated.

Chapter Nine

THE MORTAL GOD
1 1 0 1 1 1 1

ρ

The old man smiled when he saw Thana.

"Humphrey!" she called.

"Thana, precious girl, you've come back to visit!"

He was taller than he'd looked from the distance and there was a gentle power about him. His face was stern, yet kind, and although his leathery skin showed deep lines around his neatly trimmed white beard, he was far from feeble. I waited while the old friends shared an embrace.

When they separated Thana turned and introduced us. "Humphrey, I'd like you to meet Jason Tardin."

"Good to meet you, sir." I offered my hand.

His eyebrows furrowed and his glowing eyes seemed to darken. "What do you want with me?"

"I've come a long way, by horse and by foot, to speak with you. It is a matter of great consequence."

He scowled at me and grunted.

Thana put her hand on his arm. "He's all right, Humphrey. I promise."

Still scowling the old man examined me with a critical eye. "All right," he said with a toss of his hand, "but I'll not go on any fool crusades with you. I'm a man of peace. And a tired man at that!"

I tried to be diplomatic. "All I seek is information. Whatever you are willing to share will be appreciated."

He gave a slight nod. "Then come in and rest your bones." He offered his arm to Thana. "And grab a few of them logs if you don't mind," he said, pointing to the pile next to the chopping block.

I stacked some sticks in my arms and trailed along behind.

Humphrey's cabin was neat and orderly, and although sparsely decorated, had all the comforts of home. A pleasant piney odor hit me as I entered. Instantly the warmth of the cabin's rustic beauty enveloped me. "Where do you want these?" I asked.

"In the basket by the fireplace," he said over his shoulder as he guided Thana into the kitchen. I figured he wanted to grill her with questions about me, but she came back out rather quickly, with thick slice of bread and a large glass of milk.

"What do you want in your coffee?" she asked.

"A spoon of sugar will be fine."

"One sugar," she called into the kitchen. "I'm going to wait out here, okay, Humph?"

Humphrey returned with a, "Yup!"

"He likes you," she whispered.

"He does?" I said, completely surprised. "What makes you say that?"

"He would have turned you away outside if he didn't. And he wouldn't offer coffee unless he wanted you to stay a bit. He used to make a cup for Gaza before their long discussions, but he even turned him away a few times before finally giving in."

"Well, I am certainly honored."

We stopped speaking as Humphrey rounded the corner.

"Mind if I take your bed tonight, Humph?" Thana asked.

"Not at all. You must be tired after your long trek."

"You have a bed?" I asked.

"Yes. It doesn't get much use though. On occasion I try lying down to see if sleep takes me."

100

"Any success?"

"No, but I keep hoping."

Thana headed for the bedroom. "I'll leave you two alone to talk about god stuff. I'm exhausted. I'll catch up with you in the morning."

"Good night, Thana," I said. "Dream for us all."

She nodded her head in the affirmative.

Humphrey handed me a cup of steaming coffee.

"That didn't take long."

"I put the pot on before you arrived."

"Ahh."

"Have a seat, young Mister Tardin," he said, waving his hand at a rocking chair. "What brings you out this way?"

I sat and placed my cup on the end table. "As I said, I've come seeking information."

"Uh-huh. What kind of information?" He perched on the edge of the woodbox.

"Well, two days ago Kitaya and I used an event cell to re-live a portion of Vrin's history. Kitaya witnessed a discussion between Gaza and Rath where Gaza was threatening to destroy this world if Rath did not do his bidding. She didn't get all the details, but Gaza was talking about searching for a woman and a girl child. We were hoping Gaza might have mentioned them to you."

Humphrey furrowed his brow. "He believes his wife and daughter died in a car accident in his previous existence. That might have something to do with it. But I don't know why he'd be searching for a woman and child in this world."

"He mentioned something about an exact match. Do you think he was referring to them?"

"It's possible. He could have made replicas of them to ease his pain."

"No. --That wouldn't make sense. He's *searching* for them, for an exact match. If he *made* replicas he

101

wouldn't have to search for them." I gave Humphrey a quizzical look. "Right?"

"This world is extremely complex." Humphrey picked up an iron poker and began stirring the fire. "There could be a great many explanations. Gaza mentioned many details of its creation but most of it was gibberish to me."

"Did he mention his search?"

"No, but it wouldn't surprise me if he is searching for them. Their deaths weigh heavily on his mind."

"Why do you think he would enlist Rath and no one else? If he wanted to find them so badly, why not bring us all in on it?"

"I have no idea." Humphrey looked into the fire. "He never mentioned Rath to me."

I studied the old man's profile. "Well-- do you think he'll follow through on his threat?"

Humphrey shook his head. "I don't know. Gaza is something of an enigma. There is no disputing the fact that he is a genius, but his mind is tortured, his reasoning impaired. I spent many a night trying to help him through his questions." Humphrey stood and began to pace. "He is angry with God. He blames God for the death of his family, but it goes beyond reason. It's a fixation. I believe he is between calms." Humphrey stopped and looked out the window.

"I'm sorry? I've never heard that expression."

"That's because I made it up," he said gruffly.

"Could you-- elaborate?"

He started pacing again. "In a person's life there is a flow, or as I call it, a calm. You find the path that is most pleasing and you follow it." He looked at me.

I nodded, hoping I looked like I knew what he was talking about.

"Unfortunately," he went on, "things happen, devastating things: the death of a loved one, a debilitating accident. Events like these suck the wind out of a person, leaving them in the emptiness between calms. Most find the strength to stand again, their paths irrevocably changed, but others never regain their calm. Gaza's physical body has probably long healed but who he is refuses to return. The pain of his experience is holding him back. If he could work through the fear he would be free to return to his body. But he can't, so he's stuck. He's unable to continue on into eternity, yet he cannot return to the physical."

"It sounds like you're saying he's a ghost." I let out a small laugh.

"He's as close to a ghost as a physical being can be. His path is wrought with uneasiness and loss. I believe his search is nothing more than a desperate attempt to retrieve his calm."

I shook my head. "How can you sound so sure?"

"Have you not realized? This is a spiritual place. We are no longer in our physical bodies as we understand it. I'm not sure what I would call it, but the best I can come up with is purgatory, a spirit plane between the physical and eternity."

I squinted at him. "You think we're *dead?*"

He nodded slowly. "I'm not certain-- but yes. I think we're dead."

I looked him in the eye. "With all due respect, sir, I believe you are wrong, because just last night I had a conversation with a scientist who would disagree with you."

He looked genuinely astonished. "You've talked with people-- on the *physical* plane?"

"Yes, and although I haven't figured out what this place *is,* I'm pretty sure we're not dead."

He walked back to the window. "This is very odd," he said softly. "I've had some enlightening conversations with my soul, and it mentioned nothing of being able to talk to the other side."

"Your *soul?*"

103

"Yes. Occasionally I have brief conversations with it." He reached out and rubbed a spot on the window. "It said I was on the edge of the physical world and that I had more to accomplish. It said this place was special. There is so much doubt in the world, so many questions. We are an inquisitive species. Without this place we would lose our way. What we learn here we bring here. What we carry with us we made under God's watchful eye."

Again I shook my head. "With all due respect, sir, I don't need any more riddles. My life is complicated enough."

"You wanted to know where we are!" He turned to face me. "I'm telling you what I know!"

"Well I don't buy the fact that I'm dead."

"We're not dead. I was mistaken. It hadn't occurred to me before because I never bothered looking for clarification on the matter. I believe we are on the edge of death. Yes, that's it."

"The *edge* of death?"

"Ask your scientist friends! What I say is true, to the best of my knowledge."

All was quiet for a moment.

"Do you-- want me to try to contact them now?" I said, examining his face for a response. "I'll need to use the power."

He hesitated, then nodded slowly. "As long as you do not effect this world or its people. And I thank you for your consideration."

"No problem. Will you be joining me?"

"I will observe."

I pulled my concentration back in on itself and the web appeared. The thread I had used before was long gone, so I chose another, stretched it, and tracked down the remark. A new message read, "Waiting for a response."

I answered, "I'm here," then created two clamps and pulled a thread taut between them.

104

After a few moments the thread began to vibrate. "Robert?" came the voice of Dr. Solomon.

"I'm here, Doctor."

"What happened? We lost communication with you."

"I was interrupted. Sorry. I got back to you as soon as I could."

"We were worried about you." He sounded genuinely concerned.

"Well you should be. But I'm fine for the moment. Look, I'm going to ask you a question and I want a straight answer. It is *very* important that you answer this question."

"I'll do my best."

"Am I dead?"

Silence. Then I heard an audible burst of air escape from his mouth.

"Doctor, am I *dead?*"

"No, Robert, you're not dead. You are very much alive. I was just surprised by your question. And before you ask again, as I know you will, I will tell you where you are. We discussed it with the psychologist and he said as long as we don't get into any repressed memories you should be okay." He paused.

"Well?"

"You're not dead, Robert. You're in a coma."

"--What?"

A coma. I know this will sound strange, but the world you perceive around you is being fed to your mind by a computer. You're in a simulated level four non-REM sleep state. The computer is artificially planting sensory information into your mind through electronic stimulation. The results, as you can see, are quite real."

"That explains the program."

"Yes."

"So-- you hooked ten of us up to a computer and gave us an environment we could relate to."

105

"Well, almost. We made the basic structure but you're finishing the work we started."

"Are we all in comas?"

"I'm sorry. I can't tell you that."

"Okay," I said, getting frustrated again. "Then why did you ask for me personally in the program?"

"Look, Robert, this isn't easy for me either. I want to tell you what you want to know, but I've been advised not to share certain things. You have to trust me. Our primary goal right now is to get you and the others out of there. But before we can do that we need to learn more about why you're not coming out on your own."

"I'll tell you why," Humphrey interjected.

I'd almost forgotten he was in the room.

"Our souls have lost their way back."

"Who am I speaking with?" asked Dr. Solomon.

"I don't remember my name but you can call me Humphrey, it's the name I've chosen for myself," he said, displaying his grumpy nature.

"Okay, Humphrey, are you one of The Ten?"

"Yes."

"And what makes you think your soul can't get back?"

"It told me it's trapped here."

There was an awkward pause.

"Humphrey talks to his soul, " I said.

"I see," said the doctor. "I noticed a tinge of sarcasm in your voice, Robert. Don't you believe him?"

"Well you have to admit, it sounds a little... ah... He does spend an awful lot of time alone."

Humphrey shot me a look and opened his mouth to speak.

"It's very likely Mr. Humphrey is correct."

Humphrey looked as surprised as I was.

"Come again?" I said.

"I know it sounds far fetched but hear me out. In

106

order to design this system we needed to conduct extensive tests on brainwave activity. As I'm sure you both know there are countless chemical and electrical operations that take place within the human body. We had the arduous task of mapping those electrical pathways. The computer is using the map we developed in order to feed impulses to your brain, and your brain is interpreting these impulses as sight, touch, and so forth. Right now you are using the portion of your brain, which controls your sense of hearing. When I speak my voice is translated into the computer as electrical impulses, which your ear *would have* sent to your brain. In a sense I am talking directly to your brain. And in turn you are sending back vocal responses, which are translated and reproduced by a synthesizer. The computer is monitoring all of these sensory operations."

"O-*kay*. But-- what does this have to do with Humphrey talking to his soul?"

"I'm getting to that," he said, showing restraint. "So far we've isolated all of the electrical signatures and their corresponding responses. That is, all except one. We call it the phantom signature. When we tested normal subjects this phantom signature was a source of much frustration because it caused a bleed over into the other channels. But when we tested coma patients we found this particular signal to be absent. Some of my colleagues believe a person will go into a coma when there has been major damage to the portion of the brain which generates this phantom signal. When the signal is removed consciousness ceases to exist. We don't understand how or why. It just does. And this energy leaves the entire body not just the brain. Something definable departs. --So, why not call it the soul?"

Humphrey looked skeptical.

"But he's not really *talking* to his soul. Is he?" I asked.

"He believes he is and his perception is very

107

important to his recovery. The mind holds a great many secrets and we have only begun to scratch the surface. If we can somehow guide his soul back to his body perhaps his brain will turn the function back on."

"It's more than that!" Humphrey protested.

"I would be the first to agree with you, Humphrey," said Dr. Solomon. "I'm sure it's more than just a chemical process. I would love to be able to claim fame as the man who discovered the soul. But from a scientific point of view we can't prove anything."

"I'm done listening to this technical mumbo jumbo," said Humphrey heading into the kitchen.

"You'll have to excuse him, Doctor. He's easily agitated."

"I can see that."

"I should let you go. I'll contact you later."

"Okay but don't keep me hanging long, I have questions too."

"I'll get back to you as soon as I can." I let the web disappear and went after Humphrey. "What's wrong?" I asked rounding the corner.

"I don't care what he says. I know what I know."

"He was agreeing with you."

"He was humoring me!"

"Well you do have to admit it does sound a little… Do you hear hoof beats?"

Humphrey quickly moved to the window and pushed the curtain aside. Orange light cascaded in. With a jolt he burst from the kitchen. I followed to see him leap out into the night air and down the front steps. Staying in the shadows, I watched as several dark figures on horseback came out of the forest. Their heads were covered with black hoods. Each carried a torch.

"*What do you want?!*" Humphrey waved a wooden staff in the air. "*Get away!*"

"Greetings old sot," the first one hissed in a

nightmarish whisper. "Nice night for a fire isn't it?" The dark figure moved his horse in sideways waving his torch toward Humphrey. "Why don't you use your power, old man? Oh that's right, you don't *use* your powers *do you?"*

"You have no business being here!" Humphrey pounded the ground with the staff. "Now go away if you know what's good for you!"

"What are you going to do, hit me with your *stick?"*

Humphrey swung the staff toward the figure.

The rider retreated with a quick kick and a pull on the reins. "That was not wise," he hissed. His hand disappeared into his cloak. "We do not have time for your feeble threats, however *amusing* they may be." His hand reappeared holding a blue glowing ball. It sparked and whined.

Before I could respond the horseman had hurled the orb at Humphrey's chest. The impact sent the old man flying backwards.

"No!" I screamed, jumping from the shadows of the porch. Instantly the web ignited around me. My anger took the form of an explosive wind and the shock wave knocked the dark figure and his horse to the ground. I leaped through the air, landed full force on the sprawling phantom, and struggled to get my hands on his throat. One of the others came in from the side and took me to the ground. "You like to play with *fire?"* I grabbed his cloak and it ignited in a ball of flames. He let out a startled scream and began clawing at his garments. I set my foot on his chest and pushed him from me.

Another figure advanced. With a quick jab I pushed my fingers into the hard soil. The ground began to tremble as a jagged outline quickly formed around me. He struggled to keep his balance as I rose high into the air on a pillar of earth.

I needed a better view.

I stood and peered down at the remaining

109

marauders. Two were frantically trying to snuff out their flaming friend so I turned the ground beneath them into quicksand. Two more were attempting to set fire to the cabin. I pinched a thread, sending my energy into the frame of the house. Two rectangular slabs bolted outward and connected with their faces. They were knocked cold. With a sweep of my arm I brushed their lifeless bodies into the pit of quicksand.

A sharp pain shot through my shoulder. I looked down to see an arrow sticking from the socket. "Who the... ?" I looked up and saw a figure poised to fire. With a thought a shield formed in front of me and the bolt glanced off of it. Using the threads around the creature and the sheer force of my will, the threads took on a substance of their own and coiled around his chest and arms. I lifted him high in the air before me.

"Now I'm *REALLY angry!*"

He clutched frantically at the hidden cables as I launched him into the air. If the initial tug didn't break every bone in his body, the fall certainly would.

The remaining three, including the one who had attacked Humphrey, began circling the land pillar. "You took me by surprise. That will not happen again," he hissed.

"We'll see about *that!*" I said, turning myself invisible.

He continued to look right at me, while his associates looked around.

I was unable to hide my surprise. "Are you-- one of The Ten? Are you *Gaza?*"

"Gaza would not waste his time with you."

"Then who?"

"You are in no position to ask questions," he hissed.

As we talked I searched for a thread that would bring me in behind him. With a flash of blue energy, I transported, reached up, and hauled him off his horse.

"How's this position?" I said with a grunt.

He disintegrated from my grasp.

I looked up at the figure on the horse next to me. *"You want a piece of me?!"* I lunged at him an his horse reared. I brought up the web and spun about. "Where'd you go, *coward!"*

"Watch out!" That was Thana's voice.

I dove to the side as a huge block of granite hit the ground where I had stood.

"As much *fun* as this is," came the raspy voice of my enemy, "I am being summoned. You will live a while longer." I saw a puff of smoke. Then the two remaining horsemen disappeared into the forest.

I fell to my knees. The pain from the arrow was catching up with me. Placing my hand on the shaft I concentrated on its material and turned it to air. Fortunately it hadn't hit any major organs; I didn't know how to fix a heart or a lung. As I sealed up the wound Thana came to my side. I looked up at her. "How's Humphrey?"

She could barely reply. "I- I think he's dead."

We walked over to where Humphrey lay. His chest was still smoldering from the attack. I examined his structure.

"Can you heal him?"

I looked at her. And sadness welled up inside me. "I'm sorry, Thana, there's too much damage. Even if I use my power I don't know enough about anatomy to heal him."

A single tear trickled down her hard cheek. Here was a girl who was no stranger to pain. She knelt down and took his hand in hers. "Good night, great one," she whispered. "I will look for you in the light."

Chapter Ten

THE DARKNESS EMERGES
1 1 1 0 0 1 0

O

The smell of death hung in the air like a dark cloud.

After a brief memorial service for Humphrey we placed his body in a grave near the waterfall. Thana said it was his favorite spot. I did not know Humphrey very well but I missed him anyway. A deep sadness pulled at my heart and I couldn't help but think that my chances of leaving this world may have perished along with him. His death signified a new era of darkness and confirmed my deepest fear. We *could* die in this place.

Our trip back to Ristol was quiet and uneventful. Thana's quest was over but mine had just begun. When we arrived I thanked her for her company, and although I didn't mention Humphrey again I was sure she could see the sorrow in my eyes. We shared a hug and parted ways.

At a reasonable distance from the town I reached out with my mind to Kitaya. I was anxious to tell her all I had been through and everything I'd learned. But there was no response. I repositioned the thread and tried again. Still nothing.

I tried Corel. My mind pushed out into the expanse of the web and I connected with her presence. She was worried.

"Corel, what's wrong?"

"Now is a bad time, Jason!"

"Where are you? I'll come."

"Not a good idea! Go to the castle and wait for us!"

I felt her push me from her mind.

That was odd. I couldn't reach Kitaya and Corel was in trouble. My heart sank as a disturbing vision formed in my mind. I saw Kitaya, lying broken on the cold dry earth. I would not believe it! She was okay. She had to be!

I found the thread that would take me to Armadon's castle and pushed my energy into it. In a flash of blue I was on the battlement-- what was left of it. The castle was in ruin, with smoke billowing forth from every broken orifice.

Down on the ground I saw a man trapped underneath a hefty stone. I went to him. His eyes pleaded up at me. Touching the threads of the stone I transformed the granite exterior into air and the man gasped as the hollow wire frame rolled off him. I stripped away the textures of his clothing and flesh in order to examine his internal structures. His ribs were broken in many places and one had nearly punctured his lung. I placed my hands on his chest and molded the threads of his body to fix the damage then applied tissue to where tissue had been lost. Soon the man was breathing easier.

"Are you okay?" I asked.

"Yes. Thank you," he responded dryly.

"What happened here?"

"Kric' tu." I believe was his response, but it could just as well have been blood gurgling in the back of his throat.

"Is that a name?"

"Yes," he breathed. "The Dark One. His army attacked soon after Armadon left for Stormhaven."

I thought for a moment. "Rath's castle?"

"Yes."

"I've never heard of Kric' tu. Does he go by another name?"

"Not that I know of."

"Is he one of The Ten?"

"No. He is the maker of darkness."

That didn't sound good.

I helped the man to his feet then went about looking for other survivors. In the courtyard the putrid smell of flesh rose from a raging fire. I stripped away the texture of the flames and through the dancing threads saw two figures fighting for safety from the smoke and heat. I pushed my energy into the threads and transformed the flames to water. It splashed to the ground. A large cloud of steam billowed upwards. I repeated this process with every fire I could find, healed as many as I could, then turned the thick dark smog into clean fresh air. With the smoke removed I could see that the devastation was complete. The ground was littered with lifeless bodies. I made one last search for survivors and healed the few I found.

Finally I pushed my mind out into the web. This time I would talk with Armadon. I felt his mind. He was very strong, his will impressive.

"How are you faring?"

"Rath has aid," he said shortly.

"Who?"

"Some say Kric'tu, others say Gaza."

"What do you think?"

"I say both." The link became weak.

"Armadon?"

He was distracted. *"We can't hold out m..."*

The connection was lost.

I stood staring down at the carnage desperately considering my options. Kitaya was unreachable and I was unfamiliar with Tiko. If Armadon and Corel fell I would be left alone. I could not let that happen.

It was time for the god of reason to make a formal appearance at the capital. With a flash of energy I stood in front of the capital building at Oonaj, where I had attached a thread earlier. I emerged from the bushes and walked up to the gate. Two guards followed me with their eyes.

"I am Sam' Dejal," I stated in my best god-like

voice. "I wish to speak with Sajin Barrows."

One stood with his mouth gaping but the other recovered quickly. "Yes, right this way, lord." He bowed and gestured toward the doors. I followed him in through the huge iron doors, down winding corridors-- past open-mouthed patriots and wide-eyed diplomats. When the doors to the great chamber were opened, every face turned toward us.

"Gentlemen," I announced, "there is a battle going on and we need your help."

Sajin gave a startled glance to the man at his left, a stately man with a gray mustache and beard wearing a regal blue suit.

The man spoke. "Greetings, Lord Tardin. I am Daru, Prime Median of Vrin. What is the nature of this conflict and why would a god need the help of mortal men?"

"I don't know what Mr. Barrows has told you of the current situation between Gaza and the others but things have quickly gone from bad to worse. Gaza and Rath have enlisted the aid of Kric' tu and as we speak Armadon and Corel are engaged in a deadly battle against them. Humphrey is dead and Kitaya is missing. Although we have many powers we need your support to balance the scales. We need your numbers to help even up the fight. And we fight more for your sake than our own. If Vrin melts away the gods will go on but your people will suffer the ultimate cost. Not only will your lives be lost but your world will cease to exist. I beg you, decide quickly; time is of the essence."

Daru stroked his beard in contemplation. "Your words have great meaning." His wisdom was evident in his vivid speech. "I am in favor. Does anyone oppose?" He looked around the twelve-edged table applying his steady gaze to each individual. None made even the slightest hint of resistance. He looked back at me. "Your words ring clear and true, lord. We will support you." As he rose he addressed the men. "You know what to do. Prepare our forces. We move against darkness!"

The men pushed away from the table and speaking in one voice, cried, "For Vrin!"

I released a breath.

The men rushed past bowing as they went. Sajin brought up the rear. He also bowed.

"I need a private room to prepare some things," I said to him in a low voice

"Yes, lord, this way." He motioned with his hand.

Once inside I brought up the web and designed a subprogram which would allow me to repeat processes in mass numbers. Whenever I made armor or weaponry for myself, with a thought, the web would make duplicates for each of the soldiers under my command. This would free me up so I could better concentrate on the battle.

I made one more attempt to contact Kitaya. There was still no response.

I headed back out to the wide granite steps. It didn't take long for the four-hundred or so troops to amass. Sajin informed me that a good number of them were veterans. Many looked like experienced soldiers but most were townsmen and women with old weaponry or farm tools. They were a motley crew but they had a passion for the cause, and in my opinion that was better than experience.

I stood on the marble steps with the multitude of pensive fighters below me. There was movement and discussion but as I raised my hands the crowd fell silent.

I was unsure of what to say. I hoped they weren't expecting some fantastic speech from their sacred tome, of which I knew nothing. I didn't want to say the wrong thing and take the chance of alienating them, so I decided on a brief yet potent prologue. "For Vrin!" I pushed my fist into the air. That got them going. "For justice!" Waves of enthusiasm. "For *reason!*" That brought them to a frenzy. Any more would have been too much so I motioned with my hands, and they quieted.

I had chosen the words I knew were on their minds. I called upon their faith in their world, the promise of the gods, and then punctuated it with the hope of reason, for which I was after all, its god.

Supplies were readied and the soldiers began to chant my name as I set about the task of transporting them to the site. I would move them to the battleground in the same way Corel had transported us to Armadon's fortress. I ordered them to move in close and to take each other's hands. Every person's attention was focused upon my glowing form as I stepped down to the edge of the massive crowd. I pushed my power outward into the structure of the assembly. Once I was sure every thread was energized, I closed my eyes and visualized Pagnia.

The ground began to pull away from our feet and we rose as one unit high into the sky, passing above the clouds, and moving away from the planet until it was nothing more than a globe far below. Fear was in the eyes of my troops but they stood their ground and held tight. Responding to my desire Vrin rotated until Pagnia was in view. As the ground rushed back up at us I chose the area I remembered from the event cell, the site on top of Mount Dastra. With the softness of a feather pillow we touched down on the cliff.

I made my way to the edge and scouted the area to the right of the castle. The battle was raging and the sight was as beautiful as it was horrific. Lightning crashed and fires flared. Wind whipped and rain came down in torrents. Troops fought in the middle of a muddy field while the elements wreaked havoc around them. Hordes of evil looking beasts pushed in against a shield of a thousand human bodies.

A mighty stone wall arose around the forces of man. Creatures attempted to scale it but powerful gusts of wind and rain forced them down. A hole appeared in the side of the stone barrier but disappeared as quickly as it had formed. Parts of the ground began to move as if floating on water but the troops continued their battle. As one god made a change another corrected or transformed it. I spotted what looked like the lead outpost of Gaza's forces. That was where we needed to strike.

It was time to suit up for battle.

I examined my hand as the transformation took place. Flesh turned to metal as scales protruded from skin. Soon my entire body was covered in strips of steel alloy. I squeezed my hand into a tight fist and the armor flexed in its creases. Every joint moved as a well-oiled machine. It was an unnatural thing of beauty. It pleased me to look upon my handiwork. This time I would be ready for Gaza. I checked my back. The feathery wings had grown nicely and were magnificent to behold. I stretched their graceful lines to their fullest expanse and turned to survey my troops.

My visage was greeted with complete and utter shock.

"Do not fear! We need to armor ourselves for battle! The demons will not be able to tear at *this* flesh." I tapped my steel chest. "In a moment each one of you will experience the same transformation."

Cries of amazement were heard as their bodies took shape. Soon each soldier sported a sleek outfit of armored skin as well as a beautiful set of magnificent wings. Their startled expressions spoke volumes.

"You are now protected!" I called out. "This battle will be won by the strength of your wills! Now join me in victory!"

As my words sunk in the oddness of their new forms dissipated and the excitement of the event took hold. Weapons were raised as the war cry of four-hundred soldiers thundered across the valley.

Adrenaline pumped rapidly through the veins

beneath my steel skin as I was caught up in the moment. A knight approached and handed me a hefty sword. "This is from the Prime Median," he screamed over the cries of the troops. Deep, beautiful runes were etched into its tempered steel blade. The brazen black hilt bore an arc of precious rubies. He let go, its weight pulled my hand toward the ground. The tip dug into the dirt.

I smiled at the soldier. "I can fix that." I lightened the materials and the blade lifted. "There, much better."

Everything was set. Now was the time. With a flick of my wrist I closed my visor and with a vigorous thrust pushed my sword skyward. "Let us end the age of madness now and forever!"

The crowd cheered as my mighty white wings caught a strong updraft and I was lifted from the safety of the ground. My muscles flexed as the wings beat with thunderous force. I marveled at how easily they moved. But my fascination needed to be set aside, the war below was turning bad. As I'd expected my troops were confused at first but it wasn't long before the strongest took position directly behind me and the rest followed suit.

We swarmed down through the humid air, descending on the main camp of darkness with the justice of the cause fueling our courage. A thousand glints of metal and eight-hundred mighty wings must have made quite a sight for those on the ground. We were truly a vision worthy of the sacred tome.

I imagined the text:

The sky filled with a multitude of armored angels as the mighty army of Sam' Dejal descended from the heavens. The forces of darkness cowered and trembled in the shadow created by their blessed forms, for the god of reason brought justice in his wake.

I chuckled at how pleased I was with myself-- and the feeling produced a memory. I had always been pleased with myself. In life I was *very* smart, bordering on genius. I excelled in everything and accomplishment was a familiar feeling. I knew it well. But as soon as it had come the memory vanished. *What was I just thinking?*

--Whatever it was, it was gone.

I shook the encounter from my mind and refocused on the battle below. I was eager to meet Gaza, questions concerning Humphrey and Kitaya burned in my mind, questions only he could answer. We hit the ground a short distance from the five tents but as soon as my feet dug into the ground a stone wall pushed up in front of us.

With a thrust from my new appendages I rose to the top of the wall and surveyed the zombie-like creatures forming on the other side. Arrows glanced off my armor as motioned for the others to join me. With graceful ease we propelled over the demons and landed beyond them. Immediately they surrounded us.

Anger and hatred burned in their lifeless eyes. I swung my hefty sword and body parts fell away from my attackers. I pushed forward and slammed one directly in the chest. His ribs crackled and popped like dry logs on a fire. The air was filled with arrows moving in all directions. I quickly tucked my wings in for safety. The others followed my lead but for some it was too late. The arrows, and the demons hacking mercilessly with rusty axes had already clipped a few. I designed a shield to protect my wings in their tucked position. The program reacted and instantly all of my soldiers had a similar shield.

My sword cut back and forth as I took on four creatures at once. Blue threads began to glow as my energy filtered into the web and I did the easiest thing I could think of. The four dropped from view as I removed the ground from below their feet. *That was easy. Now what to do with the rest?*

I rose up into the air and began creating a thousand giant shards of glass above the struggling mass. Upon my command the pieces crashed down in a rain of devastation.

Demons screamed as their bodies were diced. The armor and visors of my soldiers protected all but a few outstretched wings. A cheer rose up.

I dropped to the bottom of the hill and spun toward the tents. Something hit me hard in the chest throwing me to the ground. I struggled to breathe and was dazed for a second. Someone had created a large log and let it roll down the incline. My limbs trembled as I got to my feet. My chest had suffered considerable damage but it was surface damage and easily fixed.

Through the smoky air I saw a figure standing by the tents at the top of the hill. I advanced cautiously and five men took up positions beside me. The figure produced a fireball, which shot down at us, but I applied a counter force of wind. The fireball hovered then dissipated. The ground became slippery but before I could lose my balance I lifted myself into the air. The others took my lead.

Two can play at that game, I thought and focused on the grass below my adversary. I attempted to turn it into wet cement, but he was apparently preserving the shape and form of the ground beneath him. I created a thick beam from the web behind him. It began to fall with deadly force-- but before it made contact a figure intercepted it and the log slammed to the earth. My opponent was startled but unharmed. Through the smoke I tried to make out the figure that had saved him. Whatever it was, it was large, and it didn't look human.

I caught a current and cautiously ascended. My angel guards took formation at my sides. With the web still up I saw the threads in front of me begin to fluctuate. My opponent was up to something. I quickly turned to warn my troops but it was too late. One of them hit the wall hard and dropped from the sky in a daze. I watched as he crashed into the slippery goo below.

Pulling back I examined the situation. I could attempt to punch through the wall but I had no idea what it was made of. I could try to go around it but he could easily create new walls as I went. I was at a loss. There was no way to negate it as long as he was concentrating on it.

One of my men let out a shriek and clutched at his chest. Quickly I stripped away the textures of his body and saw that one of his ribs had been bent inward to puncture his heart. I pulled at the threads but they were immovable. Blood trickled from the man's mouth as he fell into a twisted dive. My temper flared. I pushed my energy into the three remaining men. At least they would not perish because of my inexperience.

I glanced over to check the progress of my troops on the ground. Through the thick dust and smog I saw they were fighting with Armadon's men, which made it an even match. Hate festered in my chest as I looked back at the dark figure on the mound. He looked so smug. I could almost make out a smile under his hood.

I pushed my energy into one of the threads that went over the wall and soon I had control of a network of threads surrounding him. A hollow metal ball materialized and trapped him inside. *Let's see you get out of this one.* But no sooner had the thought formed than a crackle of energy flickered next to the ball and his body materialized. It baffled me for a moment but then I realized he was maintaining the threads below him, which afforded him an escape route. The ball had remained unchanged as he simply slipped out the bottom. *Crap!*

Expecting a counter attack I held onto a thread rising up into the sky. I was finding that the more threads I controlled the more difficult it was to concentrate. And I began to realize if I continued on like this I would most certainly lose. He was far more experienced and for all I knew he was merely playing with me, like a cat with a mouse. It was time for a retreat.

I pulled away and the men followed as I flew over the battlefield to the outpost of our patriots. Hovering above I saw the camp was surrounded by a huge stone wall with a narrow doorway facing the battle. Troops traveled in and out. Some were carrying wounded. Others carried equipment. All looked filthy and tired. A muddy road stretched out to meet the battleground where demons and men fought viciously. Only a few humans were on the side of darkness, Rath's children most likely. I reached my mind out into the web and felt for Armadon's presence. *"We must pull back."*

"I agree. But will the enemy allow it?"

"We won't know until we try." I amplified my voice down into the carnage. "PULL BACK! PULL BACK!"

Shuffling backwards on shaky legs the soldiers began a slow retreat. Gradually the enemy desisted and the two sides moved away from each other, licking their wounds as they went.

I flew down inside the stone wall. Corel was standing at the entrance keeping an eye out for changes. Armadon was already healing broken soldiers as quickly as he could. The flood of wounded was tremendous so I moved in beside him. "May I assist?" I asked the hulking man.

"Please." His deep voice resonated.

I was not happy to note, that I was still intimidated by him.

We worked for over an hour, mending and saving as many as we could. The method was more like sculpture than surgery. First I exerted my will to relieve their pain then I went to work. If there was a cut I pulled the pieces together. If there was a break I fused the bone. Burn victims were easily relieved of their hideously burnt flesh. And excess blood was turned to air. There was no mess, no terror. When we were done many had died, but a far greater number had been saved.

Armadon and I went to meet with Corel at the mouth of the outpost.

"Nice armor," said Corel, looking me up and down.

I looked down at the steel bands and circular patterns. It *was* kind of fashionable. "Thank you." I smiled. "I made it myself."

It was nice to see her grin, but her eyes were worried. "We're thankful you arrived when you did. I'm glad you didn't do what I suggested."

"What happened anyway?" I asked.

She looked away. "We infiltrated the castle and retrieved the information but it was not what we expected. --Rath is in league with Kric' tu."

"So I've heard. Who is he?"

"If evil walked, it would be Kric' tu."

"That sounds bad."

"That's not the half of it," she said with grave concern. Her eyes met mine and burned into my soul. "He is *using* Gaza to destroy Vrin."

Chapter Eleven

A TWISTED KNOT

"Alganah stepped forward and spoke the words written in the ancient text of the Marathil. The sky grew dark as coal and the stones of The Circle of Ghosts began to glow. A screech emanated from within The Circle, so loud it brought the gathered people to their knees. With desperate fingers they dug at their ears. Their eyes began to bleed. The haunted stones hummed an awful accompaniment in time with the screeching wail.

"Alganah continued to speak the words of the Drahdoos. 'Te nerith oon, Tus danor bal!' His words were swallowed into the chaos forming in the center of The Circle. He spread his arms wide and his body began to shake. 'I trade my life for yours!' he screamed. Two ghostly hands pushed forth from the violent maelstrom and clutched him in their delicate grasp. With devastating force they pulled him in. The ground shook as chaos sucked up into the sky and clouds pushed away in all directions.

"When the dust cleared a man lay in the center of The Circle, naked in the rays of the sun. He had come. The prophecy had been fulfilled."

Corel reached out and turned to the next page in the thick musty book. I continued to read.

"For days we sat outside the sacred place. The dark one did not move. Men and women prayed and cried. Others went mad and leaped into The Circle in desperation. Their bodies blew apart in pieces so tiny they seemed to vanish in the air. Holy men preached and the people fasted. On the fifth day he began to stir. Rising from the ashes of his birthplace he walked in his nakedness to the edge of The Circle and stared out at the multitude. He spoke. 'I am the maker of chaos, the keeper of darkness. Why have I been summoned?'

"A holy man stepped forward. 'Thornis must be king. Only the god of power can grant his request.'

"'And if I refuse?'

"'Then I will send you back!'

"The dark one hissed, stepped backward, and lifted his arms. His body contorted into a hideous gesture. 'I WILL NOT GO BACK!' A tremendous flash blinded those who looked on. The ground trembled. And all that remained was silence, and pain."

I leaned back in my chair and looked at Corel over the dusty tattered book. Armadon paced by the door of the dimly lit tent. "The people unleashed a demon from chaos," I stated with disbelief.

"Not just any demon." Corel put her head in her hands. "Supposedly the creator of chaos."

"Are you saying he's the devil?"

"I'm not saying anything." She looked up at me. "It's the people who say it."

I got to my feet, my fingers moving across the surface of the book. "It's time I shared something with you." I chose my words carefully. "I, ah-- know the nature of this place."

Armadon stopped pacing. Corel stared on with curiosity.

I looked at them.

"Go on," they said in unison.

"We are, sort of sleeping," I stated.

"That's ridiculous!" Armadon's voice boomed out. "I haven't slept since I arrived!"

"Let me finish," I said sharply. *Wow!* He was on my

126

side and he still made me nervous. I left a wary eye on him. "Are you familiar with REM sleep?"

I looked at Corel. She nodded. I glanced over at Armadon. I gathered from his squinting eyes that he was not.

"There are four levels of sleep during the normal human sleep cycle, which takes about three hours. We go from level one to level four and back again, always in REM just before we awake. Think of it as submerging yourself in a pond. Above the surface you are awake but as you go down deeper into the water you go deeper into sleep. The shallowest is level one, which is where REM occurs. REM stands for rapid eye movement. It's where you dream all those funky things you can barely remember when you wake up. As you go down through levels two and three you go deeper into a restful sleep, the last of which is level four. Level four non-REM sleep is a rejuvenating sleep. Are you following?"

"I'm assuming there's a point," Armadon quipped.

"There is indeed. You see, we are not in level one. We are in a simulated dream state in level four non-REM. As we speak, a computer is being used to stimulate our minds into a low level active state." I walked over to Armadon. "Whenever Armadon does something the computer remembers it and alters my perception of this world to fit Armadon's change. If I were to slide this table the computer would change each of your perceptions as to where this table is." I gestured towards the roof of the tent. "The cognosphere remembers every tiny detail as we are changing things."

"All this is very fascinating, but why?" asked Corel, beginning to squirm in her chair.

"There are many whys. Can you be more specific?"

"Why are we in here and why can't we wake up?"

I paused. "Apparently the ten of us have all suffered damage to our brains. We are unable to wake up-- because we are all in comas."

Corel squinted at me. "How do you know all this stuff?"

"I've had contact with the outside, with the scientists who are conducting the experiment."

Both looked at me with faces devoid of expression. I was sure their minds reflected the same blankness.

Finally Corel stammered, "Th- that's not possible. We... Technology isn't that advanced! How is this possible?"

"Well obviously it's very possible. I don't know why, or how, but it's the truth as I know it. Why else would we have memories of another place and another life?"

"Can you prove this?" asked Armadon.

"I can let you talk to the scientists yourselves."

Armadon feigned a look out the door of the tent. "Let's assume for a moment that what you say is true. How does it fit in with the events occurring around us?"

"I've thought long and hard about that one but I'm afraid I don't know. What I do know is that these events are real to us. And as the death of Humphrey can attest, if we die in here, there's no coming back. As for the advent of Kric' tu, I don't have the slightest clue. Vrin was created by the scientists and they say we are finishing the work they started. But it would *appear* that life on this planet existed for *centuries* before our arrival. These people have lives and a history." I paused and thought a moment. "Vrin's history *could* be a series of made up events that have transpired from the intricacies of this environment. Maybe Kric' tu was just a mistake."

"A pretty *big* mistake," said Corel.

"Perhaps supernatural components were added to the program to simulate our own folklore and myth."

Corel stood. Her hands went to her hips and she began to pace. "Kric' tu is instigating events that could *destroy* this planet. Can't those scientists stop him?"

128

"I don't know. I'd have to ask." I paused. "But before doing that I'd like to know more about what happened inside the castle today."

Corel stopped pacing and fielded the question. "As you know our intentions were to find out about the woman and child, who they are and why Gaza is so interested in finding them. But we learned more than we bargained for." She shook her head in disbelief. "Rath is holding the woman and child in his dungeon. Gaza doesn't know this. And it looks like Kric' tu is calling the shots. We don't know why he doesn't want Gaza to have the woman and child but Rath has been given strict orders to hold them. We can only assume that he *wants* Gaza to go through with his threat."

I let this new information sink in for a moment, then added, "Humphrey said the two may be replicas of Gaza's wife and daughter. They died in his last existence and he has an unnatural preoccupation with them. Kric' tu may be aware of this but what doesn't make sense to me is, why would a character of this world want to destroy its home?"

Armadon interjected. "From what we know Kric' tu is the creator of chaos. It would make sense for him to destroy governments, or cause upheavals. Maybe destroying this world is *not* his main intention."

"Good point," I said. "He could be stirring things up a little to get us to play his game.

"A little?" Corel said. "He's already stirring things up *a lot.* The question is how do we stop him?"

I stepped back and looked at them. "Well, let's ask Dr. Solomon. Are you ready to meet the man in charge?"

Both nodded.

I brought up the web and followed the steps to alert the doctor of my presence. "This might take a second."

Armadon stepped over and looked at the stretched-out strand. "That's the program?"

"Yes."

"How did you find it?"

"By accident really. I had time to kill and was examining the web to better understand how it worked."

He leaned in closer. "You understand that stuff?"

"Supposedly I'm some kind of programmer, at least that's what they told me. I can read it as easily as you can read English."

The thread buzzed and came to life. "Robert?" came Dr. Solomon's voice.

"Yes, I'm here, and I have two of the others with me."

I glanced at Corel. She looked confused. "Who's Robert?" she whispered.

"Hold on a minute, Doctor." I turned toward Corel. "Robert Helm is my real name."

"Oh. --What's mine?"

"Can you tell them who they are, Doc?"

"I'm not sure. I could take a guess but I might not be right. It's complicated. You see, you are writing portions of the program we aren't able to read yet. We've been working frantically to understand the code but there's so much of it. The system was open-ended and we had no idea how to simulate an internal environment. So we let you come up with one on your own."

"I thought you said *you* created this world."

"I did. We did. Well, we made the framework, but you've changed it and adapted to it. There isn't much left of the original program."

I was puzzled. "Well then, how did you know who *I* was?"

"You're the only programmer in the system so we knew if anyone responded to our message it would have to be you. But we have a complete personality profile on each of you so perhaps if you tell me something about the other two I might be able to figure out who they are.

Corel interjected. "I like to explore, I'm into

climbing, and I love nature." Her eyes shone with excitement, like I hadn't seen since her reunion with Kitaya.

Kitaya. My mind drifted to that place which held the memory of her. When I was with her I'd felt less alone-- she had given me peace for a time. I wanted our relationship to go further but time had been so short. There was so much I wanted to tell her. I *missed* her.

"Hold on, I'm checking our dossiers. Ah, here we are. Most likely you are Helen Vandergraten, biologist, age 43."

Corel was silent.

"How about the other?" asked Dr. Solomon.

Armadon spoke up. "I don't do much of anything."

"You do a pretty good job of fighting this war," I said.

"Yes, I do seem to have a lot of knowledge about tactical movements."

"Say no more. There's a pretty good chance you are Major Ben Kendrick, age 36. You have an honorable discharge from the United States Army."

"Why don't I remember any of that?"

"We don't know. Amnesia is a strange creature."

"Well let's get back on track," I said. "The reason we contacted you is to see if you can lend us a hand. One of the characters in here has gone out of control. You said you can't locate us but can you locate the simulated characters?"

"Do you have a name?"

"Kric' tu."

"We can do a search and try to find a path for that name but it's going to be extremely difficult. The computer has assigned a number to each of the people in there including you. We would have to locate a text reference, something that was written about him, and then cross-reference it with location data stored on our time line. I think we can do it but it'll take awhile. Today for the first time we stumbled onto the text references and we're learning a great deal. It's quite fascinating."

"Yes. Well, do what you can. I'll check in periodically to see how you're progressing."

"I'll get right on it. Good luck, Robert."

The thread went limp and I let the web fade away. "Doesn't look like they're going to be much help at the moment." I looked at Corel. She seemed preoccupied. "You all right, Corel?"

She turned away from me. "Yeah, I'm fine."

"I realize it's a lot to swallow. Are you going to be okay?"

"Yes!" She snapped. "It's just... I'm not sure how to feel about all this. I just want to wake up from this *nightmare.*"

"We all do," I said gently. "But until we figure out how we need to continue with what we're doing. Kric' tu must be stopped."

"You're right." She sighed.

Armadon spoke. "We need to rescue the woman and child and bring them to Gaza."

"Yes, but someone needs to tell Gaza they are being held. He has to know they're alive or he might go ahead with his plans." I paused and looked down at the floor. "And there is still the matter of Kitaya. It concerns me we haven't heard from her."

"We suspect Tiko has her detained," said Corel.

I began moving toward the door. "Then I'll go after her."

"No." Corel was quick to respond. "I'll do it. No one knows Tiko better than me."

I wanted to object-- but realized she was right. "Okay, but let us know as soon as you find her..." I started to say more but stopped before inadvertently revealing my feelings for her.

"That leaves two tasks," said Armadon.

"Which do you prefer?" I asked.

"I've had my fill of Rath."

I nodded. "Understood. I'll try to locate the woman and child. You go to Gaza."

Corel stepped between us. "What about the war?"

"I'll fight it," came a voice from above.

Startled, our heads turned up in unison. A hole had been cut through the top of the tent and the face of a beautiful dark-skinned woman looked through. Her angelic smile was matched only by the loveliness of her vibrant blue eyes. "May I join you?"

"Who...?"

She slipped through the hole, landed solidly on the wooden table, then hopped to the floor. "I'm Lorna, the tenth. Sajin came to me this morning and explained what was going on. At first I thought he was a fruit, but since he was right about these weird powers-- and after seeing the battle ground out there my attitude has changed a bit."

"Did he explain about the war?" I asked.

"No, just basically good versus evil stuff, right?"

I smiled and nodded, then allowed my mind to reach secretly out into the web. Sajin was waiting for me.

"Greetings, Lord Tardin," came the thoughts of Sajin Barrows.

"Did you send Lorna to us?"

"Yes, I did."

"Thank you. I will be in touch."

His presence faded away into the void.

"Right. Well then," I said. "Welcome aboard, Lorna. I'm Jason. This is Armadon." I pointed. He bowed slightly. "And this is Corel." They shook hands.

I looked at Corel and Armadon. "Sajin says he sent her. That's good enough for me. Anyone have any objections?" I looked to one then to the other. "Okay then," I smiled at Lorna, "let's fill you in and get you trained."

133

Chapter Twelve

THE SOUL OF A PEOPLE
1 1 0 0 0 0 1

τ

Lorna was a quick study and the kind of woman who spoke exactly what was on her mind. I liked that about her. She was as bright as she was beautiful; within an hour she had picked up all the tricks we could think to teach her.

Preparations were made for our separate ventures. I helped the others by creating two pistols. Armadon was pleased with his. It was his first firearm since coming to this world. The weapon was dwarfed in his massive hand, but a look of satisfaction played upon his broad features. Corel, however, held her weapon like a diseased handkerchief. After I showed her how to hold it properly, and explained that it was a low caliber weapon, she appeared more at ease, but not much.

We headed out, thanking Lorna for her help, and fate for her auspicious arrival. On the tops of the walls weary soldiers stood guard. There was an eye in every direction and a sense of apprehension in the air. At any moment an attack could come. We were fortunate to have such brave, alert men fighting with us. When this war was over, we planned to reward them generously.

Behind the cover of the wall, Armadon and Corel disappeared in a flash of blue. I paused at the entrance to the compound, looking out onto the misty battlefield-- at the bodies of the dead cooling in the evening air. Soon it would be nightfall. It would be easier to hide in the dim blue light of the moons so I sat and began tossing stones, waiting for the darkness.

Behind me the sound of footfalls approached. They slowed as they neared, then stopped. "Sir?" said the voice belonging to the feet.

"Yes?" I said without turning.

"I know I'm not supposed to talk to you, but something weighs heavily on the minds of my men."

"Come then," I said kindly, "sit with me."

"Oh, no, lord. I could not."

"Sit with me, or I shall be offended."

He came around my side hesitantly then placed his helmet on the ground and perched on it. Weariness showed on his dirty young face, but he held himself up, I assumed, with a strength fueled by the cause. His chest was proud through his tattered uniform, his rank, all but melted off.

"What can I help you with?" I said, continuing to toss stones.

"Has Gaza turned his back on us?"

What an interesting question. I looked at the boy and was again struck with curiosity about these people. For the most part I was too caught up in the events of the moment to consider the implications of this world's existence, or to pay much attention to its residents. But once again I found myself in awe of their diversity. *Who* was asking this question? I could sense this boy's apprehension-- but computer simulations don't feel nervous. This boy, like Thana, appeared to be a complex living being, possessing all the strengths and frailties which make up human existence. But he wasn't *real!* If this world was an induced dream state, then *who* was responsible for this boy's question?

"Sir?" prompted the boy.

"No. Gaza has not turned his back on your people. Kric' tu is the one responsible for this conflict."

"*Kric' tu?*" The boy's face whitened. He knew the name, and he feared it.

"Do not fear. We will defeat him. Our forces are strong." After a short silence the boy began getting to his feet. But I stopped him. I wanted to get a better understanding of his design-- and pass the time before my trip. "Do you have a family?"

"Yes." He hesitated, then settled back down. "My mother and father wait for me with my youngest brother. I'm the oldest. My other brother, Finton, is here, but he is under another command."

"How do you feel about your brother being here with you?" I asked, studying his face.

"Well, at first I was angry that he enlisted behind my back. But he's getting older. I suppose it's time for him to prove himself, as it was for me."

"Do you watch out for him?"

"Yes, like an eagle," he said turning away slightly. His face was thoughtful, contemplative.

The boy's reactions were totally believable, with every mannerism completely in tune with the content of the conversation. He seemed *so real*. I suppose it was possible his emotions were feeding off The Ten, but from which of us did he draw his perception?

"Are you afraid to die?" I asked, wanting to see how he would handle a philosophical question.

"No, I do not fear it. You are with me," he said confidently.

"And what do you think I will do for you?"

His eyebrows knitted. "I don't understand."

I reworded my question. "What is it about my presence that sets you at ease?"

"Your presence provides proof that the gods do exist. The Marathil states that you will introduce our souls to the light. If I die at your side, it will only be my body. My soul will live on. Right?"

It was obvious I was making him tense with my questions. Just one more, then I'd stop. "Where do you think your spirit will go when it is released from your body?"

"I will go to live in Ethral, with the Keeper of Light, the Maker of Love" He gazed up at the sky.

I sat nodding my head. Okay, *one* more. "And what purpose do you think the god of reason serves?"

"Without you the path is broken. Why would there be a path without reason?"

"So I am the reason for the way to Ethral. Good!" I chuckled, more at my own foolishness than for the sake of easing the boy's fears. "Go tell the others that victory is inevitable. Kric' tu cannot hide the path from me, because *I* am the reason it is there."

His face lit up as he stood and bowed. "Thank you, Sam' Dejal, thank you!" Without fully raising his head, he gave a sly knowing look, then turned and bolted off.

Boys in charge of boys, I thought. *We're in trouble!*

The exchange with the young soldier left me no closer to a solution. Where were these people getting their emotional responses? Were they part of a dream scape we were feeding them subconsciously, or was Humphrey right? Was this place actually a spiritual realm somewhere between the physical world and Ethral? Since we were being artificially stimulated to dream in level four sleep, could it be we were seeing this world for the first time with our conscious minds? I was not inclined to believe in Humphrey's teachings but the evidence was beginning to weigh in his favor. First of all, I could come up with no scientific reason for the existence of such a complex and diverse people, and second, Humphrey was removed from the equation. If this was deliberate there had to be a reason-- and I was determined to find it.

I sat and watched the sun dip below the jagged teeth of the snow-topped mountains, which loomed in the distance like shadowy observers. The wind tossed my hair around in its chilly fingers as I looked toward the

137

battlefield. The dancing shadows gave subtle movement to the eerie landscape. Lights from the opposing camp pierced the night. It was time to go; it was darkest in the short space between sun and first moon.

The web lit up as I searched for my first target. There, a large rock off to the right of the battlefield; I followed a thread to it. A clump of shrubs a short distance away provided my next hiding place. Once there I had a clear view of the camp. More tents had been erected and a bunker had been built around the entire encampment. I continued on into a small wooded area just outside the town and hid behind a large tree. To get through the town unnoticed, I fashioned a thick brown woolen robe to cover every portion of my armored body, then stripped the armor away from my head and face. Earlier I had changed the program so my modifications would no longer effect the troops. The robe did a good job of covering my armor and tucked wings, but what to do with my eyes? I created a mirror, it floated in the air in front of me then fell gently into my hands. I superimposed my will on the two glowing steel orbs, but the glowing was persistent. I focused harder but they continued to resist. I tried pulling at their threads. I could easily change their shape, but the glow remained. I dissolved the mirror and created another dark band of cloth. Under the shadow of the hood it would go unnoticed, and I would be able to walk about freely without the pretense of a blind man.

I poked my head around the tree trunk and examined the stone wall between me and the entrance to the city. The main gate would be formidable for a mortal but for a god, it was a piece of cake. The web ignited as my mind pushed out into the network of strands. I still found it amazing that I was so instinctively in tune with these tiny blue lines. By touching a thread, I could tell how far it traveled. With concentration, I could see the exact make up of the entire collective. It was overwhelming to

138

comprehend. Many threads led into the city, but I needed to find one that ended somewhere discrete. I followed a number of threads with my mind's eye and found one that would work; it led into a deserted alleyway just beyond the wall. The alleyway led to the main street. *Perfect.*

In a crackle of blue energy I materialized in the empty alley; there were no windows in either building, so my passage went undetected. Even stepping out onto the sidewalk no one noticed me; they were preoccupied with the war effort. Soldiers were everywhere, many of the townspeople were preparing supplies. I kept to the shadows. These people didn't appear to have the motivation and dedication of my troops. Their actions were mechanical. I was sure they pushed forward out of the fear of punishment. Several times I noticed citizens eying the soldiers with suspicious glances. I wasn't sure what it meant, but there was deception in their eyes. A man caught my attention. Cautiously he looked over his shoulder, then entered a small building. I wouldn't have thought anything of it, but I recognized him; Fyousa, from the event cell, the one who wanted to stand up and fight. If I had an ally in this town, he was it.

The door was locked, so I peeled away the texture and looked at its innards. Three bars held the door in place. I shortened the bars until they no longer held, opened the door, and stepped inside. The dusky room looked like it had once been a bakery, but was now nothing more than a hollowed out hull, at which even a rat would turn up his nose. A lone candle burned on a nearby table. I grabbed it and moved across the room to an open door. A set of stairs lead downward, voices and flickering lights came from below. I stopped and listened.

"Armadon's forces are holding ground. We have to act now." That was Fyousa's voice.

"My men are ready," came another.

A female voice joined in. "There are some who will

139

drop out because of Kric' tu. The men fear him more than Rath."

"We will have to take the losses. If we do not act now, darkness may very well win."

I threw caution to the wind and made my way down into the cellar, and was greeted with the tips of swords. "Perhaps I can be of service," I said, removing the hood and blindfold.

The swords dropped.

"Which are you?" Fyousa stepped forward into the light of the candles.

"I am Sam' Dejal."

A voice spoke from behind the small group. "Ahh, Mr. Tardin, the god of enigma." The group parted to reveal another man whose face I recognized from the event cell.

"I hope you have a point," I said sharply.

"Oh, I do, Mr. Tardin. If any other god had dropped into our midst, I would have been suspicious, but you, I welcome. See, we have had enough of *gods*. But you, you are not a god at all." He stepped towards me. "You are just a man caught in very unusual circumstances." The light flickered in his eyebrows, causing shadows to dance on his face. "Those are your words, are they not?"

It took me a second, but then I remembered. I had said those words to Thana. "Yes," I said, feeling exposed, "those are my words." Where was he going with this?

"Your words have traveled far and you do not understand the impact they have had on my people. In your ignorance you brought first confusion and then enlightenment. You see, when the gods came, they brought with them the promise of peace and prosperity, but promise after promise was broken, and my people were left to consider the implications of the inconsistency. We hoped for a divine plan, but there wasn't one. We did not know that men, not gods, had brought the promises. We didn't want to believe it, but then in the midst of our greatest

140

confusion, there appeared a ray of hope, a spark of truth. 'I am not a god!'" He turned to the others in proclamation. "'I am but a man caught in very unusual circumstances.' That statement, along with Humphrey's death, provided our people with the hope we needed to stand up against our aggressors. The gods we feared, were not gods at all. They were mortal, and they *could* die.

"And now we are graced with the presence of the god who would be a man. If there is one among you who speaks the truth, it is you. If there is one we can trust, that would also be you. We are no longer bitter at The Ten, since the war has clarified matters. As the sides are drawn, it is becoming clearer that the Marathil was correct about one thing; in the end, it is a matter of light versus darkness. We thought the gods had turned on us but we were wrong. Evil has a way with confusion, with hiding the truth. But we have seen the seed of its way and have chosen to align ourselves with Armadon and the forces of Ethral. It is not clear to us yet who The Ten really are. But one thing is certain, gods or no gods, we need your help in fighting the darkness threatening to take our world." He turned toward me and stretched out his hand. "So, Mr. Tardin, I welcome you, to the resistance."

Chapter Thirteen

PUPPETS OF THE VOID
1 1 0 1 1 0 0

β

What could I possibly say to follow *that*? I was thoroughly impressed with the man. He was old, but his charisma and intellect gave him a youthful quality which enhanced his powerful appearance.

I took his hand, and said nothing.

He continued. "SCAR was created to stop the influence of your kind on our world, but as you know, things have changed. The picture has become broader and we now consider your arrival here a blessing. We would like to offer our support to your cause, if you will have us."

"We can use all the help we can get," I said. "Your words are true, I am no god, and as far as I've seen, none of The Ten are. Our powers are limited. Your support will be a tremendous help, but I should caution you, many of our men still believe in the message of your holy Marathil. Their belief in us has carried them this far. Although you are closer to the truth than they are, I would appreciate it if you would exercise a bit of restraint. The fact we are vulnerable could be a motivator, but if they find out our cause is a lie, it would be detrimental."

"I agree. Faith has a way with some."

"Good. Then let's get to work."

The man bowed slightly. "This way. We were discussing the deployment of our troops."

Crates and barrels littered the moist stone floor of the dank, musty cellar. In the far corner, barrels had been chopped in half to make seats and crates were set as tables. He led me through the murky, half-lit room to several maps scattered about on various surfaces. I had to strain my eyes in the dim candlelight to see the map of Pagnia on the crate between us. "Are you opposed to my using my magic?" I asked.

"No. Since the death of Humphrey and the reappearance of Kric' tu, Thana now understands the need for the gods to use their power. It is no longer a simple matter of interference. Force must be fought with equal force, and I of all people would not be opposed to magic, for you see, I am a wizard."

"Then I will shed some light on this little meeting," I said, trying to appear unaffected by his statement. A *wizard?* I looked at the old man with his ruby red robe and thick white beard. He did indeed look like a wizard. But again I was at a loss. How did *magic* fit into the scenario of this world? Apparently my perception of Vrin would have to continue to fluctuate as new facts became available. These thoughts filtered through my mind as I worked to create a simple wooden table and several large candles. The room lit up and I had my first clear look at the faces gathered around. "There that's better," I said, looking across at my new acquaintance. "I'm sorry," I said, realizing he had not told me his name, "what do I call you?"

"My apologies, Mr. Tardin. I am Arganis."

"Are you the leader of these people?"

"I am only their leader because they choose to follow me."

"You are modest," I said, looking down at the map. "So, where are your troops?"

"There are some in Rath's attack force. They have been ordered to fight defensively only. Then there is Kaprisha's group. She has them concealed in this patch of woods off to the left of the battle area. And Fyousa has

143

some men in the castle, maybe a few in town as well. Right now we have a messenger on his way to inform Armadon of our intentions.

"You've been doing your homework. Are your people ready to fight?"

"Some have been shaken by Kric' tu's arrival; they fear him more than The Ten." He shook his head slowly. "If there is a genuine deity in Vrin, it is Kric' tu. I curse the day my family released him from the pit."

"*Your* family?"

"Yes, I am a direct descendant of Alganah."

"*Fascinating.* I have many questions I'd like to ask you. But I will wait until the troops are deployed."

"I will trade you, answer for answer," he said with a smirk.

"Agreed."

That made sense. According to the historical record, Alganah had exercised some form of magical talent when he opened the gateway to chaos, or whatever it was he had opened. If this man was truly a descendant of Alganah, he would most likely have inherited some sort of supernatural ability. If he were able to exercise that kind of influence on this world, his power could be comparable to ours. *Fascinating!* Before me stood a man who represented a link between these people and my own. --Yet, he was just a simulation. --Or was he? He had called *me* an enigma. But the term best suited him.

I brought myself back to the matter at hand. Lorna needed the support these people offered. "First things first," I said. "Your messenger will not find Armadon at the outpost. Lorna, the tenth, is holding our position while we tend to other matters."

"Other matters?"

"The battle is just a distraction, a distraction that must be held, but the real war is taking place elsewhere. I cannot tell you more in the face of so many unknowns. Let me contact Lorna."

"Yes. Tell her my troops will respond to the password *faith*. They will change sides immediately upon hearing that word."

"Does the messenger know this?"

"Yes."

"Got it. Hold on."

I tipped my head to the side. *"Lorna? How goes the battle?"*

"It's still quiet here. Too quiet. Have you reached your destination?"

"No, I've met with a pleasant snag. I'm here now with SCAR. Are you familiar with them?"

"Nope."

"I won't go into detail right now, but I'll say this. You can trust them. A messenger is on his way now and he will tell you the password to use is 'faith'. He will explain their position. Let him into the outpost."

"Yessir."

"They will provide extra troops."

"Good, we can use them."

"They may be able to help me gain access to Rath's castle."

"Great."

"All right, that's it for now. Good luck, Lorna, and thanks again."

"Sure. You take care of yourself."

I pushed her energy from my mind and refocused on Arganis. "She will allow your messenger into the outpost."

"Thank you." He stood to address his group. "You know what you need to do, men. May the Maker of Light be with you."

They filtered out of the room with hopeful enthusiasm. I rose to stand beside Arganis. His face was thoughtful. I could tell he cared deeply for his people.

When the last person left, I turned to my silent host. "I will need entrance to the castle. If you are indeed a wizard, perhaps you can help."

"I will do what I can."

"I would also like to know more about your abilities so I may better understand my enemy."

"You are puzzled. Have you no wizards where you come from?"

"I don't think so. Well-- only in storybooks. That's what bothers me, you are an inconsistency in the scheme of this place. Vrin is based on scientific fact taken from my world, yet you defy the very principles that make up my universe. It would be very useful to know how, and why, you are able to possess magical abilities."

"It's simple." He chuckled. "I draw from a source outside the realm of the physical world."

"Outside of *Vrin?*" I said, astonished.

"Beyond the cognosphere lies the void."

"You mean-- space?"

He furrowed his brows. *"Space-?"*

"Never mind, it would take too long to explain."

He gave me an examining look, then continued. "Vrin floats in energy. There is a point on this planet where a channel exists, a pillar into the sky called The Circle of Ghosts. A vortex there leads into the energy pool." He leveled his eyes at me. "All who have entered The Circle have died horrible deaths for the energy is unlike anything in Vrin. I call it energy, others call it magic. My ancestors learned to tap into this magic. Hundreds of years ago, Nor' Trull built a cabin next to The Circle and each day he would go and sit at the edge. He found that the vibrations from his voice would cause things to happen, and that each vibration had a different effect. He cataloged the effects in a book that was passed down through the generations. His son learned from him, as I learned from my father.

"Interesting. Is there a reason it's called The Circle

146

of Ghosts?"

"Yes. It is a portal to a place called Dantra. It is believed a race of people live within the energy. Some say they are the ghosts of our ancestors waiting to be released to Ethral, but from what my family has gathered, they do not originate from our world. We think they are an ancient race of spiritual beings. In the many years of communicating with them, my ancestors have learned a great number of things. They used this information to attain their goals, but ultimately, it was our undoing. When Alganah called on Kric' tu, the god of power, to save our royal family from being ousted, what he unleashed was not what anyone expected. And before he could send it back, it escaped into Vrin."

"They were expecting a benevolent spirit?"

"Yes. They had no way of knowing that evil existed in the void. All the spirits that had come before were loving spirits of light."

"Do you need to be at The Circle of Ghosts to use the magic?"

"No, but it is stronger there. Energy seeps from The Circle and filters into the air. It dissipates as it moves father away from its source, but it can still be very potent."

"What types of things can you do? Would you be willing to give a demonstration?"

"Yes. But then it is my turn to ask you some questions." He gave a crooked smile.

"That sounds fair."

He stood and walked to the center of the room, then repositioned toward me. With eyes shut, his hands began to caress the air methodically. They swayed about in gentle arching movements, punctuated by gestures resembling an exaggerated form of sign language. He began a deep resonating vocal hum.

A ghostly glowing fog began to materialize. His hands moved through it, forming wakes of white sparks. He

147

spread his arms wide, leaving a swirling orb of iridescent gas, then sharply brought his hands together. A brilliant flash of light blinded me.

"Impressive," I said, rubbing my eyes. "Is that the extent of your power's usefulness?"

"It's the most visual. I can lift things and move them around, basically doing things I would normally use my hands for." He paused. "But enough about me. It is my turn."

"Alright. Fair enough."

He rubbed his hands together. "I'm almost giddy," he said with an expression of childlike enthusiasm. "Let's see. --If you are not a god, then what are you?"

Always the complicated question first! I looked at him, and shook my head. "Well, it might be a little hard for you to understand, so if I cover anything you are not sure of, feel free to interrupt."

"I will."

"The Ten are human, but not human like you." I paused. "I'm not sure exactly who or what your people are. The best I can come up with, is that you are one of the characters my imagination has created.

"So-- The Ten *did* create our people?"

"I think so. Yes. As far as I can tell."

"You *thought* us, and that gave us life?"

"Well, I'm sure there's more to it than that. I was told of a foundation that was created before my arrival. It may not have been The Ten, but it was others like us who created you and your planet. You see, I am not awake like you are. I am asleep, and dreaming of you. But it is not my dream, it is being given to me by another."

He looked perplexed. "Vrin is a dream-?"

"Well. Not exactly. But it's a place I can only visit when I'm sleeping. My real body is elsewhere-- connected to a bunch of wires I'm sure."

"Like a puppet?"

"No." I chuckled. "Not like a puppet." I thought for a moment. "The wires are similar in function to a tube that you might push the energy you control through."

"You were right. It is very confusing." He furrowed his brows. "What would happen to the dream should the dreamer awake?"

"As far as I know it would continue on, at least as long as the others are here."

"So The Ten are dreamers, who dream a dream, which is being sent to them from another place?"

"Sort of."

"What is that place?"

I thought for a moment. "It's similar to the cognosphere. For all I know, it could *be* the cognosphere."

"So you are *here*-- like I would be in an event?" His eyes lit up.

I nodded. "That would be a very close analogy."

"Have these events already happened?"

"I don't know. I think I'm experiencing all of this for the first time, but I can't be sure."

"Do you know why *we're* here?"

"No, I don't. You could be here to make this place feel more like home. Or maybe your role is important to our recovery. You see, we are not here by are own choice. We are unable to wake up."

He rubbed his chin. "Why? With such power you should be able to awake with ease."

"One would think, but it hasn't happened yet." I looked him in the eye. "So until I can find a way to wake up, I'm trying to keep this world from being destroyed. Without it, I'm not sure I would be able to find a way back."

The barrage of questions ended in contemplation. Arganis stared off to the distant wall of the cellar. It was a lot to swallow, but he was faring well. I wished I could have given him what he wanted. Perhaps a lie would have

149

been more comforting. There was no end to the questions, and the road to truth was littered with emotional potholes. Perhaps my answers fell short of their esteemed goals, but all I could do was try to answer honestly, and hope he would find some stable philosophical ground to stand on.

Again he spoke. "What of our souls? Will we eventually ascend to Ethral?"

"I'm not familiar with Ethral, so I'm not sure. If you believe you do, then I don't see why not."

It was a half-truth, but who knew? The scientists could have created a convention for Ethral and chaos. Who was I to deny its existence?

"Then I choose to believe," he said defiantly, "until proven otherwise."

"And I will believe with you. Maybe together we can will it to be so."

I made two glasses of wine, and handed one to my associate. "A toast to the afterlife, and to the soul within. May its journey continue on to Ethral." There was a clink of glass, followed by a silence, which lasted long after the wine was gone.

And there we sat, two halves of an unknown coin, two voices in the hallows of eternity, stating with conviction, *we will go on.* But feeling considerably less than sure of ourselves.

Chapter Fourteen

DEEP IN THE HEART
1 0 0 0 1 1 1

ξ

What was that principle? The more you learn, the less you know? As my perception of Vrin increased, my confusion increased along with it. But as much as I wanted to wake from this agitating dream world, I couldn't help but have a fascination for its diversity. Its complexity was far beyond anything I could possibly imagine. The computer system holding the data generated by this world must have been *immense.* So I decided, if I ever did find my way back to the world on other side, I would definitely apply for a job.

Arganis returned from upstairs carrying a map in one hand and a lantern in the other. "This is a map of the castle. It has taken us a very long time to gather the information for its design. I'm sure it is not completely accurate, but it is the best I have to offer."

"It will do splendidly!" I said, taking it from him and laying it flat on a dirty crate. "I'll need to create a tunnel, the straightest point to the dungeon. And it'd be nice if I didn't have to deal with too many guards, I don't want any chance that word of my presence will get back to Rath."

"How about here?" He pointed. It was a remote spot between some bushes on the left side of the castle. "You would only have to make a tunnel fifteen or twenty feet deep."

"Very nice." I grabbed his arm with approval. "Can

you get me there undetected."

"I'm fairly certain."

"Then let's waste no time," I said, pulling up my hood. "We can use the evening mist to conceal our efforts." I rolled up the map and stuck it in my belt as Arganis went to a corner to retrieve a small backpack.

We mounted the narrow stairs and walked through the dusty room to the door. He slid back a small piece of wood and peered out. "Looks clear."

There were no soldiers in sight as we stepped out into the busy street. The denizens were loading wagons with supplies. Old and young alike labored over the tasks.

Arganis scooted off toward the castle. I followed close on his heels. Our journey took us through side passages and under wooden overpasses. All of the damaged buildings had been rebuilt. I couldn't help but admire Rath's handiwork, he had an eye for beauty. We passed many townspeople on our way. All were clad in finely crafted clothing, but not one looked happy. These people possessed great riches, but Rath had taken away their peaceful existence.

At last we reached our destination. Between several bushes a small clearing lent easy access to the side of the castle. Arganis stood back and I went to work. I pushed the ground down twenty-five feet to the lower level of the castle wall, then removed my robe and tossed it in.

Arganis had never seen wings on a human before, and curiosity got the best of him. He reached out and ran his hand down the soft white plumage. "Very nice," he said brimming with excitement.

"Thank you." I gestured to the pit. "Shall we?"

He nodded.

I wrapped my arms around him from behind and lifted him into the air. Together we descended deep into the earth. Once we had our footing, I stripped away the texture of the wall and peered inside. It was a dark hallway, and it looked deserted, so I created a large hole.

Arganis gingerly stepped in as I retrieved my cloak. Once inside, I filled the empty space with dirt, and applied the grass covering as I'd remembered it. It was nothing to replace the wall. And within seconds, I was finished.

Up and down the passageway there were no recessed areas to hide in, so we would have to make our way down before anyone came through. We listened. Then quickly stole down the slanting hallway until we reached a T intersection at the bottom.

"This way," said Arganis. The dark corridor ended at a large wooden door. "This leads to the dungeon area," he whispered. "If they are here, that is where we will find them."

I removed the texture of the door and peeked through. "One second," I said over my shoulder. "There's a guard." A nearby thread went through the door and stopped near the man's neck. I applied my influence and watched as the end twitched then attached itself behind the soldier's ear. I attached the other end to myself.

It was time to make an impression.

"YOU HAVE BEEN CHOSEN!" I pronounced forcefully into his mind.

A startled burst of thought came through the thread, allowing me to gather what I could about the man's temperament.

"I AM REASON!"

"What do you want from me?" There was a quiver in his thought.

"Spell your name and count to ten," I ordered.

"What?"

"Do it-- or face the consequences!"

I realized the statements were far fetched, but it was my intention to confuse him and keep him off guard. If he was allowed even one second to think about his allegiance to Rath, I probably wouldn't get any information.

153

"*J, A, F, U, S-- K, E, N, R, A, one, two, three, four...* "

I breathed the name to Arganis. He shook his head, he wasn't one of ours. What could I do with this guy to put him out of commission? Scare him into silence? I whispered to Arganis, "I'm going to need one of your special light displays. Can you do it through the door?"

"No. There must be a connection between my voice and the energy cloud.

"What if I made a sliver of an opening?"

"That should work."

I went back into the soldier's mind. *"YOUR SERVICES WILL BE REQUIRED!"*

"They are already spoken for." He was feigning loyalty; I sensed the indecision in the vibrations of his thought. This was not one of Fyousa's men, but there was doubt in him.

"Rath will never give you what you desire. His path leads to darkness, and all who follow him will be swallowed by the pit. I offer you a chance to join the forces of Ethral. Think hard. I will not offer again." I could feel his anxieties. He feared Rath, but was uncertain of *my* validity.

"Time for a light show," I whispered to Arganis. I examined the door and chose the section I would remove. With the appropriate fireworks, my emergence would be very convincing. --But first I needed a little more presence. I focused on my internal structure and began to grow in size until my head was almost touching the ceiling. *Now I'm an even match for Armadon,* I mused.

"Start your chant," I said to Arganis. "I will open a section here in the door. What I need from you is some swirling colored smoke and a blinding flash of light. When you do this I will step through and convince the man to join us. I hope."

Arganis nodded and began the guttural vocals of his chant. I sent a buzz into the soldier's mind to distract him

154

from the noise. The energy from The Circle of Ghosts began to glow around us, and I opened a small sliver in the door. Faster than my eyes could follow, the energy vanished inside. I opened the hole, quickly stepped through, and closed my eyes.

When I opened them, I was standing over the guard who was frantically rubbing his eyes. I reached out and put a firm, kind hand on his shoulder. He squinted up at me.

"Be not afraid, my son. If you join me, you will no longer have to do the bidding of darkness." As his vision returned, his eyes fixated on my wings. Arganis was generating a glowing light behind them. *Nice touch*, I thought.

The guard's chest filled with resolution. "I will join you Sam' Dejal."

"Good. Then help us now. We are looking for a woman and a girl child."

He nodded. "Yes. They are in the isolation chamber."

"Is that far?"

"No, I can bring you there."

"Lead us then."

The man scurried off down the hall, and I looked back at Arganis with a wink. Reputation was always stronger than reality.

He led us through the musty stone halls down into the abysmal parts of the castle, where the stones were slippery, and moss flourished in the cracks. We descended deeper still, and the corridor grew smaller until it was clear my height would be a disadvantage. I concentrated on the threads of my body and returned it to normal size.

The soldier's eyes grew wide. "You can change your size?"

"It's one of the perks of being a god." I shrugged.

He looked curious, but said nothing more.

We continued on, and it grew darker. The guard

155

picked up a torch and lit it, and we descended still deeper into the heart of the dungeon. The wail of a prisoner echoed in the distance. I winced at the sound of his screeching howls. He must have been enduring incredible pain to make such a noise. And still we continued on, it was much farther than I had expected.

The passageway ended abruptly, and the three of us stood looking out into an immensely massive cavern. In the center, an endless pillar reached from the depths of the pit to the ceiling high above. A craggy stone sphere bulged out from the pillar directly across from us, like a rocky bead on a rotted iron bar.

"That is the chamber of isolation," said the guard with a shaky finger.

I waved my hand, but the web did not come up! I placed my hand on the wall, and was shocked by what I saw. The entire cavern had been cleaned out, all of the threads were gone except those making up the structures of the cavern and the three of us. I turned and looked back up the corridor, there were plenty of threads in there.

"This doesn't look good," I said to Arganis. "It might be better if we split ways. Take this guard and travel to the outpost. I will send word as soon as I've finished."

"But there is much I can do to help."

"If this is a trap, I will be better off alone. I wouldn't want your lives being used as bargaining chips."

He nodded. "I understand. We will go." He extended his hand. "Good luck."

I shook his hand. "To you as well my friend." I turned to the guard. "Thank you Jafus. Today you have changed your life path toward the direction of light. Go with Arganis. I will be along shortly."

The man gave a sturdy nod.

My skepticism was waning. I almost believed the words I had told him. However unbelievable my circumstances, there was something magical about this place, and I couldn't help but to feel caught up in it.

Even the danger that stood before me tasted of reality. If I failed, I would let the others down. There was a chance I could die, but it didn't matter. I was on the side of justice and harmony, and it filled me with a courage I was sure I had never possessed as a mortal man. Indeed, the more time I spent here, the less I felt like a man in a coma, and the more I felt like a god on a mission.

I snatched a few threads from the hallway and attached them to my leg. If this was a trap, Rath would most likely snip them and block my escape, but it was worth a try. Pulling the strands with me, I rose up into the dusty heights of the massive cavern. The wind felt cool and moist on my face. I rounded the large stone sphere and discovered a bridge crossing from a ledge on the wall, to a small arched opening in the center of the bead.

I touched down lightly on the bridge, examining the entrance to the rocky sphere. It was conspicuously vacant of guards. This put me on edge. I moved cautiously toward the opening, and as I approached, began to hear noises emanating from within-- but couldn't figure the source of the sound. There was a grunt, and then a faint scraping noise, but it was hard to decipher through the persistent whispering of the cavern wind.

I pressed myself back against the wall and carefully peeked in. It was pitch black inside. A single beam of light cut through the darkness from a hidden source. I listened closer. There was a bump, and more scraping. I leaned in to allow my eyes to adjust to the darkness.

And without warning a figure leaped at me. I jumped back and hit the wall hard. Before I could could piece together a thought, it was on me, grotesque and vicious. At one time it had apparently been an ape, but had been modified in hideous ways. Enraged eyes flashed from underneath a rotted iron helmet. Steel claws bit into my chest plate. The scraping made a frightful noise as I flopped

157

around like a rag doll, stuck between its deadly weight and the lip of the bridge.

In desperation I sent my power into it, but the blood drained from my face as I realized, It had no threads! With no time to contemplate the meaning of this little twist, I pushed my energy into the strand attached to my leg, and in an instant, found myself hovering several feet off the bridge. I picked up the wind weakly with my wings. Blood seeped from my abdomen, accompanied by a burning sensation.

The ape danced about the bridge in a rage, beating its armored chest with clenched fists. There was no way this creature could be here. Yet there it stood. And quite ominously. Moving about the threads of the bridge, a ghost in the machine.

Then it hit me. The Circle of Ghosts! If Kric' tu could walk about in Vrin, then it made sense he could bring forces from the other side. This ape provided evidence of the realm Arganis had spoken of, the place where the ancient spirits lived. But-- was it a real place?

Maybe this creature was just a glitch in the program? It would take a seriously sophisticated computer to hold a world this enormous, and with all complex things, there were bound to be glitches...

It didn't matter.

Whatever it was, it was between me and my goal. And it was time to remove it.

I touched the edge of the railing and sent my energy into its threads, causing the bridge beneath the beast to become air. As the creature began his exit, his mighty claws dug into the rocky sides, holding him for a moment, but I graciously relieved him of his prize. With a screech of terror, it plummeted into the abyss, and I watched until it was nothing more than a tiny dot in the distance.

Returning to the bridge, I examined my armor. It was badly damaged from the impacts of the foul beast. The metal was split and torn around the mid-section. But this, and the gash in my side, was easily mended with a wave of my hand.

Again I cautiously approached the entrance, and paused to listen intently. All was silent, so I took a step in. There were no more surprises. To my left, where the single light beam filtered in, was the outline of a door. I took a section of the thread that clung to my ankle and made a thick match. As I struck it, the room lit up slightly. A bar stuck out of a circular opening in the center of the rusty iron door. Reaching out, I took hold of it. A loud clank echoed through the dark chamber. The door creaked loudly as it slid out of its stony pocket, and light pushed free from inside.

Again I paused. Everything looked okay. At least nothing was jumping out at me.

I crept in slowly. The interior was nothing like the outside. The walls were a rich tan colored stone, and the floor, black marble with creases of white. Silently I made my way down the hall, frequently glancing behind. I came to a door with a small window. Carefully I scanned around its edges for threads or traps. Finding none, I peeked in. The lighting was dim, but I could make out two figures against the far wall. Judging from their sizes, they were the two I'd come for.

My pulse raced. And the fear of the unknown gripped me for the very first time. Anything imaginable could happen. Death could be waiting for me on the other side of this door. --Funny I should start to fear death *now*.

I'd seen so much in this odd place, heard so much talk of religion and gods, good and evil. But I hadn't stopped to think about my own place in the universe. People were counting on me, and it was possible I was the only one who held the key to the way home. But was I prepared to face the greatest unknown? --It didn't matter. At this point, there was no turning back. No matter what the

159

cost, it had to be done.

It was time.

With sweaty hands, I slid aside the five dead bolts. The door swung open.

"Who's there?" came a woman's voice from within.

I stepped in and created a wedge from the threads of the hallway floor to hold the door open. "My name is Jason. I've come to set you free," I said, keeping an eye on the open door behind me.

"Oh thank the gods!" She picked the child up in her arms, and in crossing the cell, passed into the light of the torches. She carried herself in a proud, elegant manner, and was quite beautiful. Her pale features were almost perfect, with wide set green eyes, and flawless skin. The girl's features were much like those of her mother's. Both were very beautiful, but both looked exhausted. I stretched out my arm. The woman gently placed her hand in mine.

A loud *CRASH* came from behind. I twisted around to see an enormous stone block covering the door. I pushed my energy into the threads attached to my ankle, but they only brought me as far as the barrier. I laid my hands upon the stone and released my energy, but the threads did not light! In frustration I flung myself against it, but it was no use. The stone would not yield.

Turning back in toward the cell, I found the woman kneeling in its middle with her hands raised to an invisible barrier. *"Why* are you doing this?" There were sobs in her words. *"WHY won't you let us go?"* Her daughter knelt beside her in silence.

A door opened in the rock behind them and someone entered the cell. As soon as he stepped into the light, I knew him.

"Rath!"

"Ah, you remember me. Good," he taunted.

I held my tongue and fixed my stare on him.

Another figure entered, but stayed in the shadows.

160

Rath stepped up to the divider and smiled a broad sinister smile. "You have done a fine job, Sam, but it is time you took a break." I glared at him as my mind raced to find an escape. "The war is coming along nicely. You have stoked the fires, and we have accepted the challenge. But the finale is yet to come." The sarcasm was thick on his tongue.

"You can't win!"

"We've already *won.*" He laughed. "This world will dissolve, and things will continue on as if it had never existed."

"What's in it for you?"

"You wouldn't understand if I told you."

"Try me."

He sighed. "*I* will be a true god. *I* will sit at the right hand of the ancient one."

"You're *mad.*"

He laughed. "Your limited intellect cannot comprehend the magnitude of what is going on here! We will use Vrin to change the outcome."

"What? By destroying it?"

"Not by destroying it, by *transforming* it! You do not understand now, but..."

"ENOUGH!" hissed the figure in the shadow. Then it stepped forward.

My heart constricted with terror. My eyes darted back and forth looking for a weakness in the trap. But found none. Through the transparent barrier, I saw the woman and child begin to tremble. The young girl huddled in closer to her mother as they both cowered over with expressions of horror painted on their faces. I had let them down. I had let everyone down.

Dusky light fell across the grotesque disfigurement of the dark, slightly bent body of Kric' tu. More specter than man, its form was tall and thin, with dark eyes sinking into a fleshless face. Patches of dark flesh, which looked sewn on, hung from its sickly gray skin. My stomach wretched to look at it.

He moved closer, expelling an airy laugh. "Look at you, Thomas. You are so angry, yet, you don't even know what you are fighting against."

The voice was familiar, but I couldn't place it. And-- why did he call me *Thomas?*

"I am truly horrible to look at, am I not? How clever of God to represent me as such. Do you know that in Ethral I am the most beautiful of all angels?" He turned away slightly. "But things are not always as they appear."

"If you are so, wonderful..." I tried to keep my voice steady, "then why are you bent on destroying Vrin?"

"I cannot say." He took a step toward the woman and child. "He is watching. He is always watching."

"--Who is watching?" I said, hoping to stall him.

"You are strong like him, Thomas. And your power must be added to my own." He took another step. "But first you must endure the darkness. On the other side, things will be clearer. After you have made the decision."

"What *decision?"*

He hissed a laugh. "You must decide to follow your own heart, and cease being a puppet of God. Man will grow beyond the box God has put him in."

I was trying desperately to follow his riddles. If I could not properly respond, he might lose interest in the conversation, and I was not done formulating my plan. "And this world represents a threat to that process?"

"Yes," he hissed.

"So-- you would like to keep the scales balanced toward evil."

He sighed in annoyance. "We are not *evil.* We are chaos. You do not understand, but you will." He turned sharply, and with a withered hand, effortlessly pulled the child from her mother's arms. The girl let out a desperate scream and I flinched as he struck her across the face.

162

I felt so *helpless!* What could I *do?*

Kric' tu's gnarled fingers twisted into the girl's hair as she began sobbing uncontrollably. "These two pose a threat to us."

"A threat! They're *harmless.* They've done *nothing* to you!"

Kric' tu produced a knife from his long dark sleeve.

"Take *me* instead!"

Rath laughed. "We already have you!" he said, stepping forward and putting his hands on the woman's shoulders to keep her from rising.

"If they live," hissed Kric' tu, "Gaza will find the hope he searches for." He adjusted his grip on the struggling girl. "That is simply unacceptable."

"Gaza's been warned of your plot!" I said sharply.

"Armadon?" He smirked. "He has been taken care of."

"That's a lie!"

"Your army has been crushed. And now it is time to extinguish the last flame of hope for you and your so called *cause.*" The knife moved quickly to the young girl's throat.

"MOMMY!"

Pulling my pistol from the holster on the small of my back, I gripped it tightly, and began moving toward the veil. Both Rath and Kric' tu leaped back in surprise as I began firing rounds directly at Kric' tu's head. Only one bullet needed to get through. *Just one!* My anger increased. Kric' tu flinched as bullet after bullet smashed into the barrier. Round after round chewed into the shield. And my fury continued to elevate. --But then the weapon began to click.

And the power left me.

The gun was empty. Not one bullet had pierced through. I hurled the pistol at the glass. It cracked, but instantly the tiny fragments began fusing back together. Rath was fortifying it!

163

I slammed full force into it with the metal of my shoulder. But it was no use. Rath laughed, and as I glared at him with a growing hatred, a new resolve began to build within me...

But what happened next will haunt my dreams forever. Kric' tu's blade slid smoothly across the young girl's throat, and I watched in *horror* as her life's blood drained from her. The expression on her tiny face was more surprise than fear, as though she did not understand what was happening to her. He opened his gnarled fingers and her lifeless body slumped to the floor.

I beat my fists against the barrier with fevered aggression. *"Noooo! I'll kill you! I'll KILL you!"*

"Not likely," he said, with a twisted smile.

Rath dragged the woman to the girl's bloody form. She wailed and clawed at him, but he held her tight with ease. His eyes held no remorse. No guilt. *How could such a monster have been chosen for this experiment!*

Kric' tu grabbed the woman's hair and pulled her close. No! Things were moving too fast! I needed more time! There *had* to be a way to stop him! The woman's face was wet, and her pleading eyes dug deep into my soul as she mouthed the words, *"Help- me."*

I was completely powerless. *No. WAIT!* I could not manipulate the threads around me, but I still had *my* threads! I got up and turned my back to the scene. "I do not care to watch any more," I said, desperately hoping to allow myself the few short seconds I needed.

Kric' tu's voice floated in from behind me. "No stomach for reality, Thomas?" he taunted. "Perhaps you are not the man we thought you were. You're allowing your spirit to get in the way." He paused. "You know, you were not always a puppet of God. This place has done something to you. --No matter." There was finality in his voice.

I was ready. "There is one last thing I would like to say," I stated loudly.

"Yeah. *What?*" said Rath.

"This!" I turned, and falling away from the veil, rolled until I hit the far wall with a clank. What had once been my hand skittered across the floor and came to rest next to the barrier. The deafening explosion created a shock wave that pinned me against the wall. The pressure pushed in on my sealed ear passages. My armored body shook as the walls quivered.

I rose quickly and sprinted toward the barrier. Through smoke and dust, I saw an opening, hit the ground, and slid through to the other side. The ground was slippery from the young girl's blood.

Kric' tu had not yet risen from the blast. I scrambled across the floor and grabbed him with my remaining hand. He was confused, but I clarified the situation with my stump, which came rushing toward his chest with a spike protruding from it. It sank in deep.

A smile crossed his ghoulish face. His teeth were rotted, and his eyes, empty. He began making the guttural noises of Arganis, and a searing pain shot through my leg. I rolled off him and clutched at it. The burning was *unbearable* as it spread throughout my body, engulfing me! My mind locked up. The room swirled around me. And I fell into darkness.

I awoke to find myself back on the other side of the transparent barrier, with the room spinning in nauseating twists. I was unable to stabilize my vision, but could see Rath, standing just beyond the barrier, alone. His voice came to me, thick with arrogance. "That little trick with the bomb was quite clever, Sam. It will be glorious when you come to the side of chaos-- but that will have to wait." He chuckled. "Because first, you must experience the nightmare."

"You'll never hold me," I said weakly.

"What was that? I'm sorry." He jeered. "Could you say that again?"

165

Though the effort was incredible, my stubbornness would not allow me to remain silent. "You'll never hold me," I said louder through gritted teeth and spit, almost passing out from the exertion.

His laughter filled the room. "I'm afraid you are quite wrong about *that*. You see-- you are going to be my guest, for a very, *very,* long time."

I tried again to speak, but my voice would not come. He walked away-- his laughter stabbing at my heart, his form fading from view, until he was gone. As the massive stone door encased me in my tomb, the light began to fade, until I was in complete and utter darkness.

I wished for sleep, but it would not come.

Chapter Fifteen

HAVING A FAMILIAR RING

η

My first efforts to move were excruciating. So I lay still, breathing shallow breaths. An attempt at rolling to my side ended abruptly with a sharp pain stabbed into my back, informing me that my left wing was broken. I struggled to sit up, but dizziness overtook me. I fell back down against the hard sticky ground. --I guess I would have to wait a bit on the whole *moving* thing.

The room was dark as soot, but smelled of something far worse. With each breath my stomach wretched from the noxious odor assaulting my senses. To my left, was a dripping sound. At first I had to strain to hear it, but the longer I lay there, the louder it got. Each drip echoing through the chamber in a maddening rhythm, playing upon the strings of my emotions with a sinister hand.

The chill passed through my armor and into the very depths of my bones-- but I was too tired to shiver. The encounter with Kric' tu had pushed my body *far* beyond the point of exhaustion. Whatever he'd used on me caused my body to tighten so violently, every muscle had ruptured. And it wouldn't be long before the shock wore off and the process of healing began. This I dreaded, for I knew it would be extremely painful.

Pain stabbed at me again as I made another attempt to roll over, but with much satisfaction, I made it onto my stomach. The cold sticky ground offered no comfort. The pain from the wing was almost unbearable, so I reached into my mind in an attempt to remove the pain, but nothing happened. I tried again, this time making a suggestion to my subconscious, like I had done with the injured soldiers, but again I failed.

It made no sense, the technique had worked wonders for the soldiers. Why not for me? My mind struggled to understand, but there was too much interference from the searing pain.

A rush of air escaped my lungs as I tried to move to a kneeling position. It was no use, the broken wing was a dead weight against my back. I would have to remove it if I hoped to get anywhere. With this in mind, I pushed my energy out into the threads of the wing, but nothing happened. I tried again and again with the same result. The threads did not respond. My powers, were gone.

It took a moment for the reality of my situation to fully sink in, but when it did, it hit hard. And something inside me snapped. I began thrashing about, clanking and scraping and screaming at the top of my lungs. All of my anger lashed out at the universe for my stupidity! How could I have been *so* arrogant? I thought I was *untrappable!* I thought I was *invincible!* But I was wrong! And now my fate was sealed, like the door to my tomb.

Eventually my aggression dissipated, and I lay still on the chilled ground, my chest heaving with each labored breath. *What was I thinking?* This whole thing stunk of a trap. I *knew* it, and yet I'd continued on! Was it the power of the web effecting me? Was it my belief in the righteousness of the cause? I thought no one could stop me, not even Rath or his demon associate. Yet when the time came, I was powerless to stop them. *My God! The young girl! Her face! The innocence!*

I pounded my steel fist against the concrete floor. Armadon should have come. He would not have failed, but had he not failed already? *Lies! Kric'tu had to be lying!*

They wanted to destroy my hope, that was all. Armadon had made it to Gaza. It *had* to be so!

Rath's words echoed in my mind. *"First you must experience the nightmare."* The meaning of that statement was becoming clear to me now. Desolation. Loneliness. Pain. All had a way of driving a person mad, and I was no exception.

But-- if they *were* telling the truth, nothing was left to prevent Gaza from destroying Vrin. And if he did follow through with his plans, then there wouldn't be time for me to experience the nightmare intended for me. Or would the nightmare continue on after this world was destroyed? Was there pain in the destruction itself? My heart pounded in my ears. Could the destruction *be* the nightmare? Or was the statement just another *lie* to dig at my insecurities?

Assuming everything I knew was fact, where did it leave me? The goal of chaos was clear. They did not want this world here, at least not in its current form, so they were using Gaza like a puppet. *He* had the power to destroy Vrin, and would, if he couldn't make a connection with his lost family. But chaos had eliminated them. So how long would it be until Gaza made good on his promise? If Armadon *had* been stopped, then someone else had to make it to Gaza!

I pushed aside my self pity, and drew upon my anger and stubbornness. I would *not* sit around waiting for oblivion. No cage was complete. There *had* to be a way out.

It hadn't occurred to me before, but I had grown dependent on my newly acquired powers. I was addicted. The more I'd used them, the more I had needed to use them, and now that they were gone, I was experiencing withdrawals. My thoughts were erratic, and my heart was heavy with depression. A sense of futility was taking hold, but I had to fight it. I was stronger than this. There was no time for self doubt. After all, I *was* Sam' Dejal, the god of reason! If there *was* a way out, I would find it!

In searing pain, I made my way to my hands and knees, drawing upon my mortal strengths for the first time since my arrival. Then, with an equal amount of effort, I ventured to stand. The broken wing hung from my back, making it exceedingly difficult to gain my balance. I would not be able to stand for long, but needed to move around as much as possible to keep my muscles from tightening up.

I shuffled back and forth, back and forth, each step a tremendous effort. I paced for *hours* it seemed. And as time dragged on, my muscles ached more and more.

Finally, I had to sit. I found a small block of cement near a wall, and used it as a chair. The pain from my wing no longer bothered me-- the aching in my limbs far exceeded it. I leaned back, and let my body go limp.

Hours melted into each other, and pain was my only companion. I no longer had any perception of body. I was just pain, floating in darkness. Even the nasty stench had melted away into my experience. Humans have a way of coping with stress, and I had reached my threshold many times over.

As hours, and then days passed, I searched every nook, every angle of my pen, but I couldn't even find the door. I must have circled the room a thousand times, but all the walls felt the same. With meticulous precision, I trolled back and forth across the room, looking for items on the floor, but found nothing. Still I could not be certain I had covered every spot, the darkness was too complete. I hoped my eyes would eventually get used to the darkness, but there wasn't a drop of light to work with.

As the madness began to grow, my motivation dwindled. After a while, even time was meaningless. Then I waited, as the pain disappeared completely. I was sad to see it go, it was all I had to remind me I was still alive. Now I was nothing more than a ghost, as large as the universe, or as small as an atom. I wondered how long this could go on.

There was no hunger, no need for sleep. I simply existed. And that was all.

In my free-floating mind, I thought of all the possibilities of this place called Vrin. I thought of Humphrey's concepts and of Dr. Solomon's experiment. I thought of the wizard, Arganis, and his ancestral roots of magic. There was the world of Vrin surrounded by a spirit world called Dantra, and The Circle of Ghosts connecting the two. Then there was the infamous Kric' tu, commanding the threadless beasts of the vortex. What did it all mean? Or did it have meaning? Were there supernatural forces at work in this world? Or was it all a computer glitch?

And what about the frozen figure in the capital? What was his name? It eluded me, but I could see his face in my mind. I realized now, that looking at him was like looking into my own memory, as if I had once sat at the same table, reading the same book, by the same fire. That was why seeing him had effected me so profoundly. But this new found realization brought no relief. It only deepened the mystery.

Thoughts of Kitaya floated to the surface. In this whole experience, she had made the most positive impression. She was so lovely, so full of life. I cared for her with a longing that made my chest constrict. We could never be together now. Somewhere in the darkness, my fist tightened. She was unreachable, even *if* I could find my way out of this cell.

A faint sobbing broke into my perception. And once it started, it did not cease. Sobs echoed off every recess of my tomb. What I perceived as my face was replaced by a cold lake of sadness.

Before my empty vision, my days in Vrin played out in vivid detail. It hadn't occurred to me before, because I wouldn't admit it, even to myself, but I truly wanted to be a god. Although I had shown constraint with Thana, I could

171

not fight the desire to use the power. Something deep inside me wished for it.

I was given many opportunities to see this world for what it was, yet I had remained willfully ignorant. Each inconsistency in the program, and each talk with the outside, made my foolishness complete. I *knew* I was no *god,* yet I chose a lie over the truth! I was here, because of my own *arrogance,* my own pride.

I had reached the end of myself.

"God?" My voice was dry and weak. "I don't remember the last time I talked to you-- or if I've ever talked to you-- so I'm not very good at this." I choked out the words. "I- just want to say, if you can hear me, I need your help. I'm sorry. Please forgive me."

Somewhere in the emptiness, I felt a squeeze. I waited. There it was again! I tried to localize the sensation, then it came to me. *Scratch!* I had forgotten all about my little friend.

"Hello, Thomas," came a voice from the other side of the room. Kric' tu had called me that, but this was not Kric' tu's voice. "Do not be frightened. I've come to bring you home."

Home? My chest quivered with emotion. Was this another trick? The voice was not familiar, but the inflection in it was. I had heard the gentle tones before.

"You are experiencing disorientation. That is understandable, but it is over now."

I squinted into the darkness. "Who...?" I whispered.

"I have many names, but for now, you may call me Scratch." He chuckled.

I felt for the ring. It was still on my finger.

"That is merely the host God made for me."

"*God* made for you?" I whispered.

"Yes, you don't remember, because this world keeps the memories from you, but when you were brought to Vrin for the first time, he knew I could not exist in your new

172

body, so he created a ring for me. At times I tried to contact you, but your hatred drove me away. Hatred is contrary to my nature."

I remembered the canyon, and the figure in the woods. "Was that *you* in the canyon, and the forest?"

"Yes. I exited the ring to speak with you, but returned because it hurt me to be exposed to your hatred. You hate Gaza very much."

"Why do you stay at all?"

"You are a complex being, and I am a part of who you are. I can't leave you, Thomas. I *am* you."

"I don't understand."

"The complexity of God's creation is beyond your current awareness."

My weakened mind groped for the answers. "You have come-- to take me home?" I said weakly.

"Yes."

"Why did you wait so *long?"*

"I did not wait, God waited."

"What?" I could barely get the word out.

"It wasn't him. It was you. You finally called out to him. He wanted to help, but he waited until you realized your need for him. It had to be your choice. Our choice." The room began to fill with light, and I saw him for the first time, a million tiny marbles, and in each glass orb, a brilliant light. "It is time to go."

"But I have more questions."

"I know you do, but the angels of God are holding off the forces of evil. We must go now."

I felt dizzy, then in an instant, found myself peering through his eyes. We had fused together, and I was now complete. Looking down down at the broken body on the floor, I and was disgusted at the wretch I had become.

My essence began to rise up, through the dungeons, through the castle, out into the air above. Below, I could see the battle still raging. They *had* lied to me, which meant there was a chance that Armadon had made it to Gaza. I wanted to go there and see, but was unable to fight against the force acting upon me. There was a superior purpose in its design, and there was no arguing with it.

I continued to rise higher and higher, until the people below were nothing more than specks on the open battlefield. As I moved closer to the clouds, I realized, for the first time, they were not clouds at all, but a projection moving across a large sphere. I flinched as I passed through.

Outside the sphere, love and light surrounded me like water. Its current flowed through me, filling me with peace. It was a familiar feeling; I had been here before.

I travelled up a blue strand at a blistering pace, and Vrin grew smaller and smaller in the vast cavern of shifting light. Upon its surface, currents of electricity arced, like blue liquid fire boiling.

To my left, a movement caught my eye. It was at first beautiful, then horrific. Brilliant bursts of light, which should have blinded me, exploded not far from where I ascended. Colors beyond description shot forth in all directions. The beings of light were at war, but why? They collided with awesome force, creating an unimaginable shock wave. Were these the angels of God?

I looked up. High above was a gray, bumpy, stone ceiling. As I got closer, tiny pinholes became visible. The pinholes became pores, then the pores became tunnels. Billions of them, stretching off to either side as far as the eye could see.

I rushed into one of them at a dizzying pace, straight into the heart of the porous rock. Everything became a blur, and the walls slowly melted away into space and thought, until there was nothing left of form.

It was here-- that my memories returned.

Ɛ

Memories, like a mottled collage of faint footage filled my mind. I knew at once, all that I was, and the universe made sense. It was the perfect plan of a perfect Creator. I was amazed at its simplicity.

I saw the study at the mansion, but it was not the same place. It was clear to me now. The mansion had belonged to my grandparents, Jason and Rebecca Tardin. We stayed with them on weekends when I was young. My brother and I would play for hours in the warm study. It was my safe place. As long as I was there, I would not be harassed by the bullies in the neighborhood. They liked to pick on me because I was different-- because I was smart.

Another memory came to me, sharp and painful. *"Becca! Stay away from the street!"* My daughter looked back at me in her sweet innocence. Lost in her own world, it took her a second to respond. Hers was the curious age of five, and she was excited to be in the crowded city. I watched until she lost interest in the street and began exploring the various novelties of a nearby vendor.

Her mother joined her to look at some jewelry. She'd been sitting on a bench nearby, tired from carrying the extra weight of our unborn son. "Stay close to me, sweetheart," said Annie, reaching out with a gentle hand to pull her in.

I turned back to the man I had been talking to. "So how much for the painting?"

"It's a work of art, man, I couldn't let it go for less than fifty dollars."

I looked at the painting, then back up at the man. "Fifty? Tell you what, I'll give you forty for it. That's the best I can do."

The man grudgingly accepted, and I smiled to myself. I knew he would take it. Everything was a game on the city streets. Nothing went for face value.

"Rebecca *come here!*" Annie's voice was urgent.

Behind me, Becca scurried along the edge of the street in pursuit of a small puppy. I twisted quickly, and, at an awkward angle, barely got hold of the back of her shirt as she jumped off the curb. The puppy darted out into traffic.

Off balance. Tires screeching. A mail truck veered out of control. Everything began to move slowly. If I could not regain my footing, the truck would plow into us! With all my strength, I pushed my daughter from me.

The memory faded, and although I continued upward, there was no sense of movement. Above was a curtain of energy. The Separation. I knew it, and I knew its purpose. I would not be allowed to bring the memory of this place to Earth. It was here, Sam' Dejal had to stay.

And he did not like it. Not one bit.

A mild current of energy washed over me as I entered. A splitting of identity, and an *explosion* of anger. I was helpless to stop the forces of eternity as the experiences of Sam' Dejal were ripped from me, fading and screaming into the darkness, leaving only the memories of my earthly self.

And I was, once again, Thomas Tardin.

I found myself sitting in a boat with a beautiful young oriental girl. The water was as smooth as a mirror. The sun was warm in a peaceful sky. She was smiling. Why was she smiling? There was something familiar about her, but there was no name.

176

I stepped down from the carriage and turned to help the young woman to the ground. The old western town was deserted, but I paid no mind. I left the carriage and the girl, and entered the tavern in front of me. People moved about inside, sharing in whiskey and music. Several games of cards were going on, but my interest was at the bar. I moved up alongside an old man. He was drunk, and babbling about gods or something.

"You have my keys," I said to him.

He turned to me and laughed. "You'll have to find them yourself, my boy." His eyes were red from the liquor, and there was a film of moisture on his lips.

"My wife is waiting for me at home, but I can't get there without my keys."

"Why don't you ask your lady friend for them," he said, stubbornly.

I felt a pair of hands move in around my waist; they belonged to the young Asian girl. I turned, still in her grasp, and we began moving back and forth to the music. The bar was empty now, and a tranquil melody drifted from the jukebox. I put my arms around her and pulled her in close. She smelled of sweet flowers in the morning dew. The song ended, but we continued to dance. I wanted the night to last forever.

She pulled free from my grasp. "I will be back soon," she said, throwing her bags onto the black leather seat of the red convertible. I recognized the man in the driver's seat, a strikingly handsome man, with curly blond hair, brilliant blue eyes, and a faint scar on his right cheek. Where did I know him from? The girl hopped over the door and blew me a kiss. Tires screeched, and the car spun out of sight.

"Honey? What's wrong?" came Annie's voice from behind me.

"Nothing, just thinking." I turned to see my wife making breakfast in the kitchen of our old apartment. She broke another egg onto the sizzling surface, and a strange clicking noise began emanating from the pan. Annie's eyes looked at me expectantly. Her lips were moving, but the voice that came out of her was not her voice. It was the voice of a man.

"Next level, split, jump three, stop, negotiate 250 degrees..." My mind struggled to make sense of the words. But instead, the absurdity of them pushed me from the dream.

I became aware of a noise next to my right ear and attempted to open my eyes. But the room was too bright. What was I just dreaming? I tried to remember, but the images were fading fast. There was a weight on my chest and a tightness at my temple. I tried to move, but something was holding my head in place.

A voice spoke. "We've been trying for four days, and my people need some rest. I understand the importance of finding the key, but without proper sleep there are going to be more mistakes."

"Just get it done!" said another voice. "Work in shifts if you have to!"

"Understood."

I heard footsteps walking away, then a series of clicking noises intertwined with what sounded like voice commands. "Next level, split, jump three, stop, negotiate 250 degrees." *clickety click.* "Next level, skip five, negotiate fifteen degrees." *clickety click.* "Stop. Identify."

"Pattern-- *not present-?"* He sounded surprised.

"What?" *clickety click.* "Search, stop, split."

"Pattern-- not present."

"Philip come here a sec."

"What is it, Brian?" Footsteps approached.

"I was finishing up my search criteria, and check this out." *clickety click.* "Search, stop, split."

"Pattern not present."

There was a brief silence. "Are you saying-- they're

178

not in the system anymore?"

"I'm *saying,* one of the patients is *awake!"*

I cleared my throat and swallowed hard. "Are you, referring to me?" I said in a broken whisper.

"Holy crap!" was the response. (Not a very professional response if you asked me.)

"Where..." I cleared my throat again. "Where am I?"

"Hold on, ah-- Mr. Tardin. I'll get the doctor."

A doctor? Was I in a hospital? My eyes opened to a squint, allowing the piercing light in at my retina. Blurry forms began to take shape in the sea of white.

More footsteps approached. There was a faint smell of cologne mixed with fresh air. "Good morning, Mr. Tardin. How did you sleep?" The voice was familiar, but I couldn't place it.

"I'm- not sure."

"We are going to detach you from the equipment now. Don't be startled," he said soothingly.

Where had I heard that voice before?

There were hands all over me, a pinch here, a squeeze there, the pressure was released from my temples and chest. I tried to focus on the doctor, but he was nothing more than a hazy shape. The colors were slowly returning, but the definition was yet to come.

"Thank you. That will be all," he said to the others. "You will be briefed at the next meeting."

Doctors? Meetings? *A memory flickered; terror in my daughter's eyes, pedestrians moving in slow motion, everyone looking at me...*

"Do you remember dreaming while you were asleep?" There was a sense of urgency in his tone.

"What?"

"Do you remember dreaming?"

"Vaguely."

"Do you remember Vrin?"

"--What?" My mind tried to wrap around the word.

"Is that a name?"

He sighed. "Do you remember anything of a world called Vrin?"

It was then that it came to me, just beyond my perception and pushing in. I wouldn't have noticed it at all, but his words brought it to my attention. On the hard olive green surface of a metal arm near my head, was an imprint. I squinted. It read, **V**irtual **R**eality **I**nterface **N**etwork.

"I have no clue what you're talking about. What is this place?" I tried to lift my head.

He put his hand on my chest. "You're in no condition to get up, Mr. Tardin. Try to relax." His voice was soothing. "How do you feel?"

"Like a piece of lead." I squinted at him, still trying to bring him into focus.

"Are you in any pain or discomfort?" he said, gently pressing a stethoscope on my chest.

"No, not really. Why are you asking me all these questions?" I made another attempt to move, but he reaffirmed the pressure on my chest.

"Please, Thomas. try to be still." There was compassion in the timbers of his hauntingly familiar voice. "I need to check you over."

Another memory flashed. My little girl sprawled on the sidewalk. A woman screaming. A truck plowing into me... My heart jumped. "I was, in an accident." I desperately searched my memory. "Is this a hospital?"

He leaned in close. His friendly face came into focus. It was not a handsome face, but it was kind. And seeing it helped ease my panic. The wrinkles around his eyes were deep from many smiles, but the bags underneath showed that he hadn't slept well for many days.

"It's a hospital of sorts," he said. "Hold still." He shined a light into my eyes. "How is your vision? Are you able to focus?"

"It's-- coming back slowly."

"Good, very good. I'm going to take your blood pressure now."

I attempted to lift my arm, but it wouldn't move. I tried again. *"Why can't I move my arm?"* Panic gripped me. "Doctor?" I tried to control my voice, and frantically searched his face. "Am I *paralyzed?"*

He smiled kindly. "No, Thomas. You're not paralyzed."

"Then why can't I move!" Again I tried, and my fingers moved a little.

"I'm sorry, Thomas. It will take some time before you are back to normal, but please try to be patient. You've, ah... You've been..." He furrowed his brow and a look of compassion crossed his features. "You've been *sleeping,* for a long time."

I stared at him. "--How long?"

There was a notable silence.

"Doctor-?"

He gave a weak smile, and a look of sympathy. "You're not going to like this. That is, if you even believe me."

"What? A week? A *month?* How *long* have I been sleeping?*"

He sighed, and his eyes took on a look of clinical detachment. "Twenty-one years, Thomas, twenty-one years."

I searched his face. "You're joking. *Right?* Please tell me you're joking."

"I wish I were." He looked me in the eye. "You were in a bad accident, Thomas. And you've been in a coma, for twenty-one years." There was no sign of humor in the creases of his old face. Only deep concern.

"That-- that's not *possible!"* I stammered. "I- I can't..." My voice broke off.

"Under normal circumstances, you would be correct, but these are far from normal circumstances."

181

I felt his warm hand grip my wrist. He brought my arm up slowly. My hand came into view. The sight of it made my blood run cold. It was the hand of a stranger-- too thick and worn out to be my own. But it had my wedding ring on it. The skin looked rough and aged, the veins disturbingly pronounced. I moved my fingers.

It was mine.

Twenty-one YEARS! TWENTY-ONE-YEARS! I couldn't even *begin* to process... Just *yesterday* I was in the city with Annie. On vacation. My business was booming. Annie had another baby on the way... Twenty-one... Rebecca would be twenty-*six,* and my unborn son?

It couldn't be true. Someone was playing some kind of *sick* joke on me! Emotion welled up, and tears threatened to overtake me. But I bit my lip hard. I would *NOT* believe it. I pushed the thoughts away, and let my brain shut off.

"Thomas, what you're going through is perfectly normal, but it will pass and you will once again connect with the things you feel you've lost."

I turned my head away.

"Time has a way of catching up with you. And there will be many people to help you get back on track. It's not so bad living in 2032."

My throat tightened.

"Many things have changed, but if you take it slow, you'll be okay."

"Though your words are appreciated," I choked, "I don't think you can appreciate- the magnitude of my situation."

"I'm sorry, Thomas. You're right. I can't. But I do know the human spirit is strong, and yours is *incredibly* strong. To have come back from where you've been is a *miracle!* The fact we're even having this conversation at *all* is unimaginable! By all rights you should be brain dead. That's something at least, don't you think?"

182

I remained silent.

He was quiet for a time. Then spoke. "Well, I know this is going to be difficult. But how about getting you up to get your blood pumping. Maybe it will get your mind off things, for now anyway."

Get up? I didn't like the sound of *that* one bit, and my face must have shown it.

"It'll be okay if we take it easy." He went over to the wall and grabbed a wheelchair. "Here, I'll help you."

It was a long process, but he was patient with me. My limbs were like sandbags, and my head was groggy, but otherwise, I felt completely healthy, much healthier than I should have.

Slowly he helped me to a sitting position. My head pounded, but then things started to level out. I looked down and saw the two wrinkled strangers protruding from the sleeves of my medical gown. They were definitely not the hands I remembered. They were old and ugly. I hated them. Bitterness surged in my gut, but I forced it back. I had faced worse than this! Hadn't I? This was only a temporary setback. Yes. A setback. I pushed away the introspection and focused on the doctor.

"Careful now. Take it slow." The floor was cold and painful to my unused feet. He held me firmly as I put weight on my weakened legs. With a slight twist, I fell back into the chair, breathing heavily from the activity.

"Very good, Thomas. Very good." He gave me an encouraging smile and patted my back. "We'll have you climbing ladders again in no time."

What was that supposed to mean? I opened my mouth to ask, but he had moved behind me and was pushing my wheelchair up a ramp to an elevated catwalk, which encircled the room. My vision had almost completely returned, and I realized now, that I was not in a hospital at all, but in a lab filled with computers and sophisticated equipment. It was dark in this upper area,

183

except for the light that came from a myriad of tiny screens lining the walls. They flickered softly, filling the room with an ambiance, which spoke to my soul. Something about the crisp, vibrant glow of the computer screens put me at ease.

I reached out to touch the wall. Each screen displayed a different image and had its own set of glowing buttons. I was careful not to push anything. I only wanted to feel the monitors on the tips of my fingers.

From here I had a nice view of the entire lab. In the center of the room, workstations were positioned strategically around an enormous device, a giant cylinder reaching from floor to ceiling. A number of beds surrounded it, like petals on a giant flower. Patients of various shapes and sizes occupied the beds. As I studied them, I couldn't help but notice, that one of them stood out from the rest. He was the only child, a young boy of perhaps nine or ten. I could see his nameplate from where I sat. It read, "Fredrick Armadon."

My mind whispered, *Vrin*.

"Who are they?" I inquired in a low voice.

"They are other coma patients, like you. Don't worry, we will come back here soon. I promise I'll explain everything."

I nodded silent confirmation.

We approached the exit, and the doors glided open. The long gray corridor was filled with people in lab coats on various errands. The sounds of movement and conversation invaded the peaceful quiet. As we moved through the doors, everyone stopped and stared. Instantly I felt exposed in front of the sea of smiling faces.

"Where are we going?" I asked nervously.

The doctor increased his pace, and spoke with more optimism than I cared to hear. "Rehabilitation!"

Chapter Seventeen

A MEETING WITH DARKNESS
1 1 1 0 0 1 1

Ɛ

After a refreshing bath, and a couple hours of exercises designed to increase mobility, I felt *almost* human. It was still difficult to walk without the assistance of a cane, but the doctor reassured me my strength would return quickly. I was surprised at the rate of my recovery. After all, I'd been in a coma for over two *decades*.

Dr. Solomon explained as we walked through the last set of exercises. "Three times a day, seven days a week, each patient receives a thorough work-over to keep their body from degenerating muscle mass. Every muscle is systematically massaged. Each joint and tendon is flexed and stretched."

"That's a lot of massages." I attempted a smile. "This little vacation is going to cost me a bundle."

He chuckled. "In addition to the physical workouts, the computer is programmed to periodically stimulate the brain. Every hour on the hour, for ten minutes, a program tells your muscles to tighten and relax, causing a mild cardiovascular workout."

I was puzzled. "All this is done even though there's little chance the patients will ever wake up?"

"Yes, because the main purpose is to increase brain activity. The fact that it facilitates a quick recovery turns out to be a nice side effect."

Side effect? More like a *miracle*, I thought.

When we finished, I was given some clothes and

185

was allowed to change in the locker room. Dressing was difficult, but at last, I tucked my medical gown into the laundry shoot, then made slow progress over to the bathroom area. Rounding the corner, the reflection of a man in one of the mirrors caught my eye. I turned to see where the reflection was coming from-- but quickly discovered, that I was alone in the room. Slowly I turned back toward the mirror. The face before me was more like my father's than my own, with wrinkles embedded in its curves, a receding hairline, and a thickness that did not appeal to me. At all.

I stood examining every detail of my features. They had changed dramatically, but strangely, what stood out to me most were my eyes. They seemed-- *wrong* somehow. They were a greenish hazel, as they had always been, but there was a flash of blue in my memory. The feeling washed over me like a whisper, then was gone. I quickly dismissed it as imagination.

The door in the other room made a soft thud and I heard someone approaching. I stepped away from the mirror, composing myself for the visitor. It was Dr. Solomon. "Found the mirrors I see," he said with mock humor.

"So it would seem." I made no attempt to hide my disgust.

"I won't pretend to know how you feel, but I realize it must be tough," he said gently. "What do you say we go get something to eat? I can bring you up to speed on some things."

"Sure." I made an attempt to sound positive. "That sounds appealing."

He gave me a friendly smile and gripped me in a half hug. "Well, let's go do it then."

He helped me through the locker room and out into the hall. During our walk down the long white corridor, only one person passed us.

"Where is everyone?"

"I noticed your reaction when we entered the hall earlier, so I had the way cleared, and the cafeteria as well. Eventually you will feel more comfortable, but for now we'll take it one step at a time."

"Thank you." It did make me feel better. I didn't like the idea of parading around like some stone age freak show. In my weakened state, I felt like a frail old man. This was not a condition I was used to. I was a man of power and influence, not someone to be pitied.

The doors to the cafeteria opened before us and the sweet smells of breakfast filled my nostrils. My mouth watered. I hadn't noticed before, but I was extremely hungry.

Dr. Solomon headed off to the beverage table. I dug into the breakfast buffet: eggs, toast, sausage, bacon, hash browns, fruit, even pancakes. My tray was heavy under the weight of the farmer's breakfast. So I stood waiting for assistance to carry it to a table.

When the doctor returned, he looked at the tray, looked at me, and raised one eyebrow. "You've gone a *long* time without eating, Thomas. You need to start out slowly." He held out a chocolate shake in a glass. "Here, try this."

I gave it an unwelcoming stare.

"Here." He held it closer. "Give it a try."

Slowly I took it from him and had a sip. "Hmm. Not bad."

"It's organic and full of living vitamins. It will assist in your recovery." He patted me on the shoulder.

We headed toward a large window overlooking the parking lot, I blinked in the morning light. White and gray buildings littered the asphalt grounds. In the distance, a fence that looked like it surrounded the entire compound stretched out of sight. "Are all these buildings involved in this project?" I said, taking a seat across from him.

"Most, but not all."

"It must be very important."

"Some think so."

"So, what's the big deal about a few coma patients?" I took a sip from my shake.

His eyes turned down. "It wasn't always a big deal."

"Oh?" I stared out at the parking lot.

"Originally it was a small offshoot of a project my colleague and I were working on for the government. But then this colleague, who was also a good friend of mine, was severely injured in a car accident, which put him in a coma. It was my hope that by using the technology we'd designed together, I could communicate with him through the computer to find a way to bring him out."

"Communicate with him through the computer?" *That* got my attention.

"Yes. But when I proposed the project to the government, they wanted nothing to do with it. I tried to explain that Robert was an integral part of the existing project, and that it would be very useful for them to get him back, but they were less than optimistic about any chance of success. They assumed that by the time I figured out how to reach him, *if* it was even possible, that he would be a vegetable. So they refused funding."

"But you managed to get the project going anyway."

"Yes. That's where you and the others came in. You are all from wealthy homes. Your families are funding this project." He stopped and looked around cautiously. "But things have changed recently. The government brought up a legal complaint a few weeks ago, about my using technology developed for the government in a personal venture." He leaned in close. "But at that time, I had started talking with Robert, or, who I thought was Robert."

I squinted at him. "You actually *talked* with a coma patient through the computer?"

"Yes. By using part of the technology we were developing for the government, we created a system that

188

could talk directly to the human brain, and vice versa."

I looked at him sideways.

He continued. "We were unsure of how to start the dialog because the comatose mind is unresponsive, so we left the computer to input stimuli until a response was registered. I used VRIN, the virtual world we designed for the government, to create a base environment my friend could relate to. But it has changed so much that it isn't even the same creature anymore. Anyway, now that we've had some success, the government wants in again. They threatened to shut us down if I didn't cooperate, so I was forced to let them take control."

I stared at him. *"Amazing.* I can see why the government wanted back in."

"Yes, well we weren't happy about it. But if I didn't comply, they were going to take me to court, and if they won, they were going to shut me out completely. I wasn't about to let that happen, so I agreed to cooperate. The families were given the option of withdrawing or allowing the government to take over, the latter reducing their financial commitment. So everyone agreed to continue on. But now, guards are posted at the gate, security has tripled, and military experts examine every log we create. We can't even leave the grounds without an escort. It's like a *prison* in here."

"And there's nothing you can do about it?"

"No. The military gave everyone the option of staying or leaving. We're stuck here now."

"We? What about me? Are they going to try to keep *me* here?"

The seriousness in his face vanished and was replaced by a jovial expression. "Of course they will. There are many things that will amaze you about the lab." I felt a slow pressure on my foot. "There is so much to show you. It's all quite fascinating."

There was a noise near the door. I pivoted to see a

guard looking in our direction. I gave him a wave and a smile, and turned back to the doctor. "Yeah, it seems really cool," I said, trying to act oblivious to the tension in the room.

"It is that indeed," he returned, continuing to sound happy. I heard the doors open and close, and the doctor's face dropped again. "Things are much worse than I've had a chance to explain. It looks like my time with you is running out."

"I'm beginning to get a little nervous, Doc."

"I'm sorry it had to be like this. I wanted to explain everything so you would understand my position. My only intention was to help my friend. If it helped you and the others in the process, that was good too, but things are getting out of control. Strange men in suits have been showing up. Weird demands are being placed on us. It appears the project is being undermined, like they're afraid of what we might find in there."

"In where? In the computer?"

"No, in the minds of the patients. It's not about the computer anymore. Something is going on. We don't understand the implications." He paused.

"Implications...?"

"Of Vrin. It's gone far beyond the original project specifications. There are elements in the texts which are completely baffling." His face went smooth and his smile reappeared. "So are you almost finished?"

"Yes, thank you," I said, matching his mood.

"Then let's give you a tour of the lab."

As I got up, I ventured another glance at the doors. A different man was standing at the entrance. He was dressed in a dark blue suit. His face was stern. "Who's that?" I asked innocently.

"That's Mr. Philips. He is," the doctor hesitated, "ah-- responsible for security in the building."

We walked over and deposited our trays. The man

watched quietly as we passed. "Hello," I said, trying to convey a relaxed friendly bearing over my nervous interior.

We continued on into the hall and down toward the lab. "There is much more to tell," the doctor said.

I caught his double meaning.

Perhaps I should have stayed in the coma I thought. Instead of finding out about my family, here I was, stuck in some weird cloak and dagger game. I wanted to whisper more questions, but thought it prudent to wait for the doctor to resume the conversation. The doors to the lab opened and the warm light of the monitors touched my face. A few people in white lab coats were busy working, and I received a couple of curious glances, but nothing more.

"Come over here to my office," said Dr. Solomon. We stepped in and he closed the glass door. With his back to the door, he put his finger to his lips. I remained silent as he reached into his desk drawer. I heard a beep and after a few seconds, he looked up. "It's okay. We can talk for a little, but they'll be suspicious if we take too long. Have a seat, and keep your expressions neutral."

"Okay," I said, faking a smile, and looking out the glass wall of the office.

"I'm about to say something distressing. Remain calm please," he said with a straight empty face. "Your life is in danger, but I am going to help you. It is important that you trust me. Do you trust me?"

"Do I have a choice?" I found it difficult to remain expressionless.

"No." He leaned forward and slid a small pill in my direction. "Place this capsule in your mouth without drawing suspicion, but do *not* chew."

I looked out the large glass. No one was looking, so I turned slightly and inserted the capsule into the rear of my mouth.

"It is the antidote to a poison which will be administered to you. Even though the pill will work, you will feel a paralysis, and will be unable to move for a time. This is important to the illusion that you're dead."

The illusion that I'm dead? I did *not* like the sound of that one bit! He was going to poison me? *My God!* Had the world gone mad while I was sleeping?

"Okay." He smiled. "Let's go put on a show. You all right?"

"I'm scared stiff," I said, barely keeping my composure.

"I wish it didn't have to be this way. And listen. There is one thing I want you to do when you get out of here. A package will be provided for you. In it will be a green packet. Mail it to the address on the envelope."

"If this works," I said sarcastically.

He stood and opened the door. "It has to."

We stepped out onto the floor, and he guided me back to my bed. "Sit down, Thomas. There you go." He smiled as I did as he requested. "Now, we are going to do a few tests to make sure you are in full capacity, then I'll give you that tour I've been promising."

"Cool," I said, trying desperately to sound excited.

He directed me to lie back down. The bed was soft beneath me. It was hard when I first came to, but now it was soft and squishy. The doctor prepped a few things, then performed a series of tests, all the while glancing at the door. Finally, after what felt like an eternity, a green light next to the door came on. The doctor looked at me nervously. "That's almost it, now let me see your arm." He produced a needle and flicked it with his finger. "This will only hurt for a second."

I flinched as the needle sank into my arm, and within seconds the room began to spin. My joints ached and my jaw began to tighten involuntarily. I felt the pill crush between my back teeth. Bitterness filled my mouth. It was a good thing the pill was between my teeth, there wouldn't have been a second chance.

I must have lost consciousness, because instantly two figures were standing over me. I squinted and tried to focus on them. One was the man I'd seen in the cafeteria, and the other-- was my mother! Tears welled up in my eyes. She looked concerned, but I could say nothing to console her. I felt her hand take mine. Slowly I tracked her with my eyes. She had aged so much. I tried to speak but my voice was caught in my throat. "Mmmm," was all I could get out.

"Thomas?" she said, her chest heaving with emotion. "Are you okay?"

I heard the doctor's voice. "This is the most coherent he's been, and I'm afraid his condition is deteriorating. We're not sure what brought him out, but his mind has been through too much," he said gently. "I'm sorry Mrs. Tardin-- but we do not believe he will make it."

With great effort, I reached out and touched her hand. Her skin felt like rubber in my grasp. She began to cry as her body pressed down against mine. "*No!*" she said, taking me into her arms. "He *has* to make it. You've come so far, Thomas!" she sobbed. "You can do it!"

Again I tried to speak. "Maaaaam."

"That's it, Thomas! I'm here with you! You can do this!" But her words were useless. Off in the distance, I heard the heart monitor go flat line. My mother shook me tightly in her grasp. "No! *NO!* He can't die! He was *here!* He was *alive! He can't DIE!"*

The pain, and the frantic screams of my mother, were left far behind, as I drifted away into darkness.

There was a bump, and muffled voices. It was dark, and something was covering me. I was picked up, lowered to the ground, then someone unzipped the thing covering my face. I squinted at the brightness of the sun floating in the sky overhead.

"Hey there," said a young male voice.

The plastic covering fell away and I realized, to my disgust, that I was lying in a body bag. I struggled to get the hideous thing off. A strong pair of arms helped me with the task. "It's all right. It's all right. You're with friends." I squinted at the handsome face hovering before me.

"*Hurry up!* Get him in the car!" said a female voice. I turned my head to see a black sedan parked near us.

"I guess we're going to have to wait for introductions," he said. His strong hands gripped me under the arms and lifted me to my feet.

A large gray pickup started up and pulled away.

"Who was that?" I blinked, rubbing my eyes against the light.

"*That* was your ticket to freedom," he said with a gleaming smile. "Quick, let's get you into the car, we don't want you being seen." He helped me into the back seat and peeked in after me. "You want this?" He held out a cane.

"I'm all set for the moment."

He put the cane in the front, stuffed the body bag under the seat, and he got in. "Let's go, sis!" The tires squealed, and we took off down the road.

An uncomfortable quiet filled the interior of the car as I thought about the events that had just transpired. I was still alive, but now what? The woman driving kept glancing at me in the rearview mirror. The young man looked back at me with a broad smile. Over the hum of the engine, I heard the woman speak in a low voice. "This is crazy."

The young man gave her a look, like a cat who had just caught a mouse.

"It's really him," she whispered.

He gave a happy nod and again turned to look at me-- and this time, as he did so, I found myself staring at his face. I was sure I had never met him before-- but he looked, *so* familiar. He leaned in close to the woman and whispered something in her ear. There was *something* about him, the shape of his cheek, the slant of his mouth... He reminded me of... He looked like... He stole another glance at me. Then it hit me like a hammer. He looked like *me!* Emotion welled up inside my chest. Was this my unborn son?

He turned to the front, and then back again with that big handsome smile fixed on his muscular features. He was a strapping young man, strong, and apparently *very* full of life.

I looked over at the lovely woman driving and immediately recognized her. How could I *not* have recognized her? Her curly blond hair moving in the wind, her soft pale skin fairly glowing. The delicate red lips, the high cheekbones. And those eyes! She certainly had changed, but it was her. I was sure of it. My little girl! I could barely keep my composure.

"I'm Samuel!" said the man, interrupting my thoughts. He offered his hand to me. I took it firmly. It was *amazing* to look at him. He looked so *much* like me. Except for his hair, which was blonde, like his mother's. "You recognize me don't you! I can see it in your eyes!"

195

"Yes. It took me a moment. But I recognize you." I couldn't pull my eyes from his face. There was so much I wanted to say, so many questions I needed to know the answers to.

"I have to tell you, this is crazy weird for Bec and me. It must be twice as weird for you."

I pushed my emotion back and pressed my lips together. "I'm not going to lie, seeing you both grown up is-- *difficult,* to put it mildly."

"You've been asleep my whole life," said Sam. "And now you're *here,* just like that." He shook his head. "It's gonna to take some getting use to." He snapped his face back toward me. "But I'm glad!"

"I'm glad too, Samuel." My smiled trembled. "I only wish it were under better circumstances."

Rebecca looked at me in mirror. "What happened back there anyway?"

"You don't know?"

Sam twisted in his seat. "Bec and I got this note a week ago." He held out a crumpled piece of paper. "So we dropped what we were doing and headed here." He handed me the note and I opened it. It read, "He is waking. Go to him."

I folded it and handed it back. "Who was it from?"

Samuel shrugged. "We don't know. I thought it was from Solomon or one of his people, but after the phone call I got this morning, I'm thinking it had to be someone else."

"Why's that?"

"Because they didn't know you were awake 'til this morning."

I remembered back to how startled the men had been when I woke up. "I think you're right," I said. "They were definitely surprised by my waking."

"The man on the phone told me to pick you up at exactly 10:00 a.m. at the mile marker back there. That's all we know."

"Where are you taking me now?"

"Mom's house."

My heart skipped a beat. "She lives nearby?"

"Both Gram and Mom do."

"Your mom's mother or mine?"

"Yours."

My mother's desperate face flashed in my mind. They made her *believe* I was dead. *Why?* Wait-- maybe she didn't think I was dead. Maybe she was in on it to make it more believable. "Does your Gram know you came to get me?"

Sam looked at Rebecca with eyebrows raised.

"Not that we know of," said Rebecca. "Why?"

"She was there when they poisoned me."

Sam looked back in shock.

"They told her I came out of the coma, but that I wasn't going to make it." I looked out the window at the blur of the passing trees. "She thinks I died in her arms this morning."

Sam and Rebecca were speechless.

I continued looking out the window, and came to a decision. "We have to assume that Solomon wanted her to believe that I'm dead, in order to protect her. Because no doubt, she will be questioned." I looked at Samuel. "So we cannot tell her otherwise. It might put her life in danger." The thought of her grieving over me made my chest constrict. She had waited so *long*, hoping that I would come out of the coma.

Sam's face became stern. "We'll do whatever you think is best."

His willingness to trust a father he had never known moved my spirit. I was sure I would like the man he had become.

As the car cruised past open fields of grain, I attempted to piece together what I knew. It was hard to tell who knew what, since I didn't know all the players. And what I did know didn't make much sense. Solomon and his team found out I was awake this morning. They contacted Sam, but he and Rebecca had already known for a week. The people who wanted me dead couldn't have known. Could they? So-- who sent the notes to Sam and Rebecca? Who could possibly have known that I was going to come out of the coma? And *how?*

My mind locked onto another question. This one found its way directly to my lips. "Does your mother know?"

"Yes," said Sam. "She was there when I got the call."

"Does she know about the notes?"

"No," said Rebecca. "We didn't tell her. We didn't want her to know, you know, in case it was some kind of prank." She shook her head. "She's been through enough..." Her words trailed off, as if she wanted to say more, but decided against it.

What *had* she been through? Was Rebecca referring to the years I'd spent in a coma taking its toll on her? *That* was unlikely. Certainly it wouldn't have taken her twenty-one *years* to come to grips with the situation. Again my mind shifted gears, and another unexpected question emerged. This one not so easily vocalized. "Is she... Did your mother ever..."

Samuel turned to me. His face was solemn "Yes. But no. Not anymore."

"What happened?"

"He died two years ago. It was pretty rough on her."

That must have been what Rebecca had eluded to. And though my heart went out to Annie, I could barely conceal my own selfish relief. She was single! There was a chance I might win her back! Certainly the years were unrecoverable, but if I could have Annie and my kids... I sucked in a deep breath, and leaned back on the seat, soaking up the peace brought by this newfound hope.

Again we sat with our own thoughts as the car veered off the highway and followed a dirt road. Slowly the car turned and the tires crunched down a gravel driveway to a log cabin overlooking a quiet lake. A figure stood in the doorway. I immediately recognized her. From the distance, she appeared the same as I remembered her, as if no time had passed.

The car rolled to a stop. Samuel jumped out and opened my door. I looked nervously over the seat at Rebecca.

"Go ahead," she said encouragingly.

"I don't know what to say," I whispered.

"Just take one step at a time." Her genuine smile brought me comfort. In spite of all the years that had passed, she welcomed my return, and seemed excited at the prospect of my reconnecting with her mother.

I swung my legs out of the car and Samuel helped me up with a firm grasp. "Do you have my cane, Sam?"

"Right here." He grabbed it from the front seat.

I gripped the handle and rested my weight on it. Annie had come down to the bottom of the cobblestone path. Her eyes spoke volumes. She was happy to see me, but the many years stood between us like a gulf. For me it was only one day, but for her-- it was a lifetime.

She hadn't changed much. She looked considerably older, but age had done nothing to deface her beauty. Her eyes were the same brilliant sapphire, her blond hair twisted in curls to her shoulders. Pensively she stood with her arms folded over her midsection. I could tell she wanted to speak-- and yet, she remained silent.

Everything took on a new sense of realism as I stood looking at her face. It was the same feeling I'd had when I'd seen my reflection in the mirror earlier. Only this was worse. To see my beautiful bride looking so much older... How she must have suffered. And yet, in her eyes-- I actually saw a look of apology.

"Are you okay?" I said sheepishly.

"I had given up hope," she said quietly.

"It was a long time to wait. I wouldn't expect you to..."

"I waited," she said abruptly. "It hurt terribly, but I waited."

"I'm so sorry, Annie. I'm sorry you had to go through this. It must have been horrible."

"It's not *your* fault. It's just that-- seeing you is..." She squeezed herself a little tighter. "It's just not what I expected."

I studied her expression. "Is that *good,* or bad?"

"Good," she blurted. "It's just that, it's been so *long.* I didn't think I would feel *anything,* and, I didn't. 'Til just now."

Was it true? Could she possibly still have feelings for me after all these years? It was more than I dared to hope.

"You-- recovered so quickly. It's remarkable," she said, superficially.

"It's a miracle."

"Yes." She corrected herself. "A miracle." She stepped in toward me and her eyes flickered up. "Do you *remember* us? Our life together? For me it was so long ago."

I shook my head. "For me it was just last *week* I was dancing with you, my very pregnant wife, on our balcony overlooking the bay."

She became contemplative.

"It was the night you told me we were going to have a son, and that you had never been so happy in all your life."

Her eyes filled with tears.

"It was just yesterday for me. I had everything a man could desire, and more."

She looked up at me and a tear trickled down her

cheek. "It was so perfect I thought I had dreamed it." Her voice became a whisper. "Were we *that* happy once?"

"If you could find it in yourself to give me a second chance, we could be happy again." I immediately regretted the words. Talking about the past was one thing. But this was way too fast-- for someone who had lived twenty-one years since yesterday.

I started to mouth an apology. But she stopped me. "You don't need a second chance, Thomas. You never failed me the first time." She slid her arms under mine and hugged my chest. The smell of her hair had changed, but I was immediately satisfied by the new scent. This was not the wife of my memory, but she was still my Annie.

I looked up to see Rebecca standing by the back of the car, struggling to keep her emotions from overtaking her, and it was more than I could bear. My own tears began to flow. My baby girl... To me it was just yesterday she was strutting around the backyard in a paper crown, pretending to be a queen and giving orders to the dog. Now she was a grown woman! But she had not forgotten me. She had not stopped loving her daddy.

I held my hand out to her. "Come here, sweetheart."

She ran over and threw her arms around us. "I love you, Daddy," she whispered.

"I love you too, honey."

I felt Samuel's hand on my back. "Welcome home, Dad," he said, his voice cracking. "Welcome home."

Chapter Nineteen

THE PLAN
1 1 1 1 0 0 1

Inside, the light was warm and inviting. Annie had always possessed a keen eye for interior decoration. Rectangular cedar pillars held up thick rustic beams, which crossed back and forth in the spacious ceiling above. To the left, was the kitchen, to the right, a sunken living room, and straight in front of us, stairs leading up to a loft.

Annie helped me to a comfortable seat next to the kitchen table. I gripped the arms weakly and sat down.

"Be right back," said Rebecca, heading up the stairs.

"Can I get you anything?" asked Annie. Her face was still flush from our unexpectedly tearful reunion.

"A cup of tea would be nice. Earl..."

"Grey," she finished. "Yes. I remember."

I watched in silence as she pulled a cup from the cupboard. She was still very beautiful. The years had been far more gracious to her than they had been to me. Her face had thickened slightly and there was a hint of gray in her blonde hair, but other than that, she hadn't changed much at all.

"How are you feeling?" Samuel came in and leaned against the counter.

"Better than I ever could have hoped." I scanned the room. "This is a nice place."

"Mom has great taste." He smiled, but this smile was more pensive than his earlier ones. "Under better circumstances, I would bring you down and show you the lake. In the evening, it's beautiful when the moon shines on it. And you can catch fish as big as your arm."

I nodded. "Under better circumstances, I would enjoy that."

"Here you go." Annie placed a steaming cup in front of me.

I looked up at her. "That was fast."

"I used the TLD, it only takes a few seconds."

"Oh." I looked around. There were several devices on the counter I didn't recognize.

Annie took a hesitant step back. "Do you-- want to talk about it?" Her eyes studied me intently.

"What? the lab?"

"Everything. I mean... You've been practically dead for twenty-one years, and now out of the blue you wake up. And we're getting mysterious calls early in the morning." Her face tightened. "What's going on? Becky said your *life* was in danger?"

"I don't know. Dr. Solomon couldn't tell me much. He said the government had stepped in, something about them wanting to undermine the project-? I asked him why but he said he didn't know." I paused and thought a moment. "He said they were *afraid* of what they might discover inside the minds of the patients." I glanced up at Annie. She looked baffled.

Samuel spoke up. "Why? What's inside the minds of the patients?"

"I don't *know.* I don't remember."

"You don't remember anything?"

"No. There are feelings, but they're faint. I don't remember being in the coma. I remember New York, and then waking up in the lab." I looked from Samuel to Annie. "What happened? How did I end up in a lab?"

Annie pulled out a kitchen chair, sat down, and looked thoughtful. After a moment, she spoke. "Do you remember the accident?"

203

"Vaguely."

"Well, you suffered severe damage to your head and was diagnosed with terminal brain failure. So I started looking for a specialist, and I found one in Fresno. He couldn't do much for you, but he was the one who told us about the center, and about how they were developing a way to communicate with patients like you. So I called and talked to Dr. Solomon. He didn't promise anything, but it was the best option available."

"Tell him about the forms," said Sam.

"Yes. There were a *lot* of forms, stacks of them. They wanted to know *every* last detail of your life, right down to your childhood memories. It took weeks to get them all filled out. *"*

"Tell him about the programmer thing."

Annie gave Sam a look that said, I can *handle* this. He put his hands up in surrender. She looked back at me. "A friend of mine told me about a man she knew who was rejected because he was a programmer. And since I didn't want there to be any chance of you being rejected too, especially after filling out all of those papers..." She gave a sheepish look. "I lied on the forms. I told them you were a fireman who had inherited a hefty trust fund." She gave a wan smile.

"So that's what Solomon meant," I said under my breath.

"What's that?"

"Solomon made some comment about me climbing ladders. Now I know why."

"Oh." She chuckled. "Well, I wanted to make sure you got in. And you did." She smiled. "So apparently they didn't have a problem with firefighters. --Anyway, I couldn't be there when you were admitted because I was in labor with Sam..."

There were no emotions in the subtle lines of her face, only reflection. Apparently she had long since come to terms with the trauma.

"But when he was three weeks old I went to see you. That's when I learned they were going to try a new technique to see if they could talk *directly* to your brain."

"Yes. Solomon spoke of that. Sounds like something straight out of a sci-fi movie."

"I know. Exactly. But they were serious, and they seemed confident that it could be done. So, every month for the last twenty-one years, I've received a report from the center, detailed reports with graphs and statistics." She shrugged. "Most of it I don't understand. But there was never anything to make me suspicious about what was going on."

"Not even when the government took over?"

Her eyebrows lifted. "No. They had always provided the best care possible, and I saw no reason to worry. Solomon told me of the government's interest in the project, and that they were offering to reduce our cost. That was fine with me.

"So you never saw anything out of the ordinary?"

"Tell him about the priest, Mom," said Rebecca. She had come down and was sitting on the stairs.

"Yeah, that was strange," said Samuel.

I looked at Annie. "A priest?"

She rubbed her palms across the table. "On one of my visits, I overheard two men talking about Father Wentworth, one of the other patients. Solomon always referred to him fondly as, 'the religious component.' He said all the patients added something to the world you were creating together, and that his contribution was religion. Anyway, Father Wentworth..."

"W- wait a minute, sorry to interrupt, but, did you say, 'the world *we* were creating'?"

She shrugged. "I still don't really understand it. But Solomon said the virtual world he had created was changing on its own. The data indicated that you and the

205

other patients were adding to it and changing it, and that it was hardly the same thing anymore." She shrugged again. "That's what they told me."

I squinted at her, then shook my head. "O-*kay*. --So, what about the priest?"

"Well I guess he didn't take to the computer very well, and these two men were discussing whether or not he was even *in* the system. See, each of you had an activity monitor above your bed, and every time your mind told the computer to do something, it would appear on the monitor as a blip. --I used to stare at yours for hours." Her eyes became distant. "I can't begin to describe the feeling I would get when it would jump. It was like-- like you were whispering to me from the door of death, telling me you were still there, telling me everything was going to be okay." Her voice trailed off and she stared at the table. "Anyway." She shook her head. "Back to the priest. Father Wentworth's monitor had a single spike, and that was all."

"So, he wasn't responding to the treatment," I said. "What's so strange about that?"

"That's not the weird part, Thomas. The two men were talking about *extracting* him from Vrin. And the way they said it, it was like they were going to do it, from the *inside*. Like they could just go *in* and get him."

Sam interjected. "The voice, Mom, tell him about the voice."

"I'm getting to that, Sam." Annie stood up and walked to the window. "It wasn't just *what* they said, Thomas. It was how one of the men talked." She pulled the curtain aside and looked out. "It was... I know this sounds crazy, but it was like he spoke in another language, but I understood it." She turned back toward me. "And his *face*, his face was *perfect*, not handsome perfect, but, *flawless* perfect. --And the look he gave me... I'm telling you, Thomas, it made my knees weak. I almost dropped the coffee I was holding. I, I can't explain it, but-- I don't think

206

he was of this world."

I studied Annie's face. She was still shaken by the encounter. "When was this?" I asked.

"A few months ago."

"Did you tell Dr. Solomon?"

"I wasn't sure *what* to think, and it wasn't like he'd done anything wrong. He didn't say he was going to hurt the priest, just that they should *remove* him."

"Did you ever see him again?"

"No. I haven't been back."

I gripped my cane tightly and struggled to stand. Samuel helped me to my feet. I moved toward the glass doors to the back patio.

"So what do we do now?" asked Sam.

"I say we get out of the country," said Rebecca. "It's none of our business what's going on in that place."

I looked out at the lake, hoping to absorb its peacefulness. "Solomon pretended to kill me," I said "but if they discover my body is not at the morgue, they'll try to find me." I turned back to look at my family. "That means as long as you're with me, you're in danger too."

"If you think I'm letting you go anywhere without *me*, you're out of your mind," Samuel asserted.

"Thomas, we're in this together. We can all go away until this thing blows over."

I stood and looked from Annie, to Rebecca, to Samuel. I didn't think there was any way this *thing* was just going to blow over. And although I wanted to be with my family, I couldn't bear the thought of them being hurt by these people. I *didn't* want them involved. *But,* they were already involved. If I left them behind, they would be in more danger than if I took them with me. I let out a sigh. "Where could we go?"

Annie straightened up. "Well, like Becky said, I think we should get out of the country. Do you remember Stephen?"

I shot her a look. "Of *course* I remember Stephen." Immediately I gave a look of apology, realizing that her perspective was vastly different from my own. For all *I* knew, my best friend and business partner could have died *years* ago.

"Do you remember that resort we bought him in the Bahamas? Well, he's done very well for himself and has expanded to five more locations."

I let out a breath of relief. "I knew he had a mind for business."

"We could go stay in one of his bungalows in Haiti for awhile, until you recuperate."

"Haiti?" I grimaced. "Stephen has a resort in *Haiti?*"

Annie looked momentarily confused, then said, "Ooohh, you're remembering the old Haiti. It's been very stable and *very* prosperous for a long time now."

"Yeah," Rebecca spoke up. "After the big earthquake and all the rebuilding, Davata Notrals was much more available. That's when things really changed. Or so I read."

I looked at her blankly. "Oh. --Okay. So..." I said, turning back to Annie, "we should go to Stephen's resort?"

"Whatever you decide, I'll support you."

"Well, my life won't be my own until I find out why those men want me *dead.*" I shook my head. "I'll stay until I recuperate, but I'm coming back as soon as possible to find out what's going on."

Annie put her hand on my arm. "Then it's settled."

"Yes." I looked at each of them. "It's settled."

Chapter Twenty

SLEEP OF THE DEAD

The stewardess passed by on her way to coach.

"Miss, could I get a glass of water before takeoff?"

"Sure thing."

I looked down at the picture on my new passport. I still couldn't believe how much I had aged. It would be a long time before I would get used to all the wrinkles. We'd had no trouble getting the passport renewed. --Apparently they hadn't heard I was dead.

Annie peered out the window at the sun low on the horizon. It would be dark soon.

"What are you looking for?"

"The bad guys," she said, visibly troubled. She turned and looked at me, as if noticing me for the first time. "How are you feeling?"

"Exhausted. Like I could sleep for twenty years."

Her eyes narrowed. "That's not funny."

"Sorry." I offered a weak smile. "Humor is the only thing keeping me from breaking down."

She gave me a sympathetic look. "This all must be extremely hard on you. I can't even imagine."

"It's hard on everyone, I would think."

"Mom," said Sam from across the aisle, "when will we be touching down?"

"10:00 p.m."

"Thanks." He leaned back in to tell Rebecca.

"Are you sure they should be with us?" I asked.

209

"If we left them behind, they'd follow." She raised her eyebrows. "They have your stubbornness."

"You make that sound like a bad thing." I nudged her. "My stubbornness made us wealthy, even by today's standards." I thought back to the airport cafeteria: five bucks for coffee, seven for a danish! *Highway robbery!*

"Are you going to try to sleep?" Annie asked.

"Perhaps a couple of winks. Wake me when we get there."

"Okay." She reached up and waved her hand, the overhead light went off.

It was going to take a while to get used to the changes in technology. I chuckled to myself as I remembered the incident in the terminal. It didn't look like a robot before *or* after I kicked the little bugger over. I thought my bag was snagged on a baggage cart. As far as I was concerned, whoever designed carts with arms and hands should be *shot.*

I closed my eyes, but they popped back open. Perhaps the coffee had been a bad idea. I wasn't going to be doing any sleeping any time soon. I peeked over at Samuel. He was lost in a movie playing on a pair of sunglasses with earphones. There appeared to be a three dimensional aspect to the viewing as well. His head was turning, following some unknown object floating before of him.

My stomach made a twist. It was becoming painfully obvious that this new world with its gizmos and cutthroat pace would eat me alive if I didn't get a handle on things. But that wasn't the only thing bothering me.

I thought back to the name *Vrin.* There was, *something* about it. It sounded *so* familiar. Maybe it was only that I had heard it spoken repeatedly while I was in the coma-? No. There was something more. Something on the edge of my awareness, just out of reach, a certain uneasiness, an *urgency* to remember.

Another disturbing thought pushed forward. Why

did these mysterious, government, *other-worldly* people want me dead? Who was I to them? I couldn't even *remember* anything from the experience. And, besides, what kind of threat could ten people interacting in a computer be to anyone? It just didn't make sense!

A crick in my back brought me out of my thoughts. Although the airline seat was much softer than its historical counterpart, I could find no comfortable position. My body ached from disuse, and staying in one position for any length of time was not going to be easy. "You asleep?" I whispered to Annie.

"No. You can't sleep either?"

"I'm finding it hard to get comfortable, and my brain is working overtime."

"Then let's catch up," she said softly.

For the rest of the flight, we talked. She had all but forgotten many of the things I remembered clearly from the earlier years: details about college, our marriage, starting the businesses, early years with Rebecca... She sat and listened intently as it all came back to her. But then when we got to the the accident, it was her turn to share. She was careful to avoid talking about her second husband, but she told me all about the kids' growing up, and about how the businesses had grown. It was hours before we touched down, and yet, when the pilot's voice came over the intercom, we'd barely had time to scratch the surface.

We left the tiny terminal and took a cab to the ocean. The concierge greeted us at the pier and helped us move our luggage onto a charter boat. As it turned out, our bungalow was out on the ocean somewhere, on stilts, surrounded by water. This was just fine by me, the more secluded the better.

The night air was cool and refreshing, and it wasn't long before the coastline disappeared and the quiet silhouettes of several huts appeared before us. Warm yellow light softly emanated through the windows. The water glowed from lights beneath the surface. Mysterious, yet inviting.

We moored the boat to the front porch of the thatch-roofed bungalow. Rebecca was the first one out. She quickly disappeared inside. "Good! This one has two bathrooms!" she yelled from within.

The captain of the charter boat didn't wait for us to tip him but was already heading back to shore. His wake caused our motorboat to bang up against the moorings on the front of the porch.

I looked at Annie. "I think I'm finally ready to sleep," I said, stifling a yawn.

"Yes. I'm only going to stay up for a few more minutes myself. I'm exhausted."

"I'll bet you are." I gave her a sympathetic look. I started to turn, but stopped and turned back. "Ah, where should I..."

"You go ahead and take the master bedroom. I'll stay in Becca's room, for tonight anyway-- if you don't mind."

"I understand. I'm just glad you want to stay in the same *house* with me."

She smiled sweetly and gave me another hug. "Sleep well, Thomas." She shook her head. "I still can't believe you're back."

"Yeah," said Samuel. "It doesn't seem real to me either.

I made my way down the hallway, and gave Rebecca a hug on the way. She kissed me on the cheek. "It's good to have you back, Dad."

"It's good to be back, Rebecca. I'm sorry I can't stay up any longer, I guess the coffee finally wore off."

"I can't believe you stayed awake this long."

"It wasn't by choice, believe me."

She squeezed my arm. "Get some rest. We'll see you in the morning."

I entered the master bedroom, leaned my cane against the night stand, then stood looking at my reflection in the large mirror on the wall. The man looking back was hardly recognizable. He was older, stately, and was dressed *casual.* I never dressed casual. I couldn't even remember owning a pair of jeans.

The jacket Solomon had given me wasn't bad. I turned to look at it. Hard leather-- stylish. It fit well. I tried to remove it, but my stiff joints objected to the maneuver. On my second attempt, it pulled free and slid down. I turned and placed the jacket on a chair, and in so doing, noticed something brown protruding from the inside pocket. *What's this?* I pulled it out and examined it. It was the packet Dr. Solomon had spoken of. Inside the brown envelope was a smaller, green envelope. I read the name and address.

Hazel Brown
128 Pinrow St.
Marathon, Florida 03944

I placed the envelope on the night table and sat down. For a moment I stared at it. Should I open it? Was I supposed to open it? Dr. Solomon didn't say *not* to open it. I reached out and picked it up again. *Who's gonna know? I'm in the middle of the ocean.*

My hands shook slightly as I bent the metal fastening, opened the envelope, and peered inside. It was empty! *What the...?* I reached in and fished around, and something came loose. Carefully I pulled out a small piece of paper. It said, simply, "Thomas tardin."

What was *that* supposed to mean? Why would Dr. Solomon want me to deliver an envelope containing just my *name?* That didn't make sense. Who was I to Hazel Brown? --I regretted ever opening the cursed thing-- and

213

decided to contact Hazel Brown personally as soon as my strength returned.

Unfortunately, this, and many other mysteries, would have to wait until the morning, I could not keep my eyes open one minute longer. I finished undressing and climbed into bed.

The ceiling fan turned slowly, gently moving the curtains in the large open windows. Music filtered through the air from somewhere outside. Rebecca and Annie were talking in the living room, and Samuel was taking a shower. The world was alive around me-- but I felt alone and out of place. Fortunately, sleep took me quickly.

At first it was the sensation of a smile, then a face. It was a little girl. She moved away from me, disappearing into the curtains behind her. I followed.

I emerged from the rear of a covered wagon and perched myself upon the shaky wooden seat. Breathing deeply, I looked out across the wide expanse of prairie. Tall sweet grasses swayed in the gentle breeze, and the morning sun warmed my face. A young man sat next to me, smiling. "You recognize me don't you?"

I returned his smile, but did not answer.

"Thomas, could you hand me the blue dress?" I shifted in the seat to see Annie by the full length mirror in our old apartment. Her hand was stretched out in my direction.

"Well?" she said.

I stood and walked to the bed. On it lay the blue dress she had worn to our engagement party. I picked it up and held it out. "Are you sure it still fits?" I smiled.

She came in close to me, finger raised. "Listen, mister, you can be replaced you know." She pushed me to the bed and landed on top of me, the garment pressed between us. I rolled her off and we lay face to face, enjoying each other in silence. A tender peace washed over me. I held onto it.

Exhaustion enveloped my weary body as I settled into the hammock and gazed up at the palm fronds overhead. Soft music drifted from somewhere in the distance. I looked over to see Annie waving to me from a boat. Why was she leaving? My throat constricted as I strained to call out to her.

The boat drifted away and the lake began to warp and change-- until there was nothing left, but a hazy kaleidoscope of faint colors.

Slowly I became aware of a tiny light way off in the distance. It was dim at first, but gradually it increased, and then quickly became an enormous opening. I emerged from the dark tunnel into the glowing expanse of Dantra. Its beauty filled me with peace, as it had so many times before. And once again, God's love held me in a warm and familiar embrace.

Guided by an unknown force I continued deeper into Dantra, toward the planetoid known as Vrin. And I was not alone. Dozens of souls traveled with me, each one carried by the same hidden current, and each unable to travel freely about in Dantra as before. Like bottles in a sapphire river, we approached the ominous blue orb. Larger and larger it grew, until its immeasurable round surface became flat to my perception, and with a blinding flash, I entered.

I fell rapidly, but there was no sense of movement. Below, near the cusp of a mountain, stood the sparkling city of Oonaj. The place I called home. I continued down, deep into the heart of the city toward the golden dome of the capital building. When I reached it, there was no impact, I simply passed through-- and continued down through layer after layer. Until at last, I reached my destination, the warmly lit library, where my host sat motionless, awaiting my arrival.

I admired him momentarily. He was *so* different from his earthly counterpart. There was no obsession for wealth or power, no need to be a captain of industry. His life was his books. It was a much less complicated life. Yes, I liked him. I was proud of him. Through him, I had made better decisions. He was my second chance, and for that I was thankful.

A gentle and loving voice echoed inside me. "*It is time.*" The room warped and shifted as I entered my host. Air rushed into my lungs, and my eyes widened.

That part of me, which was eternal, became still.

So there I sat, wondering how long I had been staring at the same page of my book.

Chapter Twenty-one

OLD LIVES, OLD FRIENDS

σ

We stared at each other in silence-- and time passed. After all, what could we say? Our relationship had changed irreversibly from the moment I'd uttered the words. Words which now hung in the air like a cloud of strangling gas, threatening to steal away our very breath. I wished now I could take them back.

It was Sajin who spoke first. "So, *you* are Sam' Dejal." His tone was guarded.

"I-- don't know. I have his memories-- but does that make me him?"

"Perhaps it is some kind of transference. Does the holy book mention anything about this kind of phenomenon?"

"No." I looked down at the tiled floor. "Have *you* ever heard of such a thing?"

He glared at me. *"You're* the sky searcher, Charm! What do you make of it?"

Again we stared, and after a long moment of introspection, I stated, "*I am* Sam' Dejal."

Sajin stood abruptly. "This is nonsense!"

"Well, what do you want me to tell you!" I realized I had never spoken to him in this manner before.

He gave me an examining, and somewhat threatening look.

I yielded to it, and began again, this time lowering my head in respect. "They are not just memories, they are conscious choices which *I myself* made. There was no other consciousness but my own. Therefore, I must conclude, I *am* Sam' Dejal."

"But you were *here*. How could you be *there* and *here* at the same time? It doesn't make *sense.*"

"My body was here, but my soul was not."

"That's not possible."

"I remember it all, Sajin." I arose and took a position before him. "I remember you, greeting me in the study, and Dirm attempting to pierce me through with a crossbow bolt. I remember being in the presence of the gods. I remember things I dare not speak of, and I remember the *power* that once coursed through these veins-- so *don't* look at me as if I'm crazy."

I forced myself to take a step back. "I can share with you, the expression on your face when I barged into the council chambers, announcing the end of the world. *And* tell you what it was like to lead an army of angels against the forces of Kric' tu. I am *not* crazy. I *was* Sam' Dejal!"

I had known Sajin my whole life. He was my mentor and my friend. For as long as I could remember, he had always had a talent for speaking, it was one of his greatest strengths, and I had never seen him at a loss for words. Yet there he stood, unable to speak, for the third time.

I turned from him and crouched before the fire. The flames danced and bounced as I searched intently for what I knew was there, or more accurately, what I knew was not. "Sajin," I said quietly. "Would you come here please."

He walked over and crouched beside me.

"What is missing here?" I asked.

He examined the fire, then looked at me expressionless. "Whatever it is you wish me to see, I'm missing it."

"Does the smoke rising up into the chimney seem

strange to you?"

"Not especially."

"Don't you think it's strange there are no ashes rising up in the smoke stream?"

His eyes narrowed as he looked at me. "No. What's your point?"

"My point is, last week, it didn't seem strange to me either, but now it does." I put my hand on his shoulder. "I *am* different, Sajin. I am aware of things I have never been aware of before, and I'm not quite sure how to handle it. Whether I am Sam' Dejal or not is irrelevant-- I am no longer Charm."

Sajin stood and looked down into the fire. As deep orange light flickered across his stern features, there came a quiet knock at the door.

The doors to the study pushed inward, filling the room with daylight. A soldier stood silhouetted in the entrance. "Master Sajin, Lady Kitaya is here. She wishes an audience with you."

My mind wrapped around the name, and something deep within me was awakened. Perhaps it was relief at knowing she was okay. Perhaps it was something more. I wanted to go to her, but I held back. Would she know me?

"Tell her I will be there momentarily," Sajin said absently. He turned and straightened. "This conversation is going to have to wait."

"I understand."

For now, I will have your status upgraded. A servant will be appointed to you, and your quarters will be transferred to the west wing of the palace. I hope that will be adequate."

"That won't be necessary."

"I sense in you a new spirit, Charm. You will not be satisfied to contain yourself in the role you once played, so we will have to define a new one for you."

"As you wish, my lord," I said, with a subtle bow.

"But for now, I have business to attend to."

"May I accompany you?" I said too quickly.

Sajin gave me an examining stare. It was a stare I knew well, one which he employed frequently with great precision. But this time, there was a hint of defeat in his eyes. "You *have* changed," he said quietly. He turned toward the door. "You may come, but show me the courtesy of remaining silent."

We entered the capital's immense indoor garden to see Kitaya standing with her back to us. Her delicate form was shrouded in a mysterious silk dress, which flowed about her in gentle currents. Subtle shades of tan and brown melted into soft shadows of gossamer transparencies. Her braided ponytail swung gracefully behind her. She was studying a brilliant orange tulip in the center of the elaborate garden. The blossom seemed to shimmer as the sun hit it-- but perhaps it was her presence that brought the little flower to life.

"It is good to see you are well, Lady Kitaya," said Sajin, announcing our presence.

Kitaya turned slowly, revealing her brilliant blue eyes. "It is good to see *you* are well, Sajin."

I kept to the rear as she glided toward us.

"To what do we owe the honor of your visit?" Sajin took her hand into his, and feigned a kiss.

"Oh Sajin, you are so very regal, a true diplomat."

Sajin smiled.

"I have come to ask a favor of you."

"Anything you wish, my lady."

"I wish to borrow Davata Notrals," she said brightly.

Sajin showed no reaction. "You must know I can't grant that. I don't have the authority."

"Then will you bring it before the council?"

"If it is your wish." He bowed, then hesitated. "Would you do something for *me?*"

She smiled. "What would you have me do?"

"Enlighten us as to its origin?"

A slight pout developed on her face. "What do your people find so impressive about that book? It is nothing more than fairy tales about a world which doesn't exist."

"Davata Notrals contains the living text. Each time our sky searchers examine it, the text changes. Stories unfold in different ways, and the prophecies about its people change."

"But they are not your people, Sajin."

"I am puzzled Ki' Janu. Why would you create such an artifact for us to cherish, and then make light of its importance?"

"It is only important to you, because you do not understand it."

"It is important to us, because we believed it was a gift from you, and now you ask for it back?"

I knew Kitaya was bluffing, and this insight caused an involuntary smile to form on my face. Unfortunately it caught her attention.

"Who is this?" She sounded mildly annoyed.

"This is our sky searcher, Charm." Sajin kept his posture.

Kitaya moved in my direction, examining me with a cold sapphire gaze. After a few excruciating seconds, she produced a squint, and a half smile. "He has your strength, Sajin. Perhaps you should guard yourself; your career may be at stake."

"I will keep that in mind."

"So will you do as I asked?" she said, repositioning herself in front of Sajin.

"I will." He folded his arms over his chest. "Will you consider *my* request?"

"Yes, but in the mean time, may I at least *see* the text?"

"Do you wish to see the original parchments?"

221

"Yes, please."

"Is there any particular section you would like to view, or would you have it all?"

"I wish to view the book of the prophet Amiel."

"The Book of Reason," he stated with an almost imperceptible hesitation.

She nodded.

"There is a matter I must attend to. Charm can show you the text." He looked at me. My head gave a startled snap in his direction. Our eyes met in silent communication. "Is there a problem?" he asked.

"I beg your pardon, sir," I replied in my most diplomatic voice. "I merely doubt I have the proper credentials to assist Lady Kitaya in a manner befitting her stature."

"I am sure you will do just fine." He turned back to Kitaya. "If you need anything else, my lady, I will be in the council chambers."

"Thank you, Sajin." Her eyes were still on me. It was clear she didn't know what to think of me, but I suspected it was a mystery she would enjoy unraveling.

I gave her a discrete bow. "If you will follow me, your holiness."

As we headed out into the main corridor, people stopped and stared. Kitaya was intriguing to behold, and quite out of place amidst the plain clothed dignitaries. We reached a slate staircase and I looked back at her. "This way, my lady," I said, gesturing to the stairs.

They spiraled around a massive marble cylinder, which reached from the basement to the peak of the domed ceiling high above. Its thick marble railing was graced with intermittent statues. It had taken seventeen long years to build this staircase, and men had died during its construction-- but all I could think about, was the fact that I had never seen anyone dust it.

For a long time we climbed in silence.

"How goes the war?" I inquired at last.

"There seems to be no end to it," she replied passively.

"Who wages the war while you are here? Armadon, Lorna, and Corel?"

"Yes."

"Did we have any luck in getting Tiko?"

She came to a stop and looked up at me. "Did *we* have any luck? How is it you know so much about the affairs of the gods?"

I stopped and turned. "This is the capital, many rumors travel through these walls."

Her right eyebrow rose slightly. "Yes-- I suppose they do."

I looked ahead, then back at Kitaya. "We should be there soon. It's only a little farther."

She nodded, and in her eyes I saw suspicion.

How much could I tell her? I trusted her, but things were different now. Even if I did tell her, would she believe me? Would I have believed myself? It didn't matter. I could not reveal my identity. I shuddered at the thought of what Rath would do to me in my present form. My mind shifted to the unending blackness of the dungeon, and Gaza's daughter flashed into my perception. Her pleading eyes stabbed at my heart. She was dead now. Kitaya needed to know this. She needed to tell the others-- but there was no way to tell her without revealing my identity.

"Deep in thought?"

My heart skipped a beat. Was she listening to my thoughts? A wave of adrenaline passed over me. "Why do you ask?" I said, forcing a casual tone.

"You seem quiet, that is all."

"I can talk more if you wish."

"That will not be necessary, unless you care to share with me what you were thinking?"

Did she know? No. If she knew, she would not be

223

reacting so calmly. "I was- thinking about Davata Notrals, considering the Book of Barithimus. Do you think the Hestimites will be able to do what they did in the Book of Hagus. On the last recorded change to the text, it was clear they could not. What are your thoughts?"

"It is a secret," she said, looking away.

"Then I suppose I shall wait to see. Forgive me for asking," I said in silent relief.

We reached the last bend and climbed up to the final plateau. Kitaya turned and looked down over the thick railing. I stepped up beside her. The architecture was breathtaking. All the way down, beams of sunlight filtered in through thin ornate windows, filling the interior with a peaceful yellow glow. The inside of the tremendous dome surrounding us appeared as a giant honeycomb of marble and granite. Some of the openings were offices, others were meeting rooms, and in each hole there was activity.

Straight before us, cutting through the side of the dome, a circular window lent a view of the Tower of Pisa, which stood on the other side of the river amongst the ruins of old. Funny though, it seemed odd to me now-- as though it should have a lean to it.

"Beautiful view," Kitaya said softly.

"Yes it is. I have stopped to admire it many times. I don't believe there is another one like it in all of Vrin."

She let out a long sigh. "Your people are strong."

"Yes, I suppose we have been through quite a bit."

She looked up and gave a smile. Her brilliant blue eyes scanning my face, and I felt a soft brush of energy wash over me. "Have we met before?" She sounded genuinely intrigued.

"I would have remembered such a meeting, and cherished the memory of it," I replied.

Her smile widened. "So that is why they call you Charm." She winked. Then reaching down and lifted the flowing fabric of her garment, she gracefully turned toward the door. "Is this our destination?"

"Yes," I said, not able to tear my eyes from her delicate form.

"Then let us go have a look."

Chapter Twenty-two

PROPHECIES
1 0 0 1 1 0 1

 Э

The massive hardwood doors opened before us, revealing a pitch black interior. I walked forward into the dark room, to its center, where I knew a tinderbox could be found. I felt for it.

"Are you so proud that you will not ask for assistance?" inquired Kitaya. The room began to fill with soft light. I looked up and saw a brilliant yellow sphere floating overhead, like a gaseous miniature of the sun.

"Impressive."

"It is the least I could do. I am grateful for the opportunity to look at the scrolls."

"You could easily have taken them," I said, "I don't think we could put up much of a fight."

"Yes, but that is not our way."

"Would you permit me a question, your holiness?" I asked with a gentle bow of respect.

"It depends on the question." She winked.

"The scrolls are enlightenment from the gods, right? And the gods are all knowing and all powerful, so why would you require the scrolls? Do you not already know what has been written?"

"You do not ask easy questions, Charm."

"Is there such a thing?" I smiled.

She returned my smile. "I suppose not."

"So why then do you seek the scrolls?"

"If I tell you, you can never tell a soul. Do you

accept these terms?"

"Yes."

Kitaya pushed her index finger toward me, and as she did, a pulse of energy spread out to illuminate a pane of ghost-like glass. "Let me illustrate." A glowing dot expanded from under her fingertip. She dragged her finger down, creating a faint iridescent line ending at a second larger dot. She withdrew her finger. "Your people are becoming, and soon will be gods. It is the natural progression of the universe. Davata Notrals is not a book of our revelation to you. It is God's revelation to us. Through it we will become what we were fated to be. Do you understand?"

"It is Gaza's revelation?" I knew it was not.

"No. It is the scripture of the God of all."

"So the God of Davata Notrals, is the God of the gods?"

"Yes."

"Even the God of Gaza?"

"Even the God of Gaza. All creation is subject to him. But one day we will be as he is, and one day you will be as we are."

The questions began to flood my mind. Questions I could not ask Kitaya. I felt for the bench behind me, and took a seat.

As Kitaya passed through the transparency, it dispersed into gas. Softly she touched my shoulder and sat down next to me. "Why are you troubled?" she asked tenderly.

"It's complicated." I looked up at her.

She smiled sympathetically, her eyes examining every detail of my face.

I wanted to tell her. I wanted to confide in her, but it was too dangerous. I was vulnerable, I no longer had the power of the gods. My heart sank. Why had God returned me to Charm? Had I failed? I remembered the cold dungeon. The spirit told me it was time to go home, but where was *home?* This didn't seem to qualify. Why did I return to Vrin instead of exiting the simulation? If what she said was *true,* why had God taken away my power? Was I not *ready* to be Sam' Dejal?

Kitaya's expression of empathy melted away, and was replaced by a look of astonishment.

"What? What's wrong?"

"Jason?" she whispered.

The realization struck me in the chest. In my weakness, I had incited her curiosity. She must have listened to my thoughts! I had unwillingly revealed my deepest secret, and I could not take it back. Why had I let my guard down?

"Perhaps somewhere deep inside, you wanted me to know," she said softly, still reading my mind.

I gripped my head in my hands. "I am in danger in this body, terrible danger."

She took my hands into hers and squeezed them warmly. Quietly she examined my face. "You don't need to worry, I will not betray you."

"Will you withdraw your thread?"

"Yes. I am sorry. I was only trying to help."

"Thank you."

She sat staring at me. "It is really you."

"Yes. I don't know how, but it is."

"So, you are now, a character in the program?"

I looked at her intently. The others must have told her about the program and our communication with the outside. *"Am* I just a character, or is something more going on? There's a *connection* between these two worlds. I just can't put my finger on it."

She rubbed my back. "It will come."

The touch of her hand was comforting. There was something about this young lady that set me at ease. Perhaps it was the lack of pretense her youth afforded her, or maybe it was her innocence. Either way, I felt I could trust her, and with so many questions on my mind, I needed *someone* I could trust. I gave her a warm look. "I missed you."

She smiled. "I missed you too."

"What happened to you anyway? I couldn't contact you."

"I traveled to Jahazmad to find Tiko, but ended up-- being detained."

"What happened?"

"I thought I saw Tiko exiting the bazaar, but the area was crowded," she said, shaking her head. "I could not get a clear look at him. He disappeared into a building, so I followed, and found myself in an enormous room, and it was dark. On the other side was an open doorway, so, thinking that was where Tiko had gone, I headed towards it. But when I reached the center of the room, a figure stepped in front of the door. At first I thought it was Tiko, but then I realized, to my horror, it was Rath!

Of course I tried to use my power. I swung my arms around searching for the web, but there wasn't a single thread anywhere." She looked down at the floor. "And that's when he sealed me in."

"I had a similar experience."

She gave a sympathetic nod. "He left me there to rot, and I did, for a *long* time. But then I figured something he missed. I could still control *my* threads. First I made my hands glow so I could look around. I knew I could not activate the threads in the room, but I figured I could break out manually. So I removed my cloak and transformed it into a sticky putty, then pressed it onto the wall. Once I had a firm coating, I pulled a thread out and stepped back. On my command the putty turned to acid, which made a large hole in the wall."

"How long were you in there?"

"Oh forever." Her brows furrowed. "It reminded me

229

of the void."

"What happened next?"

"I found Tiko and brought him to the others."

I gave her a deep examining look. "Have we stopped Kric' tu?"

She shook her head. "We have lost ground. There seems to be no end to Kric' tu's forces. But we now have the aid of most of The Ten."

"Who?"

"Corel, Armadon, and Lorna, as you know. And Tiko joined us, but there is much tension between him and the others. Then there is Hamjin. I do not believe you know him. He is the ninth."

"Why didn't he come with Lorna?"

"He was unreachable by the mortals. It was Armadon who enlisted him."

"Armadon? Did he get in contact with Gaza?"

"No. He was unable to find him."

"Do you know about his wife and daughter?"

"Yes, our sources inside Rath's fortress informed us. They are both dead."

"So..." I stood up. "Why are we still *here?* It's obvious Rath and Kric' tu wish to force Gaza's hand, and Gaza has lost what stands between him and his threat." I shook my head. "So *why* are we still here?"

"I do not know."

"Is that why you're here?" I turned. "Does the Book of Reason hold the key?"

"It may. After our last defeat, we gathered for an emergency meeting. Although we believe your theory that we are in comas, we were all in agreement that there was more going on. None of us can speak to the outside, so I offered to go to The Circle of Ghosts to see if I could learn more about Kric' tu. It was my first time there, and it was *very* unsettling. At first nothing happened, but then as I was getting ready to leave, a man appeared in the center of The

230

Circle. He was transparent, like a ghost, and he said *God*
wished to speak with me!"

"Wow."

"He warned me not to look at God, because if I did,
I would be destroyed. I was terrified! I dropped to my
knees and did *not* look up. The ground shook and a brilliant
light appeared. When he spoke, I could not tell if it was
coming from inside my head, or from The Circle. But I will
never forget what he said. First, he said, we are greatly
loved, and second, that Vrin is important, even though it is
imperfect. And finally, he said there are answers in his
book. And that is why I am here."

"He didn't mention us becoming like him?"

"No." She bit her lip.

"So-- what was with the whole, we are becoming
like God, speech?"

She feigned a smile. "I made that up. I thought you
were Charm. I figured it would give you hope."

"A hope that one day we could rise to something
greater."

She stood up and stepped toward me. "You *are*
something greater. You hold the secret to Vrin in your very
existence. We thought the people of this world were
dreams, but you are now a part of the dream."

Her words echoed in my mind. *A part of the dream.*
I was no longer in Sam' Dejal. I was Charm. I had all of his
memories, every detail of a life lived here in this computer
generated world. Had I entered the computer, or were the
people of Vrin real? I remembered the soldier sitting on his
helmet. His concern for his brother showed complex human
emotion. A program capable of that kind of complexity was
impossible, as far as I was aware, and yet every inhabitant
of Vrin apparently possessed a similar set of programming
instructions. *Did I enter the program? Or were the people
of Vrin real?*

Kitaya was close. Yet her words were distant. "Vrin

231

is real, Jason, and *you* are the key."

The key. I was the key. I was not from Vrin, and yet here I stood. Was I from both places? When I was Sam' Dejal, Charm was frozen. Frozen over the book.

"The book!"

Kitaya jumped.

I ran to the case, which held the Book of Reason, and threw open the lid. The scroll sparkled on the rose felt cushion. I snatched it up and unrolled it.

"What is it?" said Kitaya, peering over my shoulder.

"I have studied these scrolls a million times. I know every inch of this parchment. There." I pointed. "There it is!" I could hardly believe my eyes as I read, "'Then the voice of the one true God spoke to the people, from the world in dreams beyond the darkness, and their eyes were opened. No longer did they sleep, for they knew all that God had created them to be.' That's *IT!*"

"What?"

I turned toward Kitaya. "The people of Vrin *are* real. *This* is the world in dreams beyond the darkness!"

She squinted at me. "I am not following you."

"I don't understand how, but it's the only thing that makes sense. When I was trapped in Rath's fortress, I was rescued. I was told I would be taken home, but I'm still here. I couldn't understand why I returned to Charm when I should have gone back to my body-- the one lying in a coma where Doctor Solomon is. But I must have awakened, and then returned to Vrin through sleep! This verse indicates a world in dream beyond the darkness. If the void is the darkness, then that would indicate that Vrin is some form of shared dream state."

"I thought Vrin was in the computer."

"Vrin is a computer *program,* but somehow I am able to enter Vrin without being connected to the computer, and it has something to do with dreams."

"How?"

232

"I don't know-- but it's *very* intriguing."

She smiled, then frowned. "That is all very interesting, but does that scroll mention anything about how to stop Gaza?"

I thought for a moment, then lifted a finger. "Yes, I believe it does."

I unrolled the scroll again, and read. "In those the last days, God rose up the prophet Tardin, who having the secret to The Circle, turned the tide of darkness. And God banished Kric' tu with Rath in flames."

Her eyebrows rose. "Are *you* the prophet Tardin?"

I looked at her with wide eyes. "Apparently, and as long as this verse remains unchanged, I will learn the secret of The Circle, which will turn the tide of darkness.

"The *secret* to The Circle?"

"Yes. Which means I will have to travel to see my friend Arganis. The wizard."

"May I join you?"

"Yes." I put the scroll back in its case. "But first I need to speak with Sajin."

"Then I will go check on the others and return when you call for me." She placed a thread delicately on my neck.

"Kitaya?"

"Yes, Jason?"

"You cannot reveal my identity to anyone."

"I won't," she said, slipping her arms around me. She placed her head against my chest. "I am glad you are alive."

The energy engulfed me, and I found myself standing on the bottom floor of the capital building, hugging thin air. I was mildly embarrassed, but recovered quickly.

"Charm!" It was the voice of Sajin. I turned and saw him walking up the stone corridor toward me. "Where is Kitaya?"

"She had other business."

"That is unfortunate. The council decided to allow her request."

"She will be glad to hear that."

"Do you have a moment?" He gestured toward his office.

"I do."

"I still have questions."

Sajin's office was not nearly as royal or regal as the other council members'. He was a man of the people, and as such, kept his office comfortable and simple. I walked over to the tall narrow window looking out over the many gardens of the capital building.

"Would you like a drink?" he offered.

"Juice would be well received. I can barely remember the last time I ate or drank."

Sajin popped the cork from a bottle of raspberry juice and gave me a pensive look. "So tell me, Charm. What was it like being a god?"

"Have you told the others?" I continued to look out the window.

"No, and I don't think they would believe me anyway."

"It's imperative that you do not." I turned back toward him. "It would place my life in danger."

"Yes, I am aware of the ramifications."

"You were always the wise one."

"Here." He handed me the juice and gestured to his black leather couch. "I have many questions, as I'm sure you are aware."

"I don't think you will like the answers, but I will give them."

"Fair enough."

I took a sip from my drink.

"So everything we believe is a lie. Would that be a fair assumption?"

"That would be an unfair assumption."

He gave me a curious glance.

"We assumed a great many things. We assumed the gods would be all knowing and all powerful, and we assumed Davata Notrals was not for us. But as it turns out, things are progressing as they should."

"Really." He sounded sarcastic.

"The Marathil says the gods will deliver us to Ethral, well, that is a half truth. They are not gods, but they have already begun to band together to destroy the evil of chaos. I don't truly know how it all fits together, but whoever inspired the writing of the Marathil knew future events, because they are unfolding just as the book describes. And Davata Notrals is even more amazing, because it describes events here as well as places beyond here."

"I'm no sky searcher, Charm, but even I see inconsistencies."

"Because you do not have the whole picture."

There was a knock on the door and Sajin let out a sigh. The annoyance was clear in the firm lines of his face. He went to the door and opened it. *"What!"*

I heard muffled words from the other side. Sajin's eyes widened. "Send her in," he said, then turned to look at me. "You're not going to like this."

An older lady appeared in the doorway. Her skin was deep brown, her eyes as dark as coal. "Thank you, young man," she said, gently closing the door behind her. Turning, she gave each of us a look, then stated smoothly, "Gentlemen, I'm Hazel Brown."

"Welcome, Hazel." Sajin looked intently at her, then back at me. "The guard says you know *who* Charm is?"

I felt a shiver run down my spine.

"A lot of people know who Charm is," he continued. "He is very well known."

She gave him a scowl. "The fact you allowed me in, proves what I know is true." She turned to me. "And no, I ain't told no one you Sam' Dejal. Sajin figured 'cause I said I know *who* you are, I probably know other stuff I shouldn't."

Sajin began to speak, but Hazel cut him of.

"I s'pose you gonna go on with some crazy notion about how you have no idea what I'm talkin' about. Well save it."

Sajin shot me a glance.

I stood, and chose my words carefully. "Hazel. Did you come just to tell me you know who I *am,* or, do you have something else to share?"

She looked at me tenderly. "Charm, I think Doc Solomon may be dead."

I stared at her. "What? How.. Why do you think he's dead?"

Sajin stepped forward. "What's going on, Charm? Who's Doctor Solomon?"

"Hold on." I held up my hand. "Hazel, why do you think Solomon is dead?"

"'Cause we was talkin' on the phone, and it went dead."

"Wait a second. You spoke with Solomon-- through the threads?"

"Heaven's no. We talk when I'm awake, on Earth. Sajin's expression reflected utter confusion.

"*Earth?*" I said, "I don't understand."

She leveled her eyes at me. "*I* can remember."

I squinted at her. "Who *are* you?"

"Hazel Brown." She put her hands on her hips. "I already tol' you that. And now I'm tryin' to tell you I remember stuff. You see, I have a condition that makes my brain all wrong, it makes me remember stuff I wish I didn't have to. Here, there, awake, asleep. I remember it all."

I let this information sink in a moment. "You, *remember* the world *outside* Vrin? Where Solomon is?"

"Yeah. It's kinda weird really."

"Wait. How do you even know Doctor Solomon?"

"We been talkin' for some time now, watchin' you. And he said one of the ten woke up. So I checked with my sources here in Vrin, and sure enough, you awake.

Again I stared at her. *"What?"*

"There was only four of ya. It's pretty easy to figure. One's awake, the others all still frozen like a cube a ice."

"So, there are others frozen?"

"Yep. Took me some time to find 'em all. Near's I can tell, there's three others. I pieced it together. I know one of the patients woke up, so I goes and sees if any of the ice cubes awake, cause I need me a name. The book tells me stuff, but I need to tell it stuff."

Sajin and I looked at each other. This was getting weirder by the second. "And what *book* would that be?"

"Davata Notrals. It tells me stuff. It knows what's gonna happen. It changes in here, but it *don't* change out there."

"Davata Notrals, tells you stuff," I said flatly.

237

"I puts in a word, and it tells me what's gonna happen in the future. There's a code hidden in the spaces."

"I'm going to pretend like I know what that means." I put my hand to my head. "What do *I* have to do with this?"

"I need a name. Your name."

"Why?"

"Cause I need to know what Tardin's gonna do. He's the key, the prophet. But I don't know who he *is* in Vrin, so I can't ask the book what he's gonna do. And if I don't know what *he's* gonna do, I don't know what *I'm* s'pose to do."

I began to pace in frustration.

"I know you struglin' with this, son. I wish it wasn't so confusin'."

"How do you ask the book questions?"

"Well, it's complicated."

"Give it a shot."

"I use a computer. It has a program what was given me by a man in the NSA. He works in cryptography. It lets me look for words in the book. It skips letters. Like I put in Charm, and it finds it in a sentence that has the letters, but they don't appear normal. It might look for the letters every tenth letter, or twentieth letter. That's why we don't see it when we read it normal. It's hidden."

"So-- what's the big deal? What does it matter if you can find *my* name in the book?"

"It's what's 'round it that matters. If I find your name, then I looks at what's before and after it, in the same letter spacin'. Then I know what's gonna happen."

"Have you tried all the names of the frozen people?"

"Yep, and yours was the most interestin'. But I needed to know you was Tardin before I went and did somethin' crazy."

Sajin spoke up. "So you know the future?"

238

She smiled. "Yup."

"Can you prove it? What does the book say will happen next?"

She winked. "It wouldn't be fair for me to tell y'all how it ends."

Sajin did not look pleased.

"O-*kay,*" I said, formulating my question. "Do you know the *nature* of Vrin?"

"Since I was a child. I could remember where we go when we sleep. Well, we don't actually *go* anywhere, we stay in our mind. But that's beside the point. What I wanna tell you is, I was here *before* Vrin, and so was you. See, on earth-- that is, when I'm awake, I have a rare form of autism. In many ways I'm simple, but the part of my brain what controls and remembers Dantra, is smart."

"*Dantra-?*" Arganis had spoken of The Circle being connected to that place. "What *is* Dantra?"

"It's the spirit world outside Vrin. It does appear to be another thing altogether, but it ain't. Vrin's made of the same stuff as Dantra. Vrin is thought energy. Robert Helm started it."

Robert Helm? I was Robert Helm. I opened my mouth to speak, but she gave me a look as if to say all my questions would be answered.

"Robert Helm is Gaza."

I gave my head a quick shake, my brain was starting to hurt.

Hazel continued. "'Cause Gaza can form Dantra with his mind like clay, the computer used his mind to form Vrin. I knew this cause of my condition. You see, most people don't understand they in Dantra. They make Dantra into what they like, and can't see it for what it is. When I saw Vrin growin' like a big ball of blue fire in the middle of Dantra, I knew it was unlike *anythin'* I'd seen before. It *scared* me, so I went to the elders. They tol' me the conflict between God and Kric' tu was comin' to an end, and that

239

Vrin was the last battlefield. They tol' me I had a special place in God's plan, and that I would go into Vrin with others chosen by God. It was hard for all of us once we was in here, 'specially for me, 'cause I could remember. But the history of Vrin was put into the other's minds by the computer, and they took it as real."

"So the people of Vrin *are* real."

"Real as anythin'. I started to search for information 'bout Vrin on the inside and the out. This led me to Solomon. He didn't believe me at first, but after awhile he couldn't deny what I knew. And he became grateful, 'cause I knew things he couldn't see. When Solomon started Vrin, he could see what was goin' on, but when God chose others to go into the program, it changed the code, and he couldn't see in anymore. The best he could do was track the data bein' stored on the main frame and read it. And as you know, he also sent a message. When *you* responded, he thought you was Robert 'cause you understood the programmin'. Anyway, since he made a connection, he could see into the program again. He tracked you in the system as a number, and sorted out which of the ten you was while buildin' a visual representation of the data. It took a while, and the computer figured out who you really was. That was just before you came out of the coma. So I came to make sho' you was Tardin, and you confirmed it for me."

"So I *did* wake up from the coma-?"

"Yup. But came back to Vrin when you went to sleep."

"I knew it!" I started pacing again. "So now that you have what you came for, what's next?"

"Now I check the code again, and make sho' I'm doin' what I'm s'pose to."

I remembered back to the scriptures I'd read to Kitaya. Was *I* the one to stop Gaza, or would the prophecy change? "So on the outside the book stays the same?" She nodded. "Can you check a verse for me and tell me what it says?"

Her eyes lit up and she pointed at me. "I knew you was gonna ask that!" She took a journal out of her belly pocket. "What is it?"

I gave her the verse.

"I'll let you know tomorrow," she said tucking the pad back in her pocket.

"Are you going to come back here?"

"No. You comin' with me."

I gave her a look.

"Charm. Gaza prob'ly knows you're here. You'll be safer with me."

"No offense, but I don't even *know* you." I sized her up again. "That makes it a little difficult for me to trust you with my *life*."

"Oh, you'll wanna see my work. Once you see it, you'll understand everthin'. Listen. I'm an old woman, what am I gonna do, bite you?"

"It's not you I'm worried about, it's those you would turn me over to that frighten me."

"If I wanted to turn you in, you wouldn't a seen it comin', son."

"Go with her," said Sajin. "It seems she has information that will help us bring this conflict to a close."

I looked at Sajin and considered his words. "All right." I turned back to Hazel. "How far do we have to travel? Time is precious."

"It's jest the next town over."

"Then let's be on our way. Sajin I know you have more questions."

"That's an understatement." He reached out and gripped my hand. "Just give me the courtesy of keeping me informed."

"I will do my best." I shook his hand firmly.

"You have a fantastic journey ahead. Our thoughts

and prayers go with you."

"Thank you, Sajin. I'll try to not let you down."

Chapter Twenty-four

GAZA
1 1 0 1 0 0 1

ι

I let Kitaya know I would be delayed, and then sat on the front steps of the capital building. The brilliant sunset was sending dazzling cascades of gold and orange across the structures to the east. As Charm, this was the time of day I enjoyed the most. Many an evening I'd sat on these very steps, watching the radiant fusion of color playing on the coliseum, the Eiffel, the Sphinx... Tonight however, it was the Statue of Liberty who caught my eye. She was a symbol of unity for the people of Vrin. Her proud form had always spoken to me of freedom and harmony. --But now, she was just another structure in the skyline. Vrin simply wasn't the same. Her beauty was waning in my heart.

A horse drawn coach pulled up to the steps. The driver tipped his hat to me, and I headed down to greet him. "Have you been instructed?" I asked the gentleman.

"Yes, sir. We are to go to Bagidar."

"Very good." I stepped up into the carriage.

"Uh-- Sir?"

"Yes? What is it?"

"I was told you would be traveling with a companion."

"Yes. She will meet us at the gate."

"Yes, sir."

The thin door closed with a metallic click and I took a seat in the darkened carriage. Across from me, a shadowy figure sat, a guard I assumed.

"What is your name, soldier?" I asked, trying to sound authoritative.

"What's wrong, Jason?" came a hollow voice from the darkness. "Don't you recognize the creator of Vrin?"

My heart quickened. I wanted to leap from the carriage, but knew it wouldn't do any good. Instead I began an internal counting to keep from bringing any thoughts to the surface for Gaza to prey upon. "I'm sorry? Have we met?" *One, two, three, four...*

Casually he opened his eyes and looked out the window, only passively involved in our meeting, as if my presence was an irritation for him. I was immediately shaken by his eyes. They were not blue like the rest of the gods', but green, like two smoldering emeralds.

...eight, nine, ten, eleven...

"You have created for me a conundrum." His distant, lifeless voice held an eerie quality.

"How is that?" I asked cautiously. *One, two, three, four...*

"Your reanimation is a paradigm." He shifted in his chair. "Are you comfortable in your former habitation?"

"I don't understand." *One, two, three, four...*

"You are Charm once more. How do you feel about this?"

"What do you mean?" *...five, six, seven, eight...*

His eyes darted to his right and his hand rose to a fixed and invisible destination. Quickly his fingers wiggled in the air. A sigh escaped his lips. "Your confidant approaches, but our business has not yet concluded; you have information which I require." He tipped his head slightly. "Your attendance, of course, is non-negotiable." His hand snapped out and grabbed my wrist. I felt his power enter my body, and the world exploded in blue fire.

The room spun like a carnival ride as tiny aftershocks erupted randomly across my back. Glowing

244

objects streaked past my eyes, leaving visual trails on my retina. Colors pooled with colors in a blur of pulsating substance.

I needed something solid to fixate on, something I could use to rebuild my visual perception. I felt a groove in the floor and slid my fingers lengthwise across it to let the sensations register. They encountered an intersection. Slowly and methodically I followed the downward path. With effort, I slid my body until I was hovering above the floor tile. As my mind grasped the shape, it began to perceptually construct the floor. Soon the room took shape around me, and the spinning in my head subsided.

Just in front of my eyes were four wheels, and above them, a red seat. I drew the chair toward me. It let out a series of gentle squeaks. Gripping the cushion, I hefted myself onto it and sat up. Hovering on the desk in front of me was an illuminated screen within a glass box. Iridescent numbers rose line upon line. I reached out and touched the cold surface. Slowly my finger slid across the glass cube and my mind deciphered the information with unexpected efficiency. I had seen this text before. It was the very essence of Vrin.

Where was Gaza? I scanned the room. Many more illuminated glass plates balanced on metal stands, filling the room with a ghostly glow. I looked from one panel to the next, and as I studied each image carefully, I began to notice a theme. Gaza was watching. Not only was he tracking me and the other gods, but also Sajin, and several others I did not recognize. Gaza could see and hear everything!

Frantically I searched for Rath. If Rath was here, then Gaza knew! Or did he? Was he watching when his daughter was killed? My eyes darted from one image to the next. Then stopped.

Floating before me, frozen in time, was the horrifying moment I wanted so desperately to forget. The little girl's face filled the screen. Her eyes pleaded through the ghostly glass as the gnarled fingers of Kric' tu gripped her tiny forehead, and the knife pressed deep into her delicate neck. The image was so real I felt I could reach out and touch her tears.

"Looking for something?"

I twisted around in panic and met Gaza face to face. He appeared completely indifferent to my total lack of composure. "I imagined you would be longer recuperating. It appears I miscalculated," he said in the same cold, impersonal manner he'd displayed in the carriage.

"I was just..."

His hand lifted, and an invisible force squeezed my throat. "You are only alive because I have not grown tired of you. It would be auspicious of you to retain that perspective. Now," he said, releasing me, "you have information I need, and I do not have a great deal of time."

"I'm here to help," I said, rubbing my neck.

"You were taken to the realm outside of Vrin by a spirit being, yet you do not remember this place?"

"No. I don't remember anything."

"And now you are Charm again."

"So it would seem."

He turned and examined the wall of monitors. "You have been quite the busybody, Jason. I have watched your exploits with great interest." He tossed me a shadowed glance. "In fact, I have watched *you* most intently."

He gestured, and the screen holding the image of the girl pushed forward and expanded.

"I tried to save her," I said reflexively.

"This is not my daughter," he said with distaste. "Her sacrifice was a charade intended to lure you to Kric' tu. He has dark plans for you, plans that would make your blood run cold." With a twist of his wrist, the monitor returned to its original position.

"Plan? What could Kric' tu possibly need me for?"

"To stop me." He laughed.

I let these words sink in, then stated cautiously, "With all due respect, sir, that's ridiculous. Even *if* I were able to stop you, why the charade? Why not just *ask* my help? And besides-- I was *already* trying to stop you."

"His plan is confusing, is it not?"

What plan? How could I possibly help Kric' tu accomplish *anything?* The frustration welled up inside me until I could not contain it. *"What plan?"* I snapped. Lucky for me, Gaza was enjoying my agitation.

"Does this information trouble you?" He gave a sinister grin. "Do you have a *problem* with a higher being using you as a plaything? You and I are not all that dissimilar on that particular point."

He turned and drew another monitor from the wall. On this one, an aerial view of the battle raged. Kric' tu's forces had more than tripled. The only ones holding them back were the gods. The mortal army had been completely destroyed.

"Where are they coming from?" I asked.

"The Circle of Ghosts. And they will keep coming until they have conquered every last city in Vrin. But he is not content to rule only Vrin. That is why he needs you."

"To go, *beyond* Vrin?"

Gaza smiled. "You are probably of no use to him anymore, but *I* have use for you. It's funny really. I didn't have a use for you as Sam' Dejal, but as Charm..." he said, lifting his hands into the air for drama, "Charm has *much* to offer."

He began to circle. I turned warily to face him. "I created your kind and called you *sky searchers*, a nomenclature describing a scholar who studies the cognosphere, which I also created. It is this role that has caused you to develop a familiarity with something of interest to me." He wiggled his fingers in my direction and a book materialized in the air. It fell to the ground before me. "Do you recognize this item?"

"Yes. It is Davata Notrals."

"This, I did *not* create."

I squinted at him. "Then who...?"

He leaned an ear in toward me. "Who created it? *God* did. Tell me, Charm. Do you believe in the prophecies?"

"--Yes."

"But they *change!* This does not pose a *problem* for you?"

"I haven't put much thought toward it. I've been, kinda busy."

He rapidly drew in close. *"Your schedule is about to open up!"* He struck me in the chest and energy coiled through my insides.

"AAAAARGG!" I fell to the floor, clutching my chest.

"Put some *thought* toward it!" he shrieked, then began pacing.

I clutched at my gut and rocked back and forth. "It, ah, changes here in Vrin, but does not on the outside."

"Why!"

"I don't know. I only know it speaks of things as if they have already happened."

"I created Vrin from the very essence of the void! Every detail of this world came from *my code*. Nothing exists that I did not make-- except this wretched book!"

"So why would you seek to destroy that which you have created?"

My question took us both by surprise.

"Are you so dim?" He chided. "This world is nothing but a tool to return what was stolen from me."

"Your-- wife and daughter?" I stated cautiously. "Who stole them from you?"

Gaza's body shook as the words erupted from him. "GOD STOLE THEM FROM ME!" The room bent and expanded.

Terror stabbed through my chest.

"We are play things in an evil child's sandbox! Puppets for his *amusement.* What could God *possibly* gain from taking my family and leaving me imprisoned in the void! Was it not enough to take them?" He shook his fist at the ceiling. "What *crime* did I commit to deserve *emptiness* and *despair!*"

He no longer acknowledged my presence, but directed his speech to the stained glass windows above. "What *crime* did I commit to deserve *torture* in the abyss? What did I do to *YOU?* You *sit* on your throne as humanity squirms for your amusement! But you didn't expect me to escape! You didn't expect a *human* could wield power in your realm. But you were *wrong!* And your wretched book is *wrong!*"

He stiffened, and his gaze returned to me. In his burning green eyes, I saw confusion. "Stay here!" he said, then turned and walked away.

Metal straps emerged from the floor and clasped my feet firmly. I crouched to pull at them, but there was no give. They were part of the floor, and very tight. My eyes darted frantically in search of something to free myself, but nothing presented itself. The room was barren except for the panels and the glass cube sitting on a simple desk several feet in front of me. As I examined the desk, an image flashed in my mind. I saw a glowing screen, similar to the cube, and a panel with letters and numbers. *A keyboard! That's it!* That was how information was entered into the system. But *this* cube had no input device. How did he enter information into the system? Was this a terminal or merely a monitor? Maybe it would respond to voice commands.

I directed my voice toward the cube. "Activate!" I said. No response. "Expand!" To my absolute astonishment, it began to grow in size. "Stop!" I said involuntarily. The cube became still. I shot a glance toward the doors, then back to the cube. "Expand!" The cube grew until I could make out the program on the screen. "Stop!"

Now what?

"--Search." Nothing happened. I tried again. "Find." A box opened on the screen. "Charm." The screen went crazy. Entry after entry scrolled by, faster than my eyes could scan.

"Stop!" The screen became still. I glanced at the door. I needed to find myself in the program, in *this* room, with the metal straps holding me. The only method I had employed with any accuracy was the action category. If I could alter the location or state of an object, maybe I could track that object in the program based on it being the only object in Vrin that had changed in that way at that moment.

I fished in my pocket and pulled out a coin. Quickly I placed the coin in my mouth then spit it back into my hand. "Find wet coin," I said. The screen blinked with three entries.

Q5T33KL, coin, gold, wet, water, 280, trunk
J224FT, coin, gold, wet, water, 4, pocket
H034A33, coin, silver, wet, saliva, 1, hand

"Locate H034A33"

The response appeared. Grid3U9Y9K1.

That was hardly any help! "Help commands," I said. A list appeared on the screen.

I searched and scrolled, and searched... Until finally, I found what I needed. "Visual 3d grid3U9Y9K1" The room built itself on the screen in a matter of seconds. Every detail was depicted precisely, including myself.

"Transform metal straps to water." The straps melted away from my feet.

Off in the distance, something hit the floor with a

thud. I dropped to my knees and looked under the desk. There was no movement, so I crawled past the line of illuminated images, then stood. In front of me was a table filled with maps and photographs. And in front of that, a chair with its seat sitting on the floor, in a puddle of water.

In the center of the table was a screen displaying two prominent pieces of information. The first was a woman's face, which crawled with activity, every detail was being measured and calculated. The second was a number, diminishing by one each time a new face appeared. One by one faces appeared on the screen and were methodically scanned. Was this how he was searching for his wife and daughter? What happened if the computer finished its task and he didn't find them? Would that be it? Would that be the end of Vrin?

Time was running out. It was vital that I be long gone before Gaza returned. But where could I run? Where could I *possibly* hide? If that number reached zero, no hiding place would be sufficient! *I needed to buy time!*

Frantically I slid the wet chair aside and dove under the table. Past the mass of wires, two tiny boxes sat on the floor. Storage devices I assumed. Taking away a storage device would stall him in his efforts! I yanked out the wires, slid out from under the table, and lifted a box. The doors to the chamber swung in. Below the panels, Gaza's feet appeared.

In a panic, I looked about. There was a window at the back of the room. I bolted toward it.

"JASON!" Gaza sounded like a parent scolding a naughty child.

Particles of glass exploded all around me as I plummeted from, what I realized now, was a *tower!* The expanse below was dizzying! I twisted around in the air to see Gaza's face materialize in the window. Mild irritation quickly melted into wide eyed despair, as he realized what I was holding in my grasp.

My mind called out to Kitaya. *"Take me to you!"*

"Hhnnnoooooo!" was the last thing I heard, before vanishing in a flash of blue fire.

In my sickened state, I could not decipher my surroundings. *"Hide me quickly! He's watching,"* was all I could get out through The tender strand connecting me to Kitaya. Something soft enveloped me.

"Who is watching?"

"Continue doing what you were doing. Gaza is watching. You must get as far away from me as you can. You're in danger here."

"Not until I find out what is going on."

"I've stolen something from Gaza's fortress, something that will ensure I will never be safe again, a vital tool Gaza is using to find his wife and daughter. They were not killed. Gaza still searches for them."

"What? How do you know this?"

"I don't have time to explain, but Gaza's lost his faculties. There's no reasoning with him."

"Then all hope is lost."

"Not entirely. I have a plan. But I need to get out of here undetected, which means you'll have to leave. Gaza's watching you, and if he sees me here, we're both in danger."

"How will you protect yourself?"

"By staying as far away from the gods as possible! I'm going to seek out Arganis as I originally intended, and as much as I would like you to come with me, I need to go alone."

"I will have a servant prepare a horse and supplies for you. I will tell him I am sending Moota on a journey. Go to the stable. The horse will be left unattended."

"Thank you."

"Stay here," she whispered through the thread.

"Okay," I whispered back.

Her footsteps grew fainter, and a door slammed. I

252

thrust the cover off me and went to the window. Night had descended over Trinador. Tiny lights danced like fireflies in the trees. Good. The night would conceal my escape. It would be slow going by horse, but if I attempted to travel through another thread, Gaza might be able to track me. I looked up at the three glowing orbs in the night sky, and was thankful Gaza had a liking for moons. I would need their light. I leaned out the window and took a deep breath.

Suddenly the sky flashed a brilliant orange. I jerked my head back in. The walls began to groan with a deafening vibration. *Is this it?* I thought, gripping the windowsill. *Did I push Gaza over the edge?* The vibrations mutated into a resonating hum, and in the distance, muffled screams of terror echoed. The voice of Gaza boomed out. **"CHARM! YOU HAVE ONE DAY TO RETURN WHAT YOU HAVE STOLEN!"**

And as quickly as they had begun, the vibrations ceased, leaving me shaken, but somewhat relieved. He didn't know where I was, which meant I was safe-- for the moment.

I gathered my wits, and a measure of courage, and made my way down to the stables. My destination, Pagnia. Time was running out and it looked like the fate of Vrin rested on me.

I followed the roads but kept a hood over my head to shroud my identity. The landscape was cold and lifeless in the blue moonlight. Shadows shifted restlessly among the trees. As Charm, growing up, I could remember playing in woods like these, but now they seemed empty. It never occurred to me then to consider the lack of insects. Vrin never had such things, and I'd never noticed. Now, however, I found their absence troubling. Vrin had been my home, but now it was nothing more than an imperfect shadow of a world just beyond my memory. I wanted *my* Vrin back, the one I had built my life in.

I hunched over, and pushed the horse harder.

253

The sky was beginning to glow with the first signs of dawn as I entered the well-manicured area of Pagnia. The town was all but deserted, and as I guided my horse along, his footfalls echoed loudly through the vacant streets. When I reached SCAR's hideout, there were no signs of life, and the door was bolted, so I guided the horse around the back to find a way in.

A cellar door gave me access. I creaked it open and groped my way down the stone stairs. It was dark, except for the faint light from a lantern in the far corner. I moved in closer. And that's when I saw him. A figure lay next to the lamp on a wooden cot. But that was all I saw, before a sharp pain shot through my head, and everything went black.

I squinted. The light was bright. A river rushed past me and turned into a waterfall but I could not see its base. The sun was high in the sky and seagulls played in the wisps of cloud above. I sat down on a gray rock and absorbed the beauty of the mountain scape stretching out before me. It was peaceful here, even though I was not sure where here was.

"You have questions," said the man in white next to me.

"I always do," I replied.

"Yes, but now you have a question you have never thought to ask before, which is not surprising really, since you are no longer the person you were."

"I have been here many times haven't I?"

He smiled. "Oh yes."

"But I have never asked you what this place is."

"Right. You never asked because you never thought to. You had never known any different."

"But now I've changed."

"Yes. Now you carry in you the imprint of Thomas Tardin and this causes you to consider things you would have never thought to consider before. Thomas believes

254

this is a dream because that is what Charm believes, and Charm has never been able to see this place as it truly is. But Thomas can't understand why it is so vivid, and thus the question. I know it's disconcerting, but don't worry, we will eventually pass beyond this realm and enter into more familiar territory."

"How can we pass beyond, if we're not moving?"

He put his hand on my shoulder. "It's like riding the bus where you find yourself engrossed in a book or a conversation with the person next to you. You're oblivious to the scenery passing by outside."

"It's peaceful here. I don't want to move beyond."

"Well, you know something Thomas. The real mystery is you never really leave. It's all a matter of perception."

My brow furrowed. "I'm not following you."

"Don't worry. You will soon forget we had this conversation, and it won't matter that you don't understand."

"So why have the conversation at all?"

"The answer to your question is very complicated," he smiled, "but you're going to ask me anyway."

I laughed. "I suppose I will."

He repositioned himself on the rock. "Focus on me, and don't look away until I tell you, or it will hurt considerably."

I focused on him and immediately something began to happen in my peripheral. The scene shimmered like Jello. Lights and shapes melted around me, swirling and pulsating like a living organism.

When it stopped he said, "There we go."

My muscles loosened and I turned to examine my new surroundings. We were no longer outside on a mountain range. Instead, the mountain scene sped by just outside the window of the train. I looked back at him, and then around at the plush compartment.

"Where are we going?"

"To answer your question," he winked.

"What does that mean exactly?"

"We need to go where you can understand, which means we need to enter the void. Look- we're approaching it now."

Out the window I saw a tunnel approaching. Car after car disappeared inside, and then it was dark. The train began to slow with a steady squeal, then stopped.

"Are we there?"

He gave me a nod. "Follow me if you want your answer," he said. As he stood and stepped out of the compartment, I followed closely. He led me down a thin hallway and through a sliding metal door with a tiny window.

We were alone as we exited the train, and we soon found ourselves standing on a jet black platform watching as the long silver train disappeared into the night, taking its light with it. And then for a moment, all was still.

"Are you still there?" I asked.

"I'm here," he replied. "I'm always here."

"Are you going to answer my question now?"

"Yup. In three, two, one-"

I felt as if all of the information of the universe came flooding into my mind and I was immediately at one with it. Every question I could have ever thought to ask was answered, including the one for which we had made the journey.

The answer to my question was connected to the very nature of my existence. I was not simply flesh and bone, but a complex multi-dimensional being. As a man, I could not possibly comprehend the other aspects of myself, but they still existed, and they still effected me.

"So it's that simple?" I said.

"It's only simple here, because you are in the nexus."

Another question entered my mind, but as it occurred to me to ask, the answer was there. I wondered about the dark void I had experienced before Vrin. It had not been like this. I remembered a vast and lonely place. The knowledge which suffused me offered the answer-

I had created that void from the essence of Dantra, the same substance which Vrin itself was made of. While in Vrin, within Dantra, impulses from the computer triggered responses in my brain, and they in turn molded Dantra, using my connection to that spirit realm.

"We are nearing The Separation. You will soon pass into physical consciousness, and you will no longer be aware of me."

"Thanks for the help," I said.

I sensed a smile as I passed through The Separation into dream.

A dark feeling hung in the air on the street outside my childhood home. A soldier brushed by, wearing a World War II uniform, and clutching a rifle with a wooden stock. I followed him for a short distance, then bolted across the neighbor's yard to hide behind some barrels. I peeked out, no one saw me, so I hunched over and scooted across the lawn. Bursts of gunfire rained down on me from the neighbor's house. I ducked and rolled. The fire ceased.

I poked my head up then made my way toward the darkness past the open cellar door. Again gunfire broke out. I dropped to the ground and dirt exploded in small eruptions all around me. --But I was not afraid; I was no longer effected by the things of this world. I stood and faced the window. A shadowy figure took aim. But the barrage of bullets passed right through me.

My perspective shifted and I found myself watching from outside my body. Every shadow in the neighborhood began shifting and moving. Coming alive. Approaching from every direction. Surrounding me. Pressing in on me. Hoping to receive a touch from their holy one.

257

The last thing I saw were my glowing metal eyes--
and that was all I remembered, once I was fully awake.

Chapter Twenty-five

A SHORT REST

I squinted as the salty air washed over me. Off in the distance the sound seagulls squawking mingled with guitar music. I gripped the railing and looked down into the green ocean water. Fish shot by just beneath the surface like ghostly apparitions. I'd had a night of deep restful sleep. My joints still ached considerably, but my head was clearer and my strength was returning.

"Thomas," Annie's voice called from inside the bungalow. "Would you like some eggs or something?"

"Thanks," I yelled back through the sliding doors, "an egg sounds wonderful."

Her voice sounded strange to me, wrong somehow, and I had to remind myself, this wasn't the Annie of my memory. She was not standing in the kitchen with a big pregnant belly. And little Rebecca was not sitting on the living room floor surrounded by a million tiny toys. No, this was not the vacation we were headed to after New York City. --I had slept through that one.

I looked over at the envelope laying on the glass table next to me. This was quite the mystery I'd found myself entangled in: virtual worlds, science fiction experiments, cryptic notes... It was all just a little more than I could wrap my brain around. I was used to solving things like product launch schedules and media campaigns, not government conspiracies. --Not that I wanted to solve *anything* at the moment. *But,* I knew myself well enough to

259

know, that I could not just sit back and do nothing to try to solve this mystery. It was in my nature to solve puzzles. Some would even call it an addiction.

Again I read the name and address on the envelope. Who was this *Hazel Brown?* How did she fit into the puzzle? Was she an associate of Dr. Solomon? If she was, why wasn't she at the center? And *why* did the envelope contain my name, and *only* my name? Even with a night of restful sleep behind me, I couldn't even *begin* to make sense of that one.

I tucked the envelope back into my pocket and hefted myself out of the chair. Whatever it meant was irrelevant. Hazel Brown was my only lead, and it was with her I would start my investigation. I slid the screen door open, and followed the scent of breakfast.

Sam was intently watching a news clip glowing from the paint on the living room wall. I looked for the source of the projection, but found none. Rebecca was sitting on the couch with a book.

Whatcha readin'?"

"Davata Notrals." She looked up with a bright smile. "There was a copy in the dresser."

"Are they *still* putting those things in hotel drawers?"

"They sure are." Her smile got even wider.

"I made you one sunny side up if that's okay," Annie called.

"Yes, sounds great." I stepped into the kitchen. "It smells wonderful in here," I said, scanning the room.

"What are you looking for?"

"The phone. I want to call Stephen."

She laughed. "You're wearing it."

I padded myself down.

Her eyebrows rose. "On your wrist," she said, pointing.

"What?" I brought up my hand. "The watch?"

260

"Wow. I haven't heard it called that in awhile." She gave a crooked smile and started buttering toast.

I studied it closely; leather band, face trimmed in silver. But there were no buttons. The obsidian material inside the trimming had a life of its own. Faint numbers faded in and out in a cryptic pattern. I let out a sigh.

"Come here." Annie put down the toast and came around the counter. "I'll show you." She lifted my hand and touched the face. "Dial Stephen Andrews." The watch came to life. Annie gave me a wink, and returned to her work.

"Hello?" said the watch.

"Hi, Stephen, this is Thomas!" I spoke loudly into the watch.

"Thomas! It's great to hear your voice! Why are you yelling?"

"Oh, sorry." I pulled my hand away and lowered my voice. "Is this better?"

"Much. Hey, Annie said you were awake! How are you, man?"

"Not bad considering the circumstances."

"I can't imagine."

"Yeah, well, I need you to do something for me."

"Sure thing. What can I do for you?"

"Find a number for a woman named Hazel Brown. Her address is 128 Pinrow Street, Marathon, Florida."

Annie shot me a look of curiosity.

"You could just..." He stopped. "You know what-- no problem. Hold on a sec."

Sam looked over his shoulder. You can just ask the terminal to snatch the data."

I squinted at him. "Oh. --I'll do that next time. I'm just used to calling the office to have someone search for information."

Sam smiled. "We don't search for information anymore. We have digital servants for that."

"Thomas?" The watch spoke up.

"Yes, Stephen."

"Do you, ah, have a pen?"

Sam masked another smile. Apparently he was amused at Steven's attempt to shield me from future shock.

"No. Just give it to me. I'm good with numbers, remember?"

Steven chuckled. "Yes. I remember. I've never known anyone who could crunch numbers like you. Here it is, 818-555-3234."

"Thanks, man. Listen, I'm sorry to cut this short, but I have to let you go."

"Hey, just one thing. Some gentlemen came by a little while ago looking for you. I was going to call you."

My heart constricted. "Who- what did they want?"

"They were from the FBI, really *strange* looking guys, they wanted to know if I'd heard from you.

My heart skipped a beat. "You didn't tell them anything. And what do you mean *strange?*"

"It was like-- like they were straight out of a men's catalog or something, every hair in place, perfect clothes, *perfect* skin, a little *too* perfect. It was *weird.*"

I looked at Annie, her eyes were wide.

"But I didn't tell them anything. Annie told me what happened at the center, so I told them you were in a coma last I knew."

"When was this?"

"A half hour ago."

"Okay, Steven. Thanks, man. Let me know if anything else happens, okay?"

"Sure. And hey, when all this blows over, we need to get together. Last time I checked, you still own this company."

"Yeah," I said, distracted. "Thanks again. Give my regards to Amy."

There was a pause. "Sure, no problem, man. Take care."

I shot Annie another look. She was wincing. "I should have told you. --Amy died in a skiing accident a few years back."

"Oh," I said, lowering my arm. "I'll have to be more careful."

She set a plate back on the counter. "Those men sound like the one I saw at the center."

"I know."

"What do you think we should do?" she said, wringing her hands.

"I don't know." I studied her expression. "What do you think?"

"Well, we can't stay here." She glanced out the window. "They're probably on their way by now."

"You're really scared aren't you?"

She gave a quick nod.

"You and the kids need to disappear, just go somewhere and don't tell anyone."

"Thomas. We're staying with you."

"But you're not *safe* with me."

Sam got off the couch and walked toward us. "You're not in any condition to go anywhere by yourself. We need to stay with you."

Annie's eyes were pleading. "Sam's right, Thomas. We just got you back, I don't want to take a chance of losing you again."

I looked at Annie, then back at Sam. "Well, I *need* to find out what's going on, and that's going to draw attention to me..."

Sam gripped my shoulder. "We're in this together. This is *our* problem."

I studied them again, then let out a sigh. "Well if there's no changing your minds, at least meet me half way."

The satisfaction on Annie's face was obvious. "What is it you want us to do?" she asked gently.

"While they track me here, I'm going to scatter my

263

trail and try to find Hazel Brown."

Again, Annie gave me a curious look.

"She's the only lead I have." I pulled the envelope from my pocket and held it out. "Solomon told me to give this to her." Annie slid it from my grasp and opened it. "I know it doesn't make any sense," I said, "but it must be important somehow."

"This is it?" She held up the tiny piece of paper.

Sam came around and looked over her shoulder.

"Yeah, that's what doesn't make sense. Why would he ask me to deliver a packet, with just my *name?*"

"Are you supposed to mail it?" Sam asked.

"I don't know. Everything happened so fast, I don't remember exactly what Solomon said. But I'm guessing this Hazel Brown knows *something,* and I want to know what she knows."

They both nodded.

"Which means, I need to go to Florida to find her. And if those men tracking me are the same ones who want me *dead*, I don't want to put my family in danger."

"But you just agreed to let us..."

I put my hand up. "Annie, we can all go to Florida, but when we get to Marathon, you and Rebecca need to stay behind for a bit-- just until we know it's safe. Okay?" I looked over at Rebecca, quietly sitting on the couch.

She read my expression, then slowly nodded. "I trust you, Dad."

My whole face became a warm smile.

"Andy lives in Homestead," Annie said abruptly. "We could stay at his place. Plus, we'll have access to the Florida branch if we need it."

"We have a branch in *Florida?*"

"You always talked about how much you loved it there." She shrugged.

"You are a faithful woman, Annie Tardin."

Her eyes sparkled. "I have my moments."

Chapter Twenty-six

THE FALLEN

$$\delta$$

The trip from Haiti to Miami was surprisingly uneventful. Several times I tried to call Hazel Brown, but she was unavailable. I was, however, welcome to leave a message.

In Miami we had a company car brought to the airport under strictest secrecy. Sam and I dropped Annie and Rebecca off at Andy's in Homestead, then continued on down the Florida Keys to Marathon.

"Pinrow!" I said with a point.

"Blinker- on," said the synthetic voice of the car. "Turning- *left*- onto- *Pinrow- Street.*" The digital voice was *annoyingly* perfect.

"Can we turn that thing off?" I said, searching the dashboard. "It's getting on my nerves."

"GPS voice off," said Sam, giving me a big grin.

I gave him a big smirk. "I could have done *that.*"

Slowly we rolled down Pinrow Street to a one story white stucco home. "There it is," I said, pointing. "128."

Sam drove past it, turned around in a driveway a few houses down, then pulled to the side of the road. "Now what?" he asked.

"Well, it looks like there's no one home, but..." As I spoke a tiny compact electric car pulled into the driveway. An overweight, short, black woman in an bright orange dress stepped out. She reached into the car and came out clutching a stack of papers and a briefcase. Awkwardly, she scurried up the front steps and disappeared inside the house.

"That must be our lady," I said.

"*She* is going to help us?" Sam looked at me with eyebrows raised.

"That's the plan," I said, checking out the back window. "I'll go talk to her. You stay here, and call me if you see anything suspicious."

"O-*kay.*" He nodded. "How long will you be?"

"If I haven't contacted you in fifteen minutes, come looking for me," I said, stepping out of the car. Slowly I walked toward the house, casually scanning the area. As I reached the front steps, I took another scan of the neighborhood, then gave the doorbell a poke.

There were footsteps, then the sound of a deadlock. The door creaked open slowly. A face appeared in the crack. "Are you him?"

"I have an envelope for you."

"Come in quickly," she said, pulling on my arm.

Inside, the shades were drawn, causing the otherwise normal interior to look dark and foreboding. I followed her into an office where she sat down at a computer. She tapped a button on the desk then reached her hand toward me. "The envelope please."

"Don't you even want to know who I..."

"I know who you are." She reemphasized her outstretched hand. I handed her the envelope and she opened it quickly. A smile crossed her face. "How appropriate," she said, tapping the button again. "Load file twelve. Enter letter sequence, cap T, lower h,o,m, bold **a,** unbold, s, space, t,a,r,d, bold **i,** unbold, n."

I shook my head. Of course it was a *code.* How could I have missed it?

The screen responded to her commands and the face of Doctor Solomon appeared. "Hello, Miss Brown. I'm sorry we can no longer talk directly, but I do need more information. I have uploaded the latest data to the site. Please use this new sequence to decrypt the access code. And please tell Thomas I am sorry for our less than auspicious meeting, and that I am grateful for his assistance. I will contact you again by currier at the new address listed in the data. May the true God bless you and protect you."

The True God? Dr. Solomon was a religious man?

Hazel set the note aside. "Download Vrin encryption with access password." The screen went crazy, then became dark again. Hazel swiveled around. "We need to go!" She grabbed a transparent cube from an indent in the desk and stood up.

"Dad?" said my watch. "A black van just pulled up in front of the house."

Hazel's eyes rounded. "They were quicker this time."

Quicker? Was she referring to how fast they had gotten to the house after she accessed the information? That wasn't quick, that was impossible!

She clutched my arm. *"This way!"* We scurried down the hall and out the back door, down the steps and into a concrete cylinder, which lay sideways along the back of the house.

"Plug your ears, honey! It's gonna be *loud!"*

My fingers barely reached my ears as the shock wave of the explosion hit. The concrete creaked and shuddered. Loud thumps sounded.

"Move!" she said, scurrying out.

Dust and smoke hit my face as I climbed out on shaky limbs. And saw what was left of the house.

Together we stumbled down the street to where Samuel sat behind the wheel. Terrified. "They *walked through* the walls!" he screamed, as we climbed into the car.

"Go! *Quickly!"* Hazel ordered from the back seat.

267

"WHAT *WERE* THOSE GUYS!" Sam shrieked. His knuckles were white on the steering wheel.

"Now!"

He turned the key and peeled out onto the road. "I am *freaked out,* Dad!"

I twisted and looked over the seat at Hazel. *"What just happened?"* My voice came out in a high pitch.

She had the briefcase on her lap and was frantically typing.

"Hazel, *What just HAPPENED?"*

"Turn on to Route 1." Her voice was calm.

I looked at Sam. *"Do it!"*

"This is *nuts!* People don't just walk through walls!"

I looked over the seat. "Hazel, who..."

"Take a turn at the next light. I'll explain in a minute," she said, still typing.

I nodded at Sam. The wheel spun and the tires screeched as we took off down a canal road. I looked back at Hazel. "It's a dead end!"

"Stop here," she said, closing the briefcase.

The car skidded to a stop and Hazel climbed out. "Come on. This way!"

Sam was at my door helping me out.

"Quickly!" yelled Hazel over her shoulder as she scurried between two stucco houses and under a clothesline.

We emerged from the houses to see a dock running parallel to the road, and Hazel, frantically untying a speed boat. Sam helped me across the yard and into the boat, then grabbed the ropes from Hazel. She climbed over the edge and hobbled to the front.

"Ho! *Wait a minute!"* Sam yelled as the boat began to pull away from the dock. The boat slowed and he jumped aboard.

I made my way up to the vinyl co-pilot's seat.

"Hazel! We need some answers!"

"I imagine you do."

"*Who were those guys?*"

"Those, my friend, were the fallen ones."

I stared at her.*" --What?* You mean, like, from Davata Notrals?"

"The very same."

My head reeled. "I find that impossible to believe."

"You don't have to believe, Thomas. Truth is truth whether you believe it or not."

"Come *on!* You're telling me we're being pursued-- by *fallen angels?*"

"Yep."

Again I stared. "O-*kay.* Let's just say I believe you, which I don't, but if I did-- *why* would fallen angels be interested in *me?*"

She kicked the boat into high gear as we headed out into the Gulf of Mexico. "Because you know too much about Vrin!" she shouted above the noise of the wind.

"Vrin?" My response was almost a scream.

"All your questions will be answered soon! We need to..." Her words were lost above the roar of the engine.

The boat bounced over the waves and I held on for dear life. My tired body was *not* appreciating this. At all! Finally the engine slowed and the boat sidled up to a run down excuse for a houseboat.

"Come on," Hazel said, quickly stepping over the side. Sam jumped out and started securing the boat. "We should be safe here," Hazel added.

I clambered onto the deck; the boards creaked loudly under my feet. "I don't feel very safe," I said, looking around.

"Quick," Hazel said, gesturing impatiently from the doorway. Sam slipped his arm through mine and helped me to the door.

Inside was cramped, but tidy. Hazel put her

269

briefcase on the tiny kitchen table, stepped down into the sunken living room, and sat down in a chair next to a very thin old black woman in a recliner. The woman was intent on watching television.

"Hey." Hazel tapped her on the arm. "These men are here to see you."

The woman looked up at me with slightly yellowed eyes and a crooked grin.

I looked at Hazel, at the woman, then back at Hazel again. "--I'm sorry. I don't understand."

"Please forgive me," she said. "There was no time to explain. I'm Nan. *This* is Hazel. She's my mother."

Chapter Twenty-seven

QUESTIONS
1 1 0 1 1 0 1

Nan motioned with her hand. "Come, have a seat, Mom is eager to speak with you."

I sat down on an orange 70's style kitchen chair in front of Hazel, looked at Nan, and motioned to the TV. "May I?" I asked. She nodded, so I reached out and turned the volume down. I turned to look at Hazel.

She looked to be around seventy, was wearing a flowered print dress, and was fidgeting with a bowl of buttons in her lap. "Full o' questions," she said in a slow monotone, not making eye contact.

"Yes," I nodded.

Her lips pursed and twitched. She stared at the arm of her chair. "Want to know-- Vrin." Her voice was distant.

"Yes," I said again.

She took my hand gently into hers, dug a button out of the bowl, and slowly placed it in my palm. Carefully she closed my fingers around it.

I looked at Nan.

"My mother has autism. I know it's awkward, but she is very gifted. If you're patient, she will explain."

I looked back at Hazel.

"You are-- chased." She shook her head slightly, still not making eye contact.

"Yes. I *am* being chased."

The tone of her voice shifted slightly higher. "No danger. No danger. You safe now.

271

I shook my head, confused. "--But they tried to *kill* me."

There was an awkward pause as she seemed to contemplate a hidden puzzle. Then her eyes focused past me. She sat motionless, staring at the silent television with her head cocked, as if trying to catch a sound from it.

"That was before they knew," offered Nan.

I looked at her. "--What?"

"Before they knowed you went back," Hazel said, almost lucidly.

I gave Nan a quizzical look.

"Those men were not chasing *you,* they were following you, to get to us."

"And why would they want to do that?"

"Because my mother knows too much about Vrin."

I tried to piece the riddles together in my head. "Wh- what's the bottom line? Are they trying to kill me or not?"

"No." Hazel looked up at the ceiling. "No danger. You *impo'tant* in Vrin."

I stared at her, dumbfounded. "--But I'm not *in* Vrin," I said slowly.

"Impo'tant in Vrin!" she blurted, shaking her head again. "Jes' don't remember!"

"Remember? Remember *what?"*

"Vrin," she whispered.

Again I stared. "But I'm not *connected* to the computer. I'm not *in* Vrin." I was beginning to get very frustrated.

Hazel's eyes scanned back and forth rapidly. *"When you sleep."*

"Sleep?" I said, trying desperately to understand. "I don't think..."

She gripped my arm and stared intently into my eyes. "You must- stop him."

I pulled away and looked desperately at Nan.

272

"When you sleep you go back to Vrin," she said. "You don't need the computer, and mom says you are supposed to stop a man who is trying to destroy it."

"It?" I squinted at her.

"Vrin, the whole thing."

My brows furrowed. "O-*kay*..." I said with sarcasm. "Let me get this *straight*. You're telling me, that when I go to sleep, I travel to the *magical realm* of *Vrin* to try to save it from an evil mastermind?"

"Well it sounds stupid when you say it like that."

"It *is* stupid!" I stood up. "Wouldn't you think it was *stupid* if you were me?"

Hazel piped up. "Not stupid. Not stupid." She cocked her head slightly, hunched her shoulders, and looked up at the ceiling. "Impo'tant."

Nan reached out and placed a tender hand on her mother's arm. "It's okay, Mom. I'll explain it to him."

Hazel tapped her head lightly with her knuckles. "Okay, okay. Okay."

"Yes, Mom, it's okay."

"Okay. Good girl, Nan. Good girl."

Nan looked at me. "I know this is a lot to digest, and you're getting it thrown at you all at once, but please be patient."

"I don't mean any disrespect. But I came here to get answers. And this is *not* what I expected."

"Believe me, I understand your skepticism. I didn't believe it either, but I do now. I've seen things that would make your blood run cold."

I listened uneasily.

"My mother, as I said, has autism. Are you familiar with autism?"

"Yes. I've heard of it."

"Well, some people with autism can play the piano without ever being trained, others can figure out enormous equations in their heads-- things like that. Well, my mom

273

can remember her dreams, and what lies beyond. *That* is where Vrin is."

I responded with silence.

Nan placed her hands in her lap and straightened the fabric of her dress. "Can I get you a drink while we discuss things?"

"Do you have tea?" I said, grateful to change the subject, if even for a moment.

"Yes. Do you like herbal?"

"That would be fine, but if you have Earl Grey..."

"Yes, I believe we do have some Earl Grey around here. How 'bout you?" She gave Sam a glance.

He was sitting quietly on a chair by the door, taking everything in. "Any soda will do."

Nan turned up the TV as she passed by. "There's a lot to tell, but I don't think all of it is relevant to your situation."

I stepped up into the kitchen. "Perhaps we could address the most important question first. *Why* did those men want me dead?"

Nan put a teapot on the stove. "You were in danger in the lab because they didn't know how much, if anything, you would remember about Vrin. They don't want any information leaking out. But since your escape, you have slept and returned to Vrin. They must know now that you have returned, and that you are still important in Vrin."

"Yes, so you've said, but what does that *mean?"*

"First, let me explain what Vrin *is,* perhaps that will help."

"All right," I said, incredulously.

She paused, gathering her thoughts. "--There is a place we go when we sleep, a world that exists between life and death. When we sleep here, we go there. When we sleep there, we come here."

"Back and forth. "

"Yes. But it is extremely complicated. It isn't as

274

simple as passing back and forth." She handed a soda to Sam. "Everyone who believes and trusts in God, goes to Vrin. We believe it is the last human battlefield. There is a war going on in that realm which most are completely unaware of. However, it has devastating implications for eternity."

"But you said *I* go there when I sleep, and that I am important there. How is that possible, when I don't even *believe* in God?" As I said the words, I realized that I was unsure if it were still true. What had changed my mind, if indeed my mind had been changed?

"I don't think you truly realize your connection with God." Nan picked up a leather bound book and handed it to me. The cover read, *DAVATA NOTRALS*: *The Holy Truth.*

I stared at it. "And what do you want me to do with *this?*"

"Turn to the Book of Reason."

I hesitated, then cracked it open. "Where is it?"

"Near the end."

When I got there, she flipped one page, then pointed. The verse read, "In those the last days, God rose up the prophet Tardin, who having the secret to The Circle, turned the tide of darkness. And God banished Kric' tu with Rath in flames."

"You *are* that prophet."

I looked at her in total disbelief, then held the book out. "If this thing is from *God,"* I said, letting out a cynical laugh. "Then why is *wrath* spelled wrong?"

She smiled. "You cannot run from your destiny, Thomas."

"I'm *sorry.* This is all just a *little* too far fetched for me."

Sam interrupted. "I saw those men go *through* the walls, Dad. I'm ready to believe *anything."*

"Well *I'm* not ready," I said, sitting down. Nan and Samuel stared at me expectantly. "Okay," I said, "So let's

275

just suppose you're right, which I'm not saying you are, but *if* you were-- what does it *mean?"*

"We don't know yet," said Nan. "We're hoping the code will tell us."

I blinked at her. I did not want to ask. I did not want to know. But the word came out anyway. *"Code?"*

She reached out and took the book from me. "In this book, there is a hidden code that provides information about the future. Your *name* is in the code, and we are trying to find out what God wants us to do."

Again I stared, dumbfounded. "But what if *I* don't want to do *anything?* What if I just want to go back to my *life?"*

"I don't believe God expects anything else from you, not right now anyway. You were only meant to bring us the code."

"But I thought I was important."

"You *are* important. But in *Vrin."*

"So they'll leave me alone now?"

She frowned. "I don't know. They may try to capture you. But I don't think they'll hurt you, now that they know you returned to Vrin."

That was hardly comforting! "What about my family?"

She took the teapot off the stove. "They're not important."

Here, words could not convey my frustration and turmoil. I put my head in my hands.

She placed a steaming cup in front of me. "Everything is working out as it should, Thomas," she said gently. "You just need to trust in God. He has a plan."

"Look." I lifted my head. "I'm not a *fairy tales* kind of guy. This whole thing, although disturbingly convincing, is just a little *too* much. I'm not a prophet, and believe it or not, I have *no* interest in fighting fallen angels. I want my life back. I want to run my company. And I want to get to

276

know my family. So, with *whatever* is going on here, I wish you well. But I would appreciate it if everyone would just leave me alone."

"I don't know if they will leave you alone."

"Well I'm not going to fight them, and I'm not putting my family in danger." I looked at her defiantly.

She shrugged. "You may not have a choice."

"Then I'll just have to find a deep dark hole to hide my family in and lay low till everything passes over."

She nodded slowly. "We've been living in the last days for over two-thousand years. It can't be much longer."

I pushed my cup away. "I'll give you a way to contact me, in case you to."

"I'll let you know when it is safe to live your life again, Thomas." She stared at me intently. "You're positive you don't want to be a part of what we're doing?"

"This isn't my fight, Nan. This a war for-- *religious* people. I'm a man of science."

"Science and religion are not opposites."

"In my world they are."

She frowned, and I stood. "Come on, Sam, let's go," I said, starting toward the door.

"Actually, Dad, I was thinking." He looked at Nan. "Maybe I should stay here awhile, if Nan and Hazel don't mind."

I looked at him, aghast. "You *can't* be serious."

"I think one of us should stay close to what's happening, so if things start to stir up we'll be prepared. Besides, I like all this mystery stuff. I want to know more." He gave me a searching look. "If things get too crazy, I can always come join you." He turned to Nan. "Would you mind if I stayed?"

Her eyebrows rose. "It's pretty cramped in here, and my mom can be quite a handful. Are you *sure?"*

Sam laughed. "I mean, here in Marathon, in a condo or something-- so I can help you."

277

"Alright," she said with an approving smile. "As long as you follow my rules, and don't go bringing any unwelcomed guests back to my doorstep."

They both looked at me for approval.

I let out a long sigh. "I can't tell you what to do, Sam. But I hope you won't go doing anything crazy; we barely know each other, and that's a problem I was hoping to rectify."

Sam beamed. "So you really don't mind? You'll let me stay?" He looked at Nan, then back at me.

Nan nodded.

Reluctantly, I did the same.

I stood staring at my son for a long moment, then walked toward the living room. "It was nice to meet you, Hazel."

"Impo'tant in Vrin!" she said, not taking her eyes from the TV screen."

I closed my eyes and shook my head. "Yes, Hazel," I said slowly. "Important in Vrin." I turned and looked at Sam again. He was suppressing a smile.

"Come on," said Nan, picking up her keys. "I'll bring you back to shore."

"Thank you. I need a break. I'm definitely not ready for anything else."

Sam's eyes reflected disappointment. "Do you think you'll ever be ready?"

"Sam." My shoulders slumped. "I wish I could help, but this whole thing isn't me. This is something your mom might do. She's the one who fights the good fight, the one who struggles to make the world a better place. I'm an engineer, I invent things. I don't..." I paused, looking for words. "I don't *battle* the forces of evil."

His eyes turned soft. "You could."

I gripped his shoulders firmly. "I'm proud of you, son. You seem to be the best of your mother and me. Give me some time to rest and get my head screwed on right, okay? Then maybe we'll see if I can be the hero."

He smiled warmly. "I'll call tomorrow and give you an update."

"Okay, you do that, and keep your head down." I gave him an awkward hug.

Nan brought me back to the mainland where a cab was waiting near the canal. I struggled up the rusted, barnacle-covered ladder and stood up on the pavement. I looked back down into the little boat. "I'm sorry, Nan," was all I said.

The boat pulled away from the dock. "For what?" she asked. Then, not waiting for a reply, added, "You'll come around, you just don't know it yet."

The way she said it, it was hard to take offense. But what if I didn't *want* to come around? Didn't I have a say in the matter? What if I didn't *want* to go on some crazy crusade for God? Was it wrong for me to want my life back? God had already taken twenty-one years without asking! I didn't owe him anything. Whatever I was supposed to give back into the universe, I was sure I had already paid every penny. With interest.

"You coming, mister.?"

My eyes blinked as I turned to look at the cabbie. "Yes, sorry," I said, opening the back door. I climbed in. "Homestead, please."

He tapped the GPS screen on the dashboard, and spoke the command, "Homestead." A dollar figure appeared in the corner of the map. The cabbie put his foot on the gas, and the car took off like a golf cart.

It didn't take long to realize that sitting idle in the back of a cab for an hour and a half was a bad idea. Left with nothing to do but think, my imagination ran wild. Dark thoughts stepped on my chest-- making it hard to breath.

Why did God have to pick *me?* I had everything a man could want. I was a captain of industry. I had an adoring wife, a perfect daughter, a son on the way. And I had earned every bit of it! I had *paid* my dues, and was on the threshold of enjoying the fruits of my labor! But in the blink of an eye, everything had vanished, leaving only this nightmare, this horrible cage of circumstances. --*Why me?* Why not someone who *wanted* to do God's bidding? Sam's face flashed in my mind. Was that it? Had God picked Sam? Was he the one God wanted? The more I thought about this, the more it made sense. He had my ingenuity, and his mothers philanthropy.

I chuckled at myself. Was I actually beginning to buy into this craziness? It didn't matter-- I still didn't want to be involved. This was a matter for monks or priests-- or *whatever.* I wanted no part of it.

I committed myself to not thinking about it, and instead stared out the window at the passing urban sprawl-- looking for all the ways the world had changed while I was asleep.

Eventually, the cab pulled up in front of Andy's. I paid with my fingerprint, and the machine bleeped happily. "Thanks, man," said the cabbie. "Have a nice day."

"You too. Thanks." I stepped out and looked up at the house. I had never felt so exhausted in all my life. On shaky legs I made my way up the stone walkway, then dragged myself up the stairs, and opened the front door. Annie and Rebecca were sitting in the living room.

"Where is everyone?" I asked from the doorway.

Annie stood up and came toward me. "They're at a soccer game, the state finals. She looked past me. Where's Sam?"

"He stayed with Hazel."

Her eyes snapped up at me.

"He's fine," I said. "Hazel has insight into what's going on at the center. And Sam wants to find out everything he can."

Annie blinked. "Why didn't *you* stay?"

280

"I got all the information I wanted."

She cocked her head.

"The answers are turning out to be worse than the questions." I took her by the hand and led her to the couch. "Come, let's sit down. I'm *exhausted.* Hi, Becca. How are you holding up."

"I'm fine, Dad. How are *you? What* happened?"

"Well..." I looked at Rebecca, then Annie. "You know how Solomon set up the computer to talk directly to the minds of the coma patients? And how he created a virtual world we could share?"

They both nodded.

"Hazel says I'm still going back to that world-- when I *sleep."*

Their jaws hung slack.

"And that's not even the craziest part. Hazel's daughter, Nan, told me that it's really a place between life and death-- a *spiritual* realm." The word *spiritual* stuck to my lips as it came out.

Rebecca was wide eyed as she touched her fingers to her mouth. "That's incredible."

"If it's true," I said.

Annie leaned in toward me. "You don't believe her? *Do* you?"

"Honestly, I don't know what to believe. We got chased today, by men who Sam said walked *through* walls."

Annie and Rebecca sat frozen.

"Nan called them the fallen ones."

Rebecca's eyes grew even wider. "Like-- from Davata Notrals?"

"Fallen ones, angels, demons, whatever you want to call them. Apparently *Sam* believes it, and I can't blame him. It was all very convincing."

Annie's became thoughtful. "The man I saw at the center, the one who spoke that strange language-- could he have been-- one of those?"

"If what they say is true then, probably yes."

She stared at me. "Are we in danger?"

"I don't know. Hazel and Nan say we aren't. Nan said they were only following me to get to them."

"Why?"

"Well-- Hazel is special, she has autism. Nan says she can remember her dreams, *and* a spiritual place beyond her dreams. Apparently Vrin is *in* that place." Annie looked incredulous. "I know it sounds crazy! I don't want to believe it either. But Nan believes the fallen ones are after them because they know too much about Vrin."

A sudden fear flashed through Annie's eyes. "And you left Sam *with* them?"

"I don't exactly have any authority over him. I wasn't around to be his father."

She bit her lip. "I don't like him being there."

"Well *you* tell him to come with us. Maybe he'll receive it from you."

"What do you mean, *with us?* Where are we going now?"

"I don't know, someplace hidden, remote, a place no one knows about but us."

"You don't think *fallen angels* will know where to find us?"

"They can't seem to find Hazel."

Annie folded her arms. "I don't like it."

"Which part? The *us hiding* part?"

"I'm worried about Sam. I know him, he won't walk away from this."

"Then let him fight the battle."

Rebecca put her hand on her mothers leg. "Don't worry, Mom, God will protect him."

Annie's face was devoid of emotion.

My eyes drifted up to the clock on the wall. It was only quarter past seven, but it felt more like two in the morning to me. I let out a long sigh. "I hate to do this to you, but can we talk more in the morning? I can *not* stay awake another minute."

"Yes," Annie said blankly. "Yes, of course."

I stood awkwardly and looked toward the hallway. "Where are we staying?"

Rebecca stood up. "I'll show you."

I followed her to a room at the end of the hall, where a single mattress was made up under a full skylight. I brushed past her into the room. She leaned in and gave me a peck on the cheek. "We'll figure this out, Dad, I'm not worried."

"Well, that makes one of us." I gave her a weak smile.

"Goodnight," she said, then gently closed the door. Immediately it opened back up. "Oh, Mom and I picked up a few things for you, a robe and some other stuff. They're in the bag." She pointed.

I reached down and pulled out the robe. "Thanks, honey. Tell Mom thanks too."

"I will, g'night." She closed the door.

My eyes fell on the bed, and a heaviness pressed in on my heart. There was no peace here, only a fearful anticipation. If it was true-- if Vrin *was* a real place-- would I remember? Would I sense myself going past my dreams into that mysterious world beyond? My heart quickened at the thought.

Slowly I began to undress. Maybe I'm just dreaming this whole nightmare, I thought. Maybe at any moment I'll wake up in the hotel in New York and be heading off on our vacation. Maybe there's no such thing as Vrin, or Doctor Solomon, or Nan, or Haz..." As I removed my pants, a button fell from my pocket and rolled across the floor. It was the one Hazel had placed in my hand.

I let out a long sigh.

For a moment, I stood and thought about trying to stay awake, but quickly dismissed the idea, and climbed in under the sheet. My head pressed heavily into the pillow. My eyes burned in their sockets. I stared at the ceiling fan, dreading the thought of falling asleep, yet knowing there would be no stopping it. My body was beyond exhaustion, my head was already slipping into the warm dark. I rolled over onto my side.

Oh, well, I thought, here we go, back to the *magical realm* of *Vrin*-- to save it from an evil mastermind.

"Wake up!"

The voice seemed distant.

"Wake *UP!*"

The pain in my head was excruciating. The rope on my wrists scratched and burned. I opened my eyes a slit.

"Is he awake?" came another voice.

"Arganis?" I asked dryly. "Is that you?"

The lumbering shadow before me moved aside, revealing Arganis in the flickering light of the lantern.

" I do not know you, yet you call me by name?"

"We have met before."

"We have not. I would remember such a meeting." His voice was not as friendly as I remembered it. "--The signet on your collar tells me you are from the ruling house. Are you a spy?"

"No. I have come to seek your help."

He laughed. *"My* help? What could Daru possibly want from me, a humble peasant?"

Though painful, I forced my eyes open. From my position on the floor, I counted five, maybe six figures.

"Arganis, I need to speak with you, alone."

He crouched down before me. "You may speak freely."

"I can't. It would put my life at risk."

"If you do *not* speak, *that* will put your life at risk!"

"Look, Arganis, I'm not a spy. I am a friend of

285

Sajin's.

"Sajin made no mention of you."

"Listen. He *and* Sam' Dejal sent me here with a private message."

He gave me an examining stare. "How can I trust you?"

"Do you remember your conversation with Sam' Dejal?"

He squinted at me. "--Yes."

"Do you remember how he told you about the gods dreaming a dream, and how you pondered the meaning of this world."

"Yes, of course I remember." There was curiosity in his voice.

"Arganis. The *dreamer* has awakened."

His brows knitted. "Leave us," he stated. The room quickly emptied, and soon we were alone. "What is it you wish to tell me?"

I rolled over and sat up with a grunt. My head reeled. "Did you-- hear the voice of Gaza in the sky?"

"Yes."

"*I* am the one he is looking for."

"*You* are Charm?"

"Yes."

He looked me over closely. "Why are you here? And how do you know *me?*"

"I'm here because I need to learn the magic of The Circle of Ghosts."

His eyebrows raised. "And you think I will teach you this?"

"Yes, because with that knowledge I can stop Gaza from destroying Vrin."

He assessed me with incredulous eyes. *"How?"*

"By entering the cognosphere."

"You cannot change the past by using an event cell. What Gaza has done, is done."

286

"No, I am not speaking of changing the past. I intend to *enter* the cognosphere itself."

In the flickering light of the lantern, I wasn't sure if I saw horror, or surprise on his face. "Th- that's not *possible!*"

"It is only possible if you help me. Your magic holds the key. Once in the event cell, there will be no way for me to find my way back to my physical body, unless you help me."

"You would go mad in an empty event cell."

"You are incorrect. I would not."

"Everyone who has *ever* attempted this has gone mad, how are *you* any different?"

I leaned forward, against the objection of my restraints. I looked him directly in the eye. "Because, Arganis-- I *am,* Sam' Dejal."

His face went slack. "You are already mad!"

"Arganis, listen to me. I *know* things that only *he* would know. I can tell you the conversation we had in this very cellar. We talked about the dream, and the world beyond Vrin. We drank together and chose to believe in Ethral. Then we traveled into Rath's castle. Ask me anything. I remember it all."

He sat shaking his head slowly. "How is this possible?"

"The body of Sam' Dejal still lies deep in the heart of the Citadel, but who he was, is now in *this* body."

"If you are him," He paused, "then why do you not have his power?"

"I am no longer connected to the source of the power. I have the memories of Sam' Dejal, but in every other way, I am just like you."

Again he examined me. His eyes narrowed. "How did we enter Rath's castle?"

I suppressed a smile. "First you showed me the map with the best place to enter, then I created a hole in the ground, and we went into the dungeon through the wall."

He put his hand on his chin. "If you are so interested in my magic, then why did you not ask me to use it in the dungeon?"

"Ah, but I did ask. You created smoke and a blinding flash to make my appearance to the guard more dramatic. And it worked quite nicely, if I remember correctly."

"So..." His eyebrows rose. "The god who would be man-- is now a man?"

"Yes."

"A man who needs my help."

"Most definitely."

His whole face smiled.

I returned the smile.

"This is wonderful!"

"Not so much for me."

"I'm sorry, no, of course not." He crouched down and cut the bonds from my wrists and ankles. "It must be very hard for you to be without your powers, but the implications of this are remarkable. It means the gods are human." His head cocked and his eyes focused on a distant point. "You said you were sleeping. How could you be sleeping, in the dream."

That was a very good question. One I wished I knew the answer to. "I did not wake up where I expected, so I don't have an answer to that."

"This person you are now was not the one who was sleeping?"

"No. In fact, I met the person I am now while I was still in Sam' Dejal." I started to rise.

Arganis helped me up and into a chair, his voice prattling the whole time. "Amazing! When you were Sam' Dejal, you actually met this person you are now? Did he know you, or was he someone else before you inhabited this body?"

"He was frozen."

"Frozen? Had he always been frozen?"

"No. I froze-- I mean-- this body froze while I was reading Davata Notrals at the capital. I had lived a whole life up to that point."

"And when you left Sam' Dejal, you woke as Charm?"

"Yes, but it was not what I was expecting. I expected to awake in the place I was sleeping."

"Are you still dreaming the dream?"

"I believe I am a part of the dream now."

His furry brows danced. *"Amazing!"*

"I'm glad *you* think so."

He brushed me off. "I'm sorry for my enthusiasm. I must remind myself that you are in great danger in this body. Gaza himself is searching for you, and you are without your power. I should not be indulging my petty curiosities. Please, accept my apology."

"I am humbled by your wisdom and restraint, Arganis. It would not be so with me, if I were in your place."

"Your compliment brings me great honor."

I gripped the table and stood. "It is deserving, I assure you. Now, let's get down to business."

He stepped back and allowed me room.

I thought a moment. "The cognosphere remembers everything that has ever been done, correct?"

"Indeed." There was youthful enthusiasm in his expression.

"But it doesn't just remember the past. It places the present."

The wizard's face dropped.

"What I mean is, the cognosphere remembers where everyone was standing, how big they were, what time of day it was, the odors, the sounds-- everything, right?"

"You mean, in the past?"

289

"Yes. The cognosphere remembers everything."

"I suppose it does."

"Imagine controlling all of those things, location, weight and such, in the *present* simply by telling the cognosphere that what it is recording is *different.*"

He looked down at the table, then spoke. "It knows where this candle is, but you can tell it to remember it being elsewhere?"

"Yes. Everything in this world is recorded in a book, for lack of a better word. What has happened in the past cannot be rewritten, but the page that contains the now, the present, *that* can be changed."

"And any mortal man can tap into this power?"

"No. Only one who understand the language that the book is written in, can change what is written."

His irises looked like tiny green islands on a sea of white. "And you can write this language?"

"Yes."

"Can the other gods?"

"None that I know of, except Gaza."

"That explains why he is so greatly feared."

"Yes. And why I must learn your magic to stop him."

He squinted. "How can my magic compare to such power?"

"It doesn't. But it may be my only way back. See, when a person enters an event cell, the pages of the book are turned back, and he is brought to the page where the event is written."

"Like a storybook."

"Yes. Like a storybook. But in a blank event cell, the entire book is scrambled, and I won't know what page I'm on."

His eye grew wide. "This is when the madness sets in."

"I hope not." I grimaced. "Hopefully there's a way

290

to *order* the information. I've seen the book before, and I know what it's supposed to look like. The only problem is, getting back."

"You just close your eyes..."

"What if I don't know where my eyes *are?*"

His face turned down.

"I believe your magic will help me find my way back to this body."

"How?"

That was a good question. "I don't know. I need you to show me how it works. Maybe it will spark an idea."

He shook his head sadly. "I do not see how my magic can help. It is not of this world."

"That is precisely why I think it will help me. I'm going to leave this world."

He looked at me intently. "I don't understand, but I'll show you what I know." He went to a trunk in the corner of the cellar, and removed several items from its cover. It made an awful creak as it opened.

"This," he said, pulling a heavy book from within, "is the book I told you of. It was written by my ancestor Nor' Trull. In it is all we know about the magic." He came back over, set the enormous book on the table before me, and opened to the center. The letters and numbers were written in a faded calligraphy. "See these numbers." He pointed. "They correspond to notes on this." He pulled a tarnished metal tuning fork from his pocket. It had several tines protruding from a handle. "When I strike this instrument, it tells me what sound I must make with my voice. Such as..." He hit the tuning fork against the table. The sound resonated off the wet cellar walls, and Arganis joined his voice with it. The two became a perfect match-- and I felt something brush past me.

"What was that?"

"The magic responding to the command."

"What was the command?"

"I asked it to make a box around you."

I reached out and my hands came in contact with something. It gave way as I pushed on it. "It moves?"

"Only because we are far from The Circle. If we were closer, it would not move, and you would see it as I have envisioned it in my mind."

"You communicated what you were thinking, through music?"

He laughed. "It is not that amazing, I'm afraid. The magic can be anything I want it to be. The sound is just what tells it to listen to me. There are actually only five notes."

My jaw went slack. "Only five? How does it know?"

"The magic is like a gas, and I make it a solid. It responds to my thoughts. All I do, is give it the sound, then imagine what I want."

"What are the sounds?"

"Like I said, there are five sounds. Each corresponds with a command. The commands are: *create*, *destroy*, *move*, and *move me*."

"That's only four."

"Yes. I don't know what the fifth one is."

"Doesn't it say in the book?" I looked down at the page. "Speaking of the book, this is a large book for only five notes. I thought you said he catalogued all the vibrations."

Arganis smiled, and the smile touched into his eyes. "He didn't realize till the end of the book that it was his thoughts producing the effects." He flipped the book to the last page. On it were the five notes with their corresponding command word. The description for the fifth note was scratched beyond recognition.

"Who did this?" I rubbed my fingers where the book had been damaged.

"I do not know. My father forbade me to ask about

292

it."

"So this is it, five notes."

"Yes, and the closer you get to The Circle, the more real your creations become."

"Fascinating." I ran my eyes down the page, pronouncing the words in my head. *Create. Destroy. Move. Move me.* "The first three I understand, but what is *move me?*"

He stepped back and began to sing, and as the song filled the room, his feet lifted from the ground, and he floated to the other side of the room.

I couldn't help myself. "You're flying!"

"It will take me any way I wish to go."

I leaped to my feet. "That's it!"

"What is?"

"That's how I will return from the event cell! I'll use the fourth note!"

The wizard dropped back to the ground. "Well then," he said, smiling with satisfaction, "let's teach you how to make the sounds!"

Chapter Twenty-nine

THE COGNOSPHERE
1 1 0 1 1 0 1

9

The lesson was over, and I waited patiently. Soon the stairs began to creak, and a dark form entered the room. As he came into the light of the candles I recognized him. I could not remember his name, but the face was familiar. He was a stout bald man, and was garbed in clothing I knew well, the uniform of the Sky Searchers League. His eyes gleamed as he approached. It was clear he recognized me as well. This was not uncommon, I was sky searcher to the throne, and there wasn't a sky searcher in the kingdom who did not know my name-- a name made even more famous by my recent run in with Gaza.

"This is Gadson," said Arganis. "He is a trusted friend."

The man bowed low. "I am honored, Charm."

"It has been many years," I replied.

Arganis snapped a look at me. "You know each other."

"I believe we met once, at the capital."

"I forget, you lived many years before..."

I brought my hand up. "We should move forward with what we came to do."

I could see the apology on his face. He had almost revealed more to Gadson than I would have liked.

Arganis held his hand out toward his friend. "May I have the event cell."

Gadson took a leather bag off his shoulder and

handed it to Arganis. Arganis opened it and held it out to me. "Do you mind if Gadson stays with us? I would feel more comfortable."

"Not at all," I said, reaching into the bag. I drew out the event cell. It was cold and hard in my hands. I lifted my eyes toward Arganis. "Are you ready?"

His eyebrows raised." What's more important is, are *you* ready?"

I shrugged. "Ready as I'll ever be, I guess. If I don't come out in a few seconds, you know what to do." I began to lift the cell to my forehead.

Gadson's hand shot out and clutched my wrist. "It is empty, did Arganis not tell you?"

Arganis placed his hand on Gadson's arm. "It is alright, my friend. He knows."

Panic flashed in Gadson's eyes. But he released his grip on me, and stepped back He knew better than to probe us with questions.

I looked at each of them. "Right then. Let's get this over with." I gritted my teeth and placed the cell to my head.

--All was still.

In the distance-- a faint heart beat.

Darkness-- in all directions.

Emptiness penetrating my very being.

There was a sound, but I could not tell from where. It grew in intensity. Growing louder. Drowning out the rhythm of my heart.

Sensory input ENGULFED me, like a carnival ride out of control! *Terror* welled up. If it didn't *stop,* I would be *destroyed!* Overpowering! Intensity increasing! Beyond my ability- to process. Must see *beyond!* Beyond the madness! *I MUST access the program!* My mind reached out into the maelstrom. And I heard a voice scream, *"STOP!"*

Darkness enveloped me.

Was that *my* voice? It sounded like me.

I heard it again, way off in the distance. "List program."

The program began to scroll before me, or was it *through* me? I perceived it on many levels, all things at once: letters on a screen, smells, sounds, events... No dimension, yet all dimensions at the same time. I explored it like a thought, and it revealed its code to me as thought. In it I saw the creation of Vrin, and the end of Robert Helm.

A flash and a memory.

"Daddy?"

"Yes, Constance."

A little girl came up behind her dad, sitting amid a pile of papers on his bed. He turned, and she hugged him. She put her cheek on his. "How long are you going to work?" She pouted.

"Daddy is very busy, honey."

Another flash.

The man screamed as he floated in an empty void. Erratic smells and sounds. Nothing made sense.

Another memory.

The little girl, lying in bed, her father placing a book on the night stand.

"Daddy?"

"Yes, Constance."

"How come we don't have a secret handshake?" She looked up at him with big blue eyes.

He gave her a tender smile. "We *do*. I just haven't shown you yet."

Another flash, another scream, and another memory.

"Honey! You forgot your briefcase!"

The man ran back up the walkway, reaching for the case. But his wife held it from him. Playfully she grabbed his tie and pulled him in close. "You look sexy in your new suit."

He gave her a quick kiss and a half smile. "Sorry

about the meeting tonight."

"You are a great man, Robert. And great men must make great sacrifices." She straightened his tie. "And don't forget, we're in this thing together."

He gave her another kiss. "You always say that. I don't deserve you."

"I know." She winked.

"Daddy?"

The man crouched down. "What is it, honey?"

"You're gonna be at my party tomorrow, right?"

He smiled. "I haven't missed one yet."

She squeezed his neck, then looked up at her mother with an expectant look. The woman rolled her eyes, then obediently turned around. Grinning with satisfaction, the little girl clinched her hand into a fist, then swooped her pinkie like a J. Her dad did the same. Gently she pressed her tiny fist against her father's and whispered, "tap, tap, tap."

Another flash.

Robert Helm writhed in pain, as sensation after sensation flooded into his mind. But he held on to the memories. He could not let them go.

A light flashed in the rearview mirror. Robert reached up to adjust it. "Constance, put that flashlight down, honey. You can't flash that while I'm driving. It blinds me."

Rain pounded against the windshield.

"Robert! Look out!" his wife screamed. A large animal was standing in the road. Frantically, he twisted the wheel. The car careened out of control.

Darkness-- and a single heartbeat. The heartbeat began to fade, until it was so faint, I could barely hear it.

Somewhere off in the distance, the young girl's voice echoed. "Daddy? Are you awake? Daddy--? *Daddy!* Wake up, Daddy! Daaaaaadddddddy!"

All was silent.

297

The void surrounded me again, and in it, the mounting *anger* of Robert Helm, as fierce and dangerous as a cornered animal. And it was here-- that Gaza was born. The program probed him, and he was its teacher. But with each mistake there was pain. I watched as he created the strands, and then Vrin from them. I saw mountains rise, and rivers begin to flow.

Then I watched as he created the first inhabitant of Vrin, his wife. But she had no soul, and it only caused him pain to look at her. So he made a man, and sent the two off into Vrin.

I rose with him high above Vrin, and watched as he increased the speed of the simulation. A year was as a second, and the population of Vrin increased. Cities were built, civilizations formed. In silent amazement, I watched.

And then, something I did not expect, an error in the code. The simulations stopped obeying the program. And began rewriting it. Cities changed. Great structures were built. I watched as my beloved city of Oonaj grew and changed. The Eiffel, the Great Pyramid, the White House, all appeared in a flurry of human activity.

Then suddenly, everything stopped.

Gaza searched the code, and followed the strings-- but he could not unravel the mystery. This was not the Vrin he had created. These people were not the simulants he had prepared for this world. The ones he'd created all looked the same. But these each possessed a unique physical appearance.

I watched as Gaza retreated high into the mountains to build his fortress, then sped forward as the history of Vrin washed over me like a controlled river. I requested information, and it came out of the rushing torrent for me to analyze. I wanted to know if there was an event where Gaza had tried to effect time again. There was one, but it hadn't worked. He could no longer alter Vrin at that level.

Again I sped forward. I desired to know by what

means Gaza would destroy Vrin, but the computer did not understand the inquiry. So I changed the search criteria and requested options for shutting Vrin down. The computer ran the request, but did not give a result. According to the computer, a similar request had been made before, and rather than show me the result, it ran the logged event.

I saw Gaza in his fortress, in the same room I had been in. Only now, in the center of the room, was a circle of stones. Gaza stood in the midst of the rocks. Methodically he began to build a structure out of the web, a large metal platform with a hole in its center.

He ran to the side of the platform, and looked off the edge at a hovering monitor. It showed a cross section of a three dimensional wire diagram, a schematic of Vrin-- but I could not see all of it from my position. By the force of my will, I merged into the information on the monitor and instantly every path and every circuit was knowable to me. At once I understood it. I knew every implication of the structure Gaza was creating, and I knew why he was creating it around The Circle of Ghosts. The Circle was the key. It could save Vrin. Or it could destroy it.

Everything I had previously understood about Vrin flip-flopped in my mind. The magic leaking into Vrin from The Circle was not separate and foreign, as I had thought. Everything in Vrin was *made* from it. The computer was molding and shaping the energy according to the will of the ten coma patients; creating, in essence, a bottle. What Arganis called magic, was nothing more than unused energy. And The Circle was nothing more than the opening to the bottle. --But now it was letting more than energy in. It had let Kric'tu in. There was life outside the bottle, life which now had access to Vrin.

Gaza could have made his device with only one function, to explode and destroy Vrin, but curiously, he had not. There was a second use: the device could also implode and seal the opening, but not before sucking all of the

299

untamed energy from Vrin. He intended to save Vrin, *if* he could find his wife and daughter.

But that was impossible now. Or was it? Gaza knew Kric'tu had killed the woman and child, but he said it was a lie. Could his real wife and daughter be alive and well in Vrin? If they were, and if he found them, then he would save Vrin. But if they weren't, I would have to close The Circle myself.

I knew what I had to do.

I couldn't close my eyes, because I had no eyes. So I wiped the imagery from my mind and began making the vocal harmonic for travel as Arganis had taught me. It was faint, but enough. The void filled with a ghostlike mist. I continued with the note until three glowing figures materialized within the fog. Activating the energy with the harmonic, separated the energy being controlled by the computer, from the untamed energy.

I asked the energy to bring me toward the three figures, and it responded to my desire, just as the threads had done when I was Sam' Dejal. The figures grew closer, but, which one was me? I sensed a current in the energy and let it take hold of me. It brought me closer, and closer, until...

Air rushed into my lungs and I dropped the event cell. Arganis grabbed me and helped me to a chair. "Get him a drink, Gadson!" Footsteps trailed off as I opened my eyes. Arganis was wearing a broad smile. "You have journeyed to an undiscovered country, my friend!"

"I have to get to The Circle." My voice was weak.

"What did you see?"

"Gaza, in The Circle, building a structure. We must get to him before he completes it."

Arganis opened his mouth to speak, but closed it again.

"I'm sorry but your questions will have to wait."

"I understand. We will help in any way we can."

300

"Thank you, Arganis. You are a faithful friend."

The wizard's features beamed with pride.

"We will need the help of the gods."

Arganis looked surprised. "You still have a connection with them?"

"I know of at least one who is willing to help." I pictured her beautiful face in my mind, and called out to her. *"Kitaya?"*

"Yes, Jason, I am here."

"I'm going to need your help."

"Yes, Jason, I'm here."

That was weird. *"What just happened?"*

"I-- couldn't hear you for a second."

"--Okay, listen, I know how Gaza is going to destroy Vrin. I need you to get the gun I gave to Armadon and then come to me quickly. Can you do this?"

"Yes. I will be there shortly."

"Thank you. I'll see you soon."

The connection dropped and I looked at Arganis. "Kitaya will bring us to The Circle. Do you have a dozen men you can trust?"

"Yes."

"Please get them quickly."

"Gadson." He took the drink from the man. "Assemble twelve of our best fighters and bring them here as quickly as you can."

"Yes, sir!" Gadson turned and ran up the cellar stairs.

"This is it." I took a drink from the wooden cup, then set it firmly down on the table. "Are you ready to go head to head with the creator of Vrin?"

He looked uncertain. "I hope you know what you doing."

I nodded slowly. "I hope so too, my friend. I hope so too."

Arganis and his twelve men, Kitaya and I, simultaneously materialized on the outskirts of The Circle of Ghosts. Looming far above us, was the massive hulk of Armadon. *He* was not about to be left behind.

In the distance an immense metal structure, resembling a large oil drilling rig, surrounded The Circle of Ghosts. Upon it, a tiny figure could be seen.

Kitaya raised her hand, and the air began to howl. "Look." She pointed. Streams of red currents beat against an invisible wall of force. "The power will not work in there, Gaza is influencing the strands."

"All of them?" Armadon's voice boomed.

She looked at him and nodded. "His mental abilities must be greater than all of us combined."

"No," I said. He knows the program. He probably wrote a little piece of code to hold this area in place. It's not a problem, hopefully it will give him a false sense of security." I started walking. "Come on."

No one questioned my answer, and together we approached the border. Upon stepping inside, the wind ceased-- and I swear I could smell apple pie.

We traveled across the hot sand toward the ominous alien architecture. As we approached, bursts of energy caused the landscape to warp and bend. As though reality itself was being altered. I turned to see Arganis' men trudging behind us. They looked resolute, but I sensed their uneasiness. When I reached the foot of the enormous structure, Kitaya came up beside me, Together we began climbing the stairs. Armadon lumbered behind.

Suddenly there came a blood curdling scream. I whipped around to see one of Arganis' men lying on the ground clutching at his hand. Some of his fingers were missing! "There appears to be some kind of invisible defense wall!" Arganis said, kneeling next to the man.

"NO!" The voice of Gaza vibrated from the structure. "No simulants allowed! Just the thief!"

302

I looked at Arganis.

"I understand," he said. "We will wait here."

Armadon stepped down and placed his massive hand on the squirming man, until the agony on his face dissipated, and the man lay still.

I acknowledged his act of mercy with a firm nod. And again faced the structure. "Let's go have a talk with Gaza."

I continued trudging up the steps, with Kitaya and Armadon close behind, the steel creaking loudly under our feet. Upon reaching the top, we found Gaza standing on the far end, staring out at the horizon. Cautiously, we approached.

"Did you bring my property?" He kept his back to us.

"I have it right here."

"Bring it."

I moved forward, and motioned to Kitaya to move around and flank him.

"See." He pointed toward the distant army encampment. "The horde of Kric' tu gathers, because I blocked their entrance into Vrin. He knows the end is near."

"Why doesn't he strike?"

"Because I have not yet started the sequence."

"What if you find your wife and daughter are not here?"

"Then there is no use for Vrin. Is there?" His voice dripped with disdain.

"You don't have to do this. Why don't you just leave?"

He shifted his weight and glared at me. "Oh I have to do this. It is *my* creation that is being *perverted* by demons! But don't worry, I will create it again, and I will *not* make the same mistakes twice."

"And if your wife and daughter *are* here?"

"Then I will spare this world, and destroy the

303

infestation." He held his hand out.

I gave up the box.

With his free hand, he withdrew an eyepiece from his pocket and touched it to the top of the cube. Hesitantly, he lifted the box to his eye and looked into it-- for a *long* moment.

Had the program found his wife and daughter? I looked at Kitaya. She stood with the gun behind her back, and gave a small shrug.

Finally gaza let out a sigh and pulled his head up from the box. At first his face was expressionless, but then quickly distorted into a look of rage. He stepped away from the rail, hauled the box back, and launched it over the edge. "ARRGGHHH!"

I covered my head and jumped back. *"Now, Kitaya! Now!"*

But there was nothing. The air became still. Did the pistol misfire? Was it out of bullets? I turned and looked at her.

She was there, quietly holding the pistol. Only, it wasn't pointing at Gaza. It was pointing, at *me*. Her lovely face lit up in a sweet smile.

Then...

she pulled the trigger.

Chapter Thirty

DANTRA

$$\alpha$$

Being dead was not at all what I had expected. It was actually quite cozy. The red velvet surface beneath me was incredibly soft, and the sweetest melody from a flute was drifting from somewhere nearby.

Two faces appeared above me. One was Annie's; the other, my mom's. Both were crying.

"He looks good," said Annie between sobs. "Don't you think he looks good?"

"Yes." Mom sniffed. "Very handsome."

"I always loved that suit." Annie blew her nose. "The funeral parlor did a nice job with him."

Funeral parlor! I grabbed the side of the coffin, sat up, and hauled myself out.

Mom and Annie continued to stare down at the body in the open casket. It was me-- and I looked dead. But I did NOT look *good!* Why do people always say *dead* people look *good?*

I waved my hand in front of Annie. No reaction. I jumped up and down waving my arms. Still nothing. Was I a ghost? Was my spirit bound to earth for some crime I had committed? I turned and scanned the room. Samuel and Rebecca were sitting in the front row, dressed all in black. If they saw me, they made no indication. I walked to the edge of the platform and looked down at all the sad faces-- row after row of relatives, friends, business associates. "Huh." I shrugged. All things considered, it wasn't a bad turnout.

A face in the third row caught my attention. She looked familiar-- but I couldn't place her. Her clothing was odd, either *foreign*, or out of date, I couldn't decide which. I recognized her radiant blond hair and piercing green eyes. Yes, I knew her! Ariel! From the Abby where I'd studied for my appointment as sky searcher. *Sky searcher?* I knew the term, but, what did it *mean?* Ariel smiled at me. Could *she* see me? I stepped down from the platform and walked up the aisle toward her, all the while keeping my gaze fixed on hers.

The room began to warp and expand until I found myself alone with her in a dense forest. Her lovely face turned up toward mine. "I waited," she said softly. "I knew you were busy with your studies, but I waited."

I crouched in front of her and found myself saying, "I know it is difficult for you, but my workload is demanding."

"You will gain what you seek, Charm. I only hope I may share in your journey."

Memories like a distant dream began to surface. Memories of an entire life lived in a beautiful and peaceful world-- peaceful, that is, until the gods came.

I stood and took a step back.

Her countenance fell. "What's wrong?"

"I'm-- Sam Dejal."

"We don't have time for this," came a gruff voice from behind me.

I twisted around and was surprised that I was still in the funeral parlor. Standing before me, unmoving, was a priest with an annoyed look on his face. There was a long pause, and I began to wonder if he had spoken at all. I leaned in close-- looking for a hint of movement.

"Can we speed things up!"

"Whoa!" I leaped back.

The priest rolled his eyes.

I squinted at him. "Do I know you?" I asked.

"My *name* is Clayton P. Wentworth," he said gruffly, "but you know me as Humphrey."

I let out a laugh. "That's right! Of course you're here. You're dead too!"

"You're not dead, ya dope!"

"What?" I looked around. "Then, what's all this?"

"It's not real. You're creating this out of the substance of Dantra."

As he said the word, there was an impression. I knew Dantra. I had been here before. In my mind I saw a wide white bridge with a multitude of people moving across. Angels of God in brilliant orange flame were flying beside the bridge, protecting us from the fallen ones. Explosions of yellow plasma erupted as the ancient ones did battle. God had called us to save one man, Robert Helm.

Humphrey smiled. "That's it, that's a good memory. Hold on to that one. And let's go!"

"Please, Humphrey, I need more."

Humphrey looked past me and his brow furrowed.

"What is it?" I glanced behind.

"I have been reminded that time is not an issue, and--" his voice lowered and he looked away, "that I need to be more patient."

"Who reminded you?" I looked around the funeral parlor.

"Someone who knows and loves you," said a female voice. I felt a gentle hand on my shoulder and turned to see a familiar face. Her eyes squinted as she produced a smile.

"Becca!" I gave her a long hug, then pulled back slightly. "Are *you* real?"

"Yes." She laughed. "I'm real. What you saw before was a creation of your mind, but I'm real."

I gave her a puzzled look. "How..."

She smiled. "I'm here to explain that, but we will

have to take it slowly, because there is great pain if you are shifted through thought too quickly here. It isn't like your dreams. Here in Dantra, your thoughts become reality."

This idea made me uncomfortable.

"See. You are already beginning the struggle." She rubbed my shoulder. "It's okay. Humphrey and I are here to assist you. We're sharing your reality, and the angels are here as well."

Humphrey interjected. "Remember Arganis?"

It took me a second, but the memories were there. "Yes. I remember him."

"He taught you how to control the energy coming from The Circle of Ghosts while you were still in Vrin."

I squinted at him. *"Where?"*

"Vrin." He began to pace. "The place he created from the energy of Dantra, the energy surrounding us now, *thought* energy."

I stared at him.

He grunted, then tried again. *"Vrin* is made from thought energy. It is real, because in Dantra thought becomes real."

"So-- is *Vrin* a shared hallucination?"

"No." He frowned. "But that's pretty close."

Rebecca spoke up. "Let's see if you can follow this. I will stop if I sense any discomfort."

I nodded.

"Beyond our dreams and past the darkness is a spirit plane called Dantra. We are in Dantra right now. Here, God teaches us about ourselves, and we carry that information back through dreams. It is *why* we sleep. Do you understand?"

"I-- think so."

"Well a man named Doctor Solomon began an experiment intended to create a connection between the comatose mind of his friend, Robert Helm, and the physical world. But it did not go as expected, because the scientists had *no* idea what they were tinkering with. Each time the computer prodded Robert's mind, Robert created substance from the energy of Dantra, and as a result, Vrin came to be."

"Vrin, yes, now I remember. That's where we were going on the white bridge."

"Exactly! God sent you and the others there. So from that time on, whenever you slept, you went to Vrin instead of Dantra. And in Vrin you lived another life, a life *completely* separated from the one you were experiencing on Earth. Each night, Thomas Tardin went to sleep and became Charm. But then Thomas had an accident and was unable to wake up, which made sleeping very difficult for Charm. Because when Charm went to sleep, he could go only as far as The Separation, but was not able to get home.

For a time, Charm was plagued with sleeplessness, but was otherwise fine-- until one night when he was sitting up late reading Davata Notrals and his consciousness was ripped from his body. His mind was pulled into the void because at that moment, the same computer that had prodded Robert Helm began communicating with Thomas." Rebecca paused. "Are you remembering?"

I nodded slowly. "It's coming back-- though I'm not sure I want to remember."

"Should we take a break?"

"No. I need to know."

"Alright." She gave a warm smile. "When the computer first began communicating with you, you were terrified because you had no control over what was happening. But eventually you adapted and created an environment in Vrin, which brought you peace. It was then that Sam' Dejal came into existence. And since time does not exist in the void, it appeared that Charm froze at the exact time you became Sam' Dejal. And for a short time you were a god-- or so you thought.

"Sam' Dejal." An image flashed in my mind. "Yes.

But I wanted to be called Jason."

"Because it was a familiar name to you. But actually, you didn't know *who* you were, and in your attempt to find your identity, you became entangled in a conflict that was not your own. And with your new abilities, you began to believe you were invincible. This led you to ruin. But when you finally came to the end of yourself, God allowed you to return to Thomas Tardin."

"Yes. But only *after* I asked for help."

"Exactly!" Rebecca flashed a brilliant smile.

I stood thinking, and the memories continued to surface. "I returned to Thomas, but-- I was in some sort of danger. Right?"

"Yes. At the center Thomas' life was in danger, so Dr. Solomon helped him escape. *But* that was all Thomas needed to do; to expect any more from *him* would have been asking too much. His life was riddled with poor choices, because it was tailored to create the man Thomas Tardin would become. But don't feel bad. God knew there would be a Vrin, and he knew there would be a Charm, and Charm's life was fashioned by God to turn *you* into a hero. All Thomas had to do was fall asleep. You returned to Vrin, and it was once again up to Charm to complete the will of God. *And* Charm was doing great-- right up to the point where he got shot."

"Why don't I remember that?"

"It will come."

"So-- who am I now?"

"You are the sum of all." She smiled. "And, Dad, although you have made some poor decisions, I love you anyway."

"Thanks. I guess." I gave her a quizzical look. "So how do *you* know so much?"

"Because I have come to the knowledge of the truth. It is in the understanding of who God is, and of what he has done for us, that we may finally see Dantra for what it is. I no longer have to struggle against myself, I can now focus on the real war. But not all who come to Dantra see it for what it is, and that brings us to Constance. She needs you."

"--Who?"

"The daughter of Robert Helm."

"Why does she need *me?*"

"You are the only one she will listen to."

Humphrey broke in. "It's time to go. You have what you need to shift through Dantra. And we have work to do."

"But, I still have questions."

Rebecca gave me the most wonderfully loving look. "Humphrey's right, you need to go. But I want you to know, I am so glad to have you for my father. I'm proud of you, Dad, and I will see you when you return." Her form began to shift and flutter into ghostly transparencies, until she dissolved away completely.

My heart sank.

"You'll see her again, lad," Humphrey said, "when we've finished our work." He waved his hand and the funeral parlor dissipated, leaving us standing on the white bridge. Here we were enveloped in a light that was love. It eased the burden on my heart, and a feeling of complete peace washed over me.

Beings of light traveled in all directions, near and far. Two of them floated down to us. I stared open mouthed as they came in close. "*Where are you going, Humphrey?*" said one, with unmoving lips.

"*To see Magnus,*" replied Humphrey, in like manner.

"*Can we help?*" he said, his voice like a song.

"*You could give us a lift. Thomas doesn't completely remember yet.*"

"*Sure thing.*"

They swooped down and grabbed us by the armpits. At the being's touch, a soothing warmth flowed through me, up into my face and out into my chest, soaking me in

311

peace.

They lifted us high into the air, and in the distance I could see our destination beginning to take form; a brilliant crystal fortress with the base appearing as a frozen spire. --And beyond this, a darkness as black as night. Cries echoed from within, desperate voices crying out in tortured agony, pleading for an end to their torment. Holding the darkness in place was a transparent barrier. Powerful angels of light hovered before it, strengthening it with coils of energy from their hands. The sight of it made my skin tremble.

"Wh- what is that?" I pointed.

"*That* is the lost land."

If not for the calming effect from the being of light, I would have lost myself in panic. My eyes grew round. "Is-- *that* where we're going?"

Humphrey scowled with disgust and nodded.

The being leaned in close to my ear and spoke out loud. "You are brave to return."

Return?

My heart beat faster as we approached the fortress. The being gently placed me onto the translucent bricks at the entrance, then rose back up into the air. I lifted a hand toward him. It was meant to be a wave goodbye, but as I did it, I realized I was reaching for him, not wanting him to go, not wanting him to take away the feeling of peace. The love I'd felt back at the bridge was fainter here, and my own emotions were disconcertingly strong.

"Thank you," I said, still reaching. My voice sounded faint in my ears.

"*You are very welcome,*" he sang. "*It is not often we get to help a prophet.*"

A prophet? The word forced a memory to surface. I was *not* yet a man of God, but God had chosen me anyway. He'd sent his angels into the dark land to bring me out. I had been in Dantra-- but the struggles of life were weighing

312

me down. I remembered the pain of being in the love of God. It was painful because I held on to destructive things. Thomas was a shrewd businessman, an overachiever driven by success-- but with success came difficult choices-- choices that effected the lives of thousands...

Humphrey smacked me. "Think while you walk, lad. If you stop every time you get a revelation, we'll never get there." He turned and entered into an enormous engraved archway. Reluctantly, I followed.

Deep inside the courtyard of the crystal fortress, the light was much stronger than the light outside, and this light was also love. Love and light were the same. In my mind, words from Davata Notrals echoed: *Good lives for the day and the brightness of the sun, but evil flourishes under the dim light of the moon.* It was a metaphor. The sun was a representation of God's love. The moon was simply a reflection. Kric' tu was the moon. He was once the greatest of God's angels, but he was merely a reflection, a reflection that grew dimmer as he moved away from God. Some loved Kric' tu, because they loved darkness, they believed the darkness would hide their wicked deeds.

At the end of the courtyard was another angel and the light reflecting from *him* was blinding. Though the light was weaker here, this angel seemed to magnify its reflection.

He lifted his wings high into the air. "WELCOME!" His voice was deep and resonating. "I AM MAGNUS. I STAND IN THE PRESENCE OF THE ONE TRUE GOD. COME. I WILL TELL YOU WHAT YOU MUST DO."

"Do we *have* to do this?" I whispered.

"I don't," said Humphrey.

My throat constricted. "You're not coming with me?"

"I'm coming with you." He scowled. "I just don't have to."

We approached the foot of Magnus.

313

"DO NOT BE AFRAID. GOD HAS CHOSEN YOU, AND YOU HAVE DONE WELL. THE DAUGHTER OF ROBERT HELM IS IN THE LOST LAND-- AND YOU MUST MAKE A CHOICE. WILL YOU RISK YOUR LIFE FOR HERS, THAT YOU MIGHT SAVE YOUR ENEMY?"

Save my *enemy?* Thomas would have said no, he would have chosen his own needs. I did not like what Thomas had become, and was thankful that God had given me a second chance with Charm. He had learned the value of selflessness. I liked Charm. I chose Charm.

"Yes. I will."

"WELL CHOSEN. TAKE YOUR SWORD AND ENTER THE PORTAL."

I could see the portal behind him, swirling around in melted gold and silver spirals. But I did not see the sword he spoke of. I looked at Humphrey.

He let out an irritated sigh. "Your *sword* is in your mouth."

My tongue rolled in response.

"Words are our sword."

I gave him an uncomprehending look.

"In Dantra, even in the lost land, *truth* cannot be denied. If you speak truth, it must be obeyed."

"And--" I looked at him sideways. "What *is* truth?"

"It is what sways the hand of God. *He* is our weapon."

His reply did not answer my question, but I didn't press the point, partly because of the towering angel watching me with fierce eyes, and partly because Humphrey was already walking toward the portal. I hurried to catch up. He passed through without hesitation, but I was not so comfortable with the idea. Although this was not my first trip to the lost land, it *was* my first time entering with the understanding of what it actually *was*-- to an extent. The memory had not completely returned, but what I did

314

remember made me realize that I did *not* miss this place.

I closed my eyes tightly, and pushed through.

On the other side, was darkness. And it was complete. My short nervous breaths sounded much louder than they should have, as if the sound was reflecting off a hard surface inches from my face. I reached out my hand. But there was nothing there.

"Humphrey!" I whispered.

"What?" His voice made me jump, like he was right next to my ear.

"Why is it so dark?"

Something flashed in my face. The sound, and subsequent reduction of flash, told me it was a match-- before my heart could fully leap from my chest. Humphrey's face appeared in the orange glow, his wrinkles deepened by the harsh shadows.

My feet sloshed in water upon the hard obsidian surface we were standing on. I turned and squinted into the darkness, listening. There was no sign of life. Just me and Humphrey. In the middle of endless black. I should have been afraid, but I wasn't.

"--That's *weird.*"

"What?" The way he said the word, I realized he already knew what I was going to say.

"I didn't expect to feel God's love here."

He nodded. "His love fills Dantra, even in the lost land, but it is fainter here because the inhabitants cannot tolerate the light."

--Cannot tolerate the light. The words echoed in my mind. The idea was so familiar, so...

Humphrey smacked my arm. "Come on!"

I shook my head, and followed closely behind him, unable to take my eyes off the match. As we walked it continued to burn, but did not get shorter. I was about to comment on it, when a tortured scream broke through the darkness. I stopped abruptly and peered around. "That was

315

creepy," I said in a low voice.

"And to think," Humphrey said, half sympathetically, "you used to live here."

A memory surfaced. Pride and selfishness brought me to this dark place. I would come here to try to work through my financial troubles, always carrying my burdens with me, never able to trust God with them.

As I explored the memory, our surroundings began to flicker and change. Light filled the darkness and objects took shape in the receding shadows. Soon we found ourselves walking through an enormous office space with cubical after cubical of men and women frantically trying to get work done. The dark obsidian chamber had completely dissolved. "Did *I* do that?" I asked, startled.

"Yes, and yes."

"What?"

"Yes, you changed our surroundings, and yes, you used to be one of these people, struggling to make a name for yourself, never trusting God, only trusting in the talents God gave you."

"How? How did I do that?" He looked as though his answer was going to be a smart one, so I cut him off. "I mean, how did I make all this appear?"

He looked disappointed I had ruined his fun. "Don't get your undies in a bunch. It'll come to you."

I looked into one of the cubicles at a man in a business suit. He was staring at a screen filled with charts and graphs. In the corner of the screen, a stock ticker flashed red. He laced his fingers into his curly hair and gripped hard. His elbows dug into the desk.

Peering down at him, I suddenly realized, *I* had once been this man. In fact, I had shared this very office! I looked around at the other workers. They were all here because of the same lust, the same perceived *need* for something more. I was once one of them, constantly worrying about money, caught in a cycle of endless frustration.

I had not created this room. These were real people sharing the same reality, the same struggle. I had simply merged my reality with theirs-- but this was *not* a place I wanted to remember. The emotions were growing stronger, *painful* emotions, and I had *no* desire to revisit them. I turned toward Humphrey. "Can we leave?"

"Yes, you are in control," he answered. "You need to search for Gaza's daughter. Her mother is dead and her father's in a coma. Look for someone dealing with loss."

Could I do that? Could I find her by searching for her own personal hell? Wherever she was, she was experiencing the loss of a loved one. I thought of my love for my family, and of how I would feel if I lost them.

My soul reached out into the maelstrom of realities. In this realm, as in Dantra, thought became reality. But here, the fears and lusts of its inhabitants generated horrific self-made prisons. It was difficult sifting through the realities of unstable minds, but I realized, much to my surprise, that I had been created for this task. I could walk this realm because I had lived this realm. It spoke to something deep within me. A core belief? An insecurity? Regardless, it was the part of me that caused mistrust in my Creator, but ironically, it was the same part that allowed me to connect with these wretched souls. It was *why* I was uniquely qualified to rescue Gaza's daughter.

I latched on to the feeling of loss, and the world changed again. It was night and we were walking across a bridge. Several hopeless souls stood poised on the railing, working up the courage to jump. A young man leaned out and I reached to grab him, but Humphrey held my arm. "We can't help him. He has to work through this on his own."

I turned to Humphrey and studied his face. "We're helping Gaza's daughter, how is that different?"

"This trial is made for that man. He would not

317

respond to you."

I understood what he meant. God knew I would respond to the angels when they came for me. He knew I had come to the end of myself and was ready to receive their message. I turned from the suicides. It was pointless to try to help; I did not have the message they would hear.

"There was a car accident, right?"

"Yes," said Humphrey.

"Then maybe we're looking in the wrong place."

The bridge dissolved and a new scene took form around us, this time, a busy city street. There was a flutter and a woman screamed. I searched for her amidst the sea of pedestrians shimmering into view across the street. She was standing over a body. A crowd was beginning to form.

"We're looking for victims *inside* a car," said Humphrey.

"I *know!*" I snapped at him. "This is all new to me!"

"I'm just saying..."

"If you think this is so easy, *you* try it!"

"Now you're just being disagreeable," he said, folding his arms.

The environment shifted again and we found ourselves on a remote road. In the air, droplets of water hovered, like a million tiny tears-- as though time itself had frozen on the most tragic of moments, and nature could not contain its sorrow. I reached out and poked a drop. It left a hollow space, and ran down my finger.

Through the curtain of rain, I saw a woman kneeling by the side of the road. I approached her, creating a path through the droplets. At the bottom of the embankment was the object of her interest, a silver BMW, wrapped around a telephone pole.

I looked down upon the still and somber woman, then back at Humphrey. "She is too old."

Humphrey's brow furrowed. "She's not a little girl anymore, the accident happened over twenty years ago."

"Twenty *years?* Wouldn't she be past the grief?"

He gazed down at her. "It is not grief that brings her to this dark place. It is guilt."

I studied her for a long moment, then knelt beside her on the wet pavement. "Excuse me, Miss. What is your father's name?"

She stiffened. "I don't have a father."

"I'm sorry, what *was* your father's name?"

"Robert Helm." Her voice was distant. "Did you know him?"

"I still do."

"That's not funny!" She stood up.

"I'm not making a joke." I followed her into the road. "I know your father."

She stopped on the center line, and for a moment her eyes were uncertain. Then her face contorted in agony as she looked up into the darkness. "**HE'S *DEAD!***" The sky opened up and rain poured down in torrents so thick I had to shield my eyes to see her. She had collapsed to the pavement and was shivering in the downpour.

I knelt beside her. "Come with me, Constance!" I hollered over the roar of the rain. "I will bring you to him!"

"You lie! He's *dead!* You can't know him!"

I tangibly felt her sadness and guilt, and although she appeared as a woman, I sensed that inwardly she was a still little girl. *"Constance,* listen to me! When I saw your father, I saw him do this!" I held my pinky out and swooped it in a J shape, then tapped my knuckles together three times.

Her eyelids flicked at the rain as she looked up at me.

"I understand that it was a secret between the two of you! but *I* know about it! Please believe me when I say I *know* your father! He loves you very much, Constance. And I can bring you to him!

"But you don't *understand!* I can't *leave!* If I *leave,*

319

Mommy and Daddy won't wake up!" She looked up at the sky. "*I CAN'T LEAVE!*" The rain fell harder.

I leaned in closer and shielded my eyes from the deluge. "Come with me! The ambulance is here! They won't let anything happen to your mommy and daddy!"

The scene shifted forward in time and the car was swamped with activity. Lights flashed from the emergency vehicles, paramedics descended the embankment. Constance clutched my jacket and wept. "Please don't let anything happen to my mommy and daddy."

I gave her a hug. "Everything is going to be all right, Constance. I promise I won't let..."

A piercing screech filled the air and my head snapped around. A dark form descended onto the hood of the car. The metal gave way under the weight of its massive body. *"You do not belong here!"* It hissed.

Another creature, thin and humanoid, came out of the shadows. *"She cannot go with you."* It droned.

Humphrey stepped between us and the creatures. "Take her back to the portal! I'll meet you there!"

The creature on the car opened its deformed mouth and let out another screech.

Humphrey's face snapped back. "**Go!**"

I pulled Constance by the arm and we headed down the opposite embankment.

Through the wind and rain I heard shouting behind me. *"I am a servant of the most high God!"* Humphrey declared with confidence. *"It is HE you do battle with!"*

The air filled with a piercing shriek, but I did not hear what followed, we were in a corn field now, bursting through a flapping flurry of green. I looked over my shoulder. Through the cornstalks I caught a glimpse of a tall gray shape pursuing us. And it was gaining. If we did not get out of the field soon we would be overtaken.

I applied my will to the substance around us and the cornfield morphed into an open air field. Our footfalls echoed on the tarmac. I looked back again-- at an *army* of thin shadowy figures. My heart pounded in my chest as Constance pleaded with me to stop.

"We can't stop! It's just a little farther!"

If I had been alone I could have escaped easily because the memory of Dantra had fully returned. But Constance did not remember yet and shifting through thought quickly would be painful for her.

"This way!" I pulled her into an airplane hanger. It was large, hollow, and empty-- except for a tool table to the right. I snatched a large wrench off the table and pulled Constance toward the other side. Creatures poured into the hangar from every entrance. Constance screamed in wide-eyed terror as I pulled her toward the exit. *"This way!"*

We burst out of the hanger and were now running across rooftops. The creatures were everywhere now. Constance let out a screech as something dove at her from the side. I twisted and pulled her out of the way. *"We're almost there!"*

But it was too late. We skidded to a halt. We were completely surrounded. I swung the wrench wildly at the tall shadowy creatures. Their yellow eyes burned with hatred, their long thin fingers made clicking noises as they groped closer, and closer. Constance pressed against me. I held the wrench out menacingly, but it was no use. We were toast.

A large shadow passed over us and the creatures cowered back. I looked up to see a dark angel hovering overhead. The air from his mighty wings beat down on us.

"LET! THEM! GO!" His voice rattled the rooftops.

The creatures shrank back and I grabbed Constance by the arm and brought her to the edge of the building. She looked down and let out a shriek.

"Constance. *Constance!* Look at me! You can do this. I know it doesn't make sense to you, but you *can* do this!"

She was hysterical.

"Trust me! Everything will be okay!"

She looked down at the water far below, then clutched my jacket.

"I promise you, it's okay. You *can* do this."

She took my hand and squeezed her eyes shut. "I trust you."

Together we leaped into the void.

The water was *frigid,* and a frenzy of bubbles surrounded us. I pulled up on Constance and kicked hard until we broke the surface. Then with great effort, and a lot of coughing, we made our way up onto the sandy shore. It was still dark, but God's love was stronger here. The portal was close.

"Thomas!"

I looked up the beach. Humphrey was standing in front of a sheer cliff. "This way!" he hollered.

When we reached him, he placed his hand on the rock face. It shuddered as the portal opened, then the three of us stepped through.

"Man, am I glad to see you!" I said, grabbing Humphrey's arm.

"It was easy to get away once you took Constance," he said.

"We wouldn't have made it if you hadn't sent that angel."

He gave me a puzzled look, and a grumpy response. "I didn't send an angel."

"Well whoever sent him is okay in my book." I turned toward Constance. Her eyes were wide, her expression, one of awe.

"What *is* this place? It- it feels like church. Is this Ethral?"

"It may take a little time." I grinned. "But it will come to you."

She looked at Humphrey, then back to me. "You

know." She gave a small chuckle. "I don't even know your names."

"Well, I'm Thomas," I said, "and *grumpy* here is Humphrey."

She smiled.

He grumbled and walked away. "We have work to do. I'm supposed to take you to the overlook."

Constance and I looked at each other. "What's the overlook?" she called after him.

"Just follow me and you'll find out." Humphrey took another step, then froze in his tracks.

"What's wrong?" I approached and circled around him, but he gave no response. I looked back at Constance. She too had frozen.

Before my confusion could completely take hold, I found myself caught up in a familiar force which drew me toward the gray porous ceiling high above. Humphrey and Constance grew smaller and smaller until I could no longer make them out next to the crystal fortress far below.

Chapter Thirty-one

THE URGE
1 1 0 0 0 0 1

σ

I found myself in the darkened hallway of my old college dorm, searching for something, but I couldn't remember what. An unknown impulse drove me forward.

"Hey, Thomas, wait up!"

I turned to see my friend Stephen rushing up the hallway, with a stack of books precariously balanced in his arms. "You were supposed to get me," he said, attempting to push his glasses up with his shoulder.

I assisted him with a poke. "I'm not going to class."

"What are you talking about? We have finals."

"I'm not interested in that anymore," I said. "There are more important things."

He stared at me. "Have you lost your *mind?*"

I smiled. "No, I think I've found it."

"What exactly have you *found?*" He put the books down.

"I'm not sure, but it's peaceful." I turned and began walking through the shopping mall, passing shop after shop, with Stephen following close behind.

"We have plans," he said.

"I know, and we can continue to move forward. I just don't think it's important to put so much weight on making a buck. Too many people will get hurt."

"*What?* Have you gone lazy on me?"

"It's not the hard work that bothers me, Stephen. It's what we're working toward. I don't want to waste the talents God has given me on the selfish pursuits of money and comfort."

Stephen came to an abrupt stop. "What are you talking about? You gonna become a *monk* or something?" He kept talking, but I took no heed, I'd found what I was looking for.

The heavy metal door creaked open, revealing a huge locker room. I left Stephen standing in the corridor, his mouth gaping.

The place was filled with football players preparing for a game, but I wasn't interested in any of that. I walked past them into a row of lockers, then continued on through more lockers, past aisle after aisle, then into a huge shower area. Drawn to the other end I entered back into more rows of lockers, row upon row, until suddenly I found myself surrounded by a group of cheerleaders.

I looked down and noticed that all I was wearing was my underwear and a pair of slightly tattered wolf slippers. I looked back up in a panic. Fortunately for me, the ladies took no notice.

Under different circumstances, I might have explored this unique and rare opportunity, but regretfully, I left the scene of scantily clad women and headed toward the bathroom stalls. There were more urgent needs to attend to.

The graffiti laden door swung open-- but to my utter amazement and despair, the wall behind the toilet, was *missing* The stall was wide open. I could see out into the shopping mall. Across the way, an old woman sat staring at me, her shopping bags nestled neatly against her leg. *This* was not going to do! I stepped out and checked the next stall. It was the same. I checked the next, and the next...

Only when I turned to consider one of the sinks as a possible solution to my problem, did I realize, that I was dreaming.

I opened my eyes and with a grunt, rolled off the

mattress. I grabbed my robe, and headed for the bathroom.

My next stop was the kitchen. I wasn't hungry, but that had never stopped me from snacking before. I helped myself to a piece of chocolate cake, then walked over to the door leading to the patio. Someone was sitting on the edge of the pool. I slid the door open, walked over casually, and squatted down.

"Cake?"

"No thanks," said Rebecca.

"Having trouble sleeping?"

She swished her feet in the water. "I had a bad dream."

"About what?" I took a seat beside her.

"It was *weird.* First I was in a funeral parlor, and you were..." She looked over at me. "You were dead. --But I wasn't sad, because I knew you were okay." She paused and furrowed her brow. "Then I followed what I think was your *ghost* across this really *long* white bridge until you disappeared into a wall of swirling smoke. Beyond the wall, I could hear people being tortured, screaming for mercy." She shuddered. "Then I woke up."

"--Wow."

"I told you it was weird."

I put my arm around her shoulder. "Yeah, well, you've been dealing with a lot lately and-- dreams are always weird."

"I know, but it was still *unnerving.* " She studied my face. "So why are *you* here? You have a bad dream too?"

I smiled. "You don't want to know."

"What?" She returned my smile.

"Well, I was trying to find a place to go pee."

She laughed.

"And all I could find was a stall that was *wide* open to this shopping mall. Everyone could see me."

She laughed harder, then put her head on my shoulder.

326

We sat for a time staring at the reflections in the pool, and an overwhelming feeling of gratitude washed over me. I had lost so much, but had been given back far more than I ever could have hoped for. It made the loss almost bearable.

"It was hard for a long time," Rebecca said, breaking the silence. "But after a while I was able to let you go. Then it was awkward when I found out you were awake." She lifted her head up. "Don't get me wrong, I was happy you were awake. But I had built a relationship with a silent sleeping father. You were *everything* to me, because you were a fantasy." She looked thoughtful. "It was *that* fantasy that shut out my stepdad, and when I heard you were awake, I wondered if it would shut you out too." She shook her head. "How could you possibly live up to the expectations of a foolish little girl?"

I squeezed her. "Oh, honey..."

"I *missed* you, Dad. And I hope we can start fresh. I want to know who you *really* are. I want to replace the fantasy with something *real.*"

"I'd stick with the fantasy if I were you."

She scowled playfully.

"I'm serious. I'm not the saint your mother is. You deserve a better dad than me."

"I don't need a saint, Dad. I need *you,* the father God gave me."

"Yeah, well, you got short changed."

"Why do you say that?"

I slumped. "I don't know. I guess I'm feeling bad because I don't want to be a part of this whole *battle for humanity* thing. I feel like a selfish jerk."

"Is it so bad you want to reclaim your life? You've been through a *lot,* and besides, you need time to recuperate! I'm sure there are plenty of capable people at the center who can handle this kind of stuff. You shouldn't beat yourself up about it."

327

"What? Are you saying I'm not *action hero* material?"

She laughed. "Look at you, you're skin and bones."

"And wrinkly." I smiled. "Don't forget wrinkly."

She leaned over and nudged me with her shoulder. "You're right where you're supposed to be, Dad. The cloak and dagger games are best left to the professionals. But you know what, *you* are a remarkable man." She looked at me, her eyes smiling. "I believe God has a plan for you. I don't know what it is, but something tells me you were meant for something great.

"Well something tells me I will be spending a lot more time at home now, than at the office."

Rebecca smiled-- the smile melted into a yawn. "Sorry."

I gave her a warm hug. "Yeah. I'm tired too. I'm going back to bed. You coming in?"

She nodded. "I just hope I don't have any more nightmares."

"Yeah." I chuckled. "Me neither."

I did not dream this time, but passed quickly into the darkness, through The Separation, and beyond. When I entered the substance of Dantra, there was a shimmer in my perception, but I wasn't disturbed by it; I innately understood it as a natural result of shifting dimensions. Dantra, being a timeless environment, waited for me to rejoin it. And as my consciousness completed its shift, I found myself standing in the exact spot I had been in before I departed. Humphrey was moving, and Constance filed in behind him. I thought to tell Humphrey about the experience of shifting to Earth. But I sensed he already knew.

I was beginning to understand a great many things about Dantra, as dormant memories deep within me awakened. It felt like returning home, though, I had never

328

truly left.

We passed under the great and ancient archway of the crystal fortress. And Constance stopped.

"What is it?"

She raised her hands into the air and closed her eyes. "It is strong here."

"What is?"

"The love."

Humphrey smacked me on the arm. "Hey! Has your memory completely returned?"

"Ow! Would you stop *doing* that!" I said, rubbing my arm.

"Sorry." He winced. "Well-- has it?"

"Yes, I believe it has."

"Great! That will make things a lot easier." At once his body began to glow. Then points of light burst through cracks in his skin. Until there was nothing left, but light.

"You know," I said, "even though I can remember now, that *still* freaks me out."

Constance gasped.

I motioned for her to calm down. "It's okay, it's okay, it's just Humphrey."

She approached him and cautiously touched him on the chest. "He's tingly," she said, running her fingertips downward.

"Are you okay with this?" I said.

"You talking to me or her?" asked Humphrey.

She continued to touch Humphrey's chest, so I figured everything was cool. She did not have her memory back. That was why it had scared her. But she knew deep inside, that it was natural.

I stretched out my arms and pushed away the energy of Dantra, revealing my true form. It had been a long time since I had moved about Dantra as pure thought. It was exhilarating!

"Come, there's more to do," said Humphrey,

329

telepathically.

We lifted Constance into the air and traveled out into the brightness of Dantra. Below, the white bridge faded, and was replaced by a desert.

"There." Humphrey pointed.

We touched down in front of a single story nondescript building. Humphrey gathered the substance of Dantra and became corporal again. Reluctantly, I did the same. In the center of the building, was a single red metal door. It was chipped and rusted, with a large yellow hazard sign upon it.

We approached the tiny building, and the door slipped upward, revealing an elevator.

"Ladies first," I said, gesturing to Constance.

She stepped in. I followed. Then Humphrey stepped in and pushed the button for the one-hundredth floor.

Constance looked confused.

I nudged her gently. "Think of it as a dream, and it won't be so disconcerting."

She gave me a pensive look, and the elevator creaked into motion. The lights on the panel glowed slowly one at a time. And we waited. Finally the door opened and a blue light filtered in. I stepped out to see a metal catwalk stretching off in both directions as far as the eye could see. Beyond the railing, the enormous mass of Vrin hovered, suspended by millions of blue iridescent threads from the porous ceiling high above.

Constance came up beside me. "What *is* it?" Her eyes were wide.

"That," I stated, "is Vrin."

"I know that name," she said slowly. "Where have I heard that name?"

"Your father created it."

"Yes. I remember! *Vrin!* Virtual Reality Interface Network!" She tilted her head slightly. "But that would mean Solomon succeeded." She grabbed my arm.

330

"Solomon got through! He did it! He said he was going to use my father's technology to speak directly to his mind, and..." She shook her head in awe.

"And," Humphrey finished, "we are looking at the result of his experiment as it appears in Dantra."

"Yes. Dantra! I remember this place. --Why didn't I remember before?" She looked at me.

"Because," I explained, "you were trapped in physical thought. But now you are remembering your true nature. As a complex being, the physical is only one aspect of who you are."

She looked back at Vrin. "I remember."

"All of us remember before we pass through The Separation," Humphrey said. "But few remember here in Dantra. There was a time when Dantra was filled with glowing beings, sharing experiences, comforting one another-- but so many have been weighted down by selfish desires contrary to God. They'd rather struggle than know peace."

"But some have chosen obedience," I added. "They're not perfect, but they trust in the promises of God, and use *his* strength to protect themselves from evil thoughts. These were the ones the angels led into Vrin, to help your father complete his work."

"Why would God do that?"

"Because he *loves* your father." I leaned in toward her. "God's ways can sometimes be difficult to understand."

"God's ways are perfect," said Humphrey, clearly annoyed by my choice of words.

"What I'm saying is, God has a plan meant for our good, even though sometimes we don't understand it." I looked at Humphrey as if to say, *Will that work for you?*

He gave a little shrug.

Constance looked at Humphrey, then at me. "So-- why did you bring *me* here?"

Humphrey pointed. "See those strands reaching

331

from Vrin to the ceiling?"

"Yes."

"Your father is preparing to destroy Vrin."

Constance snapped a look at Humphrey.

"If he succeeds," Humphrey continued, "the explosion will send a tremendous shock wave up those threads. And *millions* will die in their sleep."

Her face twisted in horror. "*Why* would he do that?"

I looked at Humphrey, but spoke to Constance. "Because your father doesn't understand God's plan."

Humphrey scowled.

I looked back at Constance. "Your father believes wrongly. He thinks God is cruel. He doesn't understand his own failings, and he doesn't understand that everything occurring is actually for his good. He wants his family back, he wants *you* back, and he is willing to destroy and rebuild Vrin a thousand times to get what he wants."

She began to cry. I put my arm around her.

"You can help him," said Humphrey.

"How?" She sniffed.

"By bringing him a message. --But there is a catch." He reached out and gently lifted her chin. "You may not pass beyond the threshold into Vrin to be with your father."

"Why not?" She sniffed.

"God says you cannot."

"Why?" she asked again.

"It's difficult to understand." He shot me a glance. "But do you accept the terms?"

"Yes," she whispered.

"Good. Then it's time to go see your mother."

Chapter Thirty-two

A MESSAGE FROM ETHRAL
1 1 0 1 1 1 0

$$\Sigma$$

The living cannot pass into Ethral, so we stood at the barrier between. Shimmering transparent silver separated us from a brilliant city of crystal. In this place, God's love was overpowering, and Constance struggled with it. It was almost more than she could bear.

"I don't belong here," she said. "I have done too much. I have seen too much."

Humphrey laughed. "No one deserves to be in the presence of God. It is by his forgiveness alone that anyone can be with him."

"Someone approaches," I said, pointing.

Three figures in white flowing robes were walking toward us along a golden path. Long hoods shrouded their heads. As they neared, Constance covered her face with her hands.

Reaching the barrier, the one in the middle removed her hood. She was beautiful, with crystal blue eyes and fiery red hair that touched her shoulders in curls. Her expression was one of overwhelming compassion, and her gaze was fixed on Constance. "You do not need to be afraid, little one. You are loved."

Constance dropped her hands and looked up. "Mom?" Her voice quivered.

"Yes, honey. It's me."

Constance tried to run forward, but the barrier's energy held her back. The woman placed her hand on the

333

barrier. Constance did the same.

"You cannot enter where I am, sweetie," the woman said. "Not yet. You have work to do."

"I've missed you so much, Mom." Constance choked on the words.

"I have missed you too, honey. But we must think of your father now. He is in a very dark place."

"Yes. I know."

"You must travel to Vrin and give him a message."

"Then can we come and be with you?"

"When the time is right, but first you must do this." She looked at Constance intently. "Tell him, he is a great man, and that great men must make great sacrifices."

Constance nodded and wiped away a tear. "Yes, Mom. I will remember."

"I love you, Constance. Be a good girl." She gave a gentle smile.

"I will, Mom," Constance whispered. "I will."

One of the robed figures reached out and placed his hand softly on the woman's shoulder.

"I have said as much as you are able to bear, my darling. Come home, Constance." She covered her head. And the three turned and walked back down the path.

"I will, Mom! I will!" Constance called after them. She crumbled to the ground and wept.

We stood by quietly for a moment, allowing her to grieve.

"We must travel back to The Circle," said Humphrey over her sobs.

"Yes, I know."

"Are you ready?"

"I am." I looked down at Constance.

"It is not going to be easy," he said quietly.

"Nothing important ever is." I knelt down next to Constance. "It is time to take you to Vrin. Are you ready?"

"Yes," she said, wiping away tears. "I want to see

my father."

I helped her to her feet and the three of us headed back down the stairs to a grassy field. The sun sat high in the sky. I looked directly at it. But it didn't hurt my eyes.

We traveled across the meadow and into a leafy path through a wood where we wound our way in and out of massive oak trees, until Humphrey stopped us at the edge of a clearing. He motioned for us to duck down. In the center, beings of light swarmed around a circular structure, floating in and out amongst each other. I noted that the light emanating from them was weak and faded.

"Who are they?" I whispered.

"Malignant spirits," said Humphrey.

"Is that The Circle of Ghosts?"

"Yes."

"How do we get in?"

"Hold on. You'll see." He winked.

Suddenly, the air filled with light and the ground trembled. I looked up to see the massive form of Magnus descending. As he landed in front of The Circle, the ground split. And the lesser beings retreated.

"I AM MAGNUS! I STAND IN THE PRESENCE OF THE ONE TRUE GOD!"

"Go!" said Humphrey, gesturing wildly.

Constance and I bolted toward The Circle and Magnus allowed us to pass. In the shadows of the trees, the glowing demons paced like wild animals.

"Quickly! The fallen ones are coming!" Humphrey called after us.

I looked up to see bright flickers of yellow fire burning down through the atmosphere. And from them a haunted screech filled the air.

I looked at Constance. "Ready?"

She gave a quick nod. "I'm scared, but I'm ready."

"Remember, Thomas!" called Humphrey. "Time does not exist in Dantra. You will enter Vrin precisely the

335

moment you left, which will give you the element of surprise."

"Got it." I gave him the thumbs up.

Magnus stepped forward and gripped the structure, and in a flash of light, we found ourselves standing inside The Circle on Gaza's platform. Through a ghostly yellow veil, I watched, as if in slow motion, as the body of Charm collapsed onto the metal floor of the platform.

Kitaya, still holding the gun, also watched him fall. She turned and looked directly at me. *How did she know?* An evil grin appeared on her face as she threw the pistol aside and raised her arms in surrender.

I stepped through the veil.

Gaza's face showed anger then confusion. I was dead-- and yet there I stood. At first his eyes bore into mine, but then he looked past me-- and his expression changed. *"Constance?"*

I turned and looked back through the veil. Constance was standing in The Circle, appearing as a little girl.

"Yes, Daddy. It's me."

He brushed past me and stood before the veil. "Where's your mother, sweetheart?"

"She died in the crash, Daddy. But it's okay. She is in Ethral, waiting for us.

"In Ethral?" His voice was hollow. "But-- why didn't I go with her?"

"Because, Daddy, you are still living. The living may not pass into Ethral."

He crouched down. "Are *you* alive?"

"Yes. I am in Dantra."

"Why aren't you here? I thought I drew all the souls into Vrin."

She looked at him warmly. "You didn't draw the souls into Vrin, God sent them in to help you, so you could move beyond the pain of the void. You don't have to hold

336

on to that pain anymore, Daddy. You don't have to hang on to your anger. God did not do this to you. It just happened. Sometimes we think because God created everything, that he is responsible for all the bad things that happen to us. But the reality is, we cause darkness and pain by making bad choices, choices that go against the will of God. But God can take even our bad choices and use them for our good."

"I've been searching for you," he said softly.

The little girl's eyes filled with tears. "I was but a breath away. You couldn't see me, but I was there. --For many years I blamed myself for what happened. I convinced myself that if I had stayed by the car, they would have found you quicker and rescued you. But I was afraid, and I ran away."

As she continued to speak, she began to increase in years. "I carried the burden for such a long time, every day, cursing God for what happened. And I hid from him. I didn't want his pity, I wanted *you* back. But it's clear to me now, I don't have to fear. All things are working out as God promised. And you, Daddy, you have a purpose here. There's something God needs you to do. --Then someday we can be together in eternity."

As he contemplated her words, I interjected cautiously. "Perhaps, you were meant to stop Kric' tu."

He looked at me, then back at Constance. "Is that it? Is that what he expects from me?"

Constance closed her eyes and lifted her face toward the sky, as if in silent communication. Her eyes opened. "Yes," she stated with certainty. "That is what you were meant to do."

"Then come through, and I'll do it." His tone had changed, he sounded sincere.

"I can't enter Vrin, Daddy. And I can't go back. The fallen ones have blocked the way."

337

He squinted at her. "I don't understand. You've come this far. You must come through!"

Her eyes turned down. "I'm not allowed."

"Please don't do this to me," he said softly.

"You have to stop Kric' tu. It is what you were created to do."

His face contorted. "You don't understand. I *can't!*"

"You have to."

"**I CAN'T!**" His eyes were desperate. Then, all of a sudden, a look of realization appeared on his face. *"You!"* he said, spinning to face Kitaya.

She took a step back.

Gaza suddenly raised his arms, causing a tide of distortion to push outward. This sent Kitaya crashing back against the railing. Energy washed over her in torrents, crushing her violently against the metal rails.

She cried out, but it was not *her* voice that came out of her. It was in the voice of a man! Her body vibrated and her physical form melted away in the stream of electricity. And when the energy subsided, it was not Kitaya who lay on the metal grid of the platform. It was Rath!

Gaza's eyes glared. *"I'll destroy you for this!"*

"Go ahead! Destroy this body! And I will become a true god."

"Ha! Is that the *lie* that abomination fed you?*"*

"Kric' tu understands more than you ever will!"

"He's a *glitch* in the program. What could he *possibly* know that I do not? *I created* Vrin out of the essence of eternity."

Rath laughed. "Fool! Vrin is a *delusion.* Kric' tu is the reality. You *know* the people of Vrin are real. I know you do! You've searched *pathetically* for your wife and daughter in the program you yourself created. You *think* you know so much, but you're such a pathetic *loser,* you can't even figure out what Davata Notrals *is.* You don't have a clue!"

338

"It is also a glitch." Gaza sneered.

Rath laughed again. "It told us everything you would do. God thought himself clever to hide future events within the very structure of his book. But we found the code, *and* the code breaker."

They found Hazel?

"We can't allow you to destroy Vrin. The code revealed how we would stop you, and for now we have allowed it to be as it is written. But God will one day see that he is *wrong* about humanity, and his code will be useless. Then *I* will become a true god!"

"Not before I *break your FACE!" That* was *Kitaya's* voice.

Materializing in front of Rath, her foot recoiled and smashed him on the jaw, sending his head back with a jolt. Rath's hand shot out, bringing her to the floor with a crash. He rose above her with a clenched fist, but Kitaya's fingers became long metal pins, and he let out a blood curdling scream as she pushed them deep into his sides. He pushed himself away and blood trickled from the wounds.

Anger flared in his eyes as his fist came up again."

"Stop!" screamed Gaza. *"Or I will send you *both* back to the void!"

Rath's hand stopped. He looked up at Gaza. "You have no real power!"

"Test me." Gaza leveled his eyes at him.

Rath hovered for a moment, then slowly lowered his hand. "It doesn't matter." He rubbed his chin with his knuckles. "You've lost. Even now Kric' tu prepares his forces."

I looked out across the barren plain. There was movement in the black ranks.

Gaza turned back toward his daughter. His features racked with anguish. He knew what I knew, that closing The Circle would kill her. Rath and Kric' tu had set it all up. It was in the code that I would bring her here, and now

339

Gaza was trapped, held hostage by his love for Constance. Kric' tu was betting that Gaza would not allow his daughter to die, that he would leave The Circle open, so the forces of chaos could take over Vrin.

Gaza swung back toward Rath with a fierceness that caused both Rath *and* Kitaya to withdraw. "Did the book tell you I would do *this?*" He stretched out his hand toward them, and Rath violently erupted into a ball of flame. Gaza walked forward and hovered over the screeching burning form. "Do me a favor." He sneered. "Say hello to Kric' tu for me." And in a rage of inhuman strength, he shoved the burning mass through the metal railing. Like a comet, Rath plummeted and exploded on impact.

As Gaza peered over the rail at the smoldering form, the fury on his countenance was replaced by sorrow.

"LOOK!" Armadon's voice boomed out. He pointed to the distance. "THE FORCES OF KRIC' TU ADVANCE!"

Gaza looked up and calmly studied the horizon. His face was stern yet contemplative.

"It is time," I said. "He is coming."

Gaza spun and strode to The Circle. "You must jump through!" he yelled at his daughter.

"I told you, Daddy. I can't!"

"Why? What is preventing you?"

"I have chosen to obey God."

"Jump through!" He begged. "I can't live without you!" he said, beating his fists fiercely against the veil. But the very structure he had created would not allow him to get through.

Constance moved in close. "I want to, Daddy," she whispered. "You have to believe me."

"I can save this world if you come through." He pleaded. "If I close The Circle you will die."

"I will see you in Ethral." Her chin quivered. "Promise you will come home to me."

"I don't know how," he whispered, pressing his forehead against the barrier.

"Mom sent me here with a message for you," she said, her voice sounding surreal. "She said to tell you, you are a great man, and that great men must make great sacrifices. I know this is hard for you, but seek first the things of God, and he will give you what you need. Stop fighting, Daddy. Stop fighting-- and come home."

His expression was one of pure anguish as he turned and ran back to the railing. The army of darkness filled the horizon, completely surrounding us now. Soon we would be overtaken. Racked with emotion, he stared intently at the approaching horde. He knew there was no way to destroy Vrin without killing Constance. He also knew that sealing The Circle would do the same.

"You can't take them," I said, reading his thoughts. "There are too many."

He scowled at me. "I have resources the others do not."

"These creatures use the energy of The Circle. They are *very* powerful this close to the source."

Gaza's eyes burned emerald in their sockets. "We shall see."

He lifted his hands into the air and the earth quaked as a wall pushed up from the ground between the advancing enemy and our position. It encircled the entire structure. But an awful song filled the air, and instantly holes began appearing across the surface.

Gaza wiggled his fingers, and the ground became a sea of green acid. The creatures screamed as they entered the liquid, but again an awful song arose, and they began to sprout wings and take to the air.

Gaza waved his hand. All of the strands around the structure appeared as thin razor sharp wires. The strands stretched from the green acrid lake below to the now darkened sky above.

341

The demons wailed as the strands cut them to shreds. But there arose yet another song, and the black creatures phased into energy. Their faint outlines melted into each other, creating a dense dark cloud.

He tried again and again to thwart their advance, but they were no longer in phase with Vrin. Being this close to the power of The Circle gave them the ability to travel like apparitions through whatever Gaza threw at them.

He was becoming more frustrated.

I spoke in a calming voice. "Gaza. Your wife lives on in Ethral, and your daughter has turned toward the light as well. The question is, are you willing to give up Constance, to do what is right? Kric' tu cannot be allowed to take Vrin, it would have eternal implications. You *can* stop him."

I watched as the darkness grew closer and closer. I wanted to take action. *I* could set things in motion to destroy Kric' tu and his army-- but the ring on my finger gave a gentle squeeze, reminding me that it was not *my* decision to make.

As I stood waiting, everything suddenly came together, and I understood! *This was all a set up!* God knew exactly what would happen. He'd brought me here because he foresaw every choice I would make. He knew the choices each and every one of us would make, and *he* brought it all together. I trusted now. It *would* happen, just as it was written. Because God said so. And God was never wrong.

Gaza turned and strode back to The Circle. He reached out and touched the veil gently. "Promise me I will see you in Ethral," he said softly. It was clear in his tone, that he had made up his mind.

A single tear streaked down his daughter's cheek. "I love you, Daddy," she whispered.

His face hardened with grief. "I love you too, baby."

He turned and raised his hands into the air. The sky

shook. The Circle of Ghosts shimmered and shuddered. For a moment, eternity held its breath. Then all at once, The Circle collapsed in upon itself, causing a violent shock wave to erupt from the structure. It ripped through the ranks of the enemy. After reaching its full distance, it drew back like an undertow. Below The Circle a whirlpool began to form. The energy of Dantra was being drawn out of Vrin. Like black sand, the dark figures began to come apart and were swept into the funnel of energy below.

Soon The Circle would be sealed, just as the scripture had predicted.

I stood over Gaza and my form tore away as the whirlpool of energy pulled at it, for I too was made from the energy of Dantra.

The creator of Vrin fell to the ground, weeping bitterly. His daughter was gone. But now he had a new hope, a hope that one day he would be reunited with her in Ethral. "God forgive me," he sobbed.

It was then that I noticed a ring forming on his finger. He looked at it with surprise.

I smiled. "It is the very seal of God."

He lifted his hand and examined it closely. There was an inscription upon it.

It read, *"Come home."*